MW00987616

CAVEAT EMPTOR BUYER BEWARE

A mystery thriller
By

Paul R. M. Howell

This is a work of fiction. Names, characters, places and incidents are products of the author's imagination or are used fictitiously and are not to be construed as real. Any resemblance to actual events, locales, organizations or persons, living or dead, is entirely coincidental

Copyright © 2011 by Paul. R.M. Howell

ISBN-10: 1463711174
ISBN-13: 978-1463711177

This book is dedicated to my long suffering wife, Kate, without whom this opus would never have been published.

ACKNOWLEDGEMENTS

I am grateful to the following people for their many and varied contributions throughout the writing and re-writing of this book.

Firstly, my thanks go to Linda Friedel who read my very first rough draft and who offered much insight and encouragement at a stage when the task of writing a readable novel seemed overwhelming.

My gratitude also goes to Bill Lash for his extensive knowledge of the SAS and all matters military. His many other suggestions only improved the final outcome.

Others who took the time and trouble to read early drafts and offer their considered opinions are "Uncle Spots", Monique Heijn, Rick Linneman, Marie Robinson, Andrew LaGree, Ryan Sayles and Dr. James Thomas. To these people I give my heartfelt thanks.

To my nephew, Bobby Young, I thank you for your help with computer aspects of publishing. Those are things way over my head, dear chap.

Finally, but by no means least, I acknowledge the huge input from my wife, Kate, who not only typed, edited and corrected my mistakes but who acted as a wonderful sounding board. Her enthusiasm and encouragement not to mention her wizardry on the computer made the whole process of writing much easier and more enjoyable than I had a right to expect.

With best wishes,

Paul R. M. Havell.

ONE

8th September 1990
0830 hours

**Within hours Phillip Fairfax' well ordered life
would crumble like the walls of Jericho.**

It was six o'clock in the morning and Isabel Fairfax
woke with a smile on her face. As she lay under her warm
down filled duvet her hands explored her swollen belly
feeling for the miraculous signs of life within her. Isabel
was seven months pregnant with her first child.

It was sunny on that early September morning and
the rays of bright sunshine poured into the small bedroom.
Although it had rained hard during the night, it promised to
be another warm day. Isabel could not remember when she
had ever been so happy.

In this small rural village of Bredwardine in the
quiet corner of Herefordshire only a few leaves had shown
any inclination to don their famous autumn plumage.
Summer was still stubbornly clinging on in this bucolic
area of England which was chiefly known for its' famous
red and white beef cattle and its' fragrant hop fields.

This was a vastly different world to the one Isabel
had recently left which had been a world of high finance in
the frantic bustle of London's commercial banking district.
But despite her earlier fears she had settled down amongst
the rolling hills of the Welsh border and thoroughly

embraced 'life in the long grass' as her husband Phillip referred to it.

After a brief shower, Isabel slipped into a cotton print dress that sacrificed any pretence at style for the sake of comfort. As a precaution against mercurial weather she also put on a cashmere cardigan. She smiled as she looked at her unfamiliar reflection in the mirror.

She made herself a nourishing breakfast of poached eggs, fresh fruit and yogurt as she jotted down items she needed to buy at the Hereford market. As she did this she allowed her mind to wander. She thought of her husband Phillip, who was 'playing soldiers' with his regiment in the bleak landscape of the Brecon Beacons. Looking out of the window at the peacefully grazing sheep, Isabel imagined her future with Phillip as they raised their family together in this rural idyll. The images in her mind evoked feelings of utter contentment and a deeply fulfilling purpose to her life.

Reluctantly she dragged herself out of her reverie and tried to concentrate on the more practical aspects of the day ahead. Grabbing her grocery list and a pink dry cleaning receipt that had been affixed to the 'fridge door by a magnet extolling the virtues of using the Green Apple Sludge Company for septic waste management. It's motto, "We're the Number 1 in a Number 2 Business" had always amused Phillip. She slung her cavernous tote bag over her shoulder and headed for the door. Collecting her bunch of keys from the hall table, Isabel did a quick mental re-cap to make sure she had everything she needed. Closing the front door behind her she headed for the green Range Rover that was parked in the driveway.

Isabel Fairfax slid into the roomy leather clad interior of her husband Phillip's vehicle. Tossing her bag on the passenger seat she adjusted the steering wheel to accommodate her large belly. She adjusted the mirror and seat of the Range Rover, inserted the key and gave it a gentle turn. The powerful V8 engine immediately came to life. Checking the mirrors once more, she selected first gear and released the parking brake. Gently Isabel eased her foot off the clutch and effortlessly guided the large vehicle along the flat drive and then towards the steep slope to the main road.

The explosion shook the whole village. Every window within a half mile radius was either blown in or cracked. Burning debris shot skywards and landed on the roofs of houses either side of Isabel's. Small patches of lawn burned in every direction and pieces of smoking and jagged metal fell like arrows raining down on some ancient battle field. When the last piece had fallen, there was quiet. Total and utter quiet. Every living, breathing creature was stunned into a shocked silence. Slowly people emerged from their houses. Cautiously at first. They looked at the scene in stunned disbelief. No-one spoke.

It was said afterwards that the blast could be heard over four miles away. By the time the fire crew arrived on the scene, the Range Rover was a smoldering pile of burning rubber and twisted metal. The bonnet of the vehicle had been hurled over fifty yards from the epicenter of the bomb. It stuck, still smoking, into a neighboring lawn like a large crooked tomb stone.

Isabel, too, was some distance from the main wreckage. She lay quite still and lifeless; bloodied, burnt and blackened by fire and smoke. She was minus both her legs. Her gashed torso showed up a bright, shiny pink against her now black, charred body, which still emanated wisps of smoke. It left nothing to remind anyone of the vibrant young blond who, only minutes before, had been so happy and alive. Isabel and her baby were gone.

TWO

8th September 1990
1700 hours

The Director SAS at the 22nd Regiment, Stirling Lines, Hereford, was Brigadier John Black. He recalled Phillip from the survival course he was overseeing on the Brecon Beacons and told him all he knew of the tragedy. He thrust a large scotch into Phillip's hand and poured one for himself. He, too, had known and liked Isabel. He felt deeply for his friend.

"Here Phillip, I'll drink with you down to the label."

"John, that bomb was meant for me, wasn't it?"

"Probably. I'd be less than truthful with you if I didn't say I think it was. But it won't bring Isabel back, or the baby." John Black sat on the edge of his desk and faced Phillip.

"I know it won't but I feel so…" Phillip searched for the right word. " … So damned guilty, so damned responsible."

John Black laid his hand on Phillip's shoulder. He watched as Phillip's jaw muscles clenched and unclenched. Phillip was fighting to stay in control of his feelings.

"Don't try and make sense of it now, Phillip, because nothing makes sense at the moment." He poured another splash of scotch into their glasses.

"You've always known we run this risk. We do a dirty job and, yes, sometimes the innocent get caught in the crossfire."

John Black, as Commanding Officer, often had to deal with death. Death of his friends and comrades, death in

battle and even death during training exercises but this was something he felt ill-equipped to handle. There were, quite simply, no words of comfort he could offer Phillip. He decided just to let the scotch work its therapeutic magic.
"When I find whoever did this, and I will, John, they'll wish they'd never been born."
"I can't pretend to know what you're feeling, Phillip. Revenge? Yeah, it's normal but you know as well as I do that we'll probably never know who did this."
Both men took a long pull on their scotch.
"I know, I know. They'll just disappear into the ether and it will all be chalked up to the casualties of war. A war where the enemy is the person standing next to you on the train, a person in the grocery store, a person in the pub. I know the score."
The two men sat silently for a moment and sipped the amber liquid. John knew Phillip well. They'd both served in the Falkland's war together. John knew how courageous Phillip was but he worried that this senseless killing of the beautiful Isabel might destroy him.
"Do you know what I feel most, John?"
"What?"
"Anger."
"Only natural."
"No, you don't understand. I'm angry with Isabel and that makes me hate myself."
Phillip took a big swallow of scotch and emptied his glass. John said nothing but poured a little more whiskey into their glasses. He looked at Phillip and saw the hurt and confusion in his face.
"I always told her to look under the car before she got in but I don't think she ever did. I think she thought I was being melodramatic. God, I wish she'd done it - just this once."

Phillip too was used to death. He had seen it up close in the Falklands, and Northern Ireland. Everyone in the SAS had seen it in all its ugly forms and, in some cases, had caused it. It was never an easy thing to deal with, but it had ceased to cause the sudden shock that it once had. That involuntary sharp intake of breath, that sudden scrambling of normal thought patterns was not in the repertoire of a modern professional soldier. But this was different. This was personal. And one day someone would pay.

The enquiry into Isabel's murder and that of her baby lasted several months. It involved Scotland Yard's Anti-Terrorist Squad and also the bomb experts and ammunitions technicians from the Royal Logistics' Corp. The bomb disposal expert was known affectionately by those who worked along side him as "Felix". This was a reference to Felix the Cat, who, like all domesticated felines, was reported to have at least nine lives and he certainly needed them.

It was determined quite quickly that the car bomb or 'improvised explosive device', the IED as it's known to the police and military, was triggered by a 'mercury tilt switch' and detonated at least fifteen kilos of Semtex explosive. This type of switch, which activates a bomb when the vehicle ceases to be on flat and level ground, was, in the 1980's & 90's, a favorite method employed by the Provisional IRA terrorist. IEDs had been used numerous times in both Northern Ireland and on mainland England. They were both effective propaganda tools and lethal to the occupants of the vehicle. Their effectiveness, when placed inside a vehicle, multiplied because, for a split second, the explosion was contained. This dramatically increased its force when the chassis eventually gave way. An IED placed inside a vehicle detonated with much more power than one placed outside it.

Hollywood would have us believe that most car bombs were wired into the ignition system of a car and that as soon as the key is turned, the vehicle would explode. But in reality that way of doing things was dropped a long time ago. For one thing, it takes a lot longer to install, and it is very complex to tap into a modern electronic ignition system.

However, the most pressing reason for not using that method, quite simply, is that it's unreliable. Often the device would drain the car's battery which robbed the bomb's detonator of its power source. If the vehicle was started remotely, the assassin's target could, very often, escape without a scratch.

After all the investigations were complete the coroner handed down his verdict. "Isabel Fairfax and her unborn child were murdered by a person, or persons, unknown."

Phillip knew, of course, that she had died because of him. He realized that it had been because he was a member of the SAS. It was retribution for the things he had done as a soldier. It was he who should have died, not Isabel and their baby. Maybe the murderers had wanted it that way. They knew he'd never forgive himself, and in a way, that was more of a punishment than him dying.

From that moment on Phillip lost his appetite for making war. He no longer believed unreservedly in his role as a soldier. Phillip took the only course he felt was open to him. He resigned his commission and tried to start a new life. A life without Isabel.

THREE

For several weeks after resigning his commission Phillip struggled with his inner demons. He would drink heavily and then disappear for days at a time. He would pack his Bergen backpack and venture into the Welsh hills. When he would return from one of these jaunts, tired, dirty and unshaven, he remained pensive and uncommunicative. He vacillated between anger and despair and refused to let anybody into his private hell. His parents and younger sister left him alone. Phillip was very capable at surviving in the wilderness, even in winter, but they all worried that he seemed so disinclined to talk about Isabel's death. Phillip would face it only when he was ready.

In the following weeks Phillip relived Isabel's murder in his waking hours and in his sleep, though sleep eluded him on most nights. He imagined the bright bubbly personality being snuffed out in one devastating split second. His only small consolation was that she probably knew nothing about it. She heard nothing and felt nothing.

But what tore at his very soul was the certain knowledge that he, Phillip, the fearless soldier, the crusader for a righteous cause, had caused it to happen. Phillip continued to punish himself emotionally as he pushed himself to his physical limits, surviving in the depths of winter, living alone in the barren desolate hills on the Welsh border. And when that didn't work he dulled the pain by numbing himself with alcohol.

As the weeks passed and his mind began to accept what had happened as fact rather than a horrendous nightmare, Phillip began to think more about the 'living' Isabel, rather than the dead one. He revisited time and time again, the first occasion he ever set eyes on her.

It was the day after Christmas, Boxing Day, in 1986, and as he had done countless times since his youth, he joined the group of fox hunters who met outside his father's house. It had been a clear day with a cloudless sky, but the temperature was close to freezing. A mounted Phillip had enjoyed his traditional stirrup cup of warm rum and chatted to friends and neighbors. At the sound of the huntsman's horn, the pack of hounds and riders trotted down the long, winding gravel driveway and out through the large ornate wrought iron gates. The hunt was on.

It was then that Phillip first set eyes on Isabel. She was wrapped up warm with woolen gloves and scarf, and on her head she wore a navy blue knitted ski hat. Her long golden tresses poked out from under her head covering and between the layers of scarf around her neck. But it was her bright blue eyes that he noticed. They burned with a passion bordering on loathing for the mounted group who were off in search of blood. Isabel carried a home-made placard, crudely nailed to a pole. It read, "The unspeakable in pursuit of the uneatable", a slogan borrowed from Oscar Wilde, who like Isabel, felt the pastime of hunting to be not only ludicrous but immoral and wicked. Others in her group of protestors shouted abuse but Isabel was silent. She let her fiery eyes show the contempt she felt.

As Phillip remembered it, they pursued two foxes that day but caught neither. Phillip had almost forgotten the protestor when three days later he found himself sitting next to her at a dinner given by the Lord Lieutenant of Hereford, Sir Miles Walker.

He hadn't recognized her at first, as she was dressed in a beautiful red silk dress, but one look into her ardent blue eyes and he knew exactly who he was sitting next to. He opened the conversation, not with the usual platitudes exchanged by strangers at dinner, but with a direct question designed to ignite the fire behind those dazzling blue eyes.

"So, you don't believe in fox hunting, Miss Walker?" He said.

She'd turned on him as if he'd stuck a needle in her side.

"No, I don't" and she turned away to converse with the person on her left.

"Why not?" Phillip refused to let it go.

"Well, let me ask you something," she replied, "why do you do it? What is it you get out of it?"

"I won't give you the usual answer about how effective it is at keeping the fox population down, and foxes are a real menace to the farmers, because I don't actually believe it is the most efficient method of controlling them," replied Phillip, "but I do enjoy the thrill of riding at full gallop across miles of countryside. Jumping stone walls, hedges, streams, and anything else that I come across. There really isn't any thrill that compares to the mix of exhilaration and sheer fear."

He smiled at her but she did not return it. Instead she said in a matter of fact way,

"I'll give you a challenge, Mr. Fairfax. If you dare to ride with me across country one morning, and if you can keep up, I'm willing to bet you'll have as much exhilaration and fear as you can handle. And you won't have to kill a fox to feel it!"

Phillip couldn't help but smile at her passion, which did little to ingratiate him.

"I accept," he said, "name the day and I'll be there."

"Tomorrow morning," she said defiantly. "Eight o'clock, here, and don't be late or I'll write you off as the coward I think you are."

16

Phillip thoroughly enjoyed her feistiness and as he looked back to those early days of their relationship, he realized that he had started loving her from that moment. They did ride the next morning. They rode hard for miles and Phillip on his 17 hand hunter used every trick he knew to keep up with a fearless Isabel. Phillip did enjoy himself equally as much as if he'd been in pursuit of a fox. It was that day that marked not only his total dedication to Isabel but his total abstinence from fox hunting. He never rode to hounds again.

Phillip continued to go over every little moment he had ever spent with Isabel and, strangely, little by little, it gave him the strength and purpose to carry on living. Somehow, Isabel's defiant attitude and her love of life infused itself into Phillip's very being. He drew strength from her memory and he began to react to his predicament in the way that he knew Isabel would expect of herself, if the roles had been reversed. Oh God, how he wished they had been reversed. His love for Isabel had been, and still was, so pure, so all encompassing that he doubted – no, he knew – that he could never love anyone else as completely ever again.

Christmas 1990 was a particularly hard time for the Fairfax family. Everyone had bought things for Isabel and her baby and it seemed they all re-lived the tragedy over again as the gift wrapped presents were put in a trunk and taken up to the attic. Somehow not one person could quite bring them self to give those things away yet.

FOUR

The day after Christmas, Boxing Day, Phillip disappeared again but when he returned on New Year's Day he seemed to have found, if not exactly inner peace, then certainly a reluctant acceptance of the way things were. Even his drinking lessened although he still consumed more than was healthy. For the first time since the killing of Isabel and their baby, he spoke openly of his feelings. He began, at that point, to start living again and to think about a new future and possibly even a new career.

It was provident, therefore, that a letter from his uncle and Godfather, Sir Robert Spence should arrive at about this time, inviting Phillip to London. Phillip wasted no time in replying and accepting the offer. He needed a change of scenery and London could be just what he needed. Whilst there was a twenty five year discrepancy in their ages, the two men had much in common and considered each other, first and foremost, friends.

When Phillip had left school he had been offered a place at Cambridge University reading Art History. At school he had been a promising rugby player and it had been everyone's hope and expectation that he would win a full rugby Blue at Cambridge. But only weeks before taking his place at Cambridge, Phillip changed his mind and applied to the Royal Military Academy, Sandhurst. By September he had joined the other two hundred and seventy Officer Cadets and began his career in Her Majesty's Armed Forces.

The duration of his training was forty four weeks and upon successful completion Phillip emerged as a 2nd Lieutenant commissioned into the 2nd Battalion, Scots

Guards, a regiment that both his father, Major John Fairfax and Sir Robert had served in with distinction.

By June the following year, 1982, Phillip found himself fighting the Argentinean Army in the south Atlantic in defense of the British Falkland Islands. He left there with a promotion to Captain and the Military Cross for his bravery during the Battle of Tumbledown Mountain. He would return from the Falklands conflict with a depth of self belief and strength that only front line action can forge.

By the summer of 1985, Phillip had transferred from the Scots Guards to the Special Air Service, the famous SAS regiment, 14 Intel Company, the Mobile Reconnaissance Force. This was a special training wing whose main mission was undercover surveillance in Northern Ireland. Phillip found this work both physically and mentally challenging, yet ultimately satisfying. Once again, Phillip Fairfax excelled. The invitation that had arrived in the early days of 1991 from Sir Robert had been prompted by a discussion about Phillip with his former Commanding Officer, another friend of Sir Robert's. For some time Sir Robert, whose interests were now centered round art, had been incubating an idea for which he would need a man with Phillip's background, courage and integrity. The invitation to London was not solely altruistic on the part of Sir Robert.

It was cold and wet on the day that Phillip arrived in London. He had left Hereford, having dropped the keys to his cottage in Bredwardine into the offices of a local Estate Agent. Isabel's car, her little red Miata, he had given to his sister Christine who was starting University in Edinburgh that autumn. What small collection of furniture he and Isabel had amassed he had given away. Phillip fully intended to leave his past and his former life back in

Hereford, and, at this stage, cared not if he ever returned to either.

Arriving on the doorstep, a cold Phillip received a warm welcome from Sir Robert.

"God, my boy, it's really good to see you", said Sir Robert, grabbing Phillip's hand between the both of his. Sir Robert fixed his steel blue eyes on his Godson. Without preamble Sir Robert apologized, "I'm so sorry I was abroad for Isabel's funeral, but you know I was thinking of you."

"Yes, I do," responded Phillip and added, "It's good to see you too. I know you tried to get home for the funeral. We'd waited so long for the Coroner's decision that by the time it did come we just wanted it all over with as quickly as possible."

"Quite. Yes, of course. Now do come in and take that wet raincoat off." And with that, Sir Robert took the sodden garment and hung it on the hall stand where it proceeded to drip large puddles onto the tile floor.

They both entered Sir Robert's study where a gas fire gamely threw blue and yellow flames around artificial logs in the Adam fireplace. It only gave the illusion of warmth which was, in reality, supplied by a discreet central heating system. For anyone, like Sir Robert, who had suffered through London's infamous and impenetrable 'pea soup' fogs, this modern innovation was a godsend and a small price to pay.

Sir Robert motioned Phillip to sit and went to the mahogany credenza where he poured two schooners of sherry. He passed one to his guest and took a seat opposite him. For a full minute they both sat and looked at each other and smiled. It had, indeed, been a long time since they'd enjoyed each other's company.

"Phillip," observed Sir Robert, 'forgive me Phillip but you look like shit. You look as if you've lost a lot of weight." he added.

"Yes, I suppose I have. I find it therapeutic to tramp over the welsh hills trying to live off the land and I've probably been drinking too much too."

"I tend to do my best thinking when I have a drink in my hand," smiled Sir Robert, "so I suggest we pop around the corner for a bite of lunch and a brew. The 'Gloucester' does a very passable cottage pie and I can catch up with your news."

In reality, Sir Robert knew just about everything Phillip had been up to since Isabel's death. He had received several phone calls in recent months from his sister, Mary, Phillip's mother, and was well aware of the family's concern for Phillip's current lack of direction in life. This was not, however, bad news for Sir Robert. He had an idea, one that had been cooking in his mind since his retirement from the Foreign Office, and he needed someone with Phillip's abilities to help put into practice.

It was never clear to anyone in the family just exactly what Sir Robert's role had been at the Foreign Office. He laughingly shrugged off suggestions that he had been a spy - he called them 'spooks'- but somehow his denials seemed only to heighten everyone's suspicions.

Certainly he had traveled a great deal during his career and rarely with any explanation. It was, he maintained, the primary reason why he had never married. He had never, he said, found any woman who would tolerate his constant and sudden departures and his equally sudden re-appearances. Marriage had been sacrificed for his career, something which, in his advancing years, had brought about the occasional pang of regret. As a life long bachelor, he doubted now that he could ever submit to the disciplines required of a married man. Not, however, that several wealthy widows hadn't tried to persuade him otherwise.

By one o'clock Sir Robert and Phillip entered the *'Duke of Gloucester'* pub on Sloane Street, a ten minute walk from Sir Robert's home in Belgravia. They found a quiet corner table, despite the lunch time crowd, and Sir Robert took the liberty of ordering food for both of them.

'You must try their cottage pie, Phillip. It's truly a work of culinary genius and I know you'll love it."

Phillip happily acquiesced and they both ordered a pint of Boddingtons beer to wash it down. They chatted aimlessly for a few minutes until the plates of steaming pie and vegetables arrived. Once they started on their lunch, Sir Robert began to outline his plan and new idea to Phillip.

By three o'clock a jovial landlord had politely but firmly asked them both to leave, which they did. Sir Robert wore a large grin and Phillip Fairfax had a new career.

FIVE

1948

In 1948 more than 700,000 Palestinians were either forcibly expelled from their homes or fled in terror from Palestine, which now had become the newly created state of Israel. This exile, this dispossession and displacement, became known amongst the Palestinian refugees as *"al-Nakba,"* the catastrophe. Most of them would never see the land of their forefathers ever again.

One ten year old boy found himself carrying what few possessions his family had, heading for the Lebanese border. His name was Muhammad Diab. Muhammad, along with his father and mother and younger brother Tariq, eventually ended up at the *Shatilla* Refugee camp, in the southern suburbs of Beirut. The four of them, along with 15,000 others in a similar situation, came to call this polluted and overcrowded camp 'home'.

Life was not easy in their new country. Muhammad's father had been a motor mechanic in Palestine, but the laws of Lebanon forbade foreigners to hold good paying jobs. These were reserved for the native born. Only the lowliest and worst paying jobs were offered to the Palestinians.

Muhammad's father did what he could to put food on the table, but it was seldom enough. Gradually, Muhammad noticed how his once loving father became distant, withdrawn and embittered.

Somewhat predictably the *Shatilla* camp became a hotbed of dissent. Such an unstable population naturally turned towards violence in an effort to shake off their feelings of impotence, both political and humanitarian.

Naturally enough a generation of fanatical freedom fighters was born out of the detritus that once had been Palestine. They would become fighters in a holy cause.

Muhammad was an eager recruit to this movement, but he never considered himself a terrorist. He was, to his mind, quite simply a freedom fighter who was prepared to devote his life to the idea of one day removing the usurpers and returning to his homeland and his village of *Birwdh* as a free man.

Muhammad would never return to *Birwdh* which is now a part of Israel. His ancestral village had been bulldozed almost out of existence. The fields and olive groves that he had once played in as a child were now part of the *kibbutz Yasur*. Muhammad would not have recognized his home now, even if he had been allowed to return.

Always a fast learner and good with his hands, Muhammad rose within the organization that became known by the initials, 'PFLP". He did not marry, as many young men did, in their late teens or early twenties. Instead, Muhammad devoted his time to becoming a dedicated resistance fighter, a soldier for the *'Popular Front for the Liberation of Palestine'*. That is not to say that he was blind to the attractions of the opposite sex, but until he met Hala, he had never met anyone who possessed the same ideals and levels of commitment to the cause that had become his life.

He met Hala in 1965 when he was twenty seven years old and she was just a slip of a girl barely out of her teens. She had high cheek bones and dark eyes that burned with an intense fire stoked by her raw passion for Palestinian freedom. She wore the traditional red checked *keffiah*, a head scarf fringed with woolen tassels in the

Palestinian colors of black, white, red and green. She wore it loosely wrapped around her long shiny black hair.

Soon the two young people fell in love but rather than mellow their ardor for revenge, their love for each other intensified their hatred for those who had driven them from their homeland. Their joint commitment and readiness to make the supreme sacrifice drew the two freedom fighters even closer together. They were joined by a bond so strong that even Israel or its ally, America, could not break.

They married, after obtaining special consent from the PFLP. As a token of his love for Hala and as a reminder of their joint commitment to the cause, Muhammad placed upon her finger a ring made from a bullet casing and a hand grenade pin. But for Hala, there were difficulties in being both a wife and a revolutionary.

The men of the PFLP resented Hala for the attention she received. Many felt it was not acceptable that she should so overtly flaunt the patriarchal restrictions traditionally imposed upon Arab women. The fact that she insisted on dressing like the men, in khaki battle dress, and refused to be subservient to her husband brought strong criticism of both Hala and Muhammad. The fact that she also insisted on taking as big a part in the actual fighting as the men brought, along with the grumbles, a begrudging kind of admiration. That admiration along with her obvious commitment saved them both from being ostracized and expelled from the PFLP.

Eventually in January of 1969, Hala gave birth to a daughter whom they named Leila. In some ways, as a mother, the criticisms of Hala lessened and those that still felt uneasy with her participation in the fight were in a small minority. As a political activist Hala was even more dedicated after Leila's birth and whilst she may not have won over everyone's mind, she did, to some extent, win over their hearts.

When Leila was only three years old, Hala and Muhammad volunteered for a mission in Europe. It was designed to bring the world's attention into sharper focus concerning the plight of exiled Palestinians. A couple of years earlier a similar group had hijacked a TWA passenger jet when it had been in flight from Rome to Athens. *TWA flight 840,* a Boeing 707, was eventually blown up, without passengers or crew on board, in Damascus. The whole drama was played out in front of the world's media and placed the Palestinian cause firmly on the international stage.

Since then, the world had slipped back into apathy regarding Palestine. What was planned this time would make the whole world sit up and take notice of their plight. The world could no longer brush this dilemma under the carpet of their collective conscience.

This time an *El Al* flight from London to New York was to be blown up in the mid Atlantic. No longer were the PFLP prepared to spar with the west and its indifference. The Palestinian struggle for recognition would come through massive blood shed, if necessary.

Both Hala and Muhammad were deeply involved in the planning. Leaving Leila with her mother, they both flew to London. Here they set up a covert cell and Muhammad went about applying for a job as a baggage handler at Heathrow Airport's International Terminal. With the aid of false papers, Muhammad eventually found employment and planning in earnest began.

Despite the hardships in being separated from their young daughter, both Mohammad and Hala concentrated on their job and hoped it would bring them all closer to the day when, as a free family, they could return to Palestine.

What neither of them knew at this point was that they had already held their darling Leila for the last time. Neither of them would see her again. They would not witness her growing, nor would they be there for her triumphs or her tribulations. In turn, they would only be people in old photographs, people who featured in stories of bold adventures told by an ever increasingly senile grandmother. Never would Leila feel the warm embrace of her mother or experience a smile of happiness and pride from her father. Leila would grow up self reliant but with the very bitter taste of desertion in her soul.

Because of the efficiency of Israel's secret service, the *Mossad*, in conjunction with Britain's MI5, Muhammad and Hala died whilst trying to avoid capture. Their small one bed roomed apartment in Slough, chosen for its large neighborhood of Muslims and its convenience to Heathrow airport, was the scene of their deaths. Their last desperate act was to attempt to blow up the apartment and themselves. But for the first time, Hala's courage failed and she hesitated before she had pulled the pin on her hand grenade.

Both of them were shot twice through the mouth, '*tap-tap*', effectively removing their spine and the backs of their necks. This shot severed their spinal columns and stopped any reactionary impulse reaching the brain. Hala dropped to the ground onto her knees still holding the grenade. Muhammad Diab fell backwards without ever firing a shot.

In a few short seconds, a plan to bring the troubles of the Palestinians to the front pages of the western press and into the living rooms of an apathetic world were laid to waste. It was a moment when the little girl Leila Diab, far away in Beirut, became an orphan.

SIX

Friday
21st July 2000

Jasmine was a tall, statuesque girl in her mid thirties. Her straight blond hair hung loosely and fell down between her shoulder blades. Her fringe was cut straight and almost touched her eyebrows that shielded intense liquid brown eyes; eyes that, unlike her full lips, seldom smiled. Tonight Jasmine sat cross-legged on a tall chrome stool in the lounge bar of the Sheraton Park Tower Hotel in Knightsbridge. She was waiting as a hunter waits for its prey. She was waiting patiently.

Her short black dress rose to mid thigh as she sat side-saddle on the stool. Jasmine was revealing long, toned and well tanned limbs, guaranteed to attract attention. Two hours earlier Zachary Boyle had entered the double set of doors on the Lowndes Square side of the same hotel. He had checked into a pre-booked suite with three suitcases that each bore first class luggage tags from Air France.

Zachary was back in London after several months in the south of France. He had been working hard without a break and now he felt like making up for all those lost weekends. He wasn't an overly attractive man. He had a tendency to carry too much weight about his midriff which was only partially offset by his well tailored clothes. His fair hair was thinning on top and his eyes seemed far too small for his round head. Such physical drawbacks may have hindered most men in their quest for female companionship, but not so Zachary. He had long ago discovered that money and a willingness to spend it was a far more powerful aphrodisiac for women than a well

28

honed body. Once Zachary was in his suite, he unpacked
and meticulously arranged his clothes in the ample closet
and drawer space provided. He was a firm believer that not
only manners but immaculate clothes 'made the man.'

It had been a long and arduous time in Provence,
but a small token of his labors remained wrapped in brown
paper and was secreted in the lining of his suitcase. As he
neatly put away his clothes, he removed the small flat
package and placed it under his carefully folded shirts. It
wouldn't fool anyone who did a thorough search, but it
would at least keep it out of sight from a casual observer
like a chamber maid.

Zachary then showered and dressed. Strapping on
his gold Rolex watch, he checked his reflection in the
mirror. Turning first to the left and then to the right, he
appraised his image from all angles. Zachary was nothing
if not meticulous. It was part of what made him so good at
his job. Zachary was a master forger.

Satisfied with his appearance he descended, in the
mahogany lined elevator, to the hotel lobby. He crossed
the marble floor to the lounge bar where he took a stool at
the far corner by the piano. There were several couples
seated at the small tables dotted about the room. Business
men in Saville Row suits and ladies flushed from a days
shopping in Knightsbridge sipped their cocktails and
nibbled on complimentary snacks. Everything, reflected
Zachary as he surveyed the scene, was so very London, so
very English. It was, he thought, good to be home again.

Looking about him, it didn't take Zachary very long
to notice Jasmine sitting alone half way down the length of
an almost empty bar. He had been locked away in a gilded
cage for months, working all hours of the day and night
bereft of female company. Seeing Jasmine now, he
realized how much he had missed that.

With little or no effort at disguising his interest, Zachary appraised the long legged beauty that sat just a few feet away. He liked what he saw. She had the strong jaw line of a woman that knew her own mind. Zachary liked strong women. He slipped from his stool and approached. He was neither shy nor afraid of a rebuff. He knew the rules of the game, nothing ventured, nothing gained, and besides he considered himself well versed in the art of seduction. Zachary was a practiced voluptuary.

"Good evening," ventured Zachary, stretching his mouth wide in his attempt at a friendly smile. "Would you mind very much if I joined you? I am quite alone in London tonight and I'd dearly love some company and conversation"

Jasmine turned slowly and looked at him. Her lips parted in a smile, but her eyes remained cold and appraising.

"I am waiting for a girlfriend to join me," she replied as she continued to look him up and down. "She should be here soon, but yes, some company while I wait would be very nice."

"Excellent", expostulated Zachary with the enthusiasm of a teenager, "I'm delighted! What are you drinking?"

"Perrier water"

"Oh, we can't have that," blustered the seducer, emboldened by his initial success. "I'm celebrating! How about some Champagne?"

Jasmine appeared to hesitate, and gave the false impression that she was a vacillating female that needed help and guidance. Seeing this, Zachary jumped right in.

"I insist" he said forcefully, believing he was taking full charge of the situation.

"Oh well, I suppose I could, if you really insist. I
do love Champagne, but it does make me very silly
sometimes," replied Jasmine.

"I'm sure you're never silly," said Zachary
gallantly, 'but, yes, I do insist."

"Alright, then." said Jasmine. "I will, and by the
way, what are you celebrating?" feigning an interest she
didn't have.

"Shall we just say…..the successful conclusion of a
long and difficult job," he answered in his typically self
important and orotund way.

"How mysterious you are," admonished Jasmine as
she gently tapped his arm in mock reproof.

Zachary was now feeling very pleased with himself
and ordered a bottle of *Veuve Cliquot* which appeared in
short order. Louis, the ever attentive barman, recognized a
man who was out to impress and men out to impress
generally left large tips. Louis wanted his share of any
largesse that was going.

Somewhat belatedly, Zachary introduced himself.
Jasmine extended her slender hand revealing exquisitely
painted nails in bright red. Jasmine liked red. The color of
blood.

"Hello Zachary," she said, gently grasping his hand.
"I'm Jasmine", which she pronounced 'Yasmin', "Very
pleased to meet you," she lied.

"Do I notice a slight accent, Jasmine? Where are
you from?" he enquired.

"I'm from Argentina," her second deliberate lie,
although in fairness she had only recently returned from
there.

"I don't think I've ever met anyone from Argentina. Are all the ladies there as lovely as you are, Jasmine?" said Zachary smoothly.

Jasmine didn't blush as perhaps she had been expected to, but she had never been prone to such displays of femininity. She considered it a weakness. Instead, she did her best to look demure and treated the whole question as rhetorical.

For half an hour they talked of inconsequential things. They lied to each other, though for quite different reasons. Zachary, to make himself more interesting. Jasmine, to hide her true motive for being there. Eventually she asked him a leading question.

"Tell me, Zachary, why are you celebrating alone tonight?" she queried.

"Well, Jasmine, I hope I won't be alone tonight" he said with a genuine twinkle in his eyes. Zachary felt at home playing this game. He'd always thought he was good at it, and if the number of women who frequented his bed was anything to go by, he was an accomplished lothario. Though in all fairness, he had to admit, he rarely caught anyone in Jasmine's league.

Jasmine looked Zachary straight in the face. She looked into his watery eyes and for the first time Zachary noticed her deep brown emotionless eyes. They reminded him of a cobra's. They seemed alert but looked impervious to emotion. Impervious even to death he thought. They belied the smile that appeared on her full lips. For a second, Zachary felt unnerved, but as Jasmine gently placed her hand on his arm and leaned forward towards him so that he could breathe in her sensuous perfume, he once again became enraptured with the lovely looking lady who sat by his side.

"Perhaps," she said, leaning closer and letting her voice drop to little more than a husky whisper, "I should call my girlfriend and cancel our date?"

"That," said Zachary with a little hint of conspiracy "would seem to be an excellent idea."

With that, Jasmine slid elegantly from her perch.

"I shall be back very shortly," she said. "I think this phone call should be made in private. She's not going to be very happy."

Zachary made 'understanding' noises as Jasmine headed for the lobby. Both the ladies and gentlemen's cloak rooms were on the lower floor and Jasmine descended the circular staircase heading for the rest room. She dialed the number on the courtesy phone from memory. It was a short one sided conversation. She merely identified herself to the person at the other end and asked that a car meet her the following morning at five o'clock on the corner of Motcombe Street and Wilton Crescent. Jasmine then returned to Zachary who was, by now, on his third glass of champagne.

Jasmine and Zachary left the bar shortly after she had made her phone call, leaving Louis with a healthy tip. They headed by taxi to a small bistro in Pimlico Road. It was a favorite place for Zachary to eat when he came to London. Zachary was an ardent trencherman and he had missed his large portions of mixed grill whilst he had been in France.

Jasmine ate sparingly and only finished half her Dover sole, much to Zachary's chagrin. It wasn't just that it was expensive, and it was, but he hated to see food wasted. Had he not been out to impress Jasmine, he would, under normal circumstances, have scooped the left over fish onto his own plate. There was good reason why Zachary enjoyed a portly figure.

It was a pleasant July evening. They had, at first, wanted to eat outside on the sidewalk terrace, but whilst the weather was mild enough for a native Englishman to brave the elements, it was decidedly too cold for one brought up and used to warmer climates.

After a good meal, Zachary enjoyed a Cognac, whilst Jasmine sipped an espresso coffee, finally ending up strolling arm in arm, looking in the windows of the antiques shops that lined Pimlico Road.

After half an hour of strolling, Zachary hailed a black cab and they both entered its roomy interior and settled together on the rear seat. Zachary instructed the driver to head for Lowndes Square whilst he quizzed Jasmine as to her further plans for the evening.

"Are you staying at the Sheraton, too," he asked "or were you just waiting for your friend there?"

"No, I'm not staying there. Actually, Zachary, I'm staying with a friend in a very small and cramped little flat on Hans Crescent, but if you're offering, I'd love to come back for a night cap," she replied. "I'm sure your suite is much nicer and much larger than the cramped little box room I'm staying in."

"I cannot think of a more pleasant idea," said Zachary, as he mentally punched the air in triumph. It was, he thought, going to be a memorable night.

Apart from the night duty manager who greeted them on their return, the lobby was deserted. A few people could still be heard in the bar. Loud American voices having a great deal of fun were most prevalent and Zachary was relieved that Jasmine did not want to join in the raucous, impromptu party.

"Shall we go straight up to my suite?" asked Zachary. "I doubt we could hear ourselves think in the bar."

This, of course, was a loaded question and Zachary knew that the outcome of the evening depended very much on Jasmine's answer.

"Oh, yes, do let's," encouraged Jasmine.

Zachary felt one giant step closer to his goal of bedding Jasmine. Little did he know that it also moved Jasmine one step nearer her evenings' ultimate goal.

Entering the suite, he motioned Jasmine to sit on the floral chintz upholstered sofa. She sat amongst the plump down filled cushions and allowed a heavy sigh of contentment to escape her lips.

It did not escape Zachary's attention. Feeling now totally in control, he sloughed off his jacket with uncharacteristic disregard for his clothing and tossed it haphazardly on the back of a chair. He dialed room service and ordered another bottle of Champagne and as an after thought; he added an order for two large brandies. Jasmine smiled as he looked to her for approval.

After giving his room number and hanging up, he rejoined his companion on the sofa to continue his seduction. As they waited for room service they continued to talk of more inconsequential matters. Zachary alluded several times to Jasmine's beauty and flattered her with his observations of her obvious physical attributes. Whilst she didn't appear in the least bit offended by his remarks she constantly steered the subject back to more mundane matters.

They both continued their pattern of lying to each other. After all, wasn't that just part of the game? Zachary lied about his profession or his 'calling', as he referred to it. Jasmine lied about hers and her background. Had he known that Jasmine knew all about his 'calling', and quite honestly found it the least objectionable thing about him, he would perhaps have had an inkling of what was to come.

35

Instead, he continued his pontifications until the waiter delivered their champagne and brandies along with a complimentary basket of fruit.

Zachary could hardly wait to shove the waiter out of the door, and stuffing a crisp £20 note into his palm, he told the waiter that he could cope with opening the champagne and to just leave. Zachary opened the bottle with a pop and poured two flutes of champagne. He returned the bottle to the silver bucket of chilled ice water and raising his glass in a grandiose manner, Zachary proposed a toast.

"To new friends, may they become old friends!"

"To friends," replied Jasmine raising her glass to her lips.

They looked at each other and smiled. Jasmine smiled because she *knew* how the evening was going to end. Zachary smiled because he *thought* he knew how the evening was going to end.

After another small sip, Jasmine stood up.

"I need to freshen up," she said, and bending down gave Zachary a little kiss on the tip of his round, red nose. "I won't be long. Why don't you make yourself comfortable," she suggested with a knowing wink.

Picking up her glass of champagne and her small leather handbag, she headed into the bathroom.

Zachary took only a few seconds to start divesting himself of his shoes and socks, followed by his shirt, trousers and underwear. He put on a terry cloth robe that the hotel had so thoughtfully laid out on his king size bed. He sat back down and waited for Jasmine's return. He felt the familiar stirrings of longing and he hoped that she wouldn't take too long preparing herself.

Meanwhile in the bathroom, Jasmine did not undress. Instead she removed a glass vial from her handbag. It contained *gamma hydroxybutyric acid,* GHB,

36

otherwise known as the 'date rape' drug. It has no color
and no odor and although it also came in both pill and
powder form, Jasmine preferred the liquid. She took a
large sip of her champagne and then poured the complete
vial of GHB into her glass.

She returned to the living room and on seeing her,
Zachary rose in greeting. It was obvious as he stood up
what he had been thinking about. His robe bulged with the
instrument of his desire. Standing close to him, Jasmine
could feel his excitement pressing into her.

"Patience, my love," she whispered as she brought
the rim of her glass to his lips. She gently tilted the glass
and he drank deeply. He swallowed as she continued to
urge him to finish it all, giggling as she did so. Once
drained, she removed the glass from his mouth and stepped
back to avoid being kissed.

Turning her back to him, she said, "Unzip me,
lover."

He obliged. Turning to face him once more she
allowed her short black dress to slide from her shoulders
and fall to the floor. She ordered Zachary to sit back down
as she began to perform a slow and seductive dance full of
erotic suggestion. Zachary gazed enraptured with her
taught, athletic body.

As she continued her seductive gyrations she
reached behind her back and deftly unclipped her bra
letting that, too, to fall to the floor. Her breasts were firm
and her pink nipples, though small, stood erect. Zachary
was now fully aroused. After several minutes he could
hardly stand the suspense. Every attempt he made to touch
her soft skin as she straddled his lap was met with a firm,
but softly spoken rebuke.

"Soon, my love, soon," she'd say, as she gently
removed his hand from her body.

Zachary began to blink in order to clear his eyes. He thought that perhaps he had too much champagne. He promised himself that he would have no more alcohol until he had finally entered her. He knew that he was going to need all his strength to satisfy this woman.

Finally, Jasmine removed her panties and now fully naked, she went and knelt on the bed. She gyrated her hips and energetically thrust her pelvis towards Zachary until finally she beckoned him to join her. Zachary stood up to obey this sexy siren.

As he stood, his blood pressure plummeted and his steps began to falter as he approached the bed. He flopped down and rolled onto his back, his penis pointing straight up towards the water sprinkler that was set into the ceiling directly above the bed.

His glazed eyes looked questioningly at Jasmine as his mind grappled with the unfamiliar feeling that coursed through his body. Things were getting out of his control and he felt so tired all of a sudden. Perhaps, he thought to himself, Jasmine wouldn't mind if I had a little rest first. The increasing haze in his mind clouded any further thought and Zachary began to lose consciousness.

Those were the last lucid thoughts Zachary would ever have. A thin sheen of sweat coated his face and his eyes began to roll back into his head. By now Jasmine had retrieved her bra and panties from the floor and had once again put them back on. Now clothed only in her underwear, she knelt astride Zachary's ample stomach and stared with her expressionless eyes into his face.

She knelt there silently watching him for several more minutes. Suddenly, with very little warning, Zachary began to writhe in contorted spasms. Jasmine rode his belly like a bucking bronco and began laughing out loud. Zachary was having a seizure.

38

Jasmine had witnessed this before when she had used a large dose of GHB, but in order to finish her job completely, she grabbed hold of his nose between her forefinger and thumb and then placed the flat of her other hand over his mouth. Eventually the writhing ceased and Zachary Boyle was dead.

Wasting no time, Jasmine slipped back into her black dress and slipped on a pair of latex gloves of the type surgeons wore. She washed her champagne glass in the sink being very careful to remove any trace of GHB. She knew the hotel would be aware that Zachary Boyle had a visitor, a female companion, so there was no point in trying to hide the glass. She had been careful to note anything she may have touched and systematically went about wiping the surfaces clean.

She finished her cleaning and then went about searching in his closet and chest of drawers.

It didn't take her long to find the brown paper parcel under his pile of shirts. In his underwear drawer she also found a large amount of cash. Several thousands in British pounds, French euros and American dollars. At a glance, there was close to $100,000 worth in all. All of this she put inside a plastic grocery bag which in turn she put into a green Harrods shopping bag that Zachary had so conveniently left on the floor of his closet.

She gave the room a final glance and saw Zachary lying on his back dead to life but still with his erection. As a final gesture, she went over to the body and placed his still warm fist around his erect manhood.

Before leaving the room she looked through the 'spy hole' in the door and satisfying herself that the corridor was empty, she opened the door. Jasmine slipped silently into the corridor, placing the 'Do Not Disturb' sign on the door handle as she left.

Jasmine suspected that her progress down the hallway would be recorded on CCTV, so as she had done when she arrived, she kept her head low and walked briskly. Reaching the steel fire door she stepped through to the staircase that led down past all the hotel's floors to the lobby and the garage level beneath. However there were two floors above her that went to the roof level. Instead of descending she took the stairs going up.

Earlier, using her skeleton keys, she had unlocked the door that opened onto the roof. She pushed it open now and retrieved a brown canvas and leather knapsack. Emptying the contents onto the floor, she once again slipped out of her short black dress, her red heeled shoes and finally she removed the long blond wig. Jasmine ran her fingers through her short dark hair. It felt good to be her self again. A moist baby-wipe removed her red lipstick and her transformation was complete.

Jasmine now stepped into a pair of baggy tan cargo pants that covered up her shapely legs, and finally donned an old pair of sneakers and a grey hooded sweat shirt with 'UCLA' in bold block letters printed on the front. She pulled on a pair of black leather gloves that conveniently hid both her painted nails and her fingerprints. Her black dress, handbag, red shoes and blond wig were stuffed back into the knapsack, along with the cash and the brown paper parcel. Looking at her watch she made the time to be almost four thirty in the morning. She had until five o'clock to meet her ride which would be waiting on the corner of Motcombe Street and Wilton Crescent. It was barely five minutes walk away.

Lightly and soundlessly she skipped down the fifteen flights of stairs until she reached the ground floor. Even at this hour there was activity in the hotel. The night staff was beginning to clock off their shift just as the daytime kitchen staff began pouring through the rear delivery entrance. The area around the time clock was a hive of activity.

Jasmine had chosen this time well. She was able to slip out of the hotel, unseen and unchallenged, with the night porters, housekeeping and kitchen workers.

Soon she found herself walking along Lowndes Square heading for her rendezvous. As she approached the Daimler, a uniformed chauffeur emerged from the driver's seat and opened the rear door for his passenger.

"Good morning, Miss Diab," said the driver.

"Good morning, Max," she replied.

He handed her an envelope containing a passport and a plane ticket as soon as he was seated behind the wheel.

"I take it you want to go straight to Heathrow airport, Miss Diab?"

"Yes, please. My flight for Paris leaves at 8:00 a.m."

"Very good, Miss," said Max as he turned on the ignition of a smooth V8 engine.

In the back seat, Leila Diab smiled to herself. Soon she would be home in Provence and away from the likes of the lecherous Zachary Boyle.

SEVEN

Claude Chapon, 14th Marquis de Manville, sat back in his wicker chair satisfied with his breakfast of strong black coffee and fresh figs from his garden. He produced a solid gold monogrammed cigarette case and lit his first *Gauloise* of the day. The marquis enjoyed this relaxing time of day when the heat was not extreme and the troubles of the world had not yet encroached on his consciousness. As he sat in his garden a thin smile spread across his lips.

Claude was not a tall man. He stood only about 5' 6" tall, but he had a slim and wiry build which gave the impression he was taller. His thick, jet black hair showed no signs of graying or thinning despite the fact he was in his mid sixties. Whether this was natural or the result of chemistry was not known. His skin, although pock marked, was darkly pigmented which gave loud testament to his Arabic origins, as did his dark brown eyes. They were set deeply beneath his neatly trimmed eyebrows. His hands were delicate with long fingers that ended in exquisitely manicured nails.

Claude dressed well, even when he was lounging at home on his own, and although he was not a slave to fashion, his clothes were always impeccably tailored. Overall Claude presented himself as a quintessential member of the aristocracy with just enough idiosyncratic behavior to make him authentic most notably his penchant for wearing yellow socks with everything and on every occasion.

He had an exaggerated sense of self importance mixed with an unhealthy disregard for the feelings of others. Especially those who he felt were socially inferior, which was practically everyone.

His friends, all be they few in number, found his grandiosity and obsessive self interest too much to take in large doses. As a consequence, the Marquis found himself living a fairly lonely existence which, in actuality, quite suited him. He found other people's needs quite tiresome and tedious, far less of an interest to him than his own. He was, because of this, seldom invited anywhere but always found people, usually of an inferior social class, eager to enjoy his hospitality. He scarcely ever obliged them but on the rare occasions that he did he dispensed his *noblesse oblige* with an air of self sacrifice which existed only in his own mind. In reality, self sacrifice was not in the Marquis' repertoire.

The well tended garden and the ancient castle, Chateau de Manville, were situated in the community of *Baux de Provence* in the *Bouches-du-Rhone* department of southern France. The castle and grounds sat atop a rocky outcrop in the Alpilles Mountains and had a spectacular view overlooking the southern plains that ran down to the northern shores of the Mediterranean Sea. The castle dated back to the 12th century and although large parts of it now lay in picturesque ruins, by far the largest portion still remained gloriously intact.

In the late 15th century the ruling lords of the area began losing their grip on the local townships and villages that for centuries they had controlled. By the early 1600's the French crown claimed the castle and its lands and promptly placed the first Marquis de Manville in control. The family had resided there ever since.

The Manville fortunes grew rapidly but in 1821 they received an enormous boost when *'bauxite'*, an ore containing aluminum, was discovered on the Manville land by the French geologist, Pierre Berthier.

For the next century and a half, the red bauxite rock, named after the town, was mined extensively. As the 20th century began to unfold, the need for aluminum foil as a food wrapping, especially for chocolate, ensured the Manville fortune grew to vast proportions.

Today, however, the land produced no bauxite and hadn't for over fifty years. The Manville fortune, although still quite considerable, existed mainly in the form of the fabulous art collection that Claude's ancestors had amassed. The walls of Castle de Manville still housed that art collection, the star of which was undoubtedly Leonardo da Vinci's portrait of "*The Girl in the Red Dress.*" Reflecting on this portrait and its astounding beauty was the cause for Claude's smile, as he sat enjoying his first cigarette of the day. His smile was all the more surprising because he had been forced by financial circumstances to offer the Leonardo painting for sale by auction. Something he had vowed never to do.

A ringing telephone broke into Claude's thoughts and he listened for his servant, Albert, to answer it. The ringing stopped and very shortly afterwards Albert Guion appeared on the terrace. In both hands the stolidly bovine Albert carried the telephone and receiver on a large silver salver whilst the thin cord snaked its way back through the terrace door and into the chateau. He offered the tray to the Marquis, who took the instrument. The marquis raised his eyebrows to silently question the identity of the caller.

"Mademoiselle Leila," whispered Albert in answer to the wordless query, as he set the phone gently on the table.

"*Bonjour, ma petite choux,*" exclaimed the genuinely delighted Claude into the mouthpiece. "How is my 'little cabbage' today?"

"*Bonjour, Parrain.* I'm fine."

"How's London?" he asked, "Not too cold for you,
I hope. I hear it has been raining there since 1958!" he
joked.

"*Parrain*, you are dreadful," she laughed. "No, it
was gorgeous weather whilst I was there, but I am now in
Paris. I caught the eight a.m. flight this morning from
London. I thought I might do some clothes shopping since
I'm here and fly down to see you tomorrow."

"*Bien sur*. What lady could fly to Paris and not go
clothes shopping?" he responded jovially, and then asked,
"Did you get me a present when you were in London?"

"Yes, I did. I think you'll like it. It's a painting, a
portrait of a young girl."

"How wonderful!" he exclaimed. "Is it the work of
a contemporary artist?"

"Well, yes it is," she responded, "but I've heard that
the artist has recently died, so his work should start going
up in value quite soon."

"*Marveilleux*! The Marquis grinned. "I do have
the most thoughtful Goddaughter. I'll see you tomorrow,
ma petite! *Bon voyage* and don't spend all your money in
Paris," he gently remonstrated, and with that he hung up the
phone.

The Marquis' smile now became a fully fledged
beam as he reached for his second Gauloise of the day. He
thought, as he lit the cigarette, how clever he was. The
Marquis was a happy man and phase three of the big plan
was now complete.

EIGHT
Back to
5th January, 2000

Phase one of the Marquis' plan had begun well over nine months before. He had engaged a small time lawyer, an *advocat* from Nice, whose clientele came mostly from the underworld of petty crime. It had come as somewhat of a surprise to Monsieur Jean Basson when a personage of the Marquis renown sought him out. But Basson had been chosen, not for his skills in defending petty thieves and criminals – it's what his law practice relied upon for its existence - but more for his contacts in the murky world of crime. Basson had been enticed by the Marquis, with the aid of a few thousand Euros, to engage a thief for a specific purpose and Basson had wisely chosen Vito Gurino.

Vito was a skilled thief but more importantly he was a man of dubious moral integrity who registered zero on the ethics scale. Vito Gurino had a hypersensitive suspicion and mistrust of people which made him somewhat of a loner, but this only enhanced his suitability for the task at hand. Gurino was an Italian, darkly complected and with a perpetual sneer that was the result of a scar that ran from the top of his left ear to his lip.

Basson, on engaging Gurino, outlined the plan as specified by the Marquis. The plan required Gurino to steal from Italian churches. At first Basson had worried that such sacrilege would produce resistance from Gurino, but Gurino had no such compunctions. He cared little for the church, who he felt had never done him any favors. In fact Gurino cared little for anybody. Vito Gurino's main concern was for Vito Gurino.

His brief was to steal paintings on wooden panels from any church premises. The panels were to be only 15th century or early 16th century in date, although the subject matter was entirely irrelevant. Gurino was not an art expert but luckily the churches seemed eager to impart the information he required in their colorful tourist pamphlets.

Vito Gurino had little trouble securing paintings as he set about his bizarre pilgrimage around Italy. Within six weeks of his first church robbery he had amassed a collection of sixteen paintings that fell within the strict specifications of age, size and material. Accordingly, he telephoned Monsieur Basson and informed him that the paintings were ready for collection.

Jean Basson was not a successful lawyer. He eked out a living defending the petty criminals that preyed on the rich inhabitants and minor celebrities that swarmed to the Cote d'Azur every summer.

Basson was a short man who stood barely 5' 2" in his elevated shoes. He was only forty years old but his bald head and double chin made him look at least a decade older. He dressed badly in ill fitting suits and his garish ties showed not only bad taste, but, inevitably evidence of his last meal. He had fat, short fingers on hands that were constantly in motion. He waved his arms around as he spoke, so much so that he was somewhat cruelly referred to in the local magistrate's court as "*Le Petit Moulin*"-the little windmill.

Jean Basson cared little about what his peers thought because now he was not the subject of their taunts and derision but the object of their envy. He was the personal *advocat* for the Marquis de Manville and now enjoyed boasting socially to the upper crust of *Provençal* society. Those who had snubbed him in the past could, as he put it, "*baissez mon cue*, kiss my arse!"

During the telephone conversation with Gurino, Basson had ascertained that the paintings were ready for collection.

"We cannot do business of my office, Gurino. Tell me where you are staying and I shall come tonight and collect them."

"I'll want my money, in cash, before I'll give them to you," replied the thief. "I don't give credit."

Basson assured him that cash would be no problem and they agreed to meet at six o'clock at Gurino's temporary lodgings.

"Don't be late," snapped Gurino. "If you are, I'll burn the bloody lot of them. I don't want to get caught with all this religious crap. They'll send me down for a good long time if they catch me screwing the fucking church"

"I'll be there Gurino, and I'll have your money," assured Monsieur Basson. "Now just lay low 'til I get there."

Gurino passed on his address and hung up the phone.

Promptly at six o'clock a dark red Renault van with Basson behind the wheel, arrived at the back door of Gurino's lodgings. They were in the old port of Nice. There were few street lights and no people wandering around. Basson wondered if he had the right place but almost as soon as he had this thought Gurino appeared at the open window of his van. His sudden appearance made Basson jump.

"Shit, Gurino! Must you sneak up on me like that? You nearly gave me a fucking heart attack."

"Stop your whining," snapped Gurino, who then added "Did you bring my money?"

"Of course; I've got it here. Correct to the last euro," replied Basson, as he slipped a thick brown envelope through the opened driver's door into the eager grasping hands of Vito Gurino.

Gurino stuffed the fat wad of cash into the inside of his woolen work shirt. He didn't count it. He had no need to. If Basson had cheated him, he knew the consequences and Gurino felt certain he would not want to suffer those.

"Let's get those pictures on board straight away," said Basson, I need to be out of here. This place gives me the creeps."

Within five minutes Gurino had loaded all sixteen paintings into the back of Basson's rented van. He showed little respect for their age or fragility, although he had made some attempt at protecting them by wrapping them in old newspaper.

Basson cared almost as little as Gurino did about their fragility, and having them all loaded, he casually tossed an old blanket over the pile of antique artwork. Basson still felt uneasy and vulnerable. He just wanted to be away from this old, dark part of Nice. He was quite sure that cut-throat thieves and pirates still lurked behind every darkened doorway and in every alley.

The things he did for his clients, he thought. If he had ever harbored any thoughts about thievery as a living, they were definitely dispelled tonight. Basson was not a brave man and he was not enjoying this part of his employment by the Marquis. He seriously began to question his own sanity and wisdom in accepting the role in the first place. He hadn't, he scolded himself, passed his law exams just to end up as a 'gopher' for some self indulgent and larcenous Marquis.

As the rear door of the van slammed shut, various dogs in the vicinity started barking. Basson, without checking his mirrors, sped away as if the very Devil himself was chasing him. He soon realized that speeding was only likely to draw more attention to him so he got a grip of his frayed nerves and slowed the Renault to the legal speed limit. He weaved his way through the dark and narrow streets of the old port of Nice and headed towards the north of the town and the A8 auto route. From here he went west towards Cannes.

After a few kilometers on the busy highway, Basson began to relax. He enjoyed the anonymity of being just another vehicle amongst the sea of commuters and holiday makers that filled the four lanes towards Cannes. Basson even managed a smile as, all of a sudden, he felt quite brave and dashing. He had never thought of himself in this light before and he enjoyed the adrenalin rush that his escapade had provided. Perhaps, he mused, as he drove westward, a life of cloak and dagger intrigue might suit him after all. As quickly as he had this thought, he dismissed it. The seriousness of his predicament and the reality of his present situation suddenly dawned on him.

"Mon Dieu!" he said aloud, "I'm a lawyer! What in God's name would they do to me if they found me driving around France with a load of stolen paintings in the back of my van? Stolen from fucking churches, no less! Christ, they'd throw the book at me!"

At this point Basson began to sweat once more. Basson was not a brave man. Passing the exit for *Le Cannet* and the north of *Cannes*, Basson began to relax once again, although he kept his foot firmly on the accelerator, doing a steady one hundred and ten kilometers per hour in a westerly direction.

Between *Cannes-La-Bocca* and *Nandelieu-La-Napone*, he pulled off the highway into a refueling station.

50

He topped his tank off with *l'essence*, and walked towards the brightly lit building.

Keeping his van in sight he walked to the coffee machine outside the main door of the shop that seems to accompany all filling stations these days. He purchased a strong black coffee. Sipping at it, he found it better than he thought it might be. Finally he dropped a few coins into the telephone box that stood along side the coffee machine.

It was time to call the Marquis. As usual, Albert answered the phone.

"This is Monsieur Basson, Albert. Please inform Monsieur le Marquis that I am on my way to see him. I have some items of interest to him and hope to see him later this evening. I shall call when I am a little closer to you. Please tell Monsieur le Marquis I expect to be with him by ten o'clock tonight. *D'accord?* "

"*D'accord*," replied Albert who promptly hung up the phone.

After finishing his strong, hot coffee, Basson slipped back behind the wheel of his Renault van, and continued on his journey.

Roughly two hours after starting his journey he found himself crossing the D554. This, Basson figured, was about the half way mark. By now he became quite relaxed and although it was too dark to enjoy the scenery in this glorious part of Provence, he did enjoy the cool air that rushed in through his partially opened windows bringing with it the scent of wild sage and the Mediterranean Sea.

As he rounded the curve on the down slope of the highway, Basson's heart nearly stopped. Any feelings of security that he'd experienced shot straight out of his open windows. There, in front of him, were at least four police cars stretched across the road with all their bright lights flashing. Basson's first thoughts were to run. He felt sure

the police were after him. But where could he run to?
There were a dozen cars in front of him and several more
arriving behind, effectively blocking any escape. In his
heightened and nervous state, Basson felt that the game was
up. He was caught and he was going to jail. Gurino must
have blabbed! Oh God! Why had he agreed to take on this
job? He promised himself and his God that if he ever got
out of this mess, he'd never break the law again.

The line of cars crept forward and Basson suddenly
saw a policeman approaching each driver. The policeman
had a large flashlight and he shone it into the faces of all
the drivers and their passengers. Basson felt beads of sweat
on his forehead and his armpits began to feel damp and
sticky. A trickle of sweat ran down his side beneath his
shirt and sent an involuntary shiver through his whole
body. By now the policeman was approaching Basson who
was reaching a stage of near panic. The officer motioned
for Basson to fully lower his window as he shone his torch
into Basson's face.

"What's going on?" stammered Basson, as he
screwed up his eyes in the glare of the flashlight. His own
voice did not sound familiar to him. He had tried to sound
relaxed but he knew he had done a very poor job of it

"There's been an accident," explained the officer, as
he shone the torch first at Basson and then into the interior
of his van. "I see you have no one traveling with you,"
stated the policeman. "Are you on business or pleasure?"

"What kind of accident? I mean, yes, no, I'm on
business," stammered Basson. "Is anyone hurt?"

"It is a road traffic accident, Monsieur" said the
policeman, barely disguising his sarcasm, "and, yes, there
is someone hurt."

"Bad? I mean is he hurt badly?" said Basson, hoping to delay the moment when they'd have to discuss stolen paintings from Italian churches.

"Yes, Monsieur, but the ambulance is here. Are you a doctor?" he asked.

"No, no. I am an advocat, no, not a doctor," replied Basson.

"Ah, an advocat!" smiled the policeman. "No doubt you will want to sue the mountain, Monsieur that so inconsiderately got in the driver's way? Perhaps I should wave you through so that you can chase the ambulance!"

"No, no Monsieur. I am not that kind of lawyer. I do only wills and probate," he lied. "I am not interested in frivolous law suites."

"Good, Monsieur. We are getting too much like the Yankees, *n'est pas*?" said the policeman.

"For sure," said Basson, attempting another one of his awkward smiles.

"The idiot who tried to climb the mountain, Monsieur, probably fell asleep at the wheel. He wasn't even wearing his seat belt," continued the policeman. "I'm glad to see that you are wearing yours, Monsieur."

"Always," said Basson.

"*Bien*. Move forward when the ambulance has left." With that the policeman moved to the vehicle directly behind Basson's van.

Shortly after this encounter, another police officer appeared further up the road and began to wave the line of traffic forward with a glowing yellow baton. Basson heard the wail of the ambulance sirens as he and his little Renault van crept slowly, in a conga line, around the mangled wreckage of a Citroen.

He took a quick glance at the heap of crumpled metal and wondered how anyone could have survived.

Basson shuddered. He was not a religious man but he crossed himself involuntarily.

Basson was happy to be back on his way, all promises to his God forgotten. Basson was not a brave man, nor an honorable one.

NINE

After a further forty five minutes driving Basson found himself on the outskirt of Aix-En-Provence. He stayed on the A8, the road they called 'La Provencal', still heading in a westerly direction until he came to the junction of the A7 when he took a new direction and headed north.

At *Salon de Provence* he eventually left the four lane highway that he'd been on since leaving Nice and took the smaller A54 heading west again towards *Arles*. Long before he reached the town of Arles, made famous by the painter, Vincent van Gogh, he took an even smaller road, the A5 and started to climb up into the Alpilles Mountains.

Climbing steadily he eventually arrived at the small but delightfully ancient town of *Mausanne-les-Alpilles*. Basson, on seeing a telephone booth, pulled over and once more telephoned Albert at the chateau. He explained that he was now only minutes away and providing he didn't take any wrong turns, would be arriving on time. He was assured by Albert that the Marquis would be waiting and was anxious to see him.

Basson sighed with relief that his journey was nearly over as he climbed back behind the wheel for the last and shortest leg of his journey.

Fifteen minutes later the wheels of Jean Basson's little Renault crunched on the gravel drive in front of the Chatêau de Manville. Almost immediately a light went on over the front door and Albert's large silhouette appeared as the huge oak door swung inwards. Basson felt safe for the first time that night as he parked the van close to the front door.

Albert stepped aside as Basson rushed past him and walked into the cavernous chateau. There waiting for him under the vaulted ceiling stood the Marquis de Manville, relaxed and smoking as he propped himself against the huge carved stone fireplace. A few weak flames still licked around a large apple tree log. It gave off a sweet, inviting scent. The Marquis smiled at Basson; not so much with pleasure at seeing him but because it heralded the end of Phase One of the great plan.

"*Bon soir,* Basson, my friend. How was your drive?" enquired the Marquis, extending his hand in welcome. The Marquis could play the game when it was to his advantage to do so and tonight it was.

Basson was never quite sure if he should bow to the Marquis. He made a half hearted attempt at genuflecting but abandoned the attempt half way through. The marquis stifled a laugh at Basson's ineptitude and lack of grace, and hoping to save them both embarrassment he offered him a glass of wine.

"You must be thirsty after your long journey, Basson. Some wine?"

"*Merci*, Patron. I could do with one. It has been a long drive and encountering the police at *Brignole* nearly gave me heart failure."

"The police?" asked the Marquis, somewhat alarmed.

"Oh yes, but it was nothing to do with us, thank God. Some idiot had decided to go mountaineering in his car and when it came back down it made a hell of a mess all over the road. Police and ambulances were everywhere. Lights flashing, sirens going off…the usual drama, but it still made me break out in a cold sweat, I can tell you."

With that, Basson flopped down on the sofa and took a large mouthful of red wine. It tasted good as he allowed it to slip smoothly down his parched throat. He savored another and then, somewhat belatedly, held his glass aloft in silent salutation to the Marquis' excellent wine.

"It's from my own vineyard. I'm glad you approve. Last year was an exceptional season for the *Grenache Mourvedre* grapes, though I doubt this year will be any good at all."

"It's a superb wine, Patron, "agreed Basson, enjoying another large mouthful which almost drained his glass.

The Marquis ignored Basson's look which clearly indicated he was ready for a refill. He abhorred Basson's manners. This wine, he felt, should be sipped and savored slowly, not tossed down his throat like a ditch digger quenching his thirst.

By this time, Albert had started to bring in the paintings from Basson's van. He carefully lined them up against the wall, side by side. The Marquis bent to retrieve the first one as he placed his glasses on his nose to better inspect the paintings. Meanwhile, Albert kept a steady stream of artwork flowing into the hall.

With a note of surprise in his voice, the Marquis asked Basson how many pictures there were in total, as Albert continued to bring picture after picture into the chateau.

"I think my man said he'd acquired sixteen, but to be honest, I didn't stop to count them" responded the thirsty lawyer.

"Your man did well, Basson. You are to be congratulated. Some of these are excellent; in fact, some are even too good for the purpose I have in mind. I shall definitely keep a couple for my private collection. This one, for instance," he said, holding a portrait closer to the brass standard lamp to inspect the intricate brushwork, "is a fine example of *Bellini*'s work, if I'm not mistaken. Saint

Cecilia. Look how he's captured the piety in her eyes. Quite remarkable, quite wonderful," he said to himself as much as to Basson, whose interest lay more in the direction of the wine bottle than the ancient daubs of long dead Italian painters.

The Marquis was pleased with his new acquisitions. He rarely gave praise, however. He rarely found it warranted, but as a gesture of good will he poured Basson another glass of wine.

"Are you going to tell me now what you wanted all these old pictures for?" asked Basson, as he took another mouthful of red wine.

"All in good time, Basson. You'll know soon enough, and, in fact, I have another role for you to play later on. An even more important one, but you needn't worry about that just yet."

Inwardly Basson groaned. There were times, he thought, when he really wished he didn't work for the Marquis. So far he'd done very little legal work for him. In fact, most of what he'd done was totally *illegal*. Apart from writing a few letters demanding rent or threatening eviction, Basson had done little 'lawyering' for the Marquis at all. He rather expected that his next role would be another in the same vein as acquiring stolen art work.

Basson sometimes wished he'd never met the Marquis. However, he consoled himself with the knowledge that the pay was adequate, though not good, and it was one in the eye for all those snobs back in Nice. He got a lot of mileage out of being the personal advocat of one of France's most noble and well known names.

When Albert had all sixteen paintings lined against the wall, he quietly retired to his kitchen and his own glass of wine.

The Marquis was pleased and stood for several minutes appraising each panel in turn. He particularly liked the Bellini and two or three others that he felt deserved a place in his very special and very private collection. Naturally, he could not hang them on the chateau's walls. He was eager now for Monsieur Zachary Boyle to arrive and chose the four that he felt would best suit their purpose. The Marquis was, indeed, a very happy man.

As Basson sat enjoying his second glass of wine it occurred to him that he had not eaten since lunch. Now that he was beginning to relax, he started to feel the pangs of hunger gnawing at his ample stomach. As if he had read Basson's thoughts, the Marquis suddenly spun on his heels and faced a startled Basson.

"Basson, my dear fellow, you must forgive me. With all the excitement, I quite forgot to ask you if you'd eaten." Without waiting for a response he continued, "I shall ask Albert to prepare you some cheese and fruit. Would that suit you?"

Before Basson had replied that, yes 'he could eat a horse,' the Marquis had pulled on the silken rope that hung by the fireplace. Somewhere below in the bowels of the castle a small bell summoned Albert to the great hall.

Albert had anticipated the Marquis request and so he carried a large silver tray covered with a crisp linen cloth. On it were a selection of local cheeses, some fresh bread and a bowl of fresh fruit from the kitchen garden. All this he carried up stairs and along the corridors to answer the Marquis' summons. He had learned many years ago that anticipating the Marquis' needs and requests would save him many long walks along the dark corridors of the ancient castle. Placing the tray on a table outside the door to the hall, Albert gently knocked and stepped inside.

"*Oui*, Patron?" said Albert in his usual obsequious manner.

"Albert, please would you fix my guest, Monsieur Basson, some food? He is starving and I have been remiss as a host."

"*Oui, Patron*," responded Albert. "I imagined the Monsieur would want something to eat, so I have prepared a little cheese and some fruit."

With that he disappeared behind the door only to reappear seconds later with the silver tray which he placed on a low table in front of Basson.

"*Merci, Albert*" smiled the Marquis as Basson shook out his stiff linen serviette and tucked it into his collar.

Albert, without another word, bowed slightly to the Marquis and left.

"*Oui, merci*," muttered Basson with a mouthful of bread. Somewhat too belated to be heartfelt and sincere but Basson was too interested in his meal to worry about politeness to a servant.

Helping himself to more bread and some excellent *Banon* cheese, Basson, this time helped himself to another glass of wine. If he waited to be asked he'd die of thirst, he thought. The Marquis was far too preoccupied with examining the paintings to notice or even care. Basson felt entitled after all he'd been through on behalf of the Marquis.

After much deliberation and while Basson continued to shovel food into his face at an alarming rate, the Marquis extracted five paintings from those that lined the stone walls and placed them on a long, heavy oak table. These, he decided, were the ones he would keep for his own enjoyment in his private gallery. The rest would be for Monsieur Boyle to choose from when he arrived and

60

those left would be used for firewood. Sad though that was, the Marquis was very thorough and he would make sure that no trail would lead the authorities to his door.

"When you are finished," said the Marquis, looking somewhat disgustedly at the crumbs that littered the sofa and floor around Basson, "we need to discuss money. I shall, of course, reimburse you for your expenditure and for your trouble. I trust, naturally, that you gave 'your man' no inkling of the paintings' value or their further use."

"How could I, Monsieur le Marquis?" answered Basson, still with the masticated ruins of bread tumbling around inside his mouth. "I don't even know myself why you wanted all these old pictures of saints and what-have-you."

"Quite," agreed the Marquis. "Now Basson, I will explain to you." He sat himself in a tall wing backed chair and faced the still feeding lawyer. Placing the tips of his fingers together to form a steeple, he waited patiently until Basson had finished chewing and gave him his full attention.

"As you know, my cash flow has suffered somewhat in recent years," said the Marquis.

Basson didn't know but wisely chose to say nothing.

"Investments that once proved lucrative have produced little return in the last few years and this estate costs more and more each year to maintain." The Marquis stopped and lit a cigarette blowing the smoke carelessly in Basson's direction.

"There are constant repairs necessary to keep this venerable pile of stones intact. It is not only an honor but my duty to maintain the chateau for future generations."

60

Basson thought this last comment strange. The Marquis, as far as he knew, had no children, no future generation or even a wife.

"Thus," continued the Marquis, "I have decided to raise several million Euros to support myself, and the chateau, for the remainder of my life"

Still being no closer to understanding the Marquis' plan, a horrified Basson replied, "But you can't sell these pictures! They'd be recognized straight away and besides, they'd never fetch anything like a million, yet alone several million!" And then as doubt crept in, he added, "Would they?"

"My dear Basson," said the Marquis, as if indulging a somewhat backward child, "you surprise me with your depth of knowledge of the art world."

Basson presumed the remark was sarcastic. It was.

"You are correct," continued the Marquis, "the paintings would attract unwelcome attention and it is true, despite their age, they would fetch very little on the open market, but *that*", emphasized the Marquis, "is not my plan."

"I'm sorry, Monsieur le Marquis, I'm lost. I have no idea what you're talking about. Just how do you expect to profit by these...these.." he stuttered, looking for a word that wouldn't offend. He settled on "old pictures?" He played it safe and left his preferred description of the artwork unstated.

"Bear with me a little longer, Basson. Suppose," continued the Marquis taking in another lungful of smoke, "that I was to sell my Leonardo da Vinci painting of *the Girl in the Red Dress?*" Once again he exhaled in Basson's direction.

62

"Ah," responded Basson, "now that would fetch a tidy sum, but I still don't know why you need all those others."

"Their value to me is not in their subject matter. It is hardly desirable to have saints hanging on your walls in these modern, hedonistic times. No, their value lies in their age. They have one thing in common with my Leonardo painting. They are the same age; though, I admit, vastly inferior in execution."

Thinking this would make everything clear to Basson; the Marquis sat back in his chair and smiled as he waited for streams of congratulations to pour forth from Basson. Basson remained silent. He had to. He still had no idea what the big plan was.

"I see you have failed to make the connection," said the Marquis after several moments.

"Then I suppose I shall have to spell it out for you."

"Yes, I'm sorry Monsieur le Marquis, but I think you will."

"I need those old panels so that I can offer not one Leonardo painting but four! I have arranged to have produced, well, painted if you like, four old masterpieces by Leonardo! Now do you see? And Basson, the good bit is that you are going to sell them for me!"

Basson didn't see. In fact, once again, he was horrified by the Marquis' suggestion.

"How can I do that?!" blustered Basson, "I am not an art dealer and besides, people aren't just going to believe that four unknown paintings by Leonardo just happened to spring up out of nowhere. They'll be no...no...what's the thing called?" stuttered Basson.

"Provenance?" helped out the Marquis.

"Yes, there'll be no provenance, old valuations, no paperwork, no history…nothing! No one will buy it, literally, and I'll get the shaft for trying to sell them. No, no, Monsieur Le Marquis! I am not going to do it. I refuse!" stated Basson, who by now was somewhat red in the face with fear and indignation.

"Are you finished, Basson?" asked the Marquis calmly. "Good. Then I'll explain."

"I may not know much," continued Basson in the same vein and on the same subject, "but I can't see your idea working for a minute!"

As far as Basson was concerned the whole idea was ridiculous, ludicrous and he'd have no more to do with it. He thought the Marquis excessively naïve and quite possibly out of his mind.

The Marquis indulged his dim witted lawyer and smiled. "Let me worry about the details, Basson," he said soothingly. "Trust me. People will believe you. You will have eager buyers fighting each other to get their hands on a Leonardo. And I further promise, you'll be quite safe from any repercussions. You have my word on that" stated the Marquis emphatically, with the full expectation that this would be the end of Basson's protests.

The word of a larcenous Marquis was hardly comforting to Basson, but he decided that further argument was pointless. When the time came, he'd just refuse.

Changing the subject, "You must be tired," said the Marquis. He knew any further conversation tonight regarding his future plans would be less than fruitful. "I must let you get a good night's sleep."

"Thank you, Patron. I am tired, I admit. But you did mention earlier that I could expect compensation for my efforts…." he left the sentence hanging.

"Indeed, indeed, my friend. I have left an envelope by your bedside. I hope you think I have been generous."

Basson thanked him, but doubted that the Marquis even understood the meaning of the word 'generous'. The Marquis wished him *'bon nuit'* and told him that they would breakfast on the terrace in the morning at seven thirty. With that, he left and Basson reached for the last of the red wine and waited for Albert to appear to lead him through the castle labyrinth to his bed chamber.

TEN

12th January, 2000

Albert met Zachary Boyle at Marseilles airport and drove him in the Marquis' old Bentley to the Chateau de Manville. They arrived in mid afternoon and Albert showed Zachary straight to his quarters in the west wing of the castle. His suite, two rooms and a bathroom, provided modest comfort but it was obvious that no decorating or repair had been done in the rooms for several years. The paint was peeling on the window frames and the furniture wasn't antique or modern, merely old.

Zachary tested the bed by pushing on the mattress with both hands. The springs made a painful noise but he found the 'give' adequate. He hated hard beds. The bathroom which was situated in a round turret was equipped with a large cast iron bath, a wall mounted brass shower head the size of a soup plate and a pre-war styled pedestal sink. The sink bore green and brown stains from an old brass tap that still dripped. His toilet was located in a small room next to the bathroom and still used the pull chain method of flushing.

All in all, Zachary found his suite adequate but far from the opulent surroundings he'd envisaged. Besides his bedroom there was another adjoining room which, he presumed by the fact that it had large south facing windows and an easel, was to be his studio. In the center of this room was a large pine trestle table of immense thickness. Several odd chairs were dotted around and beside the fireplace stood an old sofa whose upholstery had seen better days. But the room was clean and a small log fire flickered in the hearth, which gave the room a homely feel.

Zachary had arrived with three large suitcases and these were eventually brought up to the suite by Albert. He wheezed slightly as he entered the room with all three cases piled up on a two wheeled sack truck. He was told by Zachary, in his very basic French, to leave the cases on the floor. His pronunciation was so atrocious that for a minute Albert stood looking blank, not knowing what he had been asked to do.

"*Ici*...here?" enquired Albert, pointing to the floor.

"*Oui*," answered Zachary, "*mais, tres gentil*... there are glass '*bouteilles*' in there." And indeed there were many glass bottles because Zachary Boyle had come fully equipped to produce fake paintings that would fool even the most skeptical appraiser.

Albert did as he was asked and left without another word. Zachary unpacked his clothes first and hung his jacket and trousers in an old armoire that unsurprisingly smelled of moth balls. His socks and underwear he neatly placed in an old oak chest of drawers that rocked badly when the drawers were pulled out. Zachary felt it could definitely benefit from some glue or a nail.

When he had unpacked his clothes, he dragged the remaining two suitcases into his new studio. He lifted the first one onto the pine trestle table that was at least twelve feet in length. He opened it up and started to withdraw the tools of his trade, all carefully wrapped in newspaper and bubble wrap.

His first act was to unpack his hog's bristle & squirrel hair brushes and his valuable miniver brushes which he used for very detailed work. Those he set, along with his mahogany palette, on a small side table next to the easel. Next, he unpacked a small stone mortar and pestle and various bottles of varnishes, siccatives, dilutants and natural oils. He also withdrew from his case a large bottle of gum turpentine, and an even larger bottle of Venetian medium which was a mixture of mastic and wax. It gave paint a satin like sheen and regulated the drying process.

The other ingredient he pulled from this suitcase was a medium he had made up prior to his visit to the Chateau de Manville. It was perhaps, the most potent weapon in his forger's arsenal. He had melted mastic varnish resin and amber into an oxidized linseed and poppy seed oil mixture which he stirred to a thick, pliable paste. This mixture resembled what was thought to be one of the secret ingredients used by the great masters, Titian and Vermeer. They mixed it with their paints to give a richer, deeper and more lustrous finish.

Jars of spike lavender to help paint adhesion and poppy oil to speed drying time and add depth to mixed colors, were all extracted from his suitcase, along with safflower oil and pressed linseed oil. All these jars and bottles he carefully lined up on the broad mantelpiece. Each was carefully labeled and made the room look more like an apothecary's workshop than an artist's studio.

Normally one of the difficulties facing any art forger is how much time and effort he will have to spend on creating his masterpiece. The problem is always that the higher the value of a painting, the more scrutiny it will receive. This naturally increases the chance of detection and neither Zachary nor his patron, the Marquis, wanted to run this particular risk.

Zachary was to create not one but four masterpieces. The time it took to achieve the best results possible - results that would fool even the most hardened and cynical examiner - was of no importance to the Marquis. The Marquis demanded only the best and for once was prepared, and expected, to pay it.

What made the project feasible for Zachary was that rather than having to invent a new, or in this case four new, Leonardo masterpieces, Zachary was only required to copy an existing one, four times. An awesome task even so, but one that Zachary felt he was well able to accomplish. Not only was the subject, something that scholars and critics would jump on, already designed for him by the great master himself, but the sale of these paintings was not his problem.

Selling his forgeries in the past had brought him perilously close to landing in the dock at the Old Bailey Criminal Courts. This time he was to be paid a flat fee, and a generous one, with minimal risk to himself. Or so he thought at the time.

Zachary continued to unpack his traveling studio. Some hours after he arrived he heard a gentle knock on his door. It was the Marquis, come to welcome his guest. Without waiting for a reply, the Marquis entered and immediately extended his hand. Zachary rose from the sofa to greet his host.

"*Bonjour* and welcome," smiled the Marquis. "I hope you find everything to your liking, Monsieur Boyle. My home is modest," he said gesturing about the room, "but I hope you will find it comfortable."

Zachary doubted that the Marquis had ever spent much time in this part of the castle and he doubted the Marquis' quarters were as spartan or as plain as these. However, he was graceful and said that, indeed, everything was just fine.

"If you need anything, please ring the bell," the Marquis pointed to a small black button on the wall by the fireplace, "and Albert, who I know you have met, will be only too happy to attend to your needs."

"Thank you," said Zachary,

"We will, of course, need to establish a few ground rules," continued the Marquis. "I'm sure you realize that your extended stay here should, how shall I put it….be not the subject of tittle-tattle in the town." He looked apologetic but added, "Therefore, I hope you won't mind if I ask you to restrict your outside activities to my garden. I regret I have to ask this but much rides on our little venture."

Hardly a *little* venture, thought Zachary, but he made no comment to the Marquis' insensitivity. He would realize in the weeks to come that the Marquis and insensitivity went hand in hand, especially in his dealings with those he considered to be of inferior birth. This to all intents and purposes included pretty much everyone.

"I understand," said Zachary. He fully intended to work long hours anyway. The sooner he was done, the sooner he was paid and back home in England.

"I do have one or two requests, actually," said Zachary. "I shall need a couple of strong lamps, preferably adjustable, so that I can work at night as well as when the light is bad."

"No problem. I shall arrange for those straight away. Was there anything else?"

"Well, yes. I shall also need, although not immediately, some sort of sun-tanning machine." He knew he'd have to explain, so he continued, "not for me personally, you understand, but it is for the paintings."

"Ah!" said the Marquis, nodding with a knowing look on his face. "Of course, I shall order one immediately, for drying the paintings. It is not a problem, Monsieur Boyle."

Zachary didn't bother to correct the Marquis. He felt it better to let him feel that he was well up on the techniques of the master forger. In fact, Zachary's need for a tanning machine was a closely guarded secret amongst his brethren in the forging business. Approximately four hundred hours bombarded by the lights of one of these machines produces the natural effects of one hundred years of the aging process in the life of a painting. Cooking the finished paintings for about three months would produce for Zachary about four hundred years of natural aging; enough to fool scientists who feel their machines capable of detecting any trick dreamed up by a lowly forger.

The Marquis' electricity bill would shoot through his ancient tiled roof, but that was of no consequence or concern to Zachary.

"And talking of drying, Marquis, I shall also need a good strong fan. It will also help to keep me cool when the weather heats up a bit," added Zachary.

"It shall be done! Now, Monsieur, if you permit me, I shall ask Albert to bring in the panels I have acquired for you and, perhaps together, we can choose those most suitable for your work."

With that, the Marquis stepped to the bell and demonstrated, with the aid of his index finger, how to summon Albert. Within minutes Albert appeared, slightly out of breath, but carrying five small wrapped painted panels under each arm. He gently placed them on the sofa and retired back to his kitchen where he waited for a further summons. The next time, he knew it would be for food, so he went about preparing a tray for the Patron's guest, just as he had done the previous week for the lawyer, Basson.

Zachary was excited to see the panels that he was to use for his 'replicas.' He gently picked up the first one and laying it on the trestle table, he carefully removed the paper protection. It was poplar wood. Perfect. Just what he had ordered. Leonardo da Vinci had preferred to paint on poplar panels, and like the *Mona Lisa*, his most famous

portrait, the *Girl in the Red Dress* was also on poplar.
Zachary immediately turned the painting over and
examined the back. It bore no marks other than an
inscription in chalk which read, "*V. Campi pinxit,
Cremona.*" This translated from the Latin meant V Campi
painted it, in Cremona." It was a fine painting by *Vincenzo
Campi* of the *Madonna and Child.*

    Zachary turned it over again and gently ran his
delicate soft fingers over the paint. It was hard and smooth,
almost like porcelain, with no loose paint except around the
very edge. This was good, as Zachary fully intended to
leave as much of the original around the edge as possible.
If chemical analysis were done on a painting, they would
always remove a miniscule piece of paint from the edge
which would normally be hidden by the frame. This gave
Zachary an even greater chance of succeeding when it
came to fooling the paint analysis scientists.

    Zachary put the panel aside and moved to the next
one. Sadly, it was on an oak panel and therefore of no use
to him. He put it back inside its paper wrapping. The next
painting he examined was a late 15th century work, again
on poplar wood, of *The Madonna of Humility with Five
attendant Angels.* It, too, was perfect on both sides.
Zachary was pleased. So far, two out of three were ideal.

    He unwrapped four others, mostly from the mid to
late 15th century Florentine school and mostly depicting the
Madonna and child, with one being the infant Saint John
the Baptist. The artwork was typical of the period but
uninspired in its execution. They perhaps came from the
hand or studio of *Andrea del Sarrto* or *Carlo Dolci* and as
such, lacked the quality that makes a painting truly great.
However, they would do nicely for Zachary.

    Throughout this process, the Marquis had said
nothing. Only when Zachary drew the curtains to block out

any fading daylight did the Marquis enquire as to his motive.

"It's so that I can examine the paintings under a 'black light' to see how much over painting and restoration they have received," explained the artist.

The Marquis responded with a nod of his head, as if he'd known all along. Of the ten he had to chose from Zachary eventually put aside the four best and most appropriate panels. He took off his magnifying visor and light and switched on the overhead brass chandelier. The process had taken almost an hour and was now complete. Zachary had his four panels. He was excited and very eager to get started.

"These," he said pointing to the four he had selected, "will be perfect, Monsieur le Marquis. However, I would really like to see the original painting before I dismiss the others entirely. I have picked the ones with clean backs so that any collector marks; etcetera on the original can be duplicated on my paintings. In this case, the back is almost as important as the front," he explained.

"Yes, yes, I agree," said the Marquis. "But I think tomorrow would be a more appropriate time to view my Leonardo. I expect you will want to have a little something to eat and then get a good night's sleep. I shall summon Albert once again. I think he will have prepared a small meal for you. Do you like wine?" he added.

"Very much," said Zachary, visibly brightening, for it was true he was both hungry and thirsty.

"Good. Then I shall send up a bottle of wine from my own vines," stated the Marquis, as he went to press the black button once again.

"We shall meet for breakfast on the terrace at seven thirty tomorrow" announced the Marquis. "Meanwhile, I

73

shall wish you '*bon appetite*' and '*bon nuit*'. I have no doubt Albert will be here within a few minutes."

With that, the Marquis turned and walked out of the studio door to return to his more opulent quarters.

Albert did appear, on cue, with a tray of food and wine. Zachary thought Albert was a rather stupid creature, almost an idiot, but he sensed that there lurked a kind of craftiness about his person. He had the demeanor of someone who had come from a long line of 'hewers of wood' and 'drawers of water', thought the uncharitable Zachary. Albert, he thought, was a peasant.

Sitting at one end of the enormous pine trestle table, Zachary lifted the lid that covered his dinner. Beneath, was a large bowl of rabbit stew that smelled deliciously of garlic, shallots and was served in a red wine sauce. A large section of baguette and a carafe of the Marquis' own wine completed his meal. With great enthusiasm, Zachary began to devour his meal, almost before Albert had left the room. He did manage a quick, "*Merci*" and "*Bon nuit*" to the disappearing back of Albert who neither cared nor responded.

The door closed with a firm click of the old iron lock and Zachary was alone with his stew, a selection of Italian religious art and his thoughts.

ELEVEN

Zachary awoke at six o'clock the next morning, and although the day promised to be a warm one, he was cold, especially his feet. He had fallen asleep without pulling the heavy velvet curtains and the morning light poured in through his window. He rose slowly and put his bare feet on the ancient oak floor. Zachary had half expected to have a stiff back; he usually did after the first night in a strange bed, but surprisingly, he felt well rested. Like most portly people who carried too much weight in front, he suffered acutely with lower back problems.

Zachary attended to his toilet, shaved and showered. He dressed in corduroy trousers and a short sleeved Polo shirt, and waited for the appearance of Albert to guide him down to breakfast. Had he set about trying to find it on his own, he knew he'd get hopelessly lost. Dutifully, Albert appeared shortly before seven thirty.

"*Bonjour, Monsieur Boy-eel*," said Albert. "Please to follow me," as he turned back and headed the way he'd come.

Zachary muttered "*Bonjour*" in his appalling accent and fell in behind the surprisingly sprightly Albert.

The Marquis was already seated at the glass topped table on the terrace. He chose not to rise as Zachary approached, but none the less, bade him a cheery "Good morning."

Zachary took his seat at the vacant place setting and proceeded to pour himself a glass of freshly squeezed orange juice.

"I hope you slept well," enquired the Marquis, to which Zachary replied that he had. He wondered if he should mention that an additional blanket would have been welcome but decided to bring the subject up with Albert later on.

"After breakfast," continued the Marquis, "I think I shall bring the Leonardo to your studio. I presume you will want to start work as soon as possible."

"I'm very eager to get started," confirmed Zachary.

"Good, then I, personally, shall bring it up to you, so that you can examine it. I will ask, of course, that you handle it as little as possible and that you wear gloves at all times when you touch it."

"Naturally," agreed Zachary. "I'm well aware what nasty oils and acids we all have on our fingers." He thought the Marquis was being excessively patronizing.

"I knew you'd understand. *Bon.*"

The Marquis sat back and without heed to Zachary's breakfast, lit his morning Gauloise cigarette.

The Marquis duly arrived at Zachary's studio at nine o'clock, holding his precious painting in white gloved hands. He set it on the easel and then produced a pair of similar gloves from his coat pocket for Zachary.

Zachary pulled the gloves on as he kept his eyes riveted on the magnificent portrait of *The Girl in the Red Dress.* Never before had Zachary been so close to such a masterpiece. To be able to touch it and peer at it through his magnifying visor was a supreme joy to him. He almost shook with the pure pleasure and excitement of the moment.

The Marquis looked on and smiled benevolently as if he was indulging a favorite son. He always enjoyed seeing the effect the painting had on people when they first cast their eyes upon it. How could anyone expect him, of all people, to part with such a treasure?

TWELVE

4th May, 2000

The telephone was ringing as Phillip came through the back door of his cottage in Oxfordshire after his morning run. Wiping the beads of sweat from his face with a fresh towel, he glanced at his watch. It was only just gone seven in the morning. It could only be one person calling at that hour.

"Hello. Fairfax here," said Phillip as he lifted the receiver.

"Good morning, Phillip. It's Robert."

"I wondered if it might be you. Don't you ever sleep?"

"Sorry, but I knew you wouldn't still be in bed. Have you seen the paper this morning?" said Sir Robert.

"No, I've been out jogging. Had one too many down the pub last night. What's so important?"

"I've just been reading in today's *Telegraph* that the Marquis de Manville is going to sell his Leonardo da Vinci painting, '*The Girl in the Red Dress*' at auction, in Paris."

"Are you going to buy it, then?" asked Phillip, somewhat tongue in cheek.

"I shouldn't think so," responded Sir Robert. "They say it will fetch over one hundred million Euros! There hasn't been such an important piece of art-certainly not by Leonardo-up for auction since *Vincenzo Peruggio* tried to flog the Mona Lisa to the *Uffizi* Gallery in Florence, after he'd purloined it from the Louvre."

"Yeah, I guess it will make a bit of a splash on the auction block, but I don't really think I'm familiar with it...the painting, I mean."

"Well, I'm not surprised. Only a very few people have ever been allowed to examine it. I went with Anthony Blunt, way back in 1956, the year he was knighted. We met after the war."

"Do you mean Anthony Blunt, the Russian spy?"

"Yes, the very same. He was Surveyor of Her Majesty's paintings at the time. Before we found out what a double crossing little shit he was. Anyway, I went down to somewhere in Provence, to this chap, the Marquis de Manville's place. Some large chateau perched on a bloody big rock, out in the middle of nowhere. Anyway, I get to view this painting. Bloody incredible. It beats the *Mona Lisa* hands down, if you ask me. More vibrant, if you know what I mean. Can't remember much about this Manville chap though. He was quite young and I seem to remember I didn't like him much. A bit too full of his own self importance. He acted a bit *nouveaux riche* which is surprising since his family's supposed to go back a few hundred years. I suppose being brought up in the Middle East didn't help.

Anyway, the last time this painting was seen in public was at the 'Paris Universal Exposition' in 1900. Of course it was the present owner's grandfather who loaned it then. I think it was housed in the Palace of Fine Arts and it caused quite a stir. After that Italian, Peruggio, stole the *Mona Lisa* from the Louvre in 1911, the family refused to loan their painting out again, or let it be photographed or even seen. That's why you're not familiar with it."

"I see," said Phillip. "This auction will be massive. Do we know when and where it's going to be held?"

"Not yet. According to the article, it probably won't be until the autumn. They need to let people know well in advance. I suppose it'll give them a chance to save up their pennies."

"They'll need to. Well, I just hope their security's up to the job."

"Yes, well, that's partly why I phoned. I think your expertise at tracking stolen art work should help them prevent another catastrophe. You know how lax some of these auction houses can be. They behave like rank amateurs, most of the time. Anyway, I'll make a few noises in the right ears and see if I can't drum up a bit of business."

"Sounds good. Stay in touch"

"Of course, dear boy. Now, get showered and have some breakfast. I'm sorry I called so early," said Sir Robert.

"No problem. Bye."

Since Phillip's lunch with Sir Robert at the Duke of Gloucester pub back in early 1991, Phillip had worked alongside his godfather tracking down stolen artwork across the globe. Phillip's training in surveillance and counter intelligence with the SAS and his love and knowledge of art proved an irresistible combination. Their success rate for recovering works of art and their quiet discretion quickly propelled them to the top of a very lucrative field. They worked mainly for insurance companies, often wealthy private owners who knew Sir Robert socially or from his job in the Foreign Office. They also worked occasionally for museums whose losses often brought a ton of bad and unwanted publicity.

Bad publicity for a museum or similar institution was not good business. It often meant fewer bequests from wealthy donors. After all, who would want to donate a masterpiece only to have it stolen off the walls? Security is expensive and often, the smaller museums are rich in treasures but poor in cash.

In recent years, art theft had mushroomed. It lies third behind drug and arms as the most lucrative illegal activity worldwide. This means billions of dollars in illicit trade per year. Sir Robert, who had first thought of the idea of forming an international art recovery force, had recruited Phillip as his major trouble shooter. Phillip was physically imposing. He had a quick brain and he'd never been known to let go once he'd sunk his teeth into a problem. He was as tenacious as he was intimidating to those who unwisely crossed his path.

After Phillip had shaved and had a light breakfast, he walked down to the village shop to collect his paper. He wanted to read for himself about the sale of Leonardo's portrait of *The Girl in the Red Dress.*

After he got home and had read the article Phillip sat behind his computer screen to get some background on the painting and also on the present Marquis. He found little of interest on the painting and even less on the present Marquis de Manville. It would appear that the first time the painting had been subjected to an exam was in 1905 by Roger Fry, the year before he took up his appointment as Curator of Paintings at the Metropolitan Museum of Art in New York. Mr. Fry found the painting to be 'flawless' and pronounced it 'every bit as engaging as the Mona Lisa.'

The next time it was examined was in 1938 by Sir Robert Witt, a co-founder of the *Courtauld* Institute in London and chairman from 1921 to 1945, of the National Art Collections Fund. He went one step further than Mr. Fry by calling the Leonardo painting "the finest portrait that has ever been painted."

It appears, however, that the present Marquis had entertained the idea of selling the painting well over two years ago, before 1998, because it had been subjected to *3D Electronic Speckle Pattern Interferometry*, a non-contact, non-invasive technique to examine it's deterioration, which, according to the website had been minimal. It had been carbon dated and x-rayed, the latter to detect any *pentimenti*. That's the alteration in a painting's composition showing how an artist may have changed his mind as to the arrangement of hands, arms, etc during the execution of the work. Whilst there seemed never to be any suggestion that it was anything other than by the hand of Leonardo himself, the painting had also been tested for both Prussian blue and zinc white paint, both 18th century pigments not known to earlier artists. It had also been subjected to x-ray diffraction to analyze the make up of the paint and x-ray fluorescence to determine if paint pigment was too pure or newer than the date given, which was circa 1501. In short, enough scientific work had been carried out to satisfy any future purchaser.

Oddly, however, there appeared no photographic likeness of the *"Girl in the Red Dress"* on any of the websites he visited. After gleaning all the information he was likely to get, Phillip concentrated on the de Manville history.

THIRTEEN

1920 France

In 1920, Jean-Paul Chapon, 13th Marquis de Manville was a captain in the French Cavalry. In July of that year and resplendent in his pale blue uniform and black high top boots, he was sent to Poland to join the staff of Lt. General Weygrand. Weygrand was there to fight and defeat the Red Army at Warsaw. Both of which he succeeded in doing.

Jean-Paul acquitted himself well in the fighting and came to the attention of his superiors. He was accepted into the *Legion d'Honneur* for 'Eminent Merit', one of France's highest orders and began to make a good name for himself as a soldier. When Weygrand, now promoted to General, was appointed as High Commissioner for Syria under the French Mandate of 1923, Jean-Paul was invited to accompany him as a staff member.

This started his love affair with the Arab nation. But the Marquis found the French rule too oppressive towards the proud Syrian Arabs. He felt their ancient culture was being stamped on by the large boot of the authoritarian French. The French franc became the unit of currency and the French language became compulsory in all the schools. The children were even required to sing the '*Marsaillaise*', the French National Anthem, as the authorities continued to pound their will into the native Syrians.

Jean-Paul began to have doubts about the French regime as they ruled this ancient land with little or no regard for its traditions and ways of life. But his chief grievance against his own people was the suppression of newspapers and civil rights, as well as the arbitrary division of the country into several separate states. This, apparently, made it easier to govern. Jean-Paul believed in the League of Nations Mandate, but only insofar as it provided eventual sovereignty for the Syrians. The French, however, seemed reluctant to make any attempt at framing a constitution.

His was a lonely voice in Damascus and when, in 1935, he married Zada al-Muktir, the youngest daughter of a Syrian merchant family, the French authorities viewed him with increasing suspicion, although by this time he had resigned from the French Cavalry.

The following year, 1936, Zada gave birth to a son, Claude Antoine Ibrahim Chapon, the future 14th Marquis de Manville. Jean-Paul was happy in those early days of marriage. Not only maritally happy but the new liberal Socialist government of France under Leon Blum had worked out a Syrian-French Treaty of Alliance. This brought renewed feeling of optimism to Jean-Paul and his newly adopted country of Syria.

Always a gifted linguist, he mastered Arabic quickly and now devoted his time to representing the Syrian cause. He did so both in person and by writing articles to foreign newspapers, mostly American, but little changed. Gradually, local government functions were given over to Syrian bureaucrats but only to those that the French themselves had trained.

At this time Jean-Paul eagerly offered his services to the Ministry of Works. But they, still seeing him as a colonialist Frenchman, and probably a spy, refused his offer. Although things started to progress politically in his adopted country, Jean-Paul knew that he would never be accepted. This beautiful country on the eastern shores of the Mediterranean Sea could never truly become his home.

There was constant bickering amongst the different factions all over Syria which, all too often, ended in violence. In September 1938 France again flexed her colonial muscles and separated the district of Alexandretta and transformed it into the new Republic of *Hatay*. This lasted only a year at which time it became absorbed into Turkey, something that again angered the Syrians, who, to this day, still regard it as their land.

But 1939 brought an even bigger problem. Adolf Hitler. Once again Jean-Paul's life was turned on its head when the Third Reich invaded Europe. When the French armies fell to Hitler's invading troops in 1940, Jean-Paul felt compelled to return to France and aid in her defense.

As much as he disliked and disapproved of France's handling of Syria and the despicable *Vichy* French Regime that subsequently took over, he still loved the land of his birth. Jean-Paul Chapon, 13th Marquis de Manville returned home to France in late 1940 some seventeen years after he had left. Zada and his small son, Claude, stayed behind in Syria

He joined the French Resistance, known locally as the '*Maqui*', and soon found himself leading a small cell of men and women in his home region of Bouche du Rhône. The chateau was eventually commandeered by the German forces, but the Marquis was allowed to remain in residence, with Albert. They were both confined to two small rooms in the servant's quarters.

As nobility, the Germans treated the Marquis with respect at first and Jean-Paul used his natural charm to ingratiate himself. This proximity to the Germans gave Jean-Paul excellent opportunities to watch, listen and report information back to the Resistance.

84

The magnificent art collection had been secreted away long before the Germans arrived. It lay for the duration of the war carefully packed and hidden in one of the secret rooms carved out of the dry Provençal rock within the fabric of the castle walls. The doorway was bricked up and a rough plaster disguised its whereabouts. Occasionally his military training came in handy and he was able to perform acts of sabotage against the unwelcome invaders but more often than not, it was his intelligence gathering that proved most useful.

For a brief period he worked in conjunction with Missak Manouchian, an Armenian and a communist who was brought up in an orphanage in French Syria. Manouchian, now an avid Resistance fighter had come to Marseilles in 1925 and knew very little of the current Syria but he and the Marquis would, on the odd occasion, share a bottle of wine and talk of the old days far away in Syria. Manouchian was eventually captured by the Germans. He was tortured for days and eventually executed on 21st February, 1944.

Shortly afterwards Jean-Paul was also arrested along with several dozen others believed to be in the Resistance. Twenty-two were eventually shot, but Jean-Paul escaped that fate. Instead, and because there was no specific evidence against him, he was sent to a Nazi labor camp, *Natzweiller-Stricthof* in eastern France. He stayed there and suffered, like so many of his countrymen. He didn't taste freedom again until the end of the war.

By the time Jean-Paul was liberated in 1945 he was a very sick man. He made slow progress at recovery and when in 1946 the Free French troops fled Syria and Lebanon, he wrote asking his wife Zada to bring herself and their son, Claude, to France.

He waited several weeks and eventually her reply came. She would not be coming to France, nor would their son Claude. Instead she demanded a divorce. Despite his many pleading letters, Zada was adamant. But Jean-Paul never agreed to her demands for divorce. Instead his health deteriorated and in June 1954, Jean-Paul, 13th Marquis de Manville, a bent old man of only 61 years, died alone in his chateau with neither his son nor his wife at his bedside.

Claude was only eighteen years old when he inherited the title of the 14th Marquis de Manville and the considerable fortune that accompanied the name.

Claude Antoine Ibrahim Chapon, 14th Marquis de Manville arrived in France to claim his birthright in October 1954. He was a slender young man with black shiny hair and a swarthy complexion that gave no hint of the French blood that coursed through his veins. He looked pure Arab.

He smoked incessantly and appeared to have a nervous disposition and strongly objected to enquiries into his private life. Unwelcome intrusions into his privacy often ended in him having violent tantrums. He produced his passport and birth certificate at Marseilles along with his parent's marriage license and set about claiming his rightful inheritance.

It wasn't generally known in France at this time, but Claude was now an orphan. Barely four weeks after hearing of the death of his father, Claude's mother was killed in an auto accident, along with her young Arab driver. Many assumed the young handsome Arab was also her lover but no-one knew for sure.

Initially there was much speculation by the authorities over his mother's death. She had plunged off a winding mountain road in the mountains of southern Syria. No other vehicle appeared to be involved. A young man,

Abdullah, her driver, was also killed in the accident. At first it was thought that the young man was Claude. He was of similar height and build, but both bodies were so badly burned and disfigured there was little hope of identifying either initially.

Claude had the horrendous task of identifying both bodies by their personal effects; his mother's wedding ring and a watch he himself had given Abdullah as a gift. If dental records existed, certainly no one in authority in that part of Syria thought to have them checked. In keeping with local tradition the bodies were buried within twenty four hours and a verdict of accidental death was recorded.

Zada's family was not informed by Claude of his mother's death until a week later. Her family had long ago left Damascus and had returned to their original lands in *Dayr az Zawr* in northern Syria on the Euphrates River. Whilst they were angry at not being informed immediately, they still offered Claude a home with them and a job working for one of his Uncle's companies that exported olives and dates.

They had never approved of Zada's marriage to a Frenchman, although they too, were Christians. Zada had to all intents and purposes, been cut off and disowned. Despite this, Zada's family was not unsympathetic to Claude. They would not punish him for his parents' transgressions. In actuality, they had never met Claude even when he was a baby. It then became an impossible journey to visit them when Jean-Paul returned to France in 1940 and Zada moved to Beirut with their son.

After his mother's death Claude returned to their modest house in Beirut and uncharacteristically hid himself away, refusing to accept callers and well wishers. He refused to meet his old friends, of whom he had many, and he resolutely refused to welcome even old family acquaintances.

After several rebuffs, the calls and callers stopped coming or caring. If Claude were to ever face the world again, they would happily see him, but for now, they felt he should just continue to wallow in his own self pity. Even his meals were brought to his room and were left outside the door by his servants. Only two friends, the brothers Tariq and Mohammad Diab were allowed inside his private sanctum and they would both arrive every day and leave late at night.

In early October, Claude left his house in the middle of the night and boarded a small boat bound for France. He had little baggage; most of what he'd owned he had given to Mohammad and Tariq. He carried only some good clothes, a new passport, his birth certificate and his mother's death certificate and marriage license. He had given no warning of his departure, but had left two or three letters that Muhammad Diab had promised to deliver. He gave no hint of his plans to anyone, or mentioned his final destination.

FOURTEEN

It took Phillip just a few minutes to glean what little information there was on the present Marquis de Manville. The 'Who's Who in France' website mentioned that he acquired his title and chateau from his father, the 13th Marquis de Manville in 1954.

It mentioned his upbringing in Syria and Lebanon but it made no mention of a university education or a military background. Although it did mention that he was fluent in both Arabic & English besides his mother tongue. It listed four or five organizations where he had board membership including two banks and also that he was President of the *Societe des Amis de Syrie*, the Friends of Syria Society. It listed his hobbies as wine making and art, and his address as Chateau de Manville, Baux de Provence, France.

Beyond that there seemed to be no other information available. Phillip sat and pondered. Pouring himself another cup of coffee, he picked up the phone and dialed Sir Robert.

"Hi, it's Phillip. I've just read the article about the Leonardo going up for sale, and then I did a little background checking."

"What did you come up with?"

"Well, not a lot, really. The painting has had some serious analysis a couple of years ago so I guess the Marquis has been planning the sale for a while."

"Well, he might have been," countered Sir Robert, "but there have been no whispers in the auction houses until today."

"Who's selling it?" queried Phillip. "It didn't mention the auction house in the article."

"No, apparently the Marquis made a press statement yesterday and merely informed them that he had decided to sell the painting. It was a prepared statement and there were no questions after the announcement," said Sir Robert.

"There's going to be one helluva scramble to get that particular plum," said Phillip and he continued. "By the way, I couldn't find any photos of the painting on the web sites. I don't suppose you know where I could look, do you?'

"Of course, dear boy, always ask your uncle," Sir Robert smiled to himself. "The *Courtauld* Institute has one in their records. An old photo, but it gives a very good likeness. Only black and white, I think, but the people who did all the recent analysis will have some. Did it say who'd done the work?"

"No," said Phillip, "but it could only have been one of about three companies capable of handling that kind of in-depth analysis and could be trusted with something so valuable. I doubt it left the country, so it was probably French. My guess would be Haussmann Fine Art Appraisers in Paris."

"Good thought, Phillip. Ill have a word with Jacques Maurice. He's head of Haussmann's and I wouldn't mind betting he'll try to have the sale held at Haussmann's Auctions in Paris, too."

"Makes sense. I'll let you get on the trail, then. Call me when you hear anything of interest."

"Naturally. Bye," said Sir Robert as he hung up the phone and began looking through the stack of papers and files on his untidy desk for his personal phone book.

Phillip, meanwhile, went back to his coffee and pondering. He mused for several minutes and wondered firstly if the French government would allow such a treasure to leave France and secondly if they could get together the necessary One hundred million Euros or more, to match the eventual purchase price, which is the only way they could stop its export to foreign shores.

"Either way", he said to himself, "not my problem"

Phillip decided the best way to spend the rest of his day, would be to get stuck into the restoration of his 1953, 2 ½ liter Riley RMF that was in several pieces languishing in his garage workshop. He found working on the car therapeutic. He often worked well into the evening, repairing, burnishing and replacing worn out parts on a car that had become his major 'love' interest. Ever since Isabel's death - no, he decided, call it what it was - ever since Isabel's *murder*, he found the idea of dating unthinkable. It held no interest for him at all.

His family often introduced him to eligible young ladies and held dinner parties so that he could meet them, but Phillip resolutely refused to take the bait. He doubted he would ever love again as he had loved Isabel. No one was ever going to take her place in his heart. For now, Phillip was content to be unattached and would stay comfortably married to Isabel's memory.

FIFTEEN

It didn't take long for the art world to become obsessed with the forthcoming sale of Leonardo da Vinci's portrait of the "Girl in the Red Dress." For weeks the art press of the world bombarded the Marquis with requests for interviews, all of which he refused.

He did, however, allow Haussmann's Auctions in Paris (Phillip was right on that score) to announce that they would be holding the sale. A photograph was also released for general publication, but by this time Phillip had already checked out the *Courtauld* Institute archives and had read, first hand, Sir Robert Witt's report.

He had also found Anthony Blunt's assessment of the painting when he and Sir Robert had viewed in back in 1956. It puzzled Phillip somewhat how Sir Robert Witt's appraisal had been done in 1938 when presumably the 13th Marquis was still in Syria. He posed the question to his uncle when they next met for lunch up in London.

"Good question, Phillip. Of course, I don't know for sure, but I believe at that time, the 13th Marquis, the present one's father, had notions of selling up all the family holdings and the castle in France and settling in Damascus or Beirut for good. He had become a bit enamored with that part of the world. Gone *native* if you like. He thought he would be better off in the eastern Mediterranean. I believe his wife, who by the way was a Syrian national, didn't want to move away from her homeland either."

"So the current Marquis is half French and half Syrian then?" asked Phillip, somewhat rhetorically.

"Precisely, although when I met him back in the 50's he didn't look to have a drop of French blood in him. He was very dark, swarthy even, and certainly didn't seem to have had the benefits of a noble upbringing. I found him rather coarse. He treated servants like dirt and wasn't overly cordial to me or Blunt."

Phillip smiled, "Blunt, I can understand."

"Well, yes, Blunt was an unmitigated shit, but I gathered he, that is, the Marquis, has acquired a few manners since those days. By all accounts he's somewhat more civil today, but still pretty arrogant and definitely borderline recluse."

"Another 'Howard Hughes' type?" enquired Phillip.

"Not that bad, I don't think….yet," concluded Sir Robert.

"Anyway," he continued, "Sir Robert Witt's recommendation was to sit tight on the sale of the Leonardo. Witt was particular friends with Winston….."

"Churchill, you mean?" asked Phillip.

"Yes, Churchill, and as you know, Winston was adamant that Hitler was up to no good. Europe was teetering on a knife's edge and Witt's advice to the Marquis was to hold off on any sale, wait and see what happens."

"Of course," continued Sir Robert on his discourse, "he and Churchill were right."

"But didn't the Marquis die in France after the war?"

"Yes, he did. He'd come back to fight the Bosch. Sorry, the Germans. He joined the resistance but ended up in some labor camp. Hardly the same man when he came home in '45. He was too ill to travel back to Syria, or anywhere for that matter. God knows what they'd done to him, but he was a spent force after the war."

"Didn't his wife and son come to France when they knew what state he was in?"

"Well, apparently, and some of this is supposition, they hadn't heard anything from him for a couple of years and so they thought he was probably dead. When he eventually wrote to them in 1945, after he'd gained a little strength, she'd already found herself a lover in Beirut and wasn't about to give him up to come home to a virtual cripple."

"Charming!"

"I agree that she hardly oozed with the milk of human kindness, but fate got the last laugh. Only five or six weeks after the Marquis eventually gave up the fight and died, his wife also sloughed off her mortal coil by going over the edge of a mountain road with her lover. They both died in a fiery inferno trapped in their car at the bottom of a deep ravine," explained Sir Robert.

"Sad stuff. Good movie material, though,"

"Too good to be a Hollywood plot, anyway, it was recorded as an accident. Barely hit the French newspapers yet alone the English ones. And then, as you know, young Claude fetches up and cops the lot, the estate, castle, Leonardo and a small fortune in a Swiss bank."

"Happy ending for someone then," said Phillip as he motioned the waiter for a bill

"Your treat, is it then Phillip?" said Sir Robert with mocked amazement.

Phillip smiled and added, "You always taught me to pay well for good information, that way, you'll always receive more!"

"I'm glad you thought the info worth the cost of a good steak and kidney pie."

Sir Robert was a hearty 'trencherman' and took his food very seriously. He much preferred honest English cooking to any 'fancy' foreign food that barely covered a fourth of the plate. He was a 'meat and two veg' kind of person and wasn't overly fussy whether he had the vegetables, as long as the meat was there in large helpings.

Phillip paid and they both shook hands warmly as they stepped out onto Beauchamp Place. Phillip hailed a taxi cab as Sir Robert strode out purposefully back to his apartment in Belgravia. He enjoyed a brisk walk after lunch and it helped him maintain his still handsomely trim physique.

SIXTEEN

The forthcoming sale of the famous, but little known painting by Leonardo da Vinci was greeted around the world with a great deal of excitement. It had been estimated to sell for eighty to one hundred million Euros. Some estimates put it as high as one hundred and fifty to two hundred million Euros. In reality, no one knew how much the treasure would sell for since a full blown Leonardo da Vinci painting hadn't been for sale in living memory or even recent history.

The critics and connoisseurs discussed at great length, or as Sir Robert put it, "*ad nauseum*", the variety of qualities that made Leonardo one of the most famous painters of all time. Magazines filled their pages with articles by illuminated experts. TVs filled their screens with the same.

Although he was a scientist, an inventor, a philosopher and an architect, it is Leonardo's paintings that have generated the greatest passions amongst his legion of admirers for the last four hundred years. He not only invented new techniques when it came to painting, though not all were successful, but his detailed knowledge of anatomy and light was revolutionary. The ways in which humans project subtle emotions and expressions became his distinct trademark as he captured them in paint. His compositions were flawless, as was his technique with the brush. He painted with an elusive quality known as, and called amongst the cognoscenti, *'sfumato'* or 'Leonardo's smoke.'

Unlike the Mona Lisa, whose plain dress is unadorned with jewelry or gold, the "*Portrait of the Girl in the Red Dress*" is dramatic for his use of color and for it's

96

abundance of jewelry which seems to sparkle with an independent light.

Rather than detract from the glowing face and hands of this innocent youth it leads the viewer's eyes directly into the soul of the sitter. The background, unlike the pastoral scene behind the Mona Lisa, appears to be the city of Florence as if seen by an angel or a bird.

Its condition was considered extremely good. This is rare for a painting of this date, especially as it had been painted on Leonardo's wood of choice, poplar. Wooden panels have generally proven over the years, to be susceptible to damp, humidity and rot and rarely remain damage free. *The Girl in the Red Dress'* had variously been described as 'breathtaking', 'the most beautiful portrait ever painted' and 'the finest work of art in the world.'

As an artist, Leonardo was a unique observer and had the ability to translate his observations into details of a face that we, in our unsophisticated way, could also see. The man came close to creating magic. His legend and his fame has justifiably lasted and has never been subject to fashion or fad, as so many 'old masters' since have been.

The world could not wait to see this hidden masterpiece for itself. The catalogue went into several printings and despite the cost of one hundred Euros, found eager collectors world wide that happily paid to have this work of reference in their art libraries.

Applications to view the painting came from every corner of the earth, such was the interest shown in this sale. It had become necessary for Haussmann's Auctions in Paris to limit the number of people invited to the auction to fourteen hundred, although huge TV screens would play the event live to thousands gathered across Paris. Those who were allowed to buy tickets had to prove intentions to bid by showing a banker's letter of intent. The rest were heads of state and other celebrities and dignitaries who would come by special invitation only.

Although the auction was still over a month away, the time expended on this one painting eclipsed all other day to day functions at Haussmann's Auctions in Paris. It was rumored that the Vatican had an interest in acquiring this work of art. Major museums world wide had increased their usual friendly rivalry. Donors and potential donors were courted at lavish parties in order to bolster the museum's purchasing abilities. It was clear to everyone that whoever owned the painting in just over a month from now would recoup its purchase price within a couple of years. The world was waiting to see "*The Girl in the Red Dress*" and was prepared to pay for the privilege.

Phillip and Sir Robert kept a casual eye on the circus that surrounded the painting and both had a small bet with each other regarding the final price. The Marquis, having refused every request for interviews, found himself, once again, sitting quietly in his chateau without the constant demand for his presence in front of the TV cameras or for 'in depth' interviews about his painting.

Regular and thorough news bulletins were handed out to the world press by Haussmann's eminently capable and charming, Mademoiselle Sophie Le Brun, who headed up their publicity department. This successfully brought the interest of TV crews away from the Marquis and back up to Paris. By this time they had all the stock footage of his chateau they needed and they geared themselves up for the major event, the sale in Paris.

The Marquis sighed with relief as the next part to his plan was definitely the trickiest and needed a clear head and room to maneuver.

SEVENTEEN

23 September 2000

As the days ticked by and the time to auction the world's most talked about painting drew closer, the Marquis received a call from Monsieur Jacques Maurice.

"Good Morning, Monsieur le Marquis. This is Jacques Maurice from Haussmann's, Paris."

"Bonjour Monsieur," replied the Marquis. "I expect you are calling to arrange the transport of my painting to Paris?"

"Precisely that, Monsieur le Marquis. I was wondering if you had any preferences. We will of course send our most experienced packers to wrap and crate the painting, but to get it from you to us here in Paris, we have two or three options."

"And they are…?"

"We could either employ a reputable security firm to drive it to Paris in their armored vehicle or we could have it delivered to Avignon Airport by, again, armored car, and then fly it up to Paris. The third option would be to fly it directly from you to us, by helicopter, providing, of course, you have somewhere they could land close to the chateau."

"I do have a very conveniently flat area where I have had helicopters land before. However, I am naturally a little concerned about its safety, should there be an accident."

"I fully understand your concerns, but should you choose any of the three methods of transport that I've just outlined, I assure you, the painting will be fully protected

99

from collision, fire…almost any tragedy you could imagine."

"Then that's fine," stated the Marquis, "I think the helicopter would be the most suitable, as long as you can really assure me that it will be safe. It's far too risky by road, I think."

"Of course, of course. I totally agree," said Monsieur Maurice.

"And," continued the Marquis," it will be fully insured whilst in your custody?"

"That, as we discussed some weeks ago, Monsieur le Marquis, will be taken care of. Once we have had our packers crate the painting, which although small, will be very well protected in a shatter proof and fire resistant container, we shall assume full responsibility until it is handed over to the new owner, after the auction."

"As you can imagine, Monsieur, this is a very emotional time for me. The painting has been in my family for so many generations that I feel I am losing a child, or certainly a beloved family member….." The Marquis did his best to sound sad, as if grieving at the loss of a loved one.

Monsieur Maurice was silent for a while to show respect and his understanding of the impending loss.

"I do understand, Monsieur le Marquis. I truly do; and of course we shall do everything possible to minimize the…the inconvenience…and of course, distress….having our men remove your work of art to Paris."

There was silence on the other end.

Monsieur Maurice, feeling that a brighter note to the conversation was needed, upped the tempo and changed the subject to one he hoped would be more uplifting.

"Now, Monsieur le Marquis, is there anything I can do in preparation for your visit to Paris? I am assuming, as the star of our gala night….." he injected a little flattery which in the past had always worked with the Marquis, "…you will be attending the dinner and auction afterwards?"

"I'm afraid, I haven't made up my mind yet," said the Marquis, as if still dwelling on his imminent loss, "I shall let you know nearer the time. I'm still getting used to the idea of losing the Leonardo and I'm not even sure if I could possibly celebrate with you. I understand," he continued, "that the efforts you are putting in are largely for my benefit, so I will promise to try to be there in person."

"There will be many celebrities present, Monsieur le Marquis," countered the head of Haussmann's, "who I know will be delighted to meet you. Monsieur Le President, also has expressed a specific wish to be introduced, as he put it, 'to the owner of the world's finest painting', so I hope, Monsieur le Marquis, that you will be able to find the courage to attend."

"I will do my best. That is all I can promise at this time," said the Marquis in a way to end the subject.

"Thank you. On one last point, I am planning to send my packers on the morning of Monday, the 2nd of October and the helicopter will arrive after lunch at about two thirty. We will have our head of security, Monsieur Pierre Cabot, accompany the packers and he will also travel with the container on the helicopter. I trust these arrangements are satisfactory?"

"Perfectly," answered the Marquis

"Excellent!" I shall have my secretary write to you today confirming these dates and arrangements. We shall have the painting ready for exhibition on the 3rd of October ready for the sale a week later, when, I hope to have the pleasure of entertaining you and our other distinguished guests at what promises to be the sale of the century."

Monsieur Maurice was pleased with his little speech but more so for bagging the greatest prize currently on offer in the art world.

The Marquis sighed into the mouthpiece.

"Yes, yes, that's all fine. I'll speak to you when the painting has left. Goodbye Monsieur." and he hung up the phone.

The Marquis somber mood dissipated immediately. He had, of course, laid it on a bit thickly for the benefit of poor Monsieur Maurice. He chuckled as he imagined the look on Jacques Maurice's face when he learns that he won't be selling the painting after all.

"My God," thought the Marquis as he imagined the scene, "the poor bastard will probably die of heart failure." The Marquis laughed out loud at the thought.

That afternoon, Leila arrived having flown back from Rome that morning. She had run a few 'errands' on behalf of her godfather and returned to plan with him the final stages of his master plan.

EIGHTEEN

"Leonardo da Vinci Theft Shocks Art World"

28th September, 2000, Le Figaro-Paris

Yesterday masked gunmen stole the Leonardo da Vinci portrait of *"The Girl in the Red Dress"* worth an estimated 150 million Euros from the Chateau de Manville, in Baux de Provence in southern France.

The heist of the famous painting, slated for auction on the 10th of October in Paris, has shocked the art world. The robbers broke into the chateau, situated in picturesque Baux de Provence in the late hours of 26th September and held the Marquis de Manville, owner of the painting, at gunpoint. A servant at the chateau, Albert Guion, was attacked during the robbery.

Two men in dark clothes and ski masks tied up the Marquis and forced him to reveal the combination of the safe where the painting was being stored prior to its' journey to the world famous auction house, Haussmann in Paris.

"This is one of the biggest art thefts in France's history, and is rivaled only by the theft of the *Mona Lisa* from the Louvre," said Bertram Lavelle, head of the police investigation.

Monsieur Lavelle went on to explain that the robbery was only noticed when a cleaning lady arrived for work the following morning and was unable to gain access to the chateau. She called the police who responded immediately.

A reward of €100,000 has been offered by Haussmann's, who was to offer the painting for sale next month.

M. Maurice, head auctioneer and chairman of Haussmann's said this morning,

"We are all totally shocked by the audacity and horror of this robbery of one of the world's most magnificent paintings. This painting cannot be re-sold, as it is too well known, especially after the world wide publicity it has received in recent weeks. Because of this, we have high hopes that the painting will be recovered very soon."

He added that he and his staff wished the Marquis de Manville a speedy recovery from this harrowing ordeal.

The Marquis was found bound and gagged in his study by police after they had gained access through a kitchen window. The Marquis, who received minor medical treatment for shock and bruising, was said to be well, but deeply distressed at the loss.

The police said they have no immediate suspects but were following several leads. They were particularly anxious to trace a red four door vehicle said to be seen driving fast through the town of Baux de Provence in the early hours after the robbery.

The story continued with a run down of other major art thefts throughout the world in the last few decades.

The *Times* and the *Daily Telegraph* in London both led with the story. They also confirmed that Interpol had been alerted and that they were leading the investigation along with the police in Marseilles and a private art recovery team from London, International Art Recovery, led by Sir Robert Spence and Phillip Fairfax.

The two armed men have not been identified except to say that one spoke French with a slight foreign accent, possibly Polish or Russian, according to the *Times,* whilst *the Telegraph* stated that the two thieves seemed to have some prior knowledge of the castle and its layout.

Both papers concurred that such a well known painting was unlikely to find a buyer and that it had possibly been stolen to order, known in police circles as a '*Dr. No*' theft, alluding to the 1963 James Bond film of the same name. In the film the villain, *Dr. No* appeared to have a stolen portrait by Goya of the Duke of Wellington hanging on the wall of his mansion. It had been stolen from London's National Portrait Gallery two years prior to the film's release.

Even before the story broke in the world's press Sir Robert had telephoned Phillip, who had been happily working on the never ending restoration of his old Riley. After getting the first brief account of the robbery, Phillip had called his friend, Daniel Masilionis of the Stolen Works of Art Unit at Interpol, in Lyon, France. He obtained the necessary papers by fax and immediately called Jarrod Wood at Staverton Airport to ready his twin engine Piper Aztec, PA23-250, for a trip to Provence.

Phillip had decided to fly directly to Avignon Airport and hire a car from there to visit the scene of the crime. It was imperative, as Phillip often said, to get on the trail as quickly as possible. Every hour delayed meant a lesser chance of catching up with the thieves. This was one case where Phillip felt he stood a good chance of recovering the famous painting and he was eager to get started.

"Woody, this is Phillip. When you've fuelled the plane could you fill out a fight plan for me? I'm on my way and I'll sign it when I get there. I'm heading to AVN Avignon Airport in the south of France. When you've filled it out, fax it to IFPS (Initial Flight Plan Processing Unit). I should be there by the time they acknowledge receipt."

"Wilco." said Woody as a contraction of 'I will comply', "Anything else you'll need?"

"No thanks, I've got all the kit I'll need already packed. I'll see you in about thirty minutes." and Phillip hung up.

The IFPS would process Phillip's flight data and store it in the CFMU database. CFMU was the *Central Flow Management Unit* which would send and distribute information about the flight to Air Traffic Controls and Air Traffic Flow & Capacity Management concerned with his flight to Avignon.

In order to have this facility Phillip had two sets of VHF transceivers installed in his Aztec each with 8.33 kilohertz channel spacing. This equipment was now mandatory for any flight above FL195-flight level of 19,500 feet. He also had 2 ILS Navigational Receivers and a RNAV system of navigation that was capable of pinpointing his position to within five nautical miles. The final update that Phillip had retro-fitted to his forty year old Aztec was an ELT-an Emergency Locator that now had become mandatory on aircraft worldwide.

Phillip arrived at Staverton, now renamed Gloucester Airport, within the hour. It lies in the heart of the Cotswold country just three minutes from the M5/A40 junction. He found Woody in the pilot's lounge. Phillip shook hands warmly with his friend and proceeded to add his signature to the paperwork Woody had filled out. He checked it all for accuracy but as usual Woody had done everything correctly.

"I've topped her off with Avgas," said Woody, "and with your long range tanks you should be able to make the trip without a refuel. You also needed a bit of sky in your rounds" he added. Being an expatriate Rhodesian - he disliked being called a Zimbabwean - Woody had left when Mugabe had taken over the country from Ian Smith in 1980. He had a colorful vocabulary of African slang and *'Sky in your rounds'* as Phillip had come to know, meant 'air in your tires'

"Thanks Woody. Yeah, I certainly hope I can get there on one tank. I need to be in Avignon as soon as possible."

Phillip then walked out with Woody to his Aztec which was parked close to the fuel pumps at stand 2. He tossed his two carry-on bags onto the middle seats of his six seater airplane and put his flight manuals, maps and check list onto the co-pilot's seat.

Phillip went about doing his external pre flight checks, although he knew that Woody had also done them only a short while before.

Phillip was a careful pilot and, as in his business life, never cut corners or took anything for granted. He completed his checks and turned to Woody who held out a brown paper bag and a can of coke.

"Thought you might need a sandwich during your trip," he said with his usual beaming smile.

"Great. That's one thing I forgot to pack. Thanks a lot Woody. I'll see you when I get back."

"Don't forget," said Woody as he turned back towards the main building, "if you walk away from a landing, it's a good one." He laughed at his own joke as if it was the first time he'd ever heard it. Woody was a jovial and likeable man.

Phillip climbed aboard and settled himself into the front left hand seat. He donned his head set and checked once more that he had all his paperwork and maps to hand.

He started the starboard engine to power up the avionics via the generator and didn't start the second engine until the avionics had been programmed with his flight plan details.

He manually adjusted the fuel mixture and cylinder head temperature and called up the control tower. He asked for permission to proceed towards the take-off point.

"Roger, Alpha Whiskey. Use runway 2-7 via Taxiway Alpha. Advise when in position."

"Alpha Whiskey, Roger."

Phillip eased the twin forward and once more did a visual check of his ailerons and tail rudder. Just prior to joining the runaway 2-7, he once more did his power checks and gave the Aztec 10 degrees of flap for take off.

"Tower, this is Alpha Whiskey. Ready on runway 27. Over."

"Alpha Whiskey, you're clear to go. Have a pleasant flight. Tower out."

With that Phillip eased the throttles forward and headed down the runway

Halfway down the 1,300 meter long, rubber streaked, asphalt Phillip had already reached take off speed. He eased back on the yoke as the Aztec gently lifted its nose skyward. At 600 ft. he turned left and began his climb to cruising altitude. Phillip then dialed up the Met Office at Exeter to re-check weather conditions and setting himself a course to coast out over Weymouth in Dorset, he relaxed and enjoyed the solitude and sense of freedom that only solo flying can give.

Some hours later Phillip approached *Avignon Caum* airport and its single runway. He joined the air traffic overhead and set his twin engine Aztec neatly on runway 35 in typical Cote d'Azur sunshine. He switched his radio from Avignon approach to ground control who guided him to a parking slot close to the main terminal. He immediately went to pay his landing fees and get all his paperwork signed, including his log book and noted, not without some pleasure, that he now had exactly 2,000 hours flying time in his Aztec.

After a much needed bathroom break he set off to find Detective Masilionis whom he had arranged to meet at the bar café situated at one end of the main terminal building.

He found the 6'5" policeman perched on a bar stool deeply engrossed in conversation with a pretty blond waitress, who evidently was not immune to the big man's charms. Few were.

"Not interrupting anything am I?" asked Phillip as he slapped the detective on his back.

Masilionis swung round on his barstool and grabbing Phillip in his huge arms gave him a bone crushing bear hug.

"Put me down Daniel!" laughed Phillip, who stood six feet two inches himself.

"Ah, you English, you must always spoil everything. Another five minutes and I would have her phone number."

"Sorry chum, but you won't have anytime for romance until we've found our painting," retorted Phillip who matched Masilionis grin for grin.

"Phillip, my friend, you are too practical. There is always time for *l'amore*. Ah, but the moment, she is now

gone. Let us get to work," and with that the two men
headed for the car park.

"Bring me up to speed, Daniel. What's the story so
far with regards to the robbery?"

Phillip was now all business. The two men knew
each other well. They had worked before on similar cases
in the past and each had developed a professional respect
for the other.

Beneath Daniel's casual, happy go-lucky façade, he
was a dedicated policeman with a pathological hatred for
the criminal classes. He was a specialized officer in the
Stolen Works of Art section of Interpol, based in Lyon,
France.

"The local police, they are rubbish. One fat *bobby*
was the first to arrive and after he call the ambulance he
call the boys from Marseilles and Aix. By the time they get
here, the Marquis and his man servant, a Monsieur Albert
Guion, were already on their way to hospital."

"The servant it would appear have a big cut on his
head and if his skull was not so thick, it probably break in
two pieces." Daniel chuckled.

"As it was he was, how you say, 'out cold' when
the first policeman he arrive. He lose a lot of blood I think."

"They were armed, I believe - the thieves?" asked
Phillip.

"Yes, but of course. However, I think they only use
the pistols to beat Monsieur Guion on his head and to
threaten Monsieur le Marquis," responded Daniel.

"What about the Marquis, Daniel? Did he receive
any injuries?"

"He say they only threaten him and make him say
where is the painting. They then threaten to shoot the
servant who was unconscious, so the Marquis, he tell them

110

the numbers to his safe, but the Marquis has one cut on his eye. Nothing serious but he still have the big shock."

The two men continued their conversation as they squeezed into Daniel's unmarked Interpol Renault.

"How did the thieves gain entry to the chateau?" asked Phillip as the two strapped themselves into their seat belts.

"It happen they break a window with the glass cutter in the dining room. There was another window also broke by the kitchen, but it was the local policeman who break it to get in. He was called by the cleaning lady."

"And now the big question Daniel. Insurance?"

"I think this too but the painting she is not insured. Never has it been. The Marquis, he say it is *trop cher*, too expensive. The auction house they have insurance, but not until they collect the painting from the chateau. It was to be on Monday, 2nd of October. So the premier motive, she is out the window."

"Okay. Well I guess we'll just have to see what the Marquis and Monsieur Guion have to say. When can I meet with them?"

"Monsieur le Marquis, he is now at his chateau. Guion, the servant, he is still in the hospital, but I hope he will be out in one, maybe two days. I will arrange for you to *see* them as soon as possible, but I do not think it can be tonight. By the way Phillip, where are you staying?"

"Haven't decided yet. I'll be fine in a hotel somewhere close by. Maybe in Saint Remy," said Phillip consulting a map of the area.

"I would invite you stay with me but, as you know, since I am not with Marie I have just one small room in Marseilles. Even that I hardly see."

"No problems," interjected Phillip. "I'd rather get a hotel room anyway. It makes it easier to come and go; and besides, if you and I shared a room, we'd probably fall out within a week," laughed Phillip.

"*C'est vrai,* my friend. Marie, she says I make a noise like a train when I sleep. I think that is why she leave me."

"Nothing to do with you and the ladies then?" suggested Phillip with a knowing look. He knew that he was probably a great deal closer to the truth."

"Can I help it if I am the full-blooded Frenchman?" said Masilionis with a typical Gallic pout and shrug of the shoulders.

Phillip wondered if Daniel really believed he was the unwitting victim of a cruel gift, an over abundance of testosterone.

At this point Daniel pulled up in front of the Eurocap Rental Car Agency and Phillip stepped out. He leaned back through the open window of the Renault and told Daniel that he would call him as soon as he found a place to stay.

"If you can arrange for us to go to the chateau as soon as possible, I'd be very grateful." said Phillip, as Daniel prepared to leave.

"*D'accord,* my friend. I shall wait for your call but I think it unlikely we shall be able to visit with Monsieur le Marquis today. Maybe tomorrow for sure. *Au revoir.* See you later." And with that Daniel sped away with a painful squeal of rubber on asphalt.

Phillip thought how comical his friend looked crammed into the interior of a very small car, but none the less he was pleased to have him around. Daniel was a very astute policeman with an incredible retention of even the minutest details of a crime scene.

Daniel Masilionis was only a second generation Frenchman. His paternal grandfather had been a carpenter in Lithuania and had moved to France in the early 1900s with his young Latvian wife, Daniel's grandmother. Daniel's father had been their third son but in many ways had been the most successful of all his five brothers, despite them all having had little formal education. Daniel's father had started work, at the age of fourteen, on a fishing boat working out of St. Malo in northern France and by the time he was thirty years old, he owned his own trawler as well as five fish monger's shops dotted along the northern coast. He died a young man at the age of forty five, but left his wife, Daniel and his five brothers, relatively well provided for.

Daniel had always wanted to be a policeman and had joined the Gendarmerie when he was eighteen years of age. At one time it had looked as if he would become an Olympic skier. He won several national championships in the giant slalom event but one too many spills at high speed wrecked not only his knees but his chances of performing at international level.

These days he confined his skiing to the warm waters of the Cote d'Azur behind a fast motor boat. No one would describe Daniel as good looking but his twinkling dark brown eyes, his almost perpetual smile and his mop of curly black hair gave his face a boyish charm that the ladies found hard to resist. Not only was Daniel tall, but approaching his mid thirties, he had filled out and by anyone's standard could now only be described as 'big'.

NINETEEN

Thirty years ago art crime was a rarity. The job Phillip now pursued did not exist. The theft of valuable paintings was about as common as cattle rustling with neither problem being a serious blight on civilized communities.

Things were different now. Art theft is definitely in the top ten of stolen personal property and generates an income for the criminal fraternity of well over three billion dollars a year. Art fraud and forgery, which is always difficult to quantify, could boost this figure to *six billion dollars* a year.

This would make the illicit dealing in stolen and forged artwork rival that of the legitimate art business worldwide. A frightening thought for art lovers everywhere. Yet despite this burgeoning trend few police forces throughout the world can afford the manpower or have the expertise to make an impact on the problem. Recovery rate is generally poor, despite it being a significant problem. Some put it as low as 6% and others as high as 20%. Either way, it was a pretty dismal record.

The victims too, are as varied as the art that's stolen. They range from banks, warehouses, museums, art galleries, private collections to inevitably, insurance companies. It was for these reasons that Sir Robert Spence started International Art Recovery almost ten years ago when he talked Phillip into being his 'point man, his principal investigator.'

Phillip had turned out to be a good investigator. He had an eye for detail and a good 'nose' for spotting lies and deceit. He was able to think like the thieves which helped make his success rate exceptionally good. Mainly due to

Phillip, I.A.R's annual success rate averages over 60%. It was a record they were all proud of.

Phillip and Sir Robert Spence now headed a company that had an excellent world wide reputation and employed no fewer than four full time investigators and six full time researchers and administrators.

The following morning Agent Masilionis was waiting, as arranged the previous night, at *Le Café Grenouille* in Baux de Provence, a small town that surrounded the rocky outcrop that the Chateau de Manville occupied.

The chateau could be seen from the small café where Daniel was sitting having his breakfast of croissant and *café au lait*, a milky breakfast coffee. At nine o'clock Phillip pulled up and parked outside. He immediately saw the large policeman sitting at a small table on the terrace enjoying his breakfast in the morning sunshine.

"*Bonjour, mon ami.*" Daniel wore his usual infectious smile. "*Ca va?*"

"*Oui, ca va.* I'm fine" replied Phillip as he sat down opposite Daniel.

Declining a waiter's offer of coffee, Phillip expressed his eagerness to get started on his quest for the stolen Leonardo painting.

"I'm ready when you are Daniel."

Daniel popped the last piece of croissant into his mouth and finished his coffee in one gulp.

"*On y va,*" said Daniel as he rose tossing several Euros onto the table.

As the two men walked to the Renault, Daniel explained that he had had a word with the waiter and owner of the café while he was waiting.

"No one in the village knows much of anything about the robbery. They all know it happen but no one know who did it" said Daniel. He continued "the chateau is a big mystery to the people of the village. No one goes up there, except the lady who clean. She was the one who first call the police. After that she know nothing. If they have fancy soiree or dinner, the Marquis he get the staff from Marseille or Aix."

"We'll need a list of those people too" said Phillip. "It could be a casual employee who noticed the painting and thought he could set up his retirement fund by stealing it or…" Phillip was now thinking out loud, "he could have supplied the information to a third party."

"All this is quite possible of course, but I think the job was quite professional."

"I agree" answered Phillip, "but we should check them all out just the same."

"It shall be done as you wish. I will ask the Marseilles police to get this information as soon as possible."

By this time Daniel and Phillip were climbing the steep mountain road which wound its way up to the gates of the chateau. It was an imposing site seen from the café but on entering the gates the towering castle took on the proportions of an immense fortress. Phillip thought that any thieves who were confronted by the massive edifice of the chateau must have had nerves of steel and big balls to pull off such a caper.

It took some time for the doorbell to be answered. When it was, it was opened by a lovely young lady who stood before them and asked, quite bluntly, what they wanted.

Daniel showed his Interpol I.D and warrant card and Phillip proffered his business card. She took both of them and examined them. She looked a little surprised when she read Phillip's name, but she said nothing. Phillip did, however, notice a slight nervousness about her and wondered why.

"I am sorry if I appeared rude, gentleman, but we have had a number of journalists in recent weeks pestering my godfather, but he is expecting both of you so please step inside."

Both men did as they were bid and waited whilst the young lady closed and bolted the massive oak door.

"Please gentleman, follow me" she said as she stepped between them.

Phillip noticed that not only was the young lady attractive and smelled delightfully of expensive perfume but also that she stood at least five feet ten inches tall herself.

Leaving the small outer vestibule, they entered into the large main hall. It had a tall vaulted ceiling that was supported by carved corbels and on the far wall hung a huge 16th century Beauvais tapestry. To their left Phillip noticed a magnificent carved stone fireplace whose ash laden grate gave the room a smoky smell of burnt apple logs. On either side of that hung two life-sized portraits, one of a handsome man in the pale blue uniform of the French Cavalry, the other of an aristocratic looking man with a bushy white beard and moustache and dressed in a long black frock coat. Phillip assumed they were ancestors of the Marquis.

Several other paintings, mostly portraits with the odd landscape thrown in, filled the remaining walls. The furniture was typically French Baroque in style having plenty of gilded decoration with marble tops on the tables and tapestry upholstery on the chairs and sofas.

Despite the formality of the furniture the room had the comfortable air of a much used room. Walking across the large Persian carpet that almost covered the entire marble floor, the two men silently followed their attractive guide. The girl opened a large mahogany door and ushered the detectives into the library. The room was fairly dark because the heavy Genoese velvet curtains were still closed. It took them a few seconds to adjust their eyes to the dimness and then they noticed a man sitting quietly behind a large mahogany desk. He spoke softly.

"*Bonjour* gentleman. Welcome to Chateau de Manville."

The young lady now stood beside the seated Marquis who offered them a seat. They sat opposite the Marquis whose face was almost entirely in shadow. The only illumination in the room was a floor standing candelabra by the fireplace with a dozen lit candles and a small desk lamp that merely illuminated the red leather top of the mahogany desk. Daniel was the first to speak.

"*Bonjour* Monsieur le Marquis. I am Detective Masilionis from Interpol and my colleague here" he gestured towards Phillip, "he is Monsieur Fairfax from International Art Recovery of London."

"Thank you for coming gentleman," responded the Marquis who neither rose from his chair nor offered his hand in greeting.

"I believe", continued the Marquis "that you have met my goddaughter, Mademoiselle Leila Diab."

The two men lifted themselves from their seats and both in turn said "*Enchante Mademoiselle.*"

Phillip noticed that her obvious physical charms had not been lost on Daniel. However, the young lady merely fixed her eyes on the seated Marquis.

Phillip now spoke. "Sir, we are here to ask you some questions which I'm sure you may have already been asked by the police. However, in order that we stand the

118

very best chance of recovering your painting, it is necessary that we both have as much information as possible."

"I understand," said the Marquis, as he looked up to his goddaughter. "I am devastated by the loss naturally and I will do whatever I can to help you find my Leonardo, but I have very little to tell you. It seemed to happen so fast. I regret I am still in a bit of shock over the whole dreadful episode."

"Naturally," said Phillip, "but every little detail can be so important, so please, I ask you to indulge us and tell us everything you can remember. For example, I understand that one of the robbers spoke French with a foreign accent?"

"I believe, yes, it was maybe Polish or Russian perhaps" answered the Marquis.

"At what time was it that they confronted you and where were you when this happened?" probed Phillip.

"I think it must have been about eleven thirty at night. I was just finishing some letters in my study when I heard a noise coming from the hall. I thought it must be Albert, my servant, starting to lock up for the night."

"Does he do this every night?" queried Daniel.

"Well, normally he would wait until I have rung the bell for him and told him that I was ready for bed but I just assumed…" he let the sentence trail off

"So if I understand it correctly, Albert normally stays in his quarters until you ring for him and then he locks up?"

"Correct." agreed the Marquis.

"What does he do when he locks up?" asked Phillip.

"The front door, of course, is always locked but he makes sure that the terrace door is locked, which it usually is too. He checks that the fire is not burning too well and fits the guard against it. He switches off all the lights and puts out any candles that may be burning. I suppose then the last thing he does is set the alarm."

"Where is the alarm panel situated?"

"I'm embarrassed to say I do not really know. It has always been Albert's job, but I think it may be downstairs by his living quarters."

"And they are where?"

"Next to the kitchen."

"So you hear a noise in the hall; you think it's Albert; then what?"

"The next thing the door opens. I expect it to be Albert, although I'm surprised he didn't knock. I look up and two men with black masks are standing there."

"Go on" encouraged Phillip.

"I see they each hold a gun which is pointed at me." At this point the Marquis looks up again at his goddaughter and she gently squeezes his shoulder in encouragement. After a second or two he continues. "One of them then asks me who else is in the house."

"Was this the one with the foreign accent?" asks Phillip.

"Yes."

"Go on."

"He asks me the question and I say 'only Albert, my servant.' I feel so bad, I should have said no one, but I wasn't thinking well. I was in shock to see two such strangers in my house, you understand. And pointing guns at me"

"We understand. Then what?" said Phillip.

"The one man, the one with the accent, asks me to call Albert. So I get up and go to the button by the fireplace and press it for Albert. I do this every evening so Albert would be expecting me to call him."

120

During his description of events, Phillip made
several notes. Daniel merely sat and observed the Marquis
as he told his story sitting in semi-darkness.
"So Albert arrives?" asked Phillip, "where were the
two gun men?"
"One moved behind the door, whilst the other one-
the one with the accent-he moved over next to me and put
the gun into my side."
"He was still wearing his mask?"
"Yes, he never removed it at all. Albert opened the
door and came into the room."
"Did he knock?" asked Phillip.
"He may have done, I don't remember. He usually
does. Anyway, he walks in and he stops when he sees me
with the masked man. The one behind the door hits him,
very hard, on the head and Albert falls to the floor,
unconscious. They tie him up with, with tape; I don't know
what you call it. It's sort of silvery and very strong and
also sticky."
The Marquis once again looked at his goddaughter.
It seemed to Phillip that the Marquis was almost saying to
her, "How am I doing?"
"I think the silvery tape you are referring to is called
duct tape," suggested Phillip. "It's very effective and as
you say very, very strong. Please continue."
"They tie him up with this 'duck tape' as you call it.
Albert moans a little and the man hits him again on the
head. They put this tape over his mouth also and his eyes.
I see that Albert is now bleeding quite badly."
"Did you say anything at this point?"
"I may have. I don't remember but I didn't know
yet why they were here."
"So they had not mentioned the painting yet?"

"No. When they had tied Albert, it was then they asked me where the Leonardo was."

"They called it 'the Leonardo', not *the* painting , or the Da Vinci or 'the painting of the *Girl in the Red Dress*'?" said Phillip.

"Yes, I'm pretty sure that's what they said. Anyway, I was left in no doubt that it was the Leonardo painting that they wanted."

Daniel and Phillip remained silent so the Marquis continued. "They said if I did not tell them immediately they would shoot Albert in the head. So, of course I told them it was in the safe. Then they told me to open the safe."

"So you opened the safe, not them?"

"Yes, the man with the accent put his gun in my face and said to open it. I went to the safe, which is behind a landscape painting in my study and opened it. The man reached in and pulled out my painting."

"Was there anything else in the safe?" This time it was Daniel who asked.

"Some papers. A little money I think but nothing of value," said the Marquis who now looked more often at Leila for reassurance. Throughout the questioning she stood silently next to the Marquis, occasionally patting his shoulder.

"When they had the painting what did they do then?" It was Phillip who resumed the questioning.

"They told me to sit back in my chair at my desk and they tied me up also with the same tape. Only they also tied me to the chair which was where I stayed until the police found me in the morning."

"Did Albert gain consciousness, do you know? I mean before the police arrived?"

"I heard a sort of muffled moan I think but he did not really move much."

"So the thieves just left you and took the picture? Did they take anything else? The chateau is full of lovely paintings. Granted not in the league of the Leonardo da Vinci, but still, they could certainly have stolen some beautiful art work worth many tens of thousands of euros."

"I suppose, but as far as I can tell nothing else is missing," said the Marquis who now was sounding very tired.

"I think my godfather has had enough questions for now," said Leila in a way that let both men know their question time had come to an end.

"That will be fine" said Phillip. "Perhaps after lunch we may come back and ask just a few more questions. We also need to speak with Albert. Do you know when he will leave the hospital?"

"We hope today," said Leila. "He feels very bad about what happened. He feels very responsible."

"Thank you very much Monsieur le Marquis. We are sorry to have to bother you at a time like this. By the way, how is your face? I understand you have a cut under your eye."

"It is nothing. It's just a small bruise. I think the gunman must have done it when he made me open the safe. I don't honestly remember."

"Marquis, with your permission, my colleague and I wish to look around the chateau. Get a feel of the place and also see how and where the robbers broke in."

"Please, be my guest. I personally cannot go into the study yet; the memory of poor Albert, the loss of my Leonardo. It's still all too painful. But you must look around all you need."

"Thank you."

"Merci." The two investigators spoke in unison.

Daniel and Phillip rose to leave. As he reached the door, Phillip turned and looked in the Marquis' direction.

"One last question Monsieur le Marquis. Do you own a gun?"

"I do not." The Marquis looked marginally peeved at the suggestion.

As the two men stepped out of the library into the vast hall, Phillip turned to Daniel and asked "What do you think?"

"It all seems a little convenient, how you say - *'slick.'* And I wonder why it was so dark in there. I could hardly see the Marquis."

"I think that was the idea" said Phillip. "It was impossible to see his eyes. I think he wanted it that way."

"But the girl, Leila, *oh-la-la*, a pretty girl, no?"

"I knew that much wouldn't escape your attention."

The first door they came to was the study, the room in which the robbery had taken place. Evidence that the finger print specialists had done their work was everywhere. The fine powder they used coated almost every surface in the room. The study itself was smaller than the library they had just left. Two large windows ran from the floor to the ceiling bathing the pale oak paneling with warm sunshine. A desk, a Louis XV *bureau plat* in kingwood adorned with gilded bronze mounts sat almost in the middle of the room. A gilded chair upholstered in fine pale blue silk was sitting behind the desk with its back to the window. Phillip bent down to examine it.

"This must be the chair that the Marquis was tied to" said Phillip, running his hand over the gilded frame.

"See here Daniel," he pointed to the back of the chair. "The duct tape has peeled off the gold leaf decoration."

124

Daniel looked on and saw the red gesso beneath the gold work standing out like a recent sore bruise.

"But it's not here on the legs" observed Daniel, "so they must have not tied his legs to the chair, *n'est pas?*"

"Doesn't look like it, does it?" agreed Phillip. "So why couldn't the Marquis have moved? Even if his legs were tied together, he would have been able to stand up and hop."

"Maybe, yes, but to where?"

"I don't know, but wouldn't you have tried to escape, get help....something?"

"It is true. I would not have just sat there all night."

Once again Phillip made notes in his notebook. As Phillip wrote, Daniel went to the bureau plat desk and tried to open the drawers. All three were locked and the key was nowhere to be seen. Removing a small leather wallet from his pocket, Daniel selected a narrow pick and within 15 seconds he had opened the right hand drawer. He did the same with the center and left hand drawers. Inside he only found writing paper, envelopes and several fountain pens, but something else caught his attention. It was a familiar smell. It was the distinct odor of gun oil.

Meanwhile, Phillip was examining the rest of the room. On the right hand wall was a large *Boulle* chiffonier in black ebonized wood with red tortoiseshell panels inlaid with etched brass decoration. On top stood a matching tantalus with three crystal decanters, each wearing a silver necklace announcing the contents of the cut glass bottles; Gin, Whisky and Brandy. He opened the cupboard door to the chiffonier. It contained an array of lead crystal glasses all neatly lined up and arranged according to size.

On top, either side of the Tantalus were two bronze statuettes of Napoleonic soldiers, each standing approximately ten inches tall on green marble bases. One

125

soldier was beating a drum whilst the other stood
nonchalantly holding his rifle in one hand and a pipe to his
mouth with the other. Phillip picked up the drummer to
admire the exquisite detail on the patinated bronze. It was
beautifully cast and although it seemed not to bear an
artist's signature, it was stamped with the round mark of a
good Paris foundry. He gently placed it back on its' marble
base. As he returned to write his observations in his
notebook, he noticed a dark reddish brown smudge on the
page he had just turned. He looked at his hand.

"Daniel, come here!" whispered Phillip.

"What have you found?"

Phillip merely offered his gloved right hand, palm
upwards. "What does that look like to you, Daniel?"

Daniel inspected the proffered hand and then the
paper on Phillip's notebook.

"You think it is blood? Well, yes...maybe."

"Have you got a swab and bag, Daniel? I definitely
want this tested" said Phillip, "It came from the statuette of
the drummer.

"We can match it, or not, with the blood stain that is
still on the carpet. I have already taken a sample of that,
too," said Daniel, as he wrote on the outside of the plastic
evidence bag.

He carefully wiped the deep crevices of the
drummer's uniform with a Q-tip which unsurprisingly
turned a reddish brown. He dropped the Q-tip inside the
bag and sealed the top.

"We'll get it analyzed and see if we get any kind of
match, but my guess it's Albert Guion's blood and it was
the statue that was used to hit him over the head, not a
gun."

"If I'm right," continued Phillip, still mulling over the implications, "why did the Marquis say Albert was hit with a gun?"

"Maybe, he thought it was a gun" stated Daniel, in his usual role as devil's advocate.

"Possibly, but why did the person put it back afterwards, neatly on its marble stand?"

"Good point, *mon ami*, but let us first get the blood tested, eh? Before we get too carried away, it is possible that it came from the cleaner, no?"

"Possible, yes, but unlikely!" said Phillip as he continued to ruminate over the details of the theft. He was beginning to feel that the Marquis had not told them everything.

"Are we done here?" asked Phillip as he slipped his notebook into his hip pocket.

"Oui, for now but I have a feeling we will be back very soon." said Daniel.

"Okay. Then let's try the dining room. See where they entered the castle. After that I need to have a good look outside."

The two men left the study and once again they entered the vast hall which they crossed looking for the dining room.

They opened a door that was directly opposite the Marquis' library. The room was in total darkness so Daniel felt for the light switch. He flicked a pair of switches and two large crystal chandeliers, festooned with multi faceted pear shaped drops, lit up the room.

"Mon Dieu," was all Daniel could think to say.

The room was the largest, apart from the hall, that they had entered so far. It was easily sixty feet long and at least thirty feet wide, with a huge table running down the center of the room. The three inch thick top was supported by a series of six heavily carved pedestals.

Around the table were arranged a set of at least forty tall backed chairs, each one upholstered in dark red embossed leather. The reason for the darkness became immediately apparent. The far wall, which consisted of five large floor-to-ceiling windows, was tightly shuttered. Phillip approached the center one and lifted the flat steel bar that held the wooden shutter closed.

As he folded back the hinged panels, sunlight streamed into the room. A large round hole had been neatly cut in the glass pane of the door sufficient for a large man to put his arm through and lift the brass catch that held the doors together. The glass doors had no locks. They would be unnecessary when the shutters were closed and barred. Phillip opened the door and stepped out onto a neat stone patio surrounded by a stone balustrade wall. To the right stood a round glass topped table and four wicker chairs. Above the table stood a tall blue canvas umbrella that offered respite from the hot sun. The patio area was festooned with potted plants and flowers. Four stone steps, between the balustrades, led down to a large tonsured lawn that stretched a good fifty yards. It ended abruptly at a low wall that appeared at one time to have been an outer defensive wall of the castle.

Approaching this wall, Phillip could just make out the town of Aix de Provence and the mountain of *Saint Victoire* far away in the distance. The clear morning air and the elevation of the castle gave a superb view of the surrounding countryside.

Peering over the edge of the low wall, Phillip saw that it fell away steeply. It would have required an experienced climber to scale such a steep and jagged rock face. At the base several hundred feet below, Phillip saw the small town of Baux de Provence where he and Daniel had met up that morning. He doubted that the intruders had come to the castle by that route. He turned to his right and followed the low wall toward the front of the castle. Although the patio and dining room windows were easily accessible from this point, it would have required the robbers to approach the front drive which was covered with thick loose gravel. Too noisy to hide foot steps and the narrow road leading up to the castle gates left no easy place to park a getaway car yet alone conceal one. The most obvious place to leave a vehicle would be a good three hundred yards down the steep winding road at a small cutaway. Risky but possible. Had the robbers done this they could have scaled the wall outside the study, and providing the curtains were closed, would not have been seen.

Phillip made his way around to that side of the house but the garden offered few opportunities to see footprints or where flowers may have been knocked over or crushed.

Had the thieves come onto the castle grounds this way they would have had to pass not only the sitting room, library and back hall, but would have also needed to climb up onto the patio via the lawn, to get to the dining room windows, which so easily could have been shuttered as they were today? All this was going through Phillip's mind as he did his walk around the castle. Some things seemed a little left to chance for a burglary of such magnitude. Or was it?

Coming round to the north side of the castle, Phillip met up with Daniel.

"What have you found?"

"Not much. I have photographed the hole in the glass. I

want to be sure that it was cut from the outside. Maybe our experts can tell these things. I hope."

"I'm a bit uneasy about this burglary Daniel. I can't see why they came in through the dining room. Why it wasn't shuttered. Where did they park their vehicle and why they didn't steal anything else? Although I suppose they could have just had a special order for the Leonardo, in which case we'll be lucky to find it, if it's gone underground."

Daniel became pensive. He stood silently staring out into the distant hills and the Mediterranean Sea beyond. Phillip knew better than to interrupt him when the cogs of his analytical brain were in full rotation. Daniel had an intellectual depth uncommon even in the most successful police investigators. Combined with Phillips ability to separate germane facts from the trifling ones -or *'peu de chose'* as the French say - the two men made an enlightened and lucent team, especially when dealing with the more fallacious element of the art world.

After a few minutes, Daniel turned to Phillip, "I think it's important we speak with the butler, Albert Guion as soon as possible. Also a few words with Miss Diab too-alone and away from the Marquis. If there's something 'fishy' about this theft, then the Marquis had help and who better than a faithful old servant or a doting goddaughter?"

"Bon, but first we eat lunch, no?"

"Whatever you say, Daniel. Heaven forbid I keep a Frenchman from his food."

With that the two men set off back to the small town of Baux de Provence and to the Café Grenouille where they'd met that morning.

Over lunch of a good local *bouillabaisse*, the two investigators discussed what they'd found so far. Not much in the way of clues, but enough to alert their suspicions that not everything was quite as straight forward as they'd previously been told. By the end of their lunch they had agreed upon one thing. Further investigation at the Chateau was essential.

Arriving for the second time that day at the Chateau de Manville, Daniel and Phillip stepped through the heavy oak door of the Chateau as once again Miss Diab was there to act as doorkeeper.

"Miss Diab," started Phillip as soon as she slid the last iron bolt back into place, "how long have you been staying here? I take it you weren't here on the night of the robbery."

"No. I was here earlier in the day but I left after lunch and returned to Cannes where I have my apartment. As soon as I heard about what happened to my Godfather, of course, I came straight back."

"How did you hear about the robbery?"

"From my Godfather. He called me from the hospital. By the time I arrived he was ready to leave but poor Monsieur Guion, Albert, was held over night."

"Have you been told how he is today and when he's due to be released?"

"Yes. The hospital spoke to the Marquis a few minutes ago and although they want to keep Albert for another day or two, he wants to leave today. So, I expect he'll be back here this afternoon, even against medical advice."

"When he does come home, and when he's rested, it's very important we get to speak with him."

"I'll certainly tell him."

"And, please call me," he handed her another business card, "as soon as he's home."

"Yes, Monsieur Fairfax. Now what else can I do for you?"

"What car do you drive, Mademoiselle?" interjected Daniel, who had been studying Leila Diab as she spoke with Phillip.

"A Volkswagen convertible."

"Color?"

"Red"

"So, that is your car in the drive?"

"Yes, it is."

"Does Albert Guion have a car?"

"No. He rarely goes anywhere except to drive the Marquis, who has an old Bentley. If he goes to the market to buy fresh produce, which he does most days, he always walks."

"Forgive my next question," Phillip looked at Miss Diab, "but you're not French. Where are you from?"

"I am Lebanese. Born and brought up in Beirut. My parents were both Palestinian. They were forced to move to Lebanon when the Israelis stole their land and kicked out all the non-Jews."

Phillip for the first time saw some passion in her dark eyes. He realized, at that moment, that his previous disinclination to find her beautiful, despite her statuesque figure, was due to the deadness in her eyes. Now he saw fire in them and her features radiated a depth of feeling that replaced her otherwise vapid personality. He knew at that instant as she jutted out her jaw in defiance, that the subject she had just touched was one that ran deep in her psyche. The hurt and even hatred that was felt in 1948 by those dispossessed of their land and birthright still bubbled with fury in the veins of their descendants. Leila's very countenance exuded a palpable sense of outrage at the thought of Israel.

"How long have you lived in France, Miss Diab?" continued Phillip.

"Since I was 18 years old mostly, although I still have an apartment in Beirut which I visit periodically. Why do you ask?"

"Curiosity Miss Diab, pure curiosity."

Phillip instinctively knew that he had touched a nerve, a still raw nerve, one that ignited the pugnacious side of Miss Diab's character, and he wondered how this would be tied into the robbery of the Leonardo or if indeed it was connected at all.

Phillip mentally filed away the information. His intuition told him somehow this was relevant to his investigation.

"I would like to speak with the Marquis again if that is convenient," said Phillip.

Leila Diab shrugged. "I think he's finished his lunch so is probably on the terrace."

Setting off in that direction, the two men silently fell in behind and once again walked through the impressive main hall of the Chateau. Daniel watched Leila's hips and *derriere* whilst Phillips attention was drawn to the lavish furnishing and tapestries that filled the chateau.

The Marquis was, as had been predicted, sitting on the terrace. He still wore a silk robe over dark blue silk pajamas. He wore sunglasses and was smoking a Gauloise cigarette when the two men stepped onto the terrace.

"More questions?" remarked the Marquis, hardly bothering to hide his disdain, "or have you come to tell me you've found my painting?"

"Regrettably not," said Phillip, as he sat, unbidden, at the round glass top table.

The Marquis made no attempt at hospitality but instead poured himself a glass of chilled rose wine from a bottle that sat in a sweating ice bucket on the table.

"I don't know what more I can tell you Mr. Fairfax. I can't help feeling that you'd be better off looking for the thieves than asking me a lot of damn fool questions; ones that the police have already asked." The Marquis was by now making no effort at disguising his contempt for Phillip and Daniels methods of investigation.

"I'm sorry you feel that way," said Phillip, "but let me ask you this. Who do you think stole your painting?"

"*Mon Dieu*, now you want me to do your job as well! I don't know who stole my Leonardo, Mr. Fairfax. If I did, I'd go and get it back."

"I understand your frustration, Marquis, but without any leads, it's difficult to know where to start looking. For example, have you had to fire anyone recently or had any part time employees; maybe from an agency? People in your house that you don't really know?"

"No, I have not. I haven't thrown a dinner party for several months and besides the catering company I use is from Marseilles and extremely reputable. They vet their staff very thoroughly. I repeat, Mr. Fairfax, I have no idea who could have done this thing. I only hope to God they don't damage it."

The Marquis stubbed out his cigarette, somewhat more forcibly than was necessary to extinguish the burning embers, and rose.

"If you gentleman have no more questions, questions that might lead somewhere, then I propose to go and lie down. I still have an awful headache and you gentleman are making it worse."

With that he turned his back on Phillip and Daniel and strode through the terrace doors.

"I think we learn nothing, eh?" said Daniel.

"Au contraire, mon brave," answered Phillip. "I think we've learned a great deal. Not about who stole the painting perhaps, but we've learned a little more about the Marquis. For instance, why do you think he is being so un-cooperative? After all, it's his painting that's been hijacked. You'd think he'd help us to find it anyway he could."

"C'est vrai, my friend," agreed Daniel. "I too find his attitude a little, how shall I say? Strange?"

"Strange indeed, Daniel. Strange indeed."

The two men once more explored the grounds but this time kept mainly to the north side of the chateau gardens.

As hard as he might, Phillip just couldn't see any easy way to enter the Chateau grounds other than by the main entrance gates. Presumably, thought Phillip, that's why they built the castle here.

As he peered over the northwest wall towards the narrow road that led from the village far below to the Chateau, Phillip noticed a lone figure walking up the winding path. His head appeared to be wrapped in a white bandage. This undoubtedly, was the unfortunate Albert Guion, returning from the hospital. Phillip continued to watch him slowly ascend the steep path until he was only fifty feet or so below him, at which point Albert disappeared from view behind a large boulder. Continuing to watch Albert's progress, Phillip fully expected Albert to reappear within seconds. He didn't.

Phillip continued to watch for Albert's re-appearance. Even assuming he'd stopped to catch his breath, it seemed odd that after five minutes he still hadn't made it around the large boulder. It then dawned on Phillip what had happened. Now he knew something more about the Marquis and perhaps something more about the robbery.

After a further half hour in the garden closely examining the wall adjoining the road to the village looking for scrapes and loosened stones, the two investigators returned to the house. They had both concluded that if anyone had ever scaled that wall from the road, it hadn't been done for over a hundred years. The moss and lichen hadn't been disturbed, and not a single stone appeared to have any scratches from a grappling hook or nylon rope.

Standing in the great hall once more, Phillip Fairfax and Daniel Masilionis were admiring the artwork that hung on the vast smooth stone walls. The fireplace remained unlit but instead was heaped with dead grey ashes. The large wicker basket, normally piled high with cut logs, lay virtually empty. Albert Guion had obviously been missed the last few days. As Phillip was taking in his surroundings Miss Diab appeared from behind the library door.

"Monsieur Fairfax? Albert has come home. He is in the kitchen if you wish to speak with him. I can show you the way."

"Thank you Mademoiselle Diab."

Leila Diab turned and strode through the door that led to the rear hall and the steps that led down to the kitchen. Phillip and Daniel once again fell in behind her.

The kitchen was a large room with a vaulted ceiling. In the center stood a plain pine farmhouse table covered with cutting boards, stoneware jars and fresh vegetables.

The walls were lined with an odd assortment of cupboards above which were hung plate racks and dozens of copper pans and iron skillets.

136

Albert was busy throwing kindling into the large ancient oven's boiler that had been built into what was once, no doubt a huge fireplace built big enough to spit roast an ox. He barely looked up when the two men were introduced to him.

Albert was a man who disliked being interrupted and he showed his displeasure by ignoring those who disturbed his labors. Phillip and Daniel waited patiently for Albert to satisfy himself that the fire was well alight. Then, and only then, did he look up and acknowledge the presence of the two investigators.

"Bonjour, Monsieur Guion."

Albert merely nodded and said nothing. Phillip continued the interview in French, although it promised to be a one sided conversation. Having established that Albert Guion was feeling well despite the large crack on his head, Phillip turned now to Miss Diab.

"Thank you Miss Diab, but please do not let us detain you any further."

She stood and looked at Phillip for a full half a minute, obviously put out that she was, in effect, being summarily dismissed. Having silently protested her expulsion, she turned and without a word walked out of the kitchen. Albert said nothing but threw another log into the roaring furnace.

"Albert- I hope I may call you that…" continued Phillip.

Throughout the interview Albert continued to go about his work. Although Phillip's French was good, he occasionally had trouble with Albert's thick Provençal accent, but Daniel was familiar with it and helped Phillip out when needed. Albert was a man of few words however, and beyond discovering that he could only remember seeing the Marquis when he entered the study and no

136

masked intruder, little more light was throw on the subject of the robbery.

On their way back to the village of Baux, Daniel and Phillip discussed the relevance of Albert not remembering seeing a masked intruder. On the surface it seemed unlikely if the man was standing next to the Marquis, but as Daniel pointed out, if the room was scarcely lit which seems to be the Marquis preference, perhaps it wasn't so unusual. Phillip remained unconvinced. Mostly because he was having increasing doubts about the Marquis's story.

The question did remain, however, as to who hit Albert on the head if there were no thieves. To Phillip there was only one possible explanation-an accomplice, which posed the next obvious question-who? Phillip had a strong suspicion he knew who it was but for the time being he kept his own counsel.

TWENTY

Back at his hotel in St. Remy, Phillip showered and changed. He poured himself a glass of red wine and dialed Sir Robert in England. Sir Robert picked up on the second ring; he was still at his desk. The two men asked after each others health and then Phillip got to the point of his call.

"Robert, can you find out anything from your buddies in the foreign office, about a woman called Leila Diab? He spelled it out. She's a Lebanese national, goddaughter to the Marquis and presently resides in Cannes. She's mid thirties I would say. Tall for an Arab too, about 5' 10". Her parents were both Palestinians. Basically, I just need to know if she has association with any undesirables."

"Is she a suspect?"

"Not exactly, no; but there are a few things that don't quite add up. The Marquis is not exactly falling over himself to be helpful and I have a hunch he knows something more than he's letting on."

"Awkward bugger, eh?"

"And not a very pleasant one. You did warn me."

"Any ideas yet?"

"Nothing concrete, no, but its early days. Get back to me as soon as you've got anything."

"Will do. Go carefully."

Phillip hung up the phone, and finished his glass of wine. He decided to wander into town to eat because later he had a mission. Phillip hoped to discover how Albert had entered the Chateau unseen, and more so, he hoped it would be another piece in the Leonardo puzzle.

At midnight, Phillip parked his rented car in the town square of Baux. It was quiet now, everyone was at home, but the occasional bar still held a few late night drinkers. The moon offered good light but was periodically obliterated by passing clouds. Phillip wore sturdy hiking boots and carried a small knapsack on his back. It contained a large flash light and a smaller pencil light. A 35 mm camera fitted with a three foot fiber optic lens with infrared capabilities, a flashlight, a set of lock picks, some electrical wire with crocodile clips, a can of WD40 penetrating lubricant and a bottle of water.

By fifteen minutes past midnight Phillip had begun to climb the steep winding road up towards the Chateau. After ten minutes he found the footpath that he had seen Albert Guion take earlier that day. The path was well worn and smooth apart from the occasional rock that had tumbled onto the path. It was steep; steeper than the roadway but a much more direct route to the castle. At approximately fifty feet below the castle wall, Phillip came across the large rock behind which Albert Guion had disappeared earlier that day. Phillip stopped and removed his backpack.

There was no sound reaching him from either the small town of Baux or the castle that loomed above him, silhouetted against the blue black sky. Removing his flashlight he shone it against the rock wall behind the boulder. There was no door. In fact the rock wall looked solid with just the normal fissures and cracks consistent with this ancient mound. Phillip continued to look around, feeling with his hands and hoping that he didn't disturb a sleeping scorpion that made its home in such a landscape.

Eventually he found not only a vertical crack in the rock face, but one that joined it and ran horizontally for about five to six feet. He traced it with his finger tips until he found another crack that ran down to the floor. There was no traditional door, but Phillip was convinced he'd found the opening that led to the chateau. He pushed the center of the rock. Nothing moved. He tried both sides but again it seemed as solid as the rest of the rock outcrop that the castle perched upon. Was this just a natural phenomenon that gave the appearance of a doorway opening? Phillip doubted it and continued to search the area for the secret to gaining entrance. A small sage bush growing like a million others from the cracks in the rocks of Provence caught his attention. Gingerly he brushed aside the fragrant branches to reveal exactly what he had been looking for.

With the aid of his torch he peered inside a round hole behind the sage and saw a black metal knob. Satisfying himself that the hole contained no sleeping creatures he reached in and pulled the knob. Soundlessly it came out at least two inches which still left it hidden in the recess. If Phillip had expected the doorway to suddenly open, he was disappointed, but a gentle push on the rock face enabled it to soundlessly pivot on a central axis. It opened revealing an entrance to a cave-like interior no wider than three or four feet, but more than sufficient for a man to enter. Phillip shone his torch inside before grabbing his ruck sack and slipping into the darkness.

The interior was roughly hewn from the solid rock and at six feet two inches tall Phillip was barely able to stand upright. He shone the torch on the walls and ceiling and saw in the far corner, not six feet away, a set of narrow stone steps leading up into the darkness.

At the bottom step an old Bakelite light switch attached to a looping wire was there to illuminate the steps leading to the castle interior. Phillip chose not to use it but instead relied upon his flashlight to guide him upwards.

141

The steps were smooth and evenly spaced but steep and narrow. Phillip could easily touch each wall as the steps wound in a gentle spiral up towards the bowels of the chateau. He proceeded slowly, feeling his way and counting the steps as he went. After climbing sixty-five steps, the stairs came to a small landing where a sturdy oak door was set into the wall.

Shining his torch around the perimeter of the old door, Phillip could see that despite the rough nature of the hewn rock, the door was a snug fit. A large keyhole had obviously been the original point of entry, but recently a new and more technically advanced lock had been installed.

Phillip debated whether he would stop and try to open the door now or continue up the steps. He reasoned that such a sophisticated lock was installed for a very good reason, and he wanted to know what the reason was. He decided, however, to just find out where the stairs led him and continued to climb the remaining few steps. After another twenty three treads the stairs came to a dead end. At a wooden wall about six feet wide and braced horizontally and vertically with two inch wide oak strips. The wall was consistent with the back of a bookcase or shelves. Phillip saw a natural crack in the wood paneling and putting his eye to it he attempted to see what room lay behind the shelves, but the darkness prevented him being able to identify it.

Removing his back pack once again, he removed the camera and fiber optic cable with the infrared lens and gently went about threading in through the narrow crack in the paneled back of the wall. Looking through the view finder, Phillip could just make out what appeared to be shelves laden with various jars and tins. Onions, smoked meats and sausages hung from hooks in the low ceiling.

What Phillip had found was Albert Guion's pantry. He doubted that any casual perusal of this small store room would indicate that it was anything other than what it appeared to be. It was, he thought, an ideal disguise for the secret stairway passage that he now stood in.

Phillip pressed the shutter button several times on his camera, adjusting the fiber optic cable between each shot. He wanted as full a record as possible of this 'secret' room. Gently he withdrew the cable and packed it away again into his ruck sack.

Phillip now retraced his steps back to the small landing where he proposed to gain entry behind the locked oak door. Shining his light onto the door he noticed that it was secured by a Medeco lock. Medeco is a good quality lock with about six or seven pins, and from experience, Phillip knew that he would have to use the *scrubbing* or *racking* technique to open it. The feel of lock picking, considered by its practitioners as an art as much a science, requires a good understanding of the relationship between applied torque and the amount of force required to lift each pin.

Most locks have mechanical design faults and for a skilled picker of locks it was relatively easy to exploit these weaknesses. Phillip inserted his tension wrench at the base of the keyhole and with his diamond pick began to rub it across the pin tumblers.

The Medeco lock was no different to the hundreds of others described as 'high security' and within forty five seconds Phillip had lifted all six pins to open the lock. Before he opened the door, Phillip removed his can of WD40 and sprayed a little on each of the four heavy duty hinges that the heavy oak barrier relied on for opening. Phillip had learned by experience that a creaking rusty hinge could produce enough ear- splitting noise to awaken anyone or anything, short of an Egyptian mummy.

Phillip was not about to announce his presence. Patiently he waited for the WD40 to work its way to all parts of the hinges. Satisfied that the lubricant had done its work, he gently grasped the solid brass handle and pushed the door inwards. What greeted Phillips eyes as he shone his flashlight into the room caused him to stop in his tracks. Whatever he had been expecting it was not this.

TWENTY-ONE

Back at his hotel in St. Remy, Phillip undressed and showered. It was gone four o' clock in the morning and much too early to call Sir Robert, so Phillip lay down on his bed to catch a couple hours of sleep.

He awoke a little more than two hours later somewhat refreshed but still trying to grapple with the meaning of his discovery the previous night. He was very unsure in what direction his investigation was leading him. It not only puzzled him but worried him that the theft of the Leonardo might only be a small part of a much bigger and more dangerous situation.

Phillip telephoned Daniel, who he suspected still had female company, and arranged to meet him at the Café Grenouille later that morning. He told him to have a good breakfast and to bring his binoculars and a telephoto lens with his camera. He warned him that it might be a long day but gave no other indication as to what he had planned.

Daniel, with his usual Gallic nonchalance, seemed happy to follow Phillips plans without question. He knew Phillip would explain it all when they met. To say too much over the phone was something neither man felt comfortable with. Their business concluded for the time being, Phillip hung up and immediately dialed Sir Robert. It was still early in London, but once again Sir Robert picked up after only the second ring.

"I thought it might be you,' said Sir Robert as Phillip got straight down to business, "get any sleep?"

"Not much, but enough," Phillip responded. "Any news from your pals in the Foreign Office?"

"About the Diab girl?" clarified Robert.

"Yes. Is she a player?"

145

"Not that we've found out so far but there is a bit of news that might interest you. It would appear that Leila Diab is the daughter of a Muhammad and Hala Diab, both known terrorists, who were killed in 1973 by our boys working in conjunction with the Mossad. Leila Diab would have been about three or four years old at the time. There was a plan, by all accounts, to plant a bomb on an El Al transatlantic flight to New York. Muhammad Diab had somehow got a job at Heathrow as a baggage handler using false papers. Anyway, Israel's Secret Service, the Mossad got to hear about it and for once shared their knowledge with our own MI 5. Between them they snuffed out the plan in the nick of time and Muhammad and Hala Diab paid the ultimate price."

Sir Robert waited for Phillip to digest this news and to decide whether it could have any possible relevance to his current investigations.

Sir Robert continued. "I believe your old mob was involved. It certainly bore the marks of an SAS take down but that bit is still classified so I can't say for sure."

Phillip made several notes as Sir Robert continued his briefing.

"Leila Diab grew up with her grandmother in Beirut and despite being from a poor family; she seemed to get a good education. She won a place at the Sorbonne in Paris but quit before getting her degree. She was studying Middle East history."

Phillip continued to take down details in his note book. "Go on Robert" he said when he had caught up.

"OK. She didn't appear to get involved with any radical groups as a student. No protest marches, no sit-ins and didn't belong to any underground organizations that we know of. She was an O.K student but not one who stood

145

out." Sir Robert could be heard taking a mouthful of his morning tea.

"After the Sorbonne she disappeared for a few years-presumably went back to Beirut-and reappeared on the social scene in Cannes about ten years ago and has been seen a few times at the fashionable clubs in London, Paris and Rome. No trace of a husband and a bit of a mystery where her money came form, but speculating, she may have slept her way into high society. And that, dear boy, is about as much as I can tell you. Does any of it fit in with your theory?"

"Well, it hasn't ruled anything out. Her parents being killed would account for her bristling at the very thought of Israel," Phillip replied, "but I can't say it puts her in the frame for the Leonardo theft; if you'll pardon the pun," said Phillip.

"You're pardoned." Robert chuckled. "Well, let me know if there's anything else you need. Meanwhile I'll keep digging, maybe check on her recent movements, flights, et cetera, but that could take some time."

"Thanks Robert. I'll get back to you soon. Take care."

"You too, my boy."

Phillip hung up the phone and went into town in search of breakfast with strong coffee.

Daniel was waiting when Phillip turned up at the café in Baux. He looked as if he'd had as little sleep as Phillip but he wore a wide grin across his face. Phillip suspected he knew the reason but felt the subject should be left alone for the time being. However, he couldn't resist a knowing wink when he enquired if Daniel had slept well.

Sitting down opposite Daniel, Phillip outlined his plan for the day. They would climb the steep and rocky slopes outside the small town where they sat and head towards the Chateau de Manville perched on top of its limestone outcrop. They would avoid the winding road that cut through the rock formation on towards the pinnacle although always trying to keep it within sight.

The southern part of the Alpilles Mountains is exposed rock, mostly formed into monstrous shapes, by centuries of erosion and the formidable winds that blast this part of Provence. The olive groves and vineyards to the southeast and the forested areas on the northern slopes don't reach the altitude of the medieval village of Les Baux de Provence, but gave way to a wilder and more hostile terrain. Phillip and Daniel, each with their packed knapsacks, left the narrow cobblestoned streets with their terraced cafes and small shops and headed for the barren, rocky landscape that surrounded the village and the castle.

It was sunny but windy as the two investigators clambered over the rocks and waded through the wild, often thorny bushes. Phillip frequently had to stop and wait for Daniel who didn't have Phillip's level of physical fitness. For this he took a certain amount of ribbing about his decadent lifestyle to which Daniel responded merely by grinning even wider.

About one hundred yards or so from the summit and the gates of the chateau, Phillip stopped and removed his rucksack. Arriving some minutes later Daniel placed his backpack next to Phillip and sat down on a rock, somewhat out of breath.

"We have arrived?' he inquired.

"*Oui*, it looks like a good place to me" responded Phillip.

"It look like a good place only for the snakes," said Daniel.

Seeing that the prospect of a snake riddled landscape didn't exactly thrill Phillip, he proceeded to

148

lecture him in great detail on the characteristics of the 'Montpellier snake', a rather aggressive poisonous creature and the '*couleuvre a echelons*' or 'ladder' snake that kills its prey by constriction rather than by venom. He polished off his dissertation with a vivid description of the *Orsin*i viper, dangerous but now somewhat rare in the south of France.
Seeing Phillip's obvious dislike of the subject he felt suitable revenge had been exacted for the taunts he'd suffered on the way up the mountainside. Acknowledging the '*touch*e' Phillip set about establishing a good view of the castle entrance whilst remaining unseen to anyone looking in their direction.

For two hours the men sat watching the Chateau through their Zeiss binoculars. Occasionally the two men sipped from a water bottle, which by now was getting rather warm, and discussed the information that Sir Robert Spence had told Phillip that morning. Phillip then explained to Daniel everything that he had discovered at the Chateau the previous night. Daniel's reaction to Phillip's revelation was predictably the same, one of great surprise.

Just at that moment both men noticed a grey Fiat followed by Leila Diab's red VW come snaking up the steep road from Baux towards the chateau. Reaching the summit both cars drove through the main entrance and parked opposite the front door. Leila Diab was the first to get out and without stopping or acknowledging the other driver she headed into the Chateau. Minutes later a short, stocky man in an ill fitting suit that looked as if he'd slept in it, emerged from behind the wheel of the grey Fiat.

"Did you get that license plate number Daniel?" enquired Phillip as he continued to observe the stout man

149

who also entered the Chateau through his powerful binoculars.

"*Oui*, my friend. It is 8-5-5 Alpha Golf Juliet zero 6. I shall call and find out who own this car."

"Thanks Daniel" said Phillip as he rummaged in his rucksack.

He withdrew two small black and yellow boxes, each about four and a half inches in length but only just over an inch wide. Each had a magnetic strip attached to one side and weighed eight ounces when the four triple 'A' batteries were inserted.

"Daniel, stay here. I'm just going up for a closer look and maybe I can fix these two tracking devices to those cars. I'd like to know where Miss Diab goes and I'd also like to know who our new friend is and what he has to do with the Marquis."

"Be careful, my friend", said Daniel. Phillip replied that he would because it could prove rather embarrassing if he was caught lurking around the two cars in the Marquis driveway.

With that Phillip set off in a low crouch and swiftly moved between the rocks and bushes as he ascended the hill towards the chateau.

It took him almost seven minutes to cover the one hundred yards to the front gates, in part due to the fact that Phillip chose a zigzag path that offered more concealment and partly because he crawled almost half the distance on his belly, despite the possibilities of a snake encounter.

Daniel had lost sight of Phillip almost immediately after he'd left and didn't, in fact, see him again until he saw his stealthy colleague slip into the chateau grounds and crouch behind Leila Diab's red Volkswagen. Feeling up underneath the wheel arch, Phillip found a section of clean metal and attached the magnetic tracking device. Making

150

sure it was firmly in place he then moved behind the Fiat and attached the second device up and underneath the rear bumper. Phillip left the drive quickly and made his way down to where Daniel was waiting. The whole operation had taken him less than fifteen minutes.

"Daniel, we will have about twenty four hours of tracking on those two cars before the batteries give out. I suggest we hike down to our cars and keep an eye on them from down in the town. When they leave the chateau- always assuming they're not staying for several days, I'll follow our new friend in the Fiat and you could please follow the lovely Miss Diab."

"It would be my pleasure to follow her" said Daniel with his usual impish grin.

"I didn't think you'd mind that assignment too much, Daniel," responded Phillip matching his broad smile.

Slipping their rucksacks onto their backs the two men set off back through the rocks and sage brush down towards their cars that were parked in Baux. As they picked their way through the rocks and bushes, Phillip handed Daniel the small receiver screen that showed the blinking red light of Leila Diab's car.

"This screen, Daniel, will show you exactly where Miss Diab's car is as she drives. You'll see it's overlaid on a map so her route will be clearly marked. It has a range of a good five to six miles so you won't need to be right on her tail but I do need to know if she makes any stops so you'll have to be no more than a half a mile behind her. In towns you can get as close as you safely can. I need to know where she goes more than where her car goes, *ca va?*"

"*Oui, ca va, mon colonel*", said Daniel, saluting, in mock derision of Phillip's orders.

"Sorry Daniel, I sometimes forget that you know as much about this business as I do."

150

"It is fine my friend, I take no offense," said Daniel
clapping Phillip on the back in a gesture of friendship. You
are British army, no? And I am just a dumb French copper,
n'est pas?" his wide grin deprecating any unintended
rancor in his statement.

"You're a good sport Daniel. I enjoy working with
you."

"You too, *mon ami*, and perhaps now you would
like to know who our new friend is?"

Without waiting for a reply, Daniel announced that
the new arrival at the chateau was a Monsieur Andre
Basson. Car registered in his name and at the business
address of Andre Basson, Advocat, 1500 Montpellier,
Nice."

"I found this out when you were hopping through
the rocks and bushes" announced Daniel. He folded the
small piece of paper with this information and handed it to
Phillip.

"He should be worth keeping an eye on," said
Phillip. "He didn't look like the type of lawyer I'd have
expected the Marquis to employ. Rather a shabby little
fellow so I guess he must be very good at his job. I'll be
interested to find out where this little man fits into all this."

"I shall leave you to find out while I follow the
delectable Miss Leila Diab. I think I have the best job, no?"

"You're definitely right there Daniel," said Phillip
as the two men strolled over to their now favorite café.

The waiter, Aaron, saw them coming and
recognizing the big tippers, immediately began cleaning
their usual table; the one that gave the best view of the
castle. They greeted Aaron cordially as they sat down at
their table. Phillip periodically peered at the castle not
through his binoculars, but through the telephoto lens of his
camera. The castle looked so majestic perched on top of

152

the huge rocks that almost every visitor to this town went home with dozens of snaps of this imposing fortress.

Recently the press had all but camped out in Baux to get footage of the famous home to the even more famous Leonardo da Vinci painting. So Phillip's constant photographing raised no eyebrows and was thought normal behavior for any tourist. Occasionally, he pointed his camera at other interesting buildings in the town in order to avert suspicion from his thorough preoccupation with the castle. Eventually he saw Andre Basson emerge from the oak doors of the chateau.

Phillip's motor drive worked overtime catching frame after frame of Monsieur Basson and the black valise that he now carried, something Phillip had not seen him with earlier. Almost immediately after Basson had reached his car, Leila Diab appeared and kissing her godfather, slipped behind the wheel of her VW.

"We're on Daniel," said Phillip as he stowed his camera onto his backpack.

Leaving two 20 Euro notes on the table Phillip bade Daniel, *'au revoir'* and wished him a safe journey.

"Keep in touch, Daniel. I'll call you to let you know where I end up and let's hope Miss Diab leads you to some interesting places too."

"Good luck, *mon ami*," replied Daniel as he too headed towards his car.

The two men waited for their targets to appear and set off behind them at a discreet distance.

For the first few miles they all followed the same road until the red VW peeled off to the east as it met up with the A8 motorway towards Cannes. Phillip continued southwards on the A7 following the grey Fiat. They were headed for Marseilles.

TWENTY-TWO

Phillip Fairfax followed Andre Basson into the short term parking lot at Marseilles' International Airport. He was able to park quite close to Basson's Fiat which made it easy for Phillip to keep him in view.

Following at a discreet distance the two men crossed, along with dozens of holiday makers and business people, between the traffic to the main terminal. The short overweight lawyer moved surprisingly quickly as he carried his black valise and small carry-on towards the Alitalia ticket desk. Basson carried no other luggage so Phillip reasoned that they were probably heading to Italy and only for a short stay. Andre Basson bought a ticket with cash, unusual in itself, and then joined the short queue for the Alitalia flight AZ7397 to Rome.

Watching this, Phillip then purchased a ticket to Rome for himself and with just his rucksack for hand luggage he too joined the queue for the 5:25 pm Rome flight. Phillip felt a little conspicuous in his choice of clothing which was designed for hiking in the Alpilles mountains rather than for strolling through the streets of Rome. Luckily he had been able to change his hiking boots for normal shoes but his multi-pocketed green cargo pants, jacket and rucksack made him look more like a Far East war correspondent than a typical tourist in Rome. Too late now, thought Phillip as the flight to Rome announced passenger boarding. It was nearly five o'clock.

Phillip had requested an aisle seat and as it turned out, so had Andre Basson. Phillip sat four rows behind but on the opposite side of the central aisle from Basson. It gave him only a partial view of the lawyer but sufficient to watch his growing agitation. Whatever errand the advocate was on, it was obvious he wanted it to be over as quickly as possible.

Phillip's traveling companion in the next seat was a vivacious young American girl who it transpired was heading to Rome to study singing under the tutelage of the well-know impresario Signore Alberto Campari. She spoke with great excitement at how difficult it was to get a place with such a world renowned teacher. Normally Phillip would have found her enthusiasm refreshing and infectious, but Phillip passed himself off as a dour history teacher, on a sabbatical year visiting the various countries dotted around the Mediterranean. His dry and fact laden dissertation about the olive trade between Rome and Carthage, and other ancient cities on the northern shores of Africa soon prompted the otherwise chatty young lady to retreat to her earphones and walkman.

This freed Phillip to devote his time to thinking, and studying Monsieur Basson. He counted the number of times Basson requested a refill of his wine glass. Four. Here was a nervous man.

Once during the flight, Basson did leave his seat. He passed Phillip on his way to the rear of the compartment where the toilets were situated. Basson still clutched his black valise rather than leave it on his seat. The look on his face told Phillip that here was a deeply troubled and unhappy man. So preoccupied was Basson that any observance of those people around him was not even a remote possibility. Basson was in a sad world of his own. Locked in his own thoughts that obviously weren't happy ones.

Phillip realized at this point that whatever clandestine errand the lawyer was on for the Marquis, he was neither happy about it nor good at it. He hoped this would make his task easier, but Phillip still couldn't understand why the Marquis had chosen someone so ill-suited to a task, which still unspecified, was doubtless dishonest in nature and required a degree of cool headedness.

At seven o'clock that evening the Alitalia jet began its descent for a landing at Rome's *Fiumicino Airport*. A flight attendant insisted that Basson either place his black leather case in the overhead bin or under the seat in front of him. At first he seemed disinclined to obey, but seeing that the fuss was drawing attention to him, he acquiesced and placed the case on the floor. He promptly placed his two feet directly on top. It seemed to Phillip that no matter what, Basson was not giving up physical contact with his black briefcase.

Landing at Italy's largest airport, everyone seemed eager to disembark. Hardly had the "fasten seatbelt" sign been switched off, than the entire aircraft population rose as one and scrambled for their possessions. All that is, except Andre Basson and four rows behind, Phillip Fairfax.

Eventually Basson joined the end of the line waiting to disembark. Phillip resuming his conversation with the young American songstress, also found an opening at the tail end of the queue and slotted the pair of them between an elderly lady and a struggling mother with two young infants.

Although the young American was an ideal 'cover' for Phillip, he positioned himself so that he always kept Basson in his peripheral vision. As this mass of passengers exited the aircraft and poured into the arrivals hall, it would be easy for Phillip to loose sight of Basson. Losing him here would mean that the whole trip had been a waste of time.

Although Phillip had visited Rome on several occasions he was not overly familiar with the busy airport.

The Fiumicino airport was the hub for the nation's main air carrier, Alitalia, and also for the package holiday carrier Ryan Air. The whole airport was a mass of humanity hurrying to get to their various destinations. It would be easy to loose Basson in the heaving throngs of people but equally as easy to tail him unobserved.

Basson, it would seem, was also unsure of his surroundings and consulted a piece of folded paper several times as he made his way through the hordes of travelers towards the rail link for the city center. Arriving on the platform both men waited for the "Leonardo Express"- what else would it be called - which would take them to the heart of Rome.

In thirty five short minutes the train arrived at the Roma Termini station. Again, Basson consulted his folded scrap of paper and returned it to the top pocket of his crumpled suit jacket.

He looked about him, not as Phillip feared, for followers, but for directions and seeing what he needed, Basson headed in the direction of the A line subway.

Phillip followed at a discrete distance and stood at the rear of a carriage whilst Basson, still clutching his briefcase close to his chest, sat near the front. At the third stop Basson left the subway getting off at the *Piazza di Spagna*. Maintaining a good distance and camouflaged by throngs of sight-seers, Phillip kept a close eye on the progress of the advocat as the nervous little man crossed the Piazza.

The scenic impact of the square, with *Bernini's Baraccia* Fountain, were lost on Basson who continued his furious pace oblivious both to Phillip and to the beauty of his surroundings. Crossing the square, Basson entered a pretty street called *Via Mairo Di Fiori* and entered the front lobby of the exclusive Hotel Condotti.

Phillip still remained convinced that Basson had not the foggiest notion he was being followed. Despite his frequent looks over his shoulder, Basson had made no evasive maneuvers nor attempted to switch back from his indicated path. So inept did Basson seem that Phillip found himself wondering if he hadn't just been led on a wild goose chase.

As Basson approached the main desk, Phillip, who entered almost directly behind him, headed for the public telephones, situated along the far wall, each encapsulated in its own oak paneled kiosk. Phillip dialed Daniel's mobile telephone number and watched as Basson turned to his right and entered the main lounge bar of the hotel. After a couple of rings Daniel answered his phone.

"*Allo, oui?*"

"Hello, Daniel, it's Phillip. I'm in Rome."

"*Mon Dieu,*, you drive fast!" joked Daniel.

"And what are you doing?" enquired Phillip, ignoring Daniel's flippancy, "besides sitting on your *derriere?*"

"I am now, Monsieur Fairfax, sitting, as you observed, on my derriere, in my car, and watching the apartment of Mademoiselle Diab. She is inside, no doubt enjoying the cool drink while I sit here bored out of my mind."

"Did she make any stops?"

"Not one .Except for *l'essence*, of course, but nothing else. You?"

"I have been following our crumpled friend, Basson, and he's led me to the Hotel Condotti in Rome. It's a nice place, and he's headed to the bar. I hope to learn something soon because so far it's been a waste of time."

"I know how you feel", responded Daniel, "so far there have been only two other peoples enter the apartments. I have photo'd them but both were old peoples. I doubt they are trouble."

"Okay Daniel, I'm off for a cold drink to keep an eye on our friend. Looks like I got the best job after all."

"My friend, I think you are right this time! *Bon courage!*"

"Good luck to you too, Daniel." And the two men hung up.

Phillip entered the main lounge and took a seat in the middle of the almost empty bar. The barman immediately placed a small round paper coaster in front of Phillip.

"*Vino rossi, por favore,*" said Phillip.

Within seconds a large glass, half filled with deep red nectar appeared in front of Phillip. Lifting his glass to his nose Phillip savored the bouquet as his eyes scanned the mirror in front of him for a reflection of Basson's whereabouts. At first he was unable to see him and wondered if Basson had managed to give him the slip after all, but just as a feeling of having been made a fool of started to engulf Phillip, he spotted the diminutive lawyer tucked into the dark recesses of a corner booth. He was alone but the ever present black valise was on the table in front of him along with a tall glass of beer.

Basson fidgeted and absentmindedly twiddled his paper coaster until it lay in a dozen torn and twisted pieces on the table in front of him.

Diving into his rucksack, Phillip produced his Leica camera and pretending to examine it, casually placed it back on the counter by his left elbow. Its lens pointed back towards Monsieur Basson in his booth. Phillip could do nothing now but wait and enjoy his drink and hope that his

159
instinct to follow Basson wasn't way off the mark.

TWENTY-THREE

Daniel Masilionis, Interpol agent, continued to sit in his small car, his camera on the seat next to him, his eyes flicking between the light in Leila Diab's apartment on the top floor and the front entrance. Daniel had decided in his own mind that he would wait until all the lights in Leila Diab's apartment had been extinguished for at least an hour, and providing nothing happened, and she didn't leave, he would risk slipping away to acquire coffee and to take a much needed pee. Almost as soon as he'd settled this plan in his mind a gentle knock at his window brought Daniels thoughts rocketing back to the present.

He lowered his window a couple of inches. A small folded note was slipped through the opening by a young man who identified himself as the son of the apartment's concierge. Having completed his task the young man disappeared back into the night.

Daniel opened the note and, grabbing his pencil flash light, read it. In neat handwriting it said,

"If you are going to watch me all night, I'm sure you would find it more comfortable to do it from my apartment. Why not join me?"

It was signed Leila.

Daniel could not resist smiling. At least the lady had a sense of humor. He switched off his flash light, got out of his car after stowing his expensive camera in the glove compartment, and locked his car doors. He was grateful to be able to stretch his legs as he strode across the road to the apartment complex.

He circled the building twice on the outside looking for anything that looked out of place. It was an affluent neighborhood judging by the cars that were parked outside but something made Daniel uneasy. On his scouting operation he only encountered one elderly lady who was walking her small dog. She bade him 'good evening' and continued on her way. Everything looked quiet, respectable and peaceful and yet his *gut* told him otherwise.

Daniel wrestled with his predicament. Should he go up to Leila Diab's apartment where he could much better keep an eye on her? He might even learn something useful. Or should he continue to sit outside and watch any comings and goings? It seemed pointless to stay outside, especially since she knew he was there, so he decided that "nothing ventured, nothing gained'

Leila Diab's apartment was on the top floor of the building as he had ascertained earlier. He pressed her door buzzer and a click immediately indicated that the main entrance door had been unlocked for him. Pushing it open, Daniel entered the marble floored lobby and headed towards the ornate iron and bronze elevator cage. He got in and pressed the button for the Fifth floor. Somewhere in the elevator shaft a noisy motor whirred into action and Daniel found himself heading upwards.

He got out at the Fifth floor and looked around. Everything was quiet. The only sounds he could hear were those from television sets or radios. He entered the staircase and again listened. Nothing. He walked slowly up the stairs and stopped at each floor to listen. All was quiet in this middle class suburban building.

Reaching the Penthouse Suite he walked to the door and pressed the button. Daniel was entering the Lion's den.

Leila Diab opened the door almost immediately. She wore very little. Daniel found himself in a spacious and open apartment, expensively decorated but devoid of color. Everything in the room was white. An open window opposite blew a gentle breeze into the room bringing with it the scent of the sea. Leila turned and went to her bar where she offered Daniel a tall flute of chilled champagne from the opened bottle that rested, chilling, in a silver bucket of ice. He refused, although the idea was very appealing to him but instead he erred on the side of caution and asked for a bottle of water. He wanted something sealed.

She handed Daniel a glass with two ice cubes and passed him an unopened bottle of Perrier water. She offered him a slice of lemon which he politely refused. He knew how easy it was to inject citrus fruit with drugs. Examining the top of the bottle he gave it a gentle twist and poured the chilled water into his glass.

Leila smiled at his caution, bit into the lemon to prove there was no poison and sat on a white leather sofa. She picked up her own flute of sparkling champagne whilst a black Sobrani cigarette smoldered in the ashtray in front of her. She wore a flimsy silk dressing robe cinched beneath her breasts but open to the floor. Underneath she wore only the flimsiest of panties. Daniel's eyes followed her every graceful move.

"I wasn't sure you'd accept my invitation." Leila Diab spoke in French.

In his native tongue Daniel too responded in French.

"How could anyone resist such a kind invitation, let alone a bored and thirsty policeman?"

Leila Diab's mouth smiled as Daniel took a thirsty drink of his sparkling water.

"Sante" he said raising it to his lips.

"Cin, cin," she replied taking a sip of hers.

Daniel took a seat opposite her and relaxed, savoring the crisp refreshing taste of his chilled water.

"So why are you watching me Daniel? I may call you Daniel, may I not?" she said looking over the top of her bubbling wine glass.

"Of course you may call me Daniel," he said, "and as for watching you, surely any man would enjoy that task," he added, allowing his usual charming grin to add the exclamation mark.

"But you don't look like a stalker. Do you think I stole the Leonardo painting from my godfather?" she countered.

"I don't know who stole it," said Daniel quite honestly. "Did you steal it?" he asked bluntly.

"No, monsieur, I did not steal it," she said quite emphatically as she rose from her seat once again.

She moved over towards Daniel. Bending over in front of him she revealed her ample bosom and taking his empty glass she returned to the bar. Daniel remained seated but his eyes remained focused on her very alluring body, which was only partially obscured by the flimsy silk dressing gown that hugged her every curve. She returned to Daniel and handing him his glass with two fresh ice cubes and a new bottle of Perrier she once again returned to her seat, where she allowed her gown to part, revealing her long, tanned and naked legs.

"So you still haven't told me why you are watching my apartment, Daniel? Are you really at such a loss as to know who stole this painting? You know it is breaking my godfather's heart," she stated taking a long pull on her cigarette.

"I'm sure it is, Leila, but there is so little to go on," said Daniel as he once again took a refreshing drink. "Surely you must have formed some ideas yourself. Who do you think stole the painting, Miss Diab?" he added.

"I'm not the detective," she replied, "but if I was able to take a guess, I'd say it was a couple of crooks who just saw an opportunity to make themselves some big money."

"Well, you could be right, and if you are, I'm sure Monsieur Fairfax and I will run them to ground," said Daniel stifling a yawn. It had been a long day, he thought.

The two people sat in silence for a while each appraising the other. Eventually Leila rose again from her couch, but this time Daniel saw not one but two sylph like figures glide silently across the room. Pinching his eyes, Daniel shook his head to clear his thoughts.

Through blurring vision he saw four other people enter the room or was it only two other people? Daniel realized at that moment, it wasn't him being tired; he had been drugged.

"*Merde!*" The bitch had spiked the ice cubes. How could he have been so stupid? She was a great deal more cunning than he'd given her credit for. He realized as his head began to swim that he had seriously underestimated her.

Trying to stand he found the room began to move. The floor rippled like the disturbed surface of a mill pond. Voices now sounded strange, as if they were being played on too slow a speed. He couldn't understand them. He felt arms holding him up. He felt hands all over his body. Just how many were there! He couldn't count. He couldn't think. He couldn't speak. Even as he tried to cry out his words just wouldn't form. Suddenly, he felt a sinking feeling and then one of almost temporary weightlessness. Daniel felt sure he was dying.

Daniel was not in fact dying but he had been right about being drugged. Two strong men now had Daniel under each arm and gradually they had coaxed him into the elevator and then out into the street. As they waited, a passing couple walking arm in arm looked at the bedraggled lump that was Daniel being propped up by two swarthy sailor types. One sailor indicated a drinking action with a free hand, an explanation that drew nods of understanding and murmurs of disgust from the inquisitive couple, who continued on their way, their curiosity sated.

Soon a large black limousine pulled up alongside the curb. Daniel was unceremoniously tossed inside where he landed half on the leather seat and half on the floor. The two sailors climbed in after him and the black stretched limousine, with deeply tinted windows, pulled away and headed down towards the old docks of ancient Cannes.

TWENTY-FOUR

Phillip was enjoying his wine and was now working on a bowl of stuffed olives as he nursed his *vino rosso* when two men walked into the bar. Phillip tried to give the impression of ignoring the newcomers but, in fact, closely studied their reflection in the mirror. The first man was small and of slight build. His hair was dark, fashionably long and naturally wavy and his features were sharp and pointed. His brown eyes, constantly in motion, could only be called 'beady'. His grey silk suit was expensive as were his polished black Italian shoes. Phillip knew instinctively at that moment that here at last was a potential customer for a stolen work of art of the magnitude of *"The Girl in the Red Dress."*

And Basson? Who better to offer the work of art than a lawyer, bound by client attorney privilege and easily sacrificed should the need arise. Maybe, thought Phillip, the choice of the bumbling and inadequate Andre Basson was a smart move on the part of the Marquis, if Phillip's suspicions regarding the theft of the Leonardo were correct.

The newcomer was in his late forties and although diminutive in size, made a great deal of noise. He shouted greetings to the few other patrons and warmly shook the hands of the hotel staff as he and his burly minder moved through the bar. He had no need to order a drink. His alcoholic preference was well known to the barman. As soon as he'd chosen a seat, the barman would bring his glass of chilled champagne. He approached the end corner booth and slid onto the red leather seats to face a somewhat startled and wide-eyed Basson.

The Italian's henchman sat next to Basson and without preamble or excuse felt inside the lawyer's jacket, felt around his back and neck and eventually, much to Basson's concern, felt up and down both sides of his legs. Wide-eyed, a stunned Basson allowed the minder to check him over for wires and weapons. Basson had neither.

Having completed his task, he nodded once to his employer that all was well and peeled off to sit a few feet away at the bar. He, too, kept an eye on the proceedings via the large mirror over the bar. He paid particular attention to Phillip. It was obvious from his demeanor that Phillip was a man of action, fit, hard, and a potential troublemaker.

For a while the small Italian sat staring at Basson, a fixed smile on his face that revealed his perfect white teeth. He reveled in Basson's growing discomfort. For him this was not an idle game. The reaction to his silent stare told him a lot about the other person. In this case, it was obvious to the potential customer that he was dealing with a messenger rather than with the principal, and therefore with someone who could not negotiate. Eventually he spoke. His voice was now soft, not loud and boisterous. Somehow the softness was even more intimidating to Basson.

"Show me what you have for me, Monsieur Wattier." The Italian spoke fluent French although with a thick Napoli accent.

Basson in his new and uncomfortable role had decided that he ought to have an alias, for his future protection. He had chosen, Wattier, his mother's maiden name.

"*Oui, oui, Monsieur,*" spluttered Basson as he fumbled with the two locks on his briefcase.

Phillip observed Basson opening the case and nonchalantly folding his right hand in front of him and into the crook of his left arm and he found the shutter button on his digital camera. It silently recorded, in hundredths-of-a-second frames, the goings on in the corner booth. Phillip hoped, as he looked in totally the opposite direction, the camera would later reveal what Basson had in his briefcase. Surely, he thought he wasn't going to produce the painting. That would be just too easy.

Andre Basson in fact pulled out a large eight by ten inch photograph from his valise and slid it over to the Italian who continued to stare at Basson. By now Basson felt beads of sweat forming on his brow. Showing an almost desultory interest in the photograph the Italian took a casual glance and then returned his stare back to Basson's face. Basson dabbed at the sweat that now began to run down both jowls.

"So Monsieur, you are expecting me to buy this painting only from this one photograph? You honestly expect me to give you, how much? Twenty-five million. Just on the strength of a photograph?"

"No, no Monsieur, of course not. But you see, that photograph of the painting is right next to the newspaper that tells of its theft. So you see Monsieur, this is merely to prove that we have the painting."

"I can see that. How do I know that it is the real painting, eh?"

"We shall bring you the painting and you may have an expert examine it. At that point Monsieur we shall expect twenty five million Euros to be deposited into our Swiss bank. When we have the money's deposit confirmed, which we shall do on a laptop computer, we shall hand over the painting. It will not leave your sight, or ours, while we await the bank transfer confirmation."

187

been released into the atmosphere around the globe. Not going too fast for you, am I?"

"Yes, but I'll try and keep up." Phillip smiled to himself as Sir Robert warmed to his subject.

"Tiny traces of cesium 137 and strontium 90 have permeated plants and the soil which eventually shows up in everything, including or especially, in the natural oils used as binding agents in oil paints."

"So they can detect this? Even in minute quantities?" queried Phillip, impressed.

"Apparently, yes, but the equipment they need is big, very expensive and doesn't exist outside of Dr. Basner's laboratory."

"Well, that's not much use to us then, is it?" said Phillip.

"Well, our Monique, clever girl that she is, is trying to build one for us here. But more importantly she's trying to develop a hand held version. Something we can carry around. A bit like those metal detecting wands they use at airports." Sir Robert sounded proud that his company was on the cutting edge of technology.

"Sounds impressive," agreed Phillip, "but technology may be able to detect a fake, but can it prove a painting is genuine?" It was a rhetorical question. "Still," continued Phillip, "everything helps. But what I really need to know is what's she like as a person? I mean, she's obviously bright. When I saw her that one time in the office, she's obviously good looking, but what about her temperament? Is she easily flustered for example?"

Sir Robert sighed, "Phillip, m'boy, do you really think I'd employ anyone who was the least bit dotty? In fact, I find her quite the opposite. She's rather cool and not very prone to showing any emotion." Sir Robert stopped and reflected for a moment.

188

"I've seen her experiments fall flat, sometimes with a loud bang and a lot of smoke and I've seen her little triumphs when everything's worked perfectly. On either occasion, she just scribbles in her book and moves onto the next phase. No, Phillip, I can definitely tell you she's not the panicky, easily flustered type," concluded Sir Robert.

"Okay, you've convinced me. If she'll do it, put her on the next plane," said Phillip. "I'll pick her up at the airport. I'll call you back this afternoon with an update on Daniel and you can let me know her arrival time then. Meanwhile I'm off to see your friend Bodoni and thanks for everything."

"Pleasure m'boy. Be careful. I'll ring Bodoni to give him a 'heads up' by way of introducing you," said Sir Robert.

"Thanks again, bye."

"Goodbye," said Sir Robert and they terminated their telephone conversation.

At two o'clock that afternoon, Phillip's taxi pulled up in front of the headquarters of Rome's Carabinieri. Having paid his taxi driver, Phillip ran up the stone steps into the impressive building that looked like an unhappy marriage between ancient and modern architecture.

Entering through large plate glass doors, that Phillip suspected were both bullet and bomb proof, he approached a security desk.

He was asked to sign the incoming sheet, and having written his name, he was required to empty his pockets of any metal objects. He did this and also removed his watch and his belt. Stepping through a metal detector, which remained silent, Phillip was directed to a waiting area and was asked to remain there until someone came to escort him upstairs.

"Signore Fairfax," said the security officer, replacing his phone in its cradle. "Colonello Bodoni will send someone soon. I have told him you are here waiting." He handed Phillip a plastic clip-on visitor's badge.

"*Multo grazie,*" said Phillip and smiled.

"*Prego,*" answered the security guard whose face remained passive and expressionless.

The boredom of his routine was easy to read in his tired demeanor. Phillip sat and watched the comings and goings of serious faced young policemen and occasionally civilians with worried looks on their faces.

Within fifteen minutes a petite young lady in the smart black uniform with red piping of the Carabinieri came to fetch him. She wore shoulder epaulettes with a single star denoting her rank as '*soltotenente*' or sub-lieutenant.

"Signore Fairfax?" she enquired.

"That's me," said Phillip springing to his feet.

"Colonello Bodoni can see you now," she said smiling the first smile Phillip had seen since he entered the building. "Please to follow me," she added.

Phillip was happy to follow her and fell in alongside. They walked down several long corridors and through several heavy doors until they came to an impressive mahogany door that bore a brass nameplate announcing the occupant behind as Colonello Alfonso Bodoni.

The young police woman knocked and without waiting for a reply, opened the door. She announced Phillip, who stepped past her and entered the large office. In the center was a large mahogany desk behind which was a wiry, grey haired man with a face that looked tanned and weathered and well lived-in.

"*Bongiorno*, Signore Fairfax," he said standing up and extending his hand, "so pleased to meet you. I received a call this morning from your uncle, Sir Robert, so I am happy to help you any way I can." His warm smile revealed a full set of straight and regular white teeth.

"Thank you so much for seeing me at such short notice." Phillip grasped the proffered hand and noticed its firm grip, the grip of a man still fit and active despite his advancing years.

"Please sit down. So, how is it that I can help you?" His face was now serious and deep furrows lined his brow as he sat down in his very large black leather chair. "Sir Robert, he tell me little of your problem. He says it better you explain, so I wait."

"I am in Rome because I followed a man, a French lawyer called Andre Basson," began Phillip. "He left the chateau of someone called the Marquis de Manville, in Baux de Provence in France."

"It is then the stolen Leonardo for which you search, yes?" interjected the Carabinieri Colonel.

"That is correct."

"Ah, I knew this name '*de Manville*.' I read much about this in the journals."

The Colonello seemed pleased to be '*au fait*' with current affairs. "But I am sorry to interrupt, please to continue."

Phillip continued. "Since he left the chateau he never left my sight. We both flew directly to Rome and I have to add that this man seems a complete amateur or totally innocent. He made no attempt to lose me and didn't even seem aware that I was following him. Anyway, we both eventually ended up yesterday at the Hotel Condotti in Rome."

The policeman nodded in recognition of this Roman landmark and jotted the name on his notepad.

"He went into the lounge bar and sat in a corner booth whilst I sat several feet away with my back to him and watched him in a large mirror behind the bartender. After maybe forty five minutes, a man, obviously accompanied by his bodyguard, entered the lounge bar and immediately sought out and sat with Basson."

"Can you describe this man, Signore Fairfax?" asked the policeman with pen poised.

"I can do better than that," said Phillip reaching into a large manila envelope and extracting a print that earlier that day he had taken off his camera's computer chip. "I have a photograph of him."

He slid a large photo of the Italian across the desk to the Colonel who studied the picture but said nothing. Phillip also produced two other prints. The second was one of Andre Basson and the third was a group shot of Basson, the Italian and his minder. He passed all of them over to the police colonel who studied each one in turn but remained silent.

He looked at Phillip and then picked up the handset of his telephone. "*Una momento*", he said to Phillip as he punched in four numbers. Almost immediately it was answered and the colonel spoke rapidly in his native tongue. Replacing the receiver he looked at Phillip once again.

"*Signore*," he said, "you have just shown me a photograph of Gianpasquale Grapponelli, known as "Nini." He is Camorra, that is to say, Napoli mafia." He waited for the fact to register with Phillip.

"This man," continued the Colonel, "he has some very bad friends. He himself does not kill men, as far as we know, but the people he work for do. And the people who work for him, they also kill. This Grapponelli man is a financier, a money-man, he washes the money from the smuggling of cigarettes, drugs, guns and even people. He deal with almost anything bad."

Phillip could not resist an inward smile at the colonel's literal translation of 'money laundering.'

"So you think he is a likely candidate to buy the stolen painting?" asked Phillip.

"Of course," exploded the colonel. "His type use these things, these precious art, and use it like money to borrow, I mean to buy, more drugs."

As the colonel got more excited, so his grip on the English language slid, but Phillip understood that in the underworld, rare antiquities and works of art, were often used instead of transporting millions and millions of dollar bills around the world. In essence, the artwork and precious treasures were used as barter, as a substitute for gold or cold, hard cash.

"Tell me please," said the colonel, "how much this painting is worth?"

"Between one hundred and two hundred million Euros. Maybe even more," Phillip explained.

The policeman let out a low whistle.

"*Si*, this is something, I think, will definitely interest our Signore Grapponelli. Do you say that this French lawyer, this monsieur….." he searched his notepad for the name, "this Andre Basson is working with or for Grapponelli?"

"No. It's not quite that simple, I'm afraid," explained Phillip. "My theory is that the robbery has been faked, made-up. It never happened."

"So why you look for a painting that you don't think has been stolen?"

"Let me explain," said Phillip, sitting back in his chair. "The Marquis de Manville reported his priceless - well, almost priceless- painting stolen by two armed men who broke into his chateau, late at night. By his account, they demanded the combination numbers for his safe; the safe where he kept his Leonardo masterpiece. But neither I nor Daniel Masilionis, an agent from Interpol, felt it had happened as stated after we had examined the crime scene. Things just didn't quite add up."

"In what way, may I ask?"

"It seemed that so much was left to chance by the robbers. Stealing such a valuable painting, that had received a huge amount of publicity, seemed the domain of professional thieves and yet we could find no concrete evidence that anyone else, besides the Marquis and his manservant, who incidentally received a very bad knock on the head, had been in the chateau."

Phillip paused and looked at the Colonel who seemed to have a look of skepticism on his face. Phillip continued his attempt to justify his instincts which he had come to trust implicitly.

"We found no tire marks outside that could not be accounted for. We found no foot prints or scuff marks, no fingerprints, no scratches from ropes or people climbing over the moss covered walls and we found no evidence to suggest that the Marquis had had his legs taped to the chair as he said they were. If they had not been taped, surely he could have moved about, at least enough to summon help."

"Certainly suspicious but hardly, how you say, conclusive," nodded the pensive Colonello.

"As I said," rebutted Phillip, "it's more a sense than actual concrete proof, but what I can't figure out is, why sell a painting on the black market, when you've got one of the world's leading auction houses, Haussmann's of Paris, lining up every multi millionaire ready to buy this fabulous masterpiece. It doesn't make a lot of sense...unless....," Phillip left the thought hanging.

"Unless what?" asked an inquisitive Colonello.

"Unless the Marquis is selling a fake!" said Phillip.

"Ah, now I see what you are saying. The Marquis, he keep the real painting and sell a forgery. But can such a good forgery be painted? Surely there are tests that can decide this, no?"

"That's true and the tests are getting better all the time, but they can only detect the bad forgeries. The really good forgeries are still hanging on the walls of museums and art galleries all over the world."

"You are, of course, much better acquainted with this than I am, so I believe what you say." The Colonel smiled.

At that moment there was a knock on the door and a fresh faced, young *Tenente* of the Carabinieri entered, laden down with files. He looked around the Colonel's office but saw not a single surface that was not already piled high with books and folders. He decided, therefore, to place everything on the floor by the desk.

"Get a chair Giorgio," said the colonel, as Giorgio stepped outside the office and grabbed an uncomfortable looking plastic molded chair. He brought it in and placed it beside his stack of files. Whilst Giorgio remained standing the Colonel thought it well to introduce the two men.

"*Signore* Fairfax, please to let me present my Lieutenant, Giorgio Gentile. Giorgio, Signore Phillip Fairfax from International Art Recovery in London."

"*Bongiorno,* Signore Fairfax."

"*Bongiorno*," repeated Phillip as he stood and grasped the young man's hand firmly.

"I should explain why I have asked Giorgio to come to this meeting. I hope this does not bother you Signore," the Colonel looked at Phillip, "but, I think he can be of more use to you than me."

"Signore Fairfax, Giorgio has been tailing Grapponelli for months. We know he is chief man for Camorra in Rome and we know he move the money for them, but I let Giorgio explain more."

The Colonel looked at Giorgio and then explained Phillip's connection and interest in Grapponelli. He gestured for Giorgio to take up the narrative.

"*Grazie, Colonello*," began the young police Lieutenant, and turning to Phillip, he addressed his remarks now to him in almost perfect English.

"The Camorra crime syndicate is very powerful and they have many resources. They have members at all levels in the government including the justices of the courts, and so it has been difficult -sometimes very difficult- to get cooperation to prosecute. Now I believe there is a good will in the government, and in the police, to put the Camorra out of business and into jail."

The young Lieutenant looked at Phillip who nodded his understanding.

Continuing he said, "One way we can hit them hard is to take away their money. It is their life blood and it is what they need to carry on their drug dealing, their cigarette smuggling and their bribery of officials to look the other way."

"Only through very good police work will we win the battle against the Camorra," interjected the Colonel, "and so Signore Fairfax, maybe you can help us as much as we can help you!"

"I'll do whatever I can to help," said Phillip, "but naturally my priority is to get to the bottom of the theft of the Leonardo. If in doing so, we can put some Camorra behind bars, then please count on my help and cooperation."

196

"*Multo bene*, excellent!" stated the Colonel who seemed satisfied that an agreement had been reached.

The *Tenente* continued, "This Nini Grapponelli comes from the town of Nola, east of Napoli-Naples as you call it. He is a member of the *Mozzarella* clan, one of the most important and influential families in the Camorra. They control drugs, cigarette smuggling and extortion, and Grapponelli is their main man for laundering millions."

The young Lieutenant stopped briefly and leafed through a large folder. He placed a small bundle of papers in front of Phillip and continued speaking. "He has infiltrated legitimate business in some cases but the amount of money he has to lose in the system makes it an enormous task for him. I am not surprised he is interested in a stolen masterpiece. We have reliable information that already he owns apartments all over Europe and America; he has cars, jewelry and even restaurants. Art would seem a natural next step."

"Excuse me interrupting," said Phillip, "but do you have anyone on the inside? I mean, anyone working for you but that is ostensibly employed by Grapponelli or the Camorra?"

The question was thrown at the elder policeman.

"Ah, that is an unhappy situation," said the Colonel. "It is difficult to find such people. The local people, who the Camorra may trust, all think we are the bad people. The Camorra, they are the good ones."

The Colonel shrugged as if he had long ago come to the regrettable conclusion that this was the way it was and this was the way it would always be.

"On the streets of Napoli, people spit and throw rocks at us when we arrest the Camorra. We did have one very good policeman. He was from Napoli, but he work for us. They find him out and…" The Colonel made a throat cutting gesture. "…and we find him. No head. A sad business, Signore. A very sad business. We still do not know how they find him out but….." he left the thought trailing.

"I'm very sorry indeed," said Phillip and he meant it.

"If we could get someone else inside," confirmed the *Tenente*," someone good who we can trust, maybe then we can jail this Grapponelli and confiscate some Camorra money. Only this way can we hope to beat them."

All the men sat silent for a moment contemplating their options. Phillip was the first to speak.

"I, too, need someone on the inside to find out more about this painting. If I come up with any ideas, I will most certainly let you know." He was not sure at this point whether he wanted to mention his plan for Monique Langer, providing she turned out to be suitable, of course.

He added, "By the way, do you know who the bodyguard is?"

"*Si*," said the Colonel, "his name is Luigi Macarini. "He also called *Mac the Knife*. It is his favorite weapon. We think, but do not know for sure, he killed our policeman."

"Another question, if I may," asked Phillip. "Do we have an address in Rome for Grapponelli? Somewhere he stays; a house or a hotel for instance?"

The *Tenente* took the question. "He has a large house here in Rome. He lives in the *Aventino* area, a very elegant and prestigious part of the city, close to the *Basilica of Santa Sabina* and the church of *Sant' Alession*. Right by the well known orange gardens."

Once again he rummaged in his stack of folders by his feet and produced a street map of Rome. He handed it to Phillip pointing to an area close to the river Tiber.

"It is his only house here in Rome, that we know, but of course, he has also houses in Napoli, France, Barcelona and New York. I have a list of his known addresses here."

The *Tenente* handed Phillip another sheet of paper. "You may, of course, keep that."

The paper not only had addresses, but phone numbers and lists of places that Grapponelli was known to frequent. Phillip realized that this would be an invaluable aid in trying to infiltrate Grapponelli's inner social circle.

Phillip was impressed by the efficiency of this young Carabinieri officer and thanked him for his willing cooperation.

"This Nini Grapponelli is, how do you say, a 'slippery' fellow, like a eel. He makes no mistakes, which we know of," he added judiciously, "and he is clever. Very clever. But also mean, a real bad man, so I urge you Signore Fairfax, to use much caution when dealing with him. We do not wish you to 'lose your head' also." The Colonel looked sternly at Phillip to show that he was serious in his warning.

"I shall be sure to keep it firmly attached to my neck," said Phillip smiling. "Finally, one last question. Do you have anyone watching him at the moment? I do not want to compromise any surveillance you currently have in place."

"Sadly Signore," said the Colonello, "we do not have the men so free to watch all the time. I wish," he shrugged, "but we have no excuses to offer the justices even to tap the telephone! If," and he looked quizzically at Phillip, "you can give us some good information then …..*maybe*, we can move against him."

"I'll certainly do what I can, "said Phillip as he rose from his chair. The two policemen did likewise, "I have to

thank you, *Colonello* Bodoni and you, *Tenente* Gentile, for
your help in this matter. You have both been very
forthright and I am very appreciative. *Mille grazie!* I shall
stay in touch and if I have any news I will immediately let
you know."

He shook the hand of the Colonel and again felt his
strong grip. He also offered his hand to the young Tenente
and noticed by contrast the softness. He guessed that the
young Gentile spent his time more on the computer than
engaging in rugged, physical pursuits.

TWENTY-SEVEN

Phillip arrived back at his hotel that afternoon and the desk clerk handed him his room key and a telephone message left by Sir Robert. It merely gave a flight number and an arrival time. So, the red-headed Miss Monique Langer was on her way. Phillip wondered if he'd made a mistake in dragging an inexperienced young lady into a business that could be fraught with danger. He dismissed the thought almost as soon as he'd had it. He reasoned that he could always just send her home again if she seemed really unsuitable.

The first thing, Phillip did on reaching his room was to telephone Interpol in Lyon. He asked for the young agent who he'd spoken to that morning. The news was not good. Daniel's car had been located. Not outside Miss Diab's apartment, but several miles away on a piece of waste ground, burned to an almost unrecognizable lump of rusted metal.

There was no sign of Daniel or his body, the latter fact being a partial relief to all concerned, but as to his whereabouts, the Cannes police and Interpol could offer no suggestions. His mobile phone, his expensive camera and binoculars were all missing too. Efforts to track his phone from the signal emitted, even when switched off, proved fruitless. It, like Daniel, had simply disappeared.

Phillip left his phone number with Interpol and asked to be called as soon as any information about Daniel became known. With a sense of foreboding, Phillip hung up and called Sir Robert. He briefed him on Daniel's update, which was little, and on his conversation with Colonel Bodoni and his Lieutenant. Phillip became more determined than ever to unravel the whole story behind the missing painting and the missing Daniel, which were now inextricably linked.

For the next couple of hours Phillip poured over some English language newspapers that he'd picked up on the way back from visiting Colonel Bodoni. There were still some articles about the stolen Leonardo, mostly speculative, and they were now relegated to the inside pages. The fickle press no longer thought of the missing masterpiece as worthy of the front page.

Monique Langer stepped through the doors of the arrival's lounge at Rome's *Fiumicino* International airport at six o'clock that evening straight off BA's flight 556.

Out of her white laboratory coat and with her long chestnut red hair cascading over her shoulders, she looked every inch a wealthy jet setter. At five feet seven inches tall she was above average height. She was elegant and slim and her slender heeled shoes added another two inches or more to her already long and lithe limbs. Her green suede skirt, worn fashionably above the knee, and her green silk blouse were both reflected in her sparkling green eyes. A camel colored cashmere coat draped over her shoulders blended artfully with the muted tones of her Louis Vuitton luggage and handbag.

Many pairs of eyes turned in her direction as she confidently strode through the throng of people waiting to greet loved ones and business colleagues from the London flight. Phillip stood amongst them and joined those who admired this red haired beauty.

Seeing Phillip, Monique smiled in recognition and headed in his direction. Upon meeting she shook his hand firmly whilst declining his offer to carry her suitcase.

"Thank you, Mr. Fairfax. I can manage quite easily."

202

"Please call me Phillip, he said, and added, "May I call you Monique?"

"Yes, Phillip" she replied matter of factly but without the customary social frills that generally irked Phillip. Her smile was warm and friendly. He found her instantly likeable.

They left terminal C and walked to the short term car park where Phillip had left his rented car. He had acquired a Fiat from Rent-a-Car through the good offices of his hotel's concierge, or in Italy, more correctly, '*il portier*'. He reasoned that it may come in handy if they needed transport in a hurry. He'd also acquired some more acceptable clothes from the fashionable Via Condotti. Phillip had also changed hotels and had moved to one closer to the Aventino district of Rome and one that featured prominently in Grapponelli's life, according to the sheet of paper that Lt. Gentile had given him that afternoon.

Phillip was hoping that an arranged 'chance' meeting with Nini Grapponelli in the expensive surroundings of the Hotel Clara might help to facilitate Monique's entry into his social circle. But first, Phillip needed to get to know Monique a little and judge her suitability for clandestine work. Although he expected her to do nothing more than report any visitors or overheard conversations, it could, non-the-less be a dangerous game; one she was not well equipped nor trained to deal with. Even now Phillip had grave doubts about the wisdom of this course of action, but without Daniel, and his ability to draw on trained Interpol agents, Phillip had to make do with an amateur. He had little choice and the more he thought about it the less he liked it. By the time they arrived at the Hotel Clara, Phillip was all but ready to send Monique home by the first flight in the morning.

"You were very quiet on the journey from the airport," said Phillip as they swept into the palm lined drive of Hotel Clara, "I expected you to be overflowing with questions for me. About why you were here," he added.

"I reasoned, Phillip," she replied. "that you would tell me when you were ready but seeing as you brought up the subject, why am I here?"

"What did Sir Robert tell you?" he countered the question with one of his own.

"Very little. He said that you needed some help in Rome because your colleague-Daniel is it?-has gone AWOL. I agreed because.....well, because I love Italy and a free trip seemed hard to pass up."

"You may come to regret that decision," said Phillip.

"You're making it all sound very sinister. Just what exactly have you got planned for me?"

"I'll explain it over dinner," said Phillip, as he pulled the Fiat under the large carved stone canopy that was the entrance to the Hotel Clara. "I hope you're hungry. I'm told they have a first class chef in the dining room."

"For Italian food-I'm always hungry," she smiled at Phillip as the uniformed doorman opened her door.

They made an elegant couple as they walked across the white Carrera marble floor of the hotel's foyer to the registration desk. Phillip stumbled with his Italian whilst Monique stood by and smiled to herself. Giving up he said the one Italian phrase he felt comfortable with, partly because he'd used it so many times in the last couple of days.

"*Parla inglese?*" he said with a look of resignation.

Monique was enjoying seeing the man who was a living legend at I.A.R. in London feeling a little out of his depth. Before the young lady behind the reception desk had a chance to reply Monique stepped forward and said, *"Buona sera. Mi scusi vorrei una singola per Signore Fairfax e 'una doppia con matrimonmiale e con il bagno private per mia, Signorina Langer. Ho riceveto dei messaggi, per piacere?*

"Si, Signorina Langer, non c'e di che," and the young raven haired receptionist reached behind and withdrew a neatly folded piece of paper that she handed to Monique.

"Grazie."

"Prego," and handing Phillip and Monique each a key card, she added, *"le chiavi, stanza quattrocentro diciotto,"* to Phillip and to Monique, *" stanza quattrocento ventuno, grazie Signorina."*

"Ciao," replied Monique, as she strode off towards the elevator with a young admiring Italian porter following hotly on her heels, who no doubt appreciated the suede enveloped sway of Monique's tight buttocks. The vision was not lost on Phillip either.

As they entered the lift, Phillip turned and looked Monique in the face. His eyes crinkled with amusement and a smile spread across his lips.

"Any more surprises you've got stored up for me, *Signorina* Langer?" said Phillip allowing a throaty chuckle to escape.

"Si, Signore Fairfax. I'm sure I've got plenty of surprises left for you to discover." She returned his smile and her green eyes sparkled. She had enjoyed showing off in front of Phillip and was glad he'd taken it so well. Male egos, she thought, could be so fragile at times.

"I had no idea you spoke Italian. Robert didn't mention it!"

205

"I doubt he even knows, although it is on my resumé but that's no doubt filed away in some dusty old cabinet in the back office."

"What else would your resumé say?" inquired Phillip as the elevator doors opened at the fourth floor. As they stepped out onto the thickly carpeted corridor, Monique turned to Phillip and said, "I'll tell you over dinner when you've explained to me just why I'm here in Rome."

"Fair enough. I'll knock on your door at eight thirty. By the way, what room am I in?"

"*Quattrocento diciotto*!" she giggled.

"Ok, you win. I give up," countered Phillip. She looked over her shoulder as she stood outside her room, number 420 and said, "Opposite me at 419." Laughing she entered her spacious double bedroom while Phillip headed for his single bedroom.

Dinner was a very pleasant affair for both of them. In between exquisite courses of mouthwatering Italian cuisine and sips of Tuscan *Sangiovese* wine, Phillip outlined his plan, such as it was, and briefed Monique on the situation to date. He explained the sudden disappearance of Daniel, partly in the hopes that Monique would realize the seriousness of the investigation and also that they were dealing with ruthless people.

People would go to any length to hide their nefarious deeds. He also learned some things about Monique. Her mother, who was Dutch and her Scottish father, a Don at Oxford University, always spoke to each other in Dutch, so Monique grew up being bi-lingual. Whether her upbringing fostered a facility with languages, she couldn't say, but she also spoke Russian, French, German and, of course Italian as witnessed in the foyer when they had first arrived. Monique had studied biochemical engineering at Cambridge University and had completed her doctorate on mass-spectrometry as applied to the detection of forged paintings.

She had Phillip's full attention when she explained to him how synthetic elements, such as einsteinium and fermium, created by neutron bombardment of uranium and plutonium during thermonuclear explosions were discovered floating around in the world's atmosphere. The presence of these new isotopes was developed into a reliable way of detecting art forgeries because scientists could now detect traces of Cesium 137 and strontium 90 which hitherto had never existed in nature.

Phillip was very impressed but half expected Monique to express reservations about her involvement. Somewhat to his surprise she did not .Instead she became incensed that such a glorious work of art, a Leonardo da Vinci portrait, should be used purely as a tool for illegal commerce. Her integrity was seriously affronted by anyone treating something that belonged to the world as a mere commodity to be traded. She expressed grave concerns that the constant handling of such a priceless masterpiece and the constant changes of atmosphere and humidity would damage it irreparably. She displayed a genuine concern for art and her passion was easy to see when she spoke of the subject that was clearly very dear to her heart.

Phillip partly allayed her fears when he described his theory that perhaps the original was still somewhere in the Chateau de Manville and that it was a forgery that was being sold. Either way they had a crime to solve and the people involved might be prepared to adopt drastic measures in order to hide their misdeeds. Despite Phillip's misgivings about involving Monique, her determination to track down either the original or its replica made Phillip realize that sending Monique back to London probably wasn't an option now. He was impressed by her demeanor and despite her fierce opposition to fraud, she was able to remain objective and not get carried away on a wave of emotion. By the end of their excellent dinner Phillip felt a great deal easier about working with her.

The next day they spent going through any information they could find on Nini Grapponelli and the Napoli Camorra. Monique visited the public library and scanned national, international and local papers on *microfisch* for stories about Grapponelli. Phillip meanwhile searched the internet and telephoned Lt Giorgio Gentile for any updates. The only notable news was that Grapponelli was known to still be in Rome. Phillip made no mention that he now had Monique helping him. The fewer people who knew about her the safer she would be.

Once again that evening Phillip and Monique dined together but this time in Monique's room as they both continued their research. By now both Phillip and Monique had acquired a great deal of information about Grapponelli. Mostly it was superficial, as his business dealings were invariably secretive, but several of his front companies, through which he no doubt laundered funds, featured in the business section of Italy's newspapers.

Their thorough research began to build a picture of a flamboyant party-goer, a lover of fine food and wine, and someone who totally embraced the concept of '*la dolce vita.*' He appeared at charity functions and fundraisers, providing the press and celebrities were also present, and generally cultivate the image, the false image, of a generous and upstanding citizen and business man.

Some articles, however, were not so flattering, especially those that dealt with his business interests. One even went so far as to mention that several of Grapponelli's business rivals had dropped out of contention for lucrative building projects "due to ill health." The article intimated, between the lines, that Grapponelli may have had something to do with their illness, though they stopped short of an actual accusation. They merely mentioned the repetitive coincidence and left the reader to draw the inference. .

Phillip had decided that the next day he would 'stake-out' Grapponelli's house. That afternoon he had gone to a builder's yard on the outskirts of Rome and acquired several red reflective cones, blue overalls and a yellow reflective sleeveless vest. He also rented a jack hammer with accompanying generator, and a workman's screen. On leaving the builder's yard, Phillip looked for a worker who was wearing similar overalls to the ones he'd just purchased.

He saw a tall man, about his height that was leaning against the cab of an old decrepit flat bed truck, leisurely smoking a cigarette. Phillip approached him and through a series of hand gestures was eventually able to convey that he wanted to swap his nice new overalls for the grubby old stained ones that the smoker was wearing. Somewhat bemused at the foreigner's strange request he acquiesced, although with some misgivings. On the surface it seemed he was getting the better of the bargain but his life's experience had taught him that if something looked too good to be true, it generally was. But being unable to find the catch he slipped out of his soiled garment and handed them to Phillip but not before taking possession of the new ones.

Phillip then rented a plain white van from a lot quite close to the builder's merchant and later stopped at a sign maker. He'd bought 2 large plastic adhesive signs that proudly announced "*Acqua Nationale.*" The telephone number printed below was the cell phone number he had acquired the day before and given to Monique. She was to field any incoming calls from the citizenry of Aventino regarding road works and would divert any suspicion's Grapponelli's people might have about road works so close to his house.

As an additional precaution he telephoned Colonel Bodoni and informed him of his intentions to keep an eye on the Grapponelli compound for a day or two. Bodoni offered Phillip the services of Lt Gentile and Phillip gladly accepted. He reasoned that it might be expedient to have a native Italian speaker if anyone should come poking around.

Phillip arranged to pick up Giorgio Gentile at the Carabinieri headquarter at 8:30 the following morning.

The doorman at the Hotel Clara was less than pleased when Phillip drove up with his white van towing a large orange generator. A swift exchange of some euros however smoothed the way and Phillip was able to park at the rear of the hotel in a small hidden lot reserved for hotel staff.

TWENTY-EIGHT

The following morning at approximately nine o'clock, Phillip and Giorgio Gentile pulled up outside the main gates of Grapponelli's house. They parked on the opposite side of the road and proceeded to set out cones and placed the screen in a small square behind the generator. In time honored fashion they then returned to the cab of the van and proceeded to drink coffee from a thermos flask and pretended to read the sports pages of the local paper.

Grapponelli's house was an impressive stone and brick structure set back from the street. A short driveway ended in a white graveled circle with a large marble water fountain in the center. Lily pads floated on the surface of the pond that surrounded the fountain and large golden koi carp swam in its dark waters.

The property was protected by large wrought iron gates. An old stone wall, at least 8 ft tall, skirted the entire perimeter of the grounds. Besides the gate was a small building, more recently built than the main house though in a complimentary style. It housed a guard who also operated the mobile security cameras that sat atop the stone pillars of the gate. Phillip noticed one camera move to look in their direction. If nothing else the guard was alert.

By 10:15 Phillip and Giorgio were back on the street and Phillip had hooked up the pneumatic drill. It burst into life when Phillip depressed the lever on the handle and the ear shattering noise broke the tranquility of this elegant Roman neighborhood.

He kept up the drilling for at least twenty minutes trying hard, but not succeeding, in creating as small a hole as possible. The soft tarmac proved no match for the jack hammer and soon Phillip had dug a hole fully two foot square and almost as deep. Satisfied that he'd inflicted enough damage to this venerable Roman highway, he sat down on the rubble behind the screen and proceeded to observe the house through a small gap in the screening with his Zeiss binoculars. It didn't take many minutes, when the drilling had stopped, for Grapponelli's guard, an extremely large man, to cross the street. As acting foreman, Giorgio Gentile tried to intercept him but not before the man had satisfied his curiosity by peering into the hole that Phillip had dug.

As the guard leaned over the screen, Phillip noticed that strapped beneath his bulky jacket was an SMG PM 98. This Polish made sub-machine gun was a compact weapon with a very high rate of fire. Phillip knew it could spit out 9mm rounds at close to 1,100 rounds per minute. Obviously Grapponelli and his cohorts were not messing around. They meant business.

Phillip left the talking entirely to Gentile and was thankful that he'd laid a short length of three inch diameter pipe at the bottom of the hole. Wedging it into the sides of the hole, Phillip had made it look as if he'd uncovered the water pipe they were digging for. A small bit of deception that he hoped would add credence to their pretence although in reality it was far too small in circumference to be a water main carrying hundreds of gallons an hour to the thirsty residents of Aventino.

Phillip hoped, as the capricious looking guard peered down the hole, that he had no knowledge of municipal plumbing. He appeared not to but still managed to embroil Lt Gentile in a loud shouting match in a way that only the Italians can do. It turned out later that the argument had been about the length of time they planned on attending to this pipe and the noise generated in doing so.

That first day they had noticed no-one entering or leaving the Grapponelli residence. To Phillip it had the air of a fortified compound. The stone wall surrounding the house and grounds was topped with broken glass shards set into cement and cameras, mounted under the eaves of the house, gave wide and comprehensive coverage of the neatly tended grounds. At night floodlights illuminated the garden and driveway. Nothing was left to chance. Nobody was entering the Grapponelli house uninvited or unannounced.

That night Phillip returned to Aventino and sat in a parked car. He watched the house until ten o clock by which time he was tired and hungry. Monique had offered earlier in the evening to bring him coffee and a sandwich which he had declined. Partly on the basis that he didn't want anything or anyone to draw attention to him and partly because he wanted something stronger to drink than coffee and was looking forward to something to eat that was more substantial than a sandwich. But by now Phillip had seen no-one arrive at the Grapponelli house and he was just about to give up for the night when he noticed a burly man open the front gates. Seconds later a large Mercedes Benz saloon came sweeping through the open gates. The lights at the entrance briefly illuminated the occupants as the vehicle turned smoothly onto the road heading down towards Rome's nightlife. The driver was the one he had seen at the Hotel Condotti and later identified by Colonel Bodoni as *Mac the Knife* Macarini and the passenger none other than Nini Grapponelli himself.

Phillip started his car and followed at a discreet distance. He also telephoned Monique on his cell phone and told her to put on her 'party dress' and to call a taxi.

He'd call back when he'd found out Grapponelli's destination. If it was somewhere he felt she could go with a viable chance of meeting the gangster, somewhere where she could expect to leave unharmed, she would have her chance to push the stagnating investigation a little further towards its goal.

Phillip listened for any sign in her voice that she was too nervous or afraid. If she was, she hid it well. Monique sounded eager yet still maintained her cool, professional attitude. Phillip was becoming quite impressed by this young, intelligent and gutsy woman.

At ten thirty Grapponelli's Mercedes pulled up outside an art gallery on the *Via Sistina*. Phillip relayed the location to Monique who was already cruising towards the center of Rome in her taxi. Phillip continued to watch the Mercedes from down the street. The driver, Macarini, opened the rear door for Grapponelli who stepped out wearing an expensive pale gray silk suit and headed towards the art gallery *Maximilian.*

Inside Phillip could see several bejeweled and bedecked men and women drinking champagne whilst smartly uniformed waiters glided between them offering silver trays loaded with canapés. The sight made Phillip more comfortable about Monique's involvement, though the sight of food reminded his stomach that it hadn't received any nourishment for nearly eleven hours.

At least, thought Phillip, Monique would be in an environment that she knew well. Within fifteen minutes Phillip saw a taxi pull up outside the gallery. The bright lights inside and the posters outside announced the opening night of a one man exhibition. From what Phillip could see, the art was abstract. Daubs of bright colors seemed to have been violently dashed against the canvases. It was the type of art that left Phillip cold, yet in his professional capacity, he acknowledged that such paintings had not only a strong following but could be worth many times that of more conventional art. Its appeal, however, still eluded him and he had never been tempted to part with his own money to hang an example on his wall.

As Monique stepped out of the taxi, Phillip was reminded, once again, of how beautiful she was. She wore a simple black dress and she had arranged her glorious thick chestnut hair in such a way as to reveal her long shapely neck. Diamond earrings in an art deco style hung from her delicate lobes and swayed and sparkled with every movement of her head. Black patent leather high heeled shoes trimmed with gold that matched a small Gucci evening bag, showed her long bare legs to their full advantage. In short, Phillip found her quite stunning and quite different from their first brief encounter in London where a shapeless white lab coat had succeeded in hiding her more physical charms.

Despite his complaining stomach, Phillip was determined to stay and keep watch over her. Even if she was unable to strike up a conversation with Grapponelli, she would obviously be a magnet for any other red blooded male at the gallery. Phillip was beginning to feel very protective of her, which was an unfamiliar emotion for him.

TWENTY-NINE

That same evening the Marquis de Manville had dined with Leila Diab in the formal dining room at the chateau. The Marquis sat in his usual place at the head of the long table and his goddaughter sat immediately to his right. Albert had prepared and served a simple but nourishing meal of chicken cooked in red wine. It was his version of a *coq au vin* which he cooked until the flesh took on a deep pink hue and fell off the bones at the mere sight of a knife and fork.

The Marquis had long lamented the fact that Albert's repertoire in the kitchen was limited to only a few dishes but consoled himself with the fact that those Albert did cook were excellent. Every attempt to encourage Albert to experiment with new recipes had been firmly resisted. The Marquis had long ago given up trying to persuade him to try something new. Simple Provencal cooking was what Albert knew and was what Albert liked. It had been good enough for the old Marquis and he felt it should be good enough for this current one too.

However, Albert's culinary skills were not forefront in the Marquis' mind that night. Andre Basson had earlier telephoned to say that he had heard from the "Italian Gentleman". Apparently he was ready to have his expert examine the painting and that the funds were ready for immediate transfer. It was exciting news for the Marquis but still news that left him feeling quite nervous. The excellence of the forgeries had not been tested as yet. Not by an art aficionado at any rate.

Although the Marquis, who considered himself a modest art connoisseur, could see no difference in any of the paintings, he naturally worried that a person with more knowledge might view them quite differently.

The risk involved in selling a fake to a man such as Grapponelli hardly seemed bearable to contemplate. He no doubt dealt with those who double crossed him with – how do they put it in the American movies? ah yes, *" with extreme prejudice"*. But the cause for which the Marquis ran this risk was too important. This was no mission for the faint of heart.

Ever the cautious planner, the Marquis had sought to minimize the risk of being caught in his duplicity by ordering one very special piece of equipment. After dinner he planned on showing it to Leila and explaining its unique features. It was, to all intents and purposes, a perfectly ordinary, though expensive, black leather briefcase. What made it so special were the custom features that the Marquis himself had designed and had had incorporated especially for the undertaking Leila was about to embark on.

After dinner when they sat sipping the last of their wine, the Marquis produced the briefcase and gently slid it across the polished top of the dining table.

"This case," he explained as Leila began to inspect it, "was specially made for me in Damascus. Made from my own ingenious design. It appears a very normal briefcase and in many ways it is. You will notice for example that as with most briefcases, it has two sets of rotating cylinder locks, each numbered from zero to nine on each wheel. This, as you know, allows you to lock and unlock the case"

Leila slightly resented being spoken to as if she was a backward child, something the Marquis was prone to do, but she allowed him to continue in his own time and in his own patronizing way.

Warming to his subject the Marquis continued.

"Please, Leila, dial the two locks to number 6 – 1 – 1 and then press the small silver buttons on either side of the locks simultaneously."

Leila did as she was asked and a firm click announced that the case was now open.

"Please now, Leila, lift the lid."

Once again she did as she was requested. The interior was fitted with a lap top computer complete with integral screen. The key board was marked, not with normal letters but instead with Arabic ones. This, the Marquis had thought, was a brilliant idea as it would preclude most people from being able to use it. Leila continued to examine it but felt that it hardly qualified as a unique piece of design. She had seen dozens of similar laptop computers all built roughly along the same lines. However, she said nothing but merely looked at the Marquis as if to say "So?"

Despite her obvious lack of enthusiasm, the Marquis remained smug.

"It is a simple computer case is it not?" He smiled. "Beautifully made, of course, but nothing out of the ordinary. Please examine it thoroughly."

Leila felt that the Marquis had been reading her mind but none the less she did a thorough exam. It became very apparent quite quickly, to Leila that there had to be more to this case and that the Marquis no doubt, still had something up his sleeve.

The Marquis was enjoying his game immensely. He then told Leila to close the lid and spin the wheels of the lock effectively locking the case once more. Leila complied.

"And now, dear Leila, please turn the numbers to read 9 – 1 – 4."

Once again Leila obeyed, but this time as she lifted the lid the computer stayed hidden as a slender compartment lined with impact absorbing foam, revealed itself. It did not escape her notice that the recess was exactly the same size as the Leonardo painting.

"And that, my dear, is how you will transport the Leonardo painting to Rome for its verification process," announced the Marquis with the self satisfied air of a magician who had pulled off an impossible trick

"Yes, I see," said Leila. "This is a brilliant way to carry the painting. It will be quite secure and quite undetectable. I have to hand it to you, you are very clever" She leaned across the table and planted a small kiss on his cheek.

"Thank you, Leila, I know. However, I have one more surprise. Please close it once more and lock it." Leila once again did as she was asked.

"Now please dial 0 – 7 – 8 and open it once again."

Leila followed her instructions and once more a firm metallic click indicated that the case was free to be opened. Again she lifted the lid and this time a second very slim compartment, identical to the last one revealed itself.

"And this, I presume, is for the copy, the fake?" She said but this time not without some genuine admiration.

"Exactly!" said the Marquis clapping his hands in delight. Delight, not in Leila's deductive powers, but at his own brilliance. "You must learn these numbers well. A mistake could be very costly. Not only might I loose my real Leonardo but it would expose our little scheme. I do not think our Italian friend would see the funny side of that particular scenario. I believe the risk of being detected whilst making the switch is quite minimal but, as you know, we must all take some risks to achieve our ultimate goal"

"I agree, Claude," said Leila, "but I think I am the one taking the risks". She fixed him with her cold dark eyes, the eyes of a killer, and the Marquis eagerly sought to change the subject.

"Quite so, quite so. Now obviously the plan is to show the real Leonardo to the expert. It *must* then be put back in the case. When the funds have cleared which you will be able to verify on the lap top, you can open the second compartment, as if it was the first, and hand Grapponelli the fake. Naturally it would be better, if not essential, that the expert was not around when the actual exchange takes place. Having closely examined it once, he may notice something different about the second painting. I can't think what, but you never know with these people. I need you to be very careful. You are so precious to me"

He laid his boney hand onto hers to emphasize his concern.

Leila, however, was under no illusion. She knew that her worth to the Marquis rested solely on her ability and willingness to do the dirty work.

The Marquis continued, "You will fly to Rome tomorrow by private jet. It is an extravagance I know, but a necessary and expedient one under the circumstances. The customs officials rarely bother with private flights providing the pilot's papers are all in order. So, my dear, get a good night's sleep. We shall breakfast together in the morning and then we shall pack the paintings together in your new case."

With that the Marquis rose from the table, kissed Leila lightly on the forehead and disappeared into his study.

220

Leila remained at the table a little longer examining the new case. She had a grudging admiration for the Marquis' design and much praise for its execution. When each secret compartment was opened it gave no hint whatsoever that there might be another one. She felt totally confident that tomorrow she could pull off the switch right under Grapponelli's nose.

220

THIRTY

Phillip waited across the street from the Gallerie Maximilian and watched the dozens of people inside chatting. They all but ignored the paintings that presumably were their reasons for being there. It was obviously the etiquette at such functions to be rather *blasé* about the work on display. Phillip decided that most people were there to be seen rather than to do the seeing.

Occasionally he caught a quick glimpse of Monique as she glided around the large open plan gallery with champagne glass in hand. She appeared very comfortable with her surroundings and her new role. Phillip realized of course that she had probably attended hundreds of such functions in the past but could not help acknowledging that this one was a bit different. He doubted that she had ever been told to try and engage a known and dangerous felon before but if she felt any nerves she certainly wasn't showing them. Phillip's respect for her was growing.

By eleven thirty the crowds were beginning to thin out as more and more people took to the sidewalk. Phillip was concerned that he might miss Monique amongst the melee but almost as soon as he'd had the thought he caught sight of her again. This time she was hanging on the arm of Nini Grapponelli. Phillip didn't know whether to be pleased or frightened at this development, but there was no doubting that she had succeeded in her mission thus far. Phillip watched as Monique was escorted to Grapponelli's Mercedes. The ever present Macarini was there to open the rear door and both she and the evil Grapponelli slid into the plush interior.

In true Italian fashion the Mercedes pulled out into the flow of traffic with little or no regard for other

222

motorists. This occasioned a cacophony of horn blowing which Marcarini totally ignored. Phillip, more cautiously, joined the flow of traffic and followed at least five cars behind. They made slow progress at first but eventually Phillip recognized the road they were travelling on. He was relieved to discover that they were heading towards the Hotel Clara. Twenty minutes later the large Mercedes swept up the driveway and stopped under the stone canopy.

Phillip was glad that his van and orange generator were parked out of sight in the rear employee's parking lot. Seeing it in front of the hotel might have raised suspicions in even the most dimwitted of bodyguards and he doubted that Grapponelli's chauffeur and minder was of that ilk.

By the time Phillip had parked his car and entered the hotel lobby, the over attentive and fawning Grapponelli had entered the lounge bar and was occupying a secluded table in a far corner with Monique Langer. Just as at the Hotel Condotti, his minder, Macarini was perched on a bar stool in close proximity sipping a coca cola. Phillip contemplated making a brief visit to the bar himself. Not only because he had a raging thirst himself but he thought that the sight of him might give Monique a degree of comfort - knowing that he was close at hand.

However, fighting this natural inclination to protect his young and inexperienced colleague, he reasoned that an appearance might do more harm than good. Should he be recognized from the Hotel Condotti for example, it might not only blow their investigation but it might put Monique in extreme danger. He decided therefore to give the bar a miss and instead opted for the dining room. His stomach, at least, was happy with the decision and even more delighted to find that dinner was still being served. Phillip had never been able to get over how late the Italians would eat their evening meal. On this occasion though, he was grateful for the custom.

He chose a table that was near the centre of the dining room. It offered him a view, not of Monique and her admirer, but at least of the entrance. At least, he felt, this way he could see when they left. He wished now that he had given her strict instructions not to leave the relative safety of the hotel with Grapponelli, but it was too late now. He would just have to believe in her good sense and judgment.

By the time Phillip was enjoying an after dinner cup of coffee, Monique and Grapponelli emerged from the bar into the hotel lobby. Grapponelli was animated. Taking hold of Monique's hand he bent a little at the waist and kissed it, all the while flirting with her with his beady little eyes. He thought himself the quintessential seducer and was using everything in the arsenal of his natural Italian charm. To Phillip, and probably most Englishmen, it came over as a rather greasy performance but, as Phillip freely admitted; he was no expert on what women liked. The uncomfortable thought that Phillip was forced to face was that he found himself bothered by the attention given to Monique. Was he developing a fondness for the lady himself? He was unwilling to acknowledge this possibility.

As Grapponelli took his leave of Monique he turned and blew her a kiss. In reply she made a grabbing motion in the air, as if to catch it. As the door closed behind the Italian, Monique rushed to the elevators and pressed a button for her floor.

Phillip signed his restaurant bill with his room number and rose from the table. He went up to his room and picking the phone up from the bedside table he called Monique's room. It rang several times before she picked it up.

"*Pronto*," she said.

"Monique, it's Phillip."

"Thank god," she replied, "I thought it was that creep again. He's already called me once since he left. Phillip, the man is a total creep."

"Sorry about that, but I did warn you that this work did have some down sides to it. Anyway I need to talk to you. Are you up for it? I really need a de-briefing tonight." Phillip tried his hardest to sound businesslike.

"A de-briefing? I've spent most of my evening trying to avoid being *de-briefed* !" she quipped, " but give me a few minutes, I need a shower , if only to wash off the stink of Grapponelli's overpowering after shave."

"You've got it." Phillip was grinning. "I'll come over to your room in about fifteen minutes or so, OK?"

"Sure, see you shortly". They both hung up their phones.

Phillip then dialed Giorgio Gentile and arranged for him to meet up near to Grapponelli's house. They decided on the Via Grimaldi, two blocks away from their road works. Phillip also outlined his plan for tomorrow to enter Grapponelli's house and plant a few radio listening bugs. It was an audacious plan and would need to be accomplished right under the noses of Grapponelli and his armed retainers. Phillip knew that the Carabinieri's involvement had to be strictly off the books but it was good, none the less, to have Giorgio's help and Colonello Bodoni's support. Phillip also requested that Giorgio bring along two other people to act as 'workers' to help facilitate the plan.

This, the young Lieutenant said, would be no problem, but a call to his Colonello would probably be advisable. Phillip agreed and after he had hung up with Giorgio he called Bodoni at home outlining the plan to him also. Colonel Bodoni thought Phillip's plan was audacious to say the least and he expressed his concerns. However, he admitted that it had a certain ingenuity that might make it work and he agreed to provide the assistance Phillip needed.

THIRTY-ONE

Twenty minutes later Monique heard a gentle knock at her door. She was wrapped in a large toweling bathrobe as she answered the door to Phillip.

"Come in," she invited, "make yourself a drink from the bar fridge. I just need to dry my hair" and with that she disappeared into her bathroom.

Phillip did as he was commanded and gratefully sank into an overstuffed armchair with a large whiskey and water. He quietly sipped at his amber drink as the muffled sounds of a hairdryer indicated that Monique was busy attending to her fiery chestnut locks.

Within ten minutes she emerged, dry and smelling delightfully of expensive soap. She had traded her bathrobe for a pair of dark blue silk pajamas. She tripped lightly across the room in bare feet and also poured herself a drink from the mini fridge.

When she had settled down on a sofa opposite him with her legs curled up beneath her, Phillip spoke. "Fire away when you're ready", he said, "tell me all you've found out about this Grapponelli fellow"

"The man is a total creep," she started, and then proceeded to tell Phillip about her evening in great detail. She had good recall and an excellent eye for detail. She felt she had made a very favorable impression on Grapponelli and fully expected him to continue pursuing her, at least until he'd bedded her. She made it quite clear that she had absolutely no intention of sleeping with him. She said therefore she thought the fledgling relationship might be strung out for about two weeks - maximum. After that she felt fairly sure he would loose interest. Monique's opinion of the man was that he was shallow, spoiled and totally self absorbed but he could be charming when it was in his best interests.

At the end of her dissertation Phillip outlined his plans for tomorrow and once again asked that she monitor the phone for *Acqua Nationale.*

Their discussion over, both Phillip and Monique felt the need for sleep. Draining the last of his whiskey, Phillip rose. He stepped over to Monique and gently resting his hand on top of hers he said, "You did a really good job tonight. Thank you." She smiled back at him but said nothing.

She looked deeply into his eyes and reaching out for his hand she pulled him gently towards her. She patted the seat next to her. He sat down and stared directly ahead. He was confused at the sudden change of pace and unsure what to do next. It had been a long time since he'd been seduced. A very long time.

Monique could sense his confusion and took control. She turned his face towards her and kissed him passionately on the lips. It awoke very dormant feelings in Phillip and he realized the reawakening was long overdue. He kissed her back.

Monique slowly began to unbutton his shirt and despite his lack of practice in recent years Phillip found himself responding appropriately and instinctively

Within minutes they had moved over to the large double bed. As tired as they both were nothing could have stopped them now.

Phillip awoke at four. Monique was lying naked next to him with her arm draped across his chest. He could hear her gentle breathing as she nuzzled his neck. He gently removed her arm and slipped quietly out of bed. He put on his shirt and trousers and looked again at the peacefully sleeping Monique. He had to admit to himself that she was

228

a very beautiful and unusual woman. Picking up his shoes, he left her room noiselessly.

.

228

THIRTY-TWO

Phillip was up at six o'clock the next morning although he had not slept since leaving Monique's room. He ordered a large breakfast of eggs and croissants with plenty of strong coffee. By seven he was showered, dressed and ready to go to work. His dirty overalls and boots he carried in a hold-all as he descended to the hotel lobby. He had given Monique a quick call before he left and had found her wide awake and ready to field any incoming calls from the residents of Aventino. Neither of them spoke of the preceding night. He had asked her to make one phone call at eight o'clock sharp and hoped that his plan for entering Grapponelli's house would work.

Meeting up with Tenente Gentile and two other young officers of the Carabinieri, Phillip went over his plan once again. He stressed that it would require swiftness, precision and a cool head from everyone concerned, but more importantly it would require a flexibility to deal with any unforeseen circumstances or even opportunities, as they arose. This was a one time opportunity, he told them. It was their only chance. They must get it right.

At precisely eight thirty the van and orange generator pulled up behind the road works opposite the Grapponelli compound. Phillip wished the three young men 'good luck' and descended from the van and down behind the screening that blocked off the hole in the road. Giorgio Gentile followed complete with clipboard and a laminated ID badge that announced him as 'works supervisor' Roberto Martini. Accompanied by the two other young men he walked across the street to Grapponelli's mansion.

To the burly guard at the gate, he explained that they were testing the new water pipe hook up and needed access to the house. The man grunted at them and went back inside his gatehouse and telephoned the main house. He was told that, indeed, someone from *Acqua Nationale* had called at eight that morning and told them to expect an inspector sometime during the morning to check their pipes. The voice from the house told the gatekeeper to check their ID badges and then to send them up to the house.

Returning to the waiting Lt. Gentile, the gatekeeper, a man of few words and menacing countenance, pointed at Gentile's ID badge which Giorgio unclipped and handed to the man. The two others did likewise. Satisfied that the photos on the badges resembled those men standing before him, the burly minder slowly opened up a single gate and pointed the three men to the main house.

Some minutes later Gentile and his men were standing inside the elaborate hall of Nini Grapponelli's mansion. A large man, who had let them in, proceeded to grill Gentile as to why such an intrusion was necessary. Giorgio proceeded to tell the story that he had been briefed on and that Monique had explained in her phone call at eight that morning, namely that in order to test that they had correctly coupled up the right pipes to the right houses they had inserted a harmless blue dye into the main junction. When the taps were turned on it was hoped that no dye would be seen. That being the case, the house was correctly hooked up and their job was done.

Gentile purposely made the explanation as technical sounding as possible and hoped that his bluff would work, for in truth, there were no road works, no new water pipes and certainly no blue dye.

Bored with the long winded explanation, the large bodyguard interrupted Giorgio just as he was waxing poetic about 'opposite flow pressure valves' and asked him just what it was he needed to do.

"We shall need to turn on all the faucets in the house – only cold water, of course," he added, "Then we shall monitor them for maybe two or three minutes. If no blue dye is seen coming out of any of the taps, we have a perfect hook up and then we can leave you in peace, Signore" Giorgio's smile was not returned.

"Well, you clowns will not be running all over the house like mad men," stated the bodyguard. "In fact you won't be allowed anywhere near the bedrooms upstairs. My men will check that for you"

"Just as you wish, Signore," said Giorgio Gentile, still maintaining his ingratiating smile.

"Is there perhaps a downstairs toilet or a wet bar somewhere that my men could check for you?"

"*Si*," said the large man, as he pointed to a door in the hallway and then took the still smiling Gentile into the study. Here he opened a large pair of doors to reveal a complete bar set up with ice machine, sink and pressurized steam washer for the glasses.

Giorgio was genuinely impressed and said so.

" Your men can watch this and the toilet", grunted the large Italian minder as he withdrew a two way radio from his pocket and called two of his colleagues, " we will watch the upstairs and the cook will watch the kitchen. *Capisce*? "

"Understood, signore, whatever you wish." In truth it didn't hurt Giorgio's plans one bit as they had wanted to place the hidden radio mikes in the main downstairs rooms, rather than the bedrooms. Fate had looked favorably on Phillip's deception and it looked to Giorgio that just maybe they would be able to succeed in duping the Grapponelli household after all. Had he been honest with himself he had serious doubts about the plan and had wondered if he'd leave the Grapponelli house with all the body bits he had come in with. He began to look more happily on his immediate future.

After a short pause Gentile continued, "Signore, once you have all the taps running please shout down to me. If everything runs clear for four or five minutes then the house is fine. But, please, if you see any blue dye in the water, let me know immediately. The dye is quite harmless, as I said, but I shall need to know which faucet it comes from in order that we can immediately correct the problem. Any questions?" Gentile looked at each of the bodyguards who said they understood and wanted to get on with it.

Giorgio Gentile hoped that the nonsense he was sprouting wouldn't trip him up. Anyone who had even the most rudimentary understanding of plumbing would realize that all the water coming into the house would be blue, if indeed they had put blue dye into the pipe from the road. But not only had they not done this, they didn't even know where the water main was. He kept his fingers crossed that enlightenment would not dawn on the two armed bodyguards, at least not until he and his men were long gone.

Each person having taken up their station started to turn on the faucets. Giorgio Gentile heard hurried steps on the floor above as the two bodyguards ran between bedrooms checking for the blue dyed water.

Meanwhile, the two Carabinieri officers downstairs set about placing their tiny round transmitters in the main sitting room and the study.

They placed them in as many strategic places as they could. They chose furniture that was placed close to the seating and stuck the miniature bugs underneath and out of sight. They had been briefed that if they moved any object or ornament, it was to be replaced in exactly the same spot as it had previously occupied. Not close, but exactly. Phillip had stressed this point in their morning briefing. He emphasized his point by telling the young policeman that even an untrained eye will immediately notice when some item is not in its familiar place. Such a revelation in these circumstances could have dire, if not deadly consequences.

Whilst the two young officers went quietly and efficiently about their task they kept up a dialogue with their 'supervisor' saying everything was still running clear. In turn Giorgio Gentile also maintained a steady flow of information from the two bodyguards upstairs and the cook in the kitchen, a floor below. This way Giorgio was able to make sure that the bodyguard's attention was still on the water taps and not on the men downstairs.

Receiving a pre-ordained code phrase from his officers telling him that they had completed the hiding of the listening devices, Giorgio called a halt to the faucet running exercise.

The first bodyguard, Macarini, appeared almost immediately and descended the stairs rapidly. Towering over Giorgio Gentile he said, "Now if you clowns are finished wasting my time you can all get out now."

"Certainly Sir," replied Giorgio and added, "if you would please just sign my work order we'll be right out of here," He held out a clipboard and his pen for a signature.

Glowering, Macarini snatched the pen and scrawled an illegible signature on Giorgio's sheet of paper.

"*Mille Grazie* and thank you for your patience Sir," said Giorgio as he ushered his two men out of the front door. Macarini merely grunted and slammed the door.

Not until the three policemen were back in the van, where Phillip had been waiting, did anyone speak. Giorgio Gentile was the first.

"Signore Fairfax, we did as you instructed and my men were able to place the microphones in two downstairs rooms, the lounge and in Grapponelli's study. We were not permitted to go upstairs."

"Excellent, Giorgio. Don't worry about upstairs, it's not overly important. It would have been icing on the cake to get one on the master bedroom but it's not essential. You men did a fine job and I thank you all."

The two officers who both spoke little English had Phillip's comments translated and both of them broke out in a wide grin. For each of the two young policemen, this had been their first taste of undercover work and they had found the experience very satisfying, a great deal more exciting than their normal routine police work.

"However," added Phillip, his face now becoming serious again, "we should visit the other houses too. I suggest the two houses either side of Grapponelli's and the three directly opposite. It would be stupid to arouse the suspicions of Grapponelli's goons by leaving after we'd only visited their house. In order to play out our roles properly we should visit his neighbors too. Do you not agree Giorgio?"

The lieutenant nodded his agreement and immediately issued his orders to the two young policemen.

Once again the three set off on their appointed rounds, leaving Phillip in the back of the van to start recording any conversation in Grapponelli's house.

THIRTY-THREE

Leila Diab and the Marquis had breakfast together at seven o'clock. Afterwards they went into the study to load the two paintings of '*The Girl in the Red Dress*' into the secret compartments of the briefcase. The real Leonardo was carefully placed in the 9-1-4 section and the fake one in the 0-7-8. Leila spun the numbered wheels thus locking the case. Surprisingly to Leila if felt no heavier than before as she lifted if off the Marquis' desk.

They spent a few minutes going over the banking procedures and the Marquis once more made sure Leila knew the codes and passwords by heart.

Satisfied that every preparation had been made and that every eventuality they could think of had been addressed, the two headed into the main hall to say goodbye. They were both somewhat preoccupied with their thoughts and their farewell lacked the warmth they usually reserved for each other.

A great deal rested on the success of this first operation and the responsibility showed in each of their faces. No doubt future deals with the other fake paintings would be easier to handle, although complacency in this game could have very costly consequences. Leila was totally focused on her role as she slid behind the wheel of her Volkswagen en route for Avignon Caum airport and her waiting Lear jet.

The journey to Rome was uneventful and by eleven o'clock Leila touched down and was taxiing to the private jet terminal at Fiumicino airport.

Macarini was waiting outside in Grapponelli's Mercedes Benz. Leila was dressed in figure hugging leather trousers and a red silk blouse. Her long blond hair,

236

her favorite wig, and large dark sunglasses completed her
ensemble. She carried no other luggage besides her black
leather briefcase and a small Gucci handbag. Macarini
noticed her immediately, as did every other male in the
vicinity, and stepping out from behind the steering wheel
Macarini opened the rear door and motioned to Leila Diab.

Approaching the vehicle, Marcarini spoke, "You are
Miss Jasmine, yes?"

"Yes," and without any further preamble or
conversation she sat in the vehicle.

Macarini tried twice to engage her in conversation
on the drive to Aventino but Leila remained resolutely
silent. After the second attempt failed Macarini gave up
and drove the remainder of the journey sulking in silence.

THIRTY-FOUR

Sitting in the van opposite Grapponelli's house, Phillip had noticed the Mercedes driven by Macarini leave the compound at about ten a.m. The two young policemen and Giorgio Gentile were still visiting houses in the neighborhood, asking them to check for blue dye in their water. But by eleven o'clock they were back in the hole that Phillip had created with his jackhammer.

Phillip had had an open line to Monique who was still at the Hotel Clara. She was on hand to translate any conversation Phillip picked up on the hidden microphones, but so far there had been none. Now that Lt. Gentile was back in the van with Phillip he severed his connection with Monique and told her to drive his rental car to *Via Grimaldi* two streets away and wait for him there.

"You'll find surveillance work, 95% boring," he had told her, "so try to stay awake!"

"And the other 5%?" she asked.

"That can either be just as boring as the 95% or downright scary. The trouble is you never know when the 5% scary is going to hit you. Staying alert is highly recommended."

"Got it, I'll be on my toes, I promise." Phillip had no doubts that she would remain totally focused.

At approximately eleven forty five Phillip noticed that the burly gate minder was once again outside preparing to open the wrought iron gates. Just as he had the second gate pinned and locked, Grapponelli's Mercedes appeared at the end of the street. Within a couple of minutes it came sweeping majestically into the drive. Phillip and Giorgio both clicked away with their cameras as fast as they could. They only had a brief glimpse of the blond passenger in the

238

rear seat but hoped that at least one frame would give a good clear shot of the visitor.

Arriving at the front door, Macarini once again stepped out of the car and opened the rear door for Leila Diab. She made no comment once again and Macarini found it hard to say nothing about her lack of respect for him. Instead he consoled himself with thoughts of what he would like to do to her. He imagined taking her forcibly and after he had satisfied his animal lust, he visualized slicing her naked flesh with his razor sharp knife. 'Death by a thousand cuts' would seem an appropriate end for this arrogant bitch. He'd make her scream out her respect for him!

By the time he'd unlocked the front door for her, he was smiling to himself. He knew one day he'd live out this fantasy, he just needed to be patient which was not easy for a man whose excessive and murderous passions could be ignited in a split second.

When the two young policemen had finished filling in the hole, they tamped it as best they could. It still left an ugly bruise on an otherwise pristine road. They then loaded the screen and cones into the back of the van. Lt Gentile hooked up the generator to the van as Phillip prepared to drive away. He drove two streets away and parked waiting for Monique to arrive with his rental car. Meanwhile Lt. Gentile was monitoring the receiver and listening for any conversation in Grapponelli's house between him and his new blond visitor. So far everything was silent except for the faint sound of a vacuum cleaner in the distance. Phillip was a little puzzled and wondered if the Carabinieri officers had done their job well enough. Within three minutes Monique arrived and pulled up behind the van and generator.

Via Grimaldi was a quiet street with few other vehicles on the road. Most were securely parked in their owners' driveways or attached garages. It was, after all, an affluent neighborhood.

Gentile had volunteered for his men to return the van and generator to the rental company. They had fulfilled their purpose and were no longer needed.

Phillip expressed his deep thanks to all three officers and promised Giorgio Gentile that he would keep him and the Colonello informed of any developments. Picking up the radio receiver and the two cameras he went to join Monique in the rental car.

"How's it going?" she asked as he sat in the driver's seat beside her.

"So far nothing of any use at all," Phillip sounded a little frustrated. "I'm just getting a few background noises but precious little else. They might as well have buried the damn bugs in the garden for all the good they're doing."

Monique was wise enough to keep her own counsel and said nothing.

Phillip continued, "We're well within range of their transmission. I just don't understand it. If they'd found the bugs we wouldn't be hearing anything. They'd have flushed them down the toilet or thrown them in the fire, but I'm only getting household background noises. Weird."

Phillip continued twiddling the tiny dials hoping to get the clearest signal possible, when suddenly the sound of a ringing telephone came through loud and clear. At last now he thought, they might start getting somewhere. It would only take a careless word or two for Grapponelli to incriminate himself. Whilst nothing could be used in a court of law, and Colonel Bodoni went to great pains to point that out, at least they would receive information from Phillip which in turn could lead to more officially

240

sanctioned and admissible wire taps. Monique stood by for translation duties.

Leila stood waiting in the hallway for Grapponelli to put in an appearance. Macarini stood watching her. His obvious dislike for her showed on his face as he too waited for his boss to appear.

Somewhere a phone started ringing and Grapponelli could be heard answering it. The conversation was brief and one sided. Grapponelli listened to the caller and after hanging up, he let out a string of invectives that would have made a merchant marine blush.

Sitting two streets away, Monique and Phillip looked at each other.

"Trust me, you don't want me to translate that outburst," said Monique. "Suffice it to say, he's one hell of a pissed off Italian."

"Did you get any idea who made the call? I mean did Grapponelli use any name?"

Phillip hoped that the Italian had revealed something in an unguarded moment.

"He did refer to 'underhanded shits' or words to that effect, but regrettably, no names," responded Monique.

At that point Grapponelli could be heard bellowing for Macarini and his other henchman.

"*Vaffanculo, stronzo. Macarini! Testa di Cazzo.!*"

"He's just called Macarini, a piece of shit and a dickhead." Monique blushed slightly.

"Now he's telling Macarini and some other guy to 'get their useless, lazy backsides' down to his study."

Monique continued to translate as Grapponelli's voice came loud and clear through Phillip's radio receiver. There followed a one sided and tense conversation in a hushed whisper which neither Monique nor Phillip could pick up. At the end of Grapponelli's muted dialogue he reverted to his normal voice. "Now find the fucking things," was how Monique translated it for Phillip.

"Well, I think he knows about our radio mikes," fumed Phillip, "Damn it, the last few days have been a complete waste of time." Phillip was frustrated.

"Bugger, Bugger, Bugger!" Phillip slapped the steering wheel of the car with such ferocity that Monique thought it might break. Phillip was frustrated beyond measure.

"Somewhere there's a bloody leak!" Phillip was spitting fire. "It's either Gentile, one of those two police constables that he chose or, heaven forbid, Colonel Bodoni." Phillip took a moment to calm down and ponder the possibilities.

"Robert speaks highly of Bodoni and I'd stake my life on Robert's judgment. So it must be one of the other three." Phillip took a deep breath.

"Well, the last couple of days have been a waste of bloody time," he said as he turned and looked at Monique, "Sorry about my outburst."

"No need to apologize. I understand and I share your frustration," said Monique, as one by one, the microphones were found and crushed by Macarini's large boot. It came across the receiver in Phillip's car as a loud crash.

Monique in an effort to inject a little optimism said, "There's still my contact with Grapponelli." Pausing, she then added, "and we also know that we probably can't trust at least one of the Carabinieri officers. So we have learned something"

"Thank God for small mercies," said Phillip. "At least Gentile and the other two don't know about our little honey trap for Grapponelli." Phillip turned and looked at Monique.

"It pretty much falls on me now, huh?" she said and flashed Phillip a confident smile. "I'm more determined than ever to get the bastard now," she added.

"We need to rethink things first," counseled Phillip. "Before we go charging ahead we need to know who the blond woman is that Macarini drove into the compound this morning. She could be nobody or she could be part of this whole plot and we need to know for sure. Let's get back to the hotel and download the photographs we took this morning." With that Phillip started up the car and, deep in thought, headed silently back to the Hotel Clara.

At this point Leila Diab, or Jasmine, as she was known today, began to feel more than a little irritated about being left standing in the hallway of Grapponelli's mansion. Just as she was about to go and find Grapponelli herself, the little Italian came flying around the corner from his study with arms outstretched in exaggerated supplication.

"Miss Jasmine, you must forgive me. I had not intended to keep such a beautiful young lady waiting but a minor crisis…you understand? Please, I beg, come and sit with me on the terrace." He took her by the arm and guided her towards the patio doors.

"Perhaps you would like something to drink?" And without waiting for a reply he clapped his hands loudly summoning an old man from the kitchen.

"Please, Miss Jasmine, would you like coffee or maybe cold, fresh lemonade?" Again, without waiting for a reply or even taking time to draw breath he dispatched the elderly man with orders to bring both coffee and lemonade onto the terrace.

Turning now to the statuesque Jasmine who towered over him, he said "now, please Jasmine, let us go

243

and relax on the terrace. We have much to discuss." He bowed slightly and with a sweeping gesture of his arm he invited Jasmine to step through the glass doors onto the sunny terrace.

The sun was shining in a cloudless sky, but the abundance of flowering trees and shrubs, and the overhanging vines gave a comfortable shade. Jasmine chose a chair situated in the corner of the terrace. The solid walls to her back gave her a semblance of comfort and protection. She did not trust Grapponelli, nor did she feel completely safe in his territory, so when risks needed to be taken, such basic precautions were advisable.

As Nini Grapponelli sat in a chair opposite her, he made no secret of his lustful appreciation of her body. His attentions were not appreciated, but Jasmine kept her feelings in check. She would make this smarmy little Italian pay for his insolence in one way or another, but for now she would just have to tolerate his beady little eyes mentally undressing her.

For some minutes the two sat in silence. Nini Grapponelli, with a fixed smile on his lips, continued to stare at Jasmine, whilst she fixed him with a stare that spelt utter contempt. The silent duel was only ended by the arrival of the elderly manservant bringing to the terrace a tray with both coffee and lemonade. Had the two been engaged in a staring competition it would have been declared a draw.

At the withdrawal of the manservant, Nini Grapponelli spoke, "*Signorina* Jasmine, I am expecting my expert to arrive any moment now. I assume that your briefcase contains the item you wish me to purchase?"

"It does."

"And you have the full powers to negotiate with me?" said Grapponelli.

"I think, Signore, you are misinformed if you think there is any room for negotiation. The price is twenty five million Euros. I have been told that you are aware of this and that you have made arrangements for this sum to be transferred into my Swiss bank. If my assumptions are incorrect, I suggest you tell me now and I can save us both a lot of wasted time and effort. Do I make myself clear, Signore Grapponelli?" Jasmine's tone was firm and resolute, but she managed to convey sufficient '*laissez-faire*' to indicate to the Italian that she had many other options open to her.

Grapponelli was impressed. He liked to spar whilst doing business and here he felt was a worthy opponent. He poured two glasses of iced lemonade.

"As you say Jasmine, I am indeed aware of your terms, but first we shall have to see if your item is worth the asking price." Grapponelli set a glass in front of Leila.

"It is," she replied, as she took a small sip of her iced lemonade.

As if on cue the doorbell rang and footsteps could be heard rushing to the front door.

"Ah, I think my expert has arrived!" said Grapponelli, leaping to his feet. "He is a very punctual man and I appreciate that in business. Do you not agree, *Signorina?*"

A minute or two later, an older man, in his mid-sixties, came onto the terrace escorted by Macarini. He was Paulo Calisti, formerly of the *Musei Vaticani*, one of the most renowned and famous cultural institutions of the *Holy See*. Signore Calisti had, at one time, been one of their most respected art restorers and historians. For forty years he had dedicated himself every day to preserving the great works of art that had been acquired over a five hundred year collecting history. Sadly his love of 15th and

16th century drawings proved too much to resist. He was caught trying to smuggle several drawings by Michelangelo and Raphael out of the museum between the pages of a newspaper.

A search of his apartment revealed that he had been indulging his passion for quite some time and he paid the price by not only losing his job and his enviable reputation but by spending the next couple of years behind bars courtesy of the Italian Government.

But secretly his vast knowledge was still sought by those who cared little about his larcenous past but desired his knowledge above all else. In this capacity he earned far more than when he was in the Roman Pontiff's employ at the museum and he worked a great deal less which gave him time to peruse the flea markets and antique shops of Rome in search of his beloved drawings. But today he knew he was in for a rare treat. He was eager to set his expert eyes on one of the world's rarest and most beautiful treasures.

"*Signorina*, may I present my expert, Signore Paulo Calisti, late of the *Musei Vaticani*," said Grapponelli proudly, as if he were introducing the Pope himself.

Jasmine remained seated as the elderly Calisti bent and brought her proffered hand toward his face. She withdrew it before he had time to touch her hand with his lips. The thought of him doing so revolted her and she cared nothing for his feelings or for this decadent Italian ritual.

"Nini, I have not slept a wink since you called me. I have been so excited at seeing your prospective purchase," said the old man. "Shall we proceed straight away? And turning to Jasmine he added, "With the lady's permission, of course."

"Indeed, Paulo. *Signorina,* if you would kindly bring your briefcase into my study, I think we should begin the exam. How long do you estimate it will take Paulo?" said Grapponelli turning to the expert.

"I shall probably know immediately I see it," said the older man, "but there are a few simple tests I must do in order to satisfy myself, and your good self. And I must make quite sure that it is in the kind of condition we expect of a great masterpiece."

No doubt, thought Grapponelli, it would also be to justify his large fee. He left the thought unspoken. As the three of them entered Nini Grapponelli's well appointed oak-paneled study, the curtains were being closed by Macarini.

"Thank you, Mac," said Grapponelli, "I assume everything in here is now fine for us to conduct some business?" He referred, of course to the removal of the transmitting radio bugs.

"*Si,* everything is good," replied the large man, still slightly sulking from his earlier rebuke which was made even more humiliating by the fact that the arrogant bitch, Jasmine, must have overheard it.

"Good, good," said Grapponelli, "perhaps you would be good enough to wait outside the door."

The big man left the room and closed the door somewhat harder than needed. Macarini was a petulant man with a short fuse and Grapponelli took note that he was reaching his limits of self control. He wondered how much longer he could afford to employ this human powder keg, useful though he undoubtedly was.

With Macarini out of the way, the Italian expert could hardly wait for Jasmine to produce his painting. Fishing in his bag he produced 3 pairs of white gloves.

Slipping a pair on over his delicate hands he said, "We cannot be too careful with such a precious artifact of such great age. I respectfully ask that you both wear these gloves before you handle the painting."

He passed a pair to Jasmine who examined them to make sure they had not been worn before. They were new, but she resisted the offer. Instead she rested the briefcase flat on the table and dialed her locks to 9-1-4. As she did so the little Italian expert retrieved a meter square piece of green felt from his tattered leather bag and laid it flat on the table top. Next he set up a small table lamp with a flexible neck and ran the lead to a convenient electrical outlet.

"Please *Signorina*, I am ready when you are," pleaded Paulo Calisti, hardly able to contain his excitement at the prospect before him.

Jasmine lifted the lid of her briefcase, but before removing the painting she acquiesced to the supplicant looks of Calisti and put on the white gloves.

As she gently withdrew the Leonardo da Vinci portrait of '*The Girl in the Red Dress*' from its soft foam cradle, Calisti held his breath.

She laid the panel on his green felt cloth. Calisti's eyes were wide with utter amazement at what he saw being placed before him.

THIRTY-FIVE

In Monique's suite at the Hotel Clara, Phillip was downloading the two camera's images taken that morning onto a laptop computer. As the first image appeared on the screen, Monique, who was leaning over Phillip's shoulder commented, "You're no Cecil Beaton, are you?" and she giggled delightfully.

Phillip was forced to admit that the image was both 'fuzzy' and badly centered, but as the various frames clicked rapidly onto the screen he began to notice something familiar in the face of the blonde woman. He ran them through twice more to be sure.

"Bingo," he said triumphantly banging his fist on the table top. "I know who she is!

And," he added, "we're right on target with this one."

Monique, who had gone back to reading more press clippings on Grapponelli, looked up.

"Great!" she exclaimed, "who?"

"It's our Miss Leila Diab, the 'supposed' goddaughter of the Marquis de Manville and she isn't a blonde. That's a wig she's wearing!"

"I guess her collar and cuffs don't match," said Monique and then blushed at her own unladylike comment.

Phillip roared with laughter, not only at Monique's risqué observation but also in relief at the much needed breakthrough.

"Tonight," said Phillip, regaining his composure, "I would like you to try and hook up with Grapponelli. See if you can get anything out of him regarding new purchases. Then I think we'll need to pay our Marquis another visit. Are you still okay with that? You know you can back out anytime, don't you? After all, the stakes have just got a little higher and I know this isn't what you signed on for with I.A.R."

"The hell it isn't!" she responded. "This is just beginning to get interesting, and besides, just because I'm an academic, doesn't mean I can't handle a little action."

"Okay, but the offer stands. If I think it's time for you to go home, I hope you'll do as you're told and go home."

"Yes sir!" said Monique standing to rigid attention and saluting.

Phillip smiled at her feistiness and added, "by the way, you salute with the right hand, not the left." They both laughed.

THIRTY-SIX

As Paolo Calisti caught his first glimpse of the Leonardo portrait he gasped out loud and both his hands involuntarily shot to his face. He stood there cupping his cheeks with eyes as wide as saucers.

"She is *bellisima!*" he exclaimed. "Truly wonderful. God himself would be hard pressed to create such a masterpiece" He crossed himself to cancel out any blasphemy as he took a small step closer.

The image of '*The Girl in the Red Dress*' glowed under the strong light of his lamp. The deep colors, still vibrant after four hundred years, leapt off the panel in an unparalleled display of artistic glory. Hardly daring to breathe he stepped a little closer still and reaching into his tattered leather bag he withdrew a pair of strong magnifying glasses. These he wore like a headband and, flicking a small switch above the lenses, shone an even brighter light onto the painting.

He bent over it and peered closely. The imperceptible brush strokes and the flawless painting of the flesh tones gave the man, who for forty years had grown accustomed to working with history's great artistic achievements, his first glimpse of pure perfection.

For several minutes he was lost in the magic that only Leonardo da Vinci could produce. Nini Grapponelli looked on at the small grey haired man as he gently, almost gingerly, turned the painting over. He was careful not to rest the painting on its painted surface as he examined the back of the panel. Paolo Calisti, still with a look of rapture on his face, muttered something about 'poplar wood' but his meaning was lost on Grapponelli and of no interest to Leila Diab. All she wanted was a positive declaration of authenticity, which she knew would be forthcoming, so that they could get on to the financial aspect of the deal.

After fifteen minutes of careful examination Calisti asked for the main lights to be switched off so that he could continue his examination under a 'black light'.

Leila Diab spoke up immediately and stated that she was not happy with the idea of being plunged into darkness with the painting lying loose on the table. Calisti assured her that the light could remain on until he had switched on his 'black light' which would illuminate the painting and show that it was perfectly safe. Having explained that the test under a black light, which was really only an ultra violet light, was the only way he could see if there had been any over-painting or restoration. She reluctantly agreed. Nini Grapponelli meanwhile was growing a little impatient himself and proceeded to switch off the main lights.

"Well, is it or isn't it genuine, Paolo?" he asked with irritation at the old man's plodding manner.

"Oh yes, most definitely genuine and the work of Leonardo. It could only be the work of the world's greatest painter but, Nini, I owe it to you to check its condition thoroughly. What appears perfect to the naked eye, even under strong light, can be undone when examined under a 'black light'. Had I any doubts whatsoever, I would suggest x-rays and chemical analysis but I assure you this painting is most definitely by the hand of the great master himself."

For a full fifteen minutes Calisti examined the work of art under the ultra violet light. Despite Calisti's bad body odor and even worse breath, Leila stood very close to him protecting her asset. She was ready to seize it in a split second if necessary. Eventually the disgraced ex Vatican employee announced that the main lights could be turned on again.

Grapponelli obliged and once again the study was illuminated by a large crystal chandelier. With a great deal of pomp Paolo Calisti announced that he was 100 per cent sure that the painting was genuine and that its condition was exceptional and 99 per cent original. Only two minor flecks on the outer edge of the panel, he said, showed any evidence of re-touching. He began to prognosticate about the various advantages and disadvantages of painting on poplar wood panels, but Grapponelli cut him off in mid flow.

"Paolo, I thank you very much for your time and, of course, your great knowledge. I have here an envelope for you," he said reaching into his desk drawer, "I shall not detain you any longer. I know what a busy man you are." With that he handed Calisti a manila envelope that contained ten thousand Euros.

"Thank you Nini but it is I who should thank you for giving me such an opportunity. Oh, the joy of seeing the magnificent work of such a great painter." He placed his hand on his heart and bowed ever so slightly.

As Grapponelli showed Calisti to the study door, he lightly touched the man's arm. Fixing him with his beady eyes and with no hint of a smile on his face he spoke softly and a little above a whisper. "I know, Paolo that our little business here today will be forgotten – and I mean totally wiped from your memory – as soon as you step out of this room. I am sure that I make myself perfectly clear"

Calisti fully understood his meaning and he knew all too well the reputation of the man whose warnings should never be taken lightly.

"*Si, si*, Nini. I only stopped by to say hello and wish you w-well." He stuttered slightly over the last word.

"Of course, Paolo, and I wish you well too."

Nini Grapponelli closed the door as Macarini re-appeared to escort the art expert to the front door.

Turning now to Jasmine he said, "I think now we have a little business to discuss. Perhaps while we talk about the payment, I could look at my prospective new purchase? I have not truly had time myself to appreciate its fine qualities."

"I will gladly show it to you and you can look at it all you want but until our financial arrangements have been concluded I think I would feel happier that it stays firmly in my possession. No disrespect intended" she added almost as an after-thought.

"As you wish, *Signorina*." Crapponelli was unused to having his wishes denied but he reasoned that he could really care less if he liked what he was going to buy or not. The important thing to Grapponelli was that it was a genuine Leonardo da Vinci painting and worth a great deal more than he was going to pay for it, even if it was stolen.

As a gesture of good faith, Jasmine put on her white gloves again as she handled the painting and returned it to the snug foam cradle in her briefcase. She closed the lid and the locks snapped shut as she spun the small numbered wheels.

"I propose, at least, to deduct the cost of my expert's advice, *Signorina*," said Grapponelli as an opening salvo in the negotiation process, "which is a paltry thirty thousand Euros." Grapponelli was of the firm belief that you should never tell the truth when a perfectly good lie will do.

"Then firstly I say, you paid far too much for the little man's opinion and secondly, I shall expect you to pay for my travel expenses, the charter of a private Lear jet which, let me see, should probably make us about even. So why don't we cut out all the crap, Signore Grapponelli" she almost spat out his name, "and just get on with the transaction. If you want to buy the painting, buy it! If not, I have other people to see. Time and patience are two commodities I have in very short supply. So do we have a deal or not?"

Grapponelli threw his arms wide and his face took on the exaggerated look of a rebuked child. "I see you are a lady in a hurry," he said now smiling widely, "but I think when you ask a man to pay you twenty five million euros, a little patience and cordiality would not come amiss". The false smile fell instantly from his face and was replaced with a dark look that spoke of his violent way of life. His small beady eyes fixed on Leila Diab's face like two laser beams.

Whilst she felt nothing but contempt for this little Italian bully she also realized that she was at a disadvantage being in his territory and on his turf. She immediately sought to soften her approach.

"Forgive me Signore if I have given any offense. It was not my intention."

"Of course, dear lady. Let us proceed, by all means, in a spirit of mutual cooperation and friendship." The plastic smile returned to his face. "As the painting has been authenticated and it appears that you possess the genuine article, I propose, as no doubt you have assumed, to purchase it from you."

"I am delighted, signore. Thank you." Her tone was now one of conciliation tinged with a slight feeling of relief.

Grapponelli was playing a game with her as a cat plays with a mouse. He continued. "*Signorina* Jasmine, I am a man of the world and I deal every day with people trying to sell me things. These are people who have spent a lifetime, as I have, learning the art of negotiating." He paused to allow the full weight of his words to sink in.

"You are out of your depth with business of this type, though no doubt you are good at your more normal work, whatever that may be. However, I am a generous man and because I like you I will make you an offer. I am also a realistic man and I know as well as you do that the painting is – how shall I put this delicately? – *the subject of much interest by the authorities."* He held up his hand as Leila began to speak and indicated that he was not finished making his proposal. He continued, "Therefore, Jasmine, I shall offer you eight million euros, BUT …" and he emphasized the 'but' – "I shall be prepared to pay my own expenses for the authentication process. You may, if you wish, take enough time to telephone and consult with any partners you may have but my offer expires in one hour."

He sat down in his maroon leather armchair and crossed his legs in a relaxed fashion indicating his complete confidence that she would accept his offer.

This came as a body blow to Leila Diab. She was a woman who was used to getting everything she demanded and if it wasn't given freely she would invariably take it. By force, if necessary. This, however, was a new experience and she was not enjoying it. Her instinct was not to cave in under the pressure.

"I regret," she said as firmly as she could, "that I have wasted your time and also a great deal of my own." She picked up her briefcase as if to leave. "Perhaps you would be good enough to ask your driver to take me back to the airport and my jet." Defiance shone from her eyes like diamonds in the flames of hell.

"Such a pity, Jasmine. I was hoping that the very least I could offer you was a little lunch and then, perhaps – and I only say 'perhaps' – my natural desire to please an attractive lady would induce me to increase my offer slightly"

"Signore Grapponelli, I came here to do business not to go to lunch and until our business is concluded I have no appetite." She remained standing but did not head for the door. She felt that the ball was now firmly back in Grapponelli's court.

"I find it hard to do business on an empty stomach so I shall increase my offer substantially to nine million euros, in the hope that you will accept and we can go to lunch". He once again reverted to putting on the face of a child beseeching an indulgent parent, knowing that in this instance he held all the aces.

"Twenty million !" she countered.

"Nine and a half. And that, my dear young lady, is my final offer and, indeed, my final word on the subject." He began to turn the screws. "It is a very fair offer, under the circumstances, and I need only make one phone call and the money can be in your account within minutes, so I suggest you think very carefully before answering"

He had her and he knew it.

So did Leila Diab.

After several minutes when Leila reviewed all of her options and wrestled with the particulars of her situation she said, "I accept". A feeling of defeat infected her speech.

"I do not think you will regret this decision, Jasmine" said Grapponelli in a tone both conciliatory and magnanimous in victory. Reaching for his telephone he added, "Now, please if you give me your bank details I shall make arrangements for the immediate transfer of the funds."

Leila handed him a small piece of paper upon which were her Swiss bank details, routing code and account number. Grapponelli gave swift and precise instructions over the phone to his banker and within a few minutes nine and a half million euros was shooting through the ether on its way to Switzerland.

It would travel a great deal further and through several different countries before the end of the day, when it would finally come to rest in an account in Beirut, Lebanon. Here it could be put to use in the ongoing fight against the Zionists in Israel. Within minutes confirmation appeared on Leila's laptop briefcase that the amount of nine and a half million euros had been credited as cleared funds into UBS Bank in Zurich, Switzerland.

With several swift strokes on her keyboard she re-sent the same amount through banks in the Cayman Islands, the Isle of Man, Jersey in the Channel Islands, Hong Kong, Lichtenstein, Damascus and finally into the Arab Bank of Lebanon in Beirut. The computer had been pre programmed with all the account numbers and passwords and it completed the task in only sixteen minutes.

Closing her briefcase she announced that everything was satisfactory and that the funds had arrived in Switzerland.

"Excellent, excellent," cried Nini Grapponelli, "and now perhaps I can be permitted to have my painting?" he added, leaping out of his chair like an over-excited adolescent at Christmas.

"Of course," said Leila smiling, for once a smile of genuine pleasure. She dialed   0-7–8 on her briefcase and with theatrical exaggeration she pulled on her white gloves. Slowly and carefully she withdrew the painting from its foam lined lair and handed it to Nini Grapponelli.

Taking it gingerly he beamed with pleasure as he looked upon the replica of "*The Girl in the red dress*" by Zachary Boyle after the original by Leonardo da Vinci.

258

Thinking that he held possibly the greatest painting ever created by the greatest Italian who ever lived, and knowing that he now owned it, brought a tear to the eye of the ruthless Italian mobster. In the dichotomous world in which Grapponelli lived, the murder of an entire family would not cause him to loose one minute of sleep but the sight of a true masterpiece of art could bring out genuine emotion. To Grapponelli it was this that moved him. Death business.

THIRTY-SEVEN

Phillip and Monique had had a late lunch and on walking back through the lobby of Hotel Clara, the receptionist called out to Monique. In Italian she explained that a gentleman had called twice and left a message for her. The receptionist handed Monique a neatly folded piece of paper. On it was written a phone number and the name *Nini* under the request '*please call*'. She showed the paper to Phillip as they entered the elevator. Entering Monique's suite, which they had been using as a temporary office, Phillip turned to face Monique and placed both his hands on her shoulders.

Looking deep into her green eyes he said, "You don't have to go through with this, you know. No-one, will think any the worst of you if you turn it in now. You've been of immense help to me already, and I'd be happy if you decided to return home."

She stared back at him and searched his eyes for any clues as to his real thoughts. His pale blue eyes gave away no sign that he was insincere.

"Are you finished, Mr. Fairfax?" she asked and he nodded. "I appreciate that little speech, I really do, but I got involved of my own free will, and whilst I can't pretend I'm not a little nervous about walking into Grapponelli's life in an unfamiliar role, I definitely want to see this through to the end with you."

"OK if you're sure," said Phillip smiling at her with admiration. "Then we had better plan a good strategy for you and a signal system if you feel things are getting beyond your comfort level. Grapponelli is a slippery little snake and like a snake he can be very venomous and aggressive. I don't want you getting bitten."

260

They both spent the next forty five minutes going over code words and signals that would indicate Monique had had enough and needed extracting from Grapponelli's clutches. They developed several signals that to an innocent observer might seem harmless but to them meant a great deal more. For instance, if Monique started twiddling her hair around her right index finger it meant that she had Grapponelli 'wrapped around her little finger' and everything was alright. If she felt in danger she was to touch her left ear lobe. The list was as comprehensive as they thought they could make it.

Phillip planned to tail her all evening and he promised that he would keep her in sight as much as was humanly possible, no matter where she went. He did insist, however, that she stay in as public a place as possible in order that he could keep an eye on her.

With everything agreed Phillip suggested she call Grapponelli, who Monique had taken to calling the "Viper" after Phillip's earlier analogy. She was going to try to arrange a meeting that evening. Picking up the phone she dialed the number that had been written on the piece of paper. It was not a number that had appeared on the list they had obtained from *Tenente* Gentile from the Carabinieri.

Grapponelli answered the phone himself.

Their conversation was animated and Monique gave the distinct impression that she was excited about seeing him again. It didn't take long for Grapponelli to broach the subject of dinner. Monique readily agreed but said she would have to cancel a business dinner she had planned with her boss who was also staying at the Hotel Clara. She told Grapponelli not to worry and that come 'hell or high water' she would be free that night.

The little Italian was delighted at her enthusiasm and ended their conversation by saying he would send a car for her at eight o' clock. Meanwhile, he said, he would be counting the seconds until they met again. Hanging up Monique gave an involuntary shudder and Phillip smiled.

"The things I'll do to get a free Italian dinner" she said and smiled back at Phillip

THIRTY-EIGHT

Grapponelli had spent the time after Leila Diab – or Jasmine, as he knew her – had left his house placing a call to Ikar Volkhovsky in St. Petersburg, the Russian city that's nestled on the Gulf of Finland. Leila had declined Grapponelli's offer of lunch which didn't unduly upset him, although he would have enjoyed having an opportunity to screw her. He found her in every way a rather 'cold fish' which, in a perverse way he found sexually arousing. But the time spent in discussion with his old friend Volkhovsky was far more profitable.

Ikar Volkhovsky was a smuggler, a thief, a drug and arms dealer and a murderer but he specialized in selling drugs and American cigarettes, or '*blondes*' as the Italians call them. Nini Grapponelli had traded with him on numerous occasions in the past and whilst he never fully trusted the man, he had found him to be someone who kept his promises. In as far as it's possible to trust a man with such a violent reputation, Grapponelli trusted Volkhovsky.

Russia has had a long history of criminals and bandits operating in the vast peripheral areas of the nation. Well armed gangs had proliferated after the breakdown of Communism but some organizations were better equipped and run than others. All of them, however, had a strong code of behavior. To break this code resulted, more often than not, in the death of the transgressor. The lucky ones were merely mutilated.

Under this code the gang members, known in Russia as '*Vory*' had to forsake all members of their family, to include parents as well as brothers and sisters. The gang was to take the place of their family and all loyalties were owed to them. The code even went as far as banning

263

members from taking wives or having children of their own. Lovers, however, were acceptable and Ikar Volkhovsky had several.

He was a large man with very large appetites. He could drink three bottles of vodka at lunch which was all the more surprising since he rarely got out of bed before lunchtime. In the late 1990s Volkhovsky took over the leadership of the *Solntsevskaya* gang, which was named after the Moscow suburb *Solntsevo* from where it originated. Its' leader at the time, Sergei Mikhailov, had just been incarcerated by the Swiss authorities. Ikar Volkhovsky who specialized in drugs, guns and cigarette smuggling, had risen through the ranks of the *Vory* mostly due to his willingness to murder anyone who got in his way. Not only was he a natural successor to Mikhailov but there were few who dared challenge him. His loud bellicose laugh, which he employed frequently, belied a cunning and cold blooded temperament. His seemingly '*laissez faire*' attitude hid an astute operator who had an uncanny gift for knowing exactly what everyone around him was thinking or planning. His network of spies, even amongst his own group, ensured that any attempt to oust him from his position as leader, was quickly and ruthlessly quashed.

When Volkhovsky discovered that one of his *vory* had secret ties to the *Tambov Syndicate* in St. Petersburg, a bitter rival in the drugs trade, he took the man out to lunch. While they tucked into a well grilled reindeer steak, a particular favorite, Volkhovsky, in one swift move, skewered both the man's hands to the table with steak knives. With his fork he gouged out both the man's eyeballs and then sent him back to his boss Vladimir Gavrillenkov but not before he'd also cut out his tongue and cut off both his ears. The message was clear; whatever the man had seen or heard would and could never be repeated.

Ikar Volkhovsky was an oligarch, that is to say he saw himself as a tycoon or a business magnate and like all Russian oligarchs he liked to show off his tremendous wealth and influence. To that end he decided to become an art collector and it was to this particular vanity that Nini Grapponelli now appealed. The acquisition of *"The Girl in the Red Dress"* by the greatest artist of all time, Leonardo da Vinci, was a prize that Nini knew Volkhovsky would pay handsomely for. Grapponelli expected to trade a great deal for this masterpiece.

Having whet Ikar Volkhovsky's appetite over the phone, Nini told him that he would fly to St Petersburg the following day and bring the painting with him. Meanwhile he had a more immediate appointment and an equally exciting prospect in the form of Miss Monique Langer.

THIRTY-NINE

Through the windshield of his rental car which was parked in the front of the Hotel Clara, Phillip saw Macarini arrive promptly at eight o' clock to collect Monique. He noticed however, that Grapponelli was not in the back seat. Macarini left the car idling under the large carved stone portico of the hotel's main entrance, and walked into the lobby.

Monique was waiting by the reception desk and was talking to the raven haired receptionist when Macarini approached. In her impeccable Italian she greeted Macarini civilly and then preceded him across the marble floor to the waiting car. She stood by the rear door until Macarini opened it for her. She slid gracefully onto the parchment leather seat, all the while conscious of Macarini's shifty eyes trying to catch a glimpse of her thighs and underwear. Monique was skilled and Macarini was disappointed.

Monique made polite conversation about the weather as most English people do when they want to avoid any deeper subject. It is always a suitable subject for general discussion and insures one avoids giving offence. It also gives someone the opportunity to appear interested in other people's opinions even when they're not. It had served the great British public for centuries and would do very nicely tonight to keep Macarini from making any improper comments.

The drive to Grapponelli's house was short and at first Monique thought that they were merely coming to pick up Grapponelli on their way to the restaurant. It was only when Marcarini switched off the car and opened the door for Monique did she realize that this was not the case. Macarini informed her that Signore Grapponelli always

liked champagne on the terrace before going out to dine
and so he led her through the main hall and out onto a large
patio that smelled of scented flowers.

Nini Grapponelli leapt out of his chair with boyish
enthusiasm when he saw Monique. With practiced charm
he scooped up both her hands in his and proceeded to kiss
them with the kind of passion that only Italians can muster.

Monique wondered if Phillip was able to see her,
though she doubted it. She did hope, however, that he was
at least within earshot should she find it necessary to
scream.

Deciding that she just had to fend for herself she
gently but firmly disentangled herself from Grapponelli's
grasp and exclaimed "oooh, champagne, my absolute
favorite!"

Grapponelli, feeling obliged to break off the
encounter, went to pour her a glass as she took the
opportunity to select and sit on a single armchair. The
thought of having to share a 'love-seat' with him did not
really appeal. She decided too, as she sat demurely waiting
for her champagne, that the floral scent she noticed on first
arriving was due in large part to Grapponelli's
overpowering cologne rather than to Mother Nature's
colorful blooms.

"Monique", said Grapponelli as he bent to hand her
a flute of chilled champagne, "I have been looking forward
to this evening all day. Indeed, I have done virtually no
work. I have merely day-dreamed of seeing you again, but
let me tell you, the reality of your loveliness tonight, is
even better than my fantasy of you. Here, I drink a toast to
my lovely new beautiful friend." He raised his glass in
salutation and after gently touching his crystal glass to hers;
he drained fully one half of his drink.

Monique smiled at him and mustering all her acting skills she said, "Nini, I too have been longing to see you tonight, so I raise my glass to celebrate getting to know you, my newest Italian friend. To friends!" she added as she took a small sip of her wine.

He responded, "To friends," and then injudiciously added, "May they become lovers."

By this time Phillip had worked his way through the neighbor's back garden that, luckily for him, was very overgrown and definitely not as well lit as Grapponelli's. He had found an old cracked terracotta flower pot sitting, unplanted except for the odd weed, on a three foot tall pedestal. Lifting the pot to the ground he tested the pedestal for strength and solidity. It appeared, in the fading light, to be made of stone or maybe concrete. In either case he felt sure it would hold his weight. It was heavy but Phillip was able to lift it and place it next to the eight foot high wall that separated the two properties. He wondered as he eased himself up onto the pedestal if broken glass was set into the wall at the sides of the garden too. It was. Taking off his thick leather jacket he placed it on top of the imbedded glass shards and very slowly raised his head until he could see over the wall. Grapponelli's garden was very neat and well tended in total contrast to his neighbors but a fruit tree of some description obscured his view of the terrace.

Moving as quietly as he could he got down from his perch, retrieved his jacket and moved the pedestal another twenty feet down the wall. Here he had not only an excellent view of the terrace and Monique but also he had the added benefit of an overhanging branch from an unpruned tree. It afforded him good concealment.

With his small and compact Zeiss binoculars he zeroed in on Monique and Nini Grapponelli as they enjoyed their champagne together. It was the kind of surveillance he had done countless times over the years but for the first time in his professional life, he felt more of a personal involvement which was a new and somewhat unsettling sensation for him. He told himself that it was from a sense of guilt at putting so inexperienced a person in harms way but deep down he knew that it was more than that. He knew he cared very much for this 'inexperienced' person and he was determined that her safety would come well ahead of the mission.

In the past Phillip's commitment to the mission's success was paramount. Today it was different. His first priority was to protect Monique from a man who was as deadly as he was lecherous. He continued to observe them both drinking and talking when suddenly he saw Macarini appear on the terrace. Phillip tensed slightly, hoping that by bringing Monique to this lair they were not trapping her. Surely, he thought, they could not suspect her of any complicity.

After a brief conversation, that Phillip was unable to hear, the two men walked back into the house leaving Monique alone on the terrace. Phillip had a desire to try and signal Monique to let her know that he was close at hand but his training told him that that was a dangerous idea. It might give Monique a degree of comfort but if seen it would not only compromise the investigation but could put her in even more danger. Just as these thoughts were coursing through his mind he saw Monique get out of her chair and tip toe into the house as well. Phillip tried to will her to stay put but the willing had no effect, as Monique slowly disappeared into the darkness of the house interior. Phillip could only wait and watch from his perch behind the tall wall.

Five minutes elapsed and Phillip's concern increased when suddenly Monique appeared again but this

269

time with Grapponelli in tow. Phillip scrutinized his body language and tried to deduce if everything was still fine between them. Judging by Monique's laughter whatever she had been up to was not discovered.

Phillip continued to watch them but as they began to make preparations to leave, he lowered himself slowly and gently to the ground. He knew even at dusk any sudden movement caught in peripheral vision by Grapponelli or one of his goons could start a hue and cry.

He made his way back through the tangled garden as quickly and quietly as he could so that he could follow them. He hoped, as he threaded his way through the overgrown shrubbery and neglected flower beds, that he wasn't going to loose them in the chaos of Rome's nighttime traffic.

He found his car sitting in the road exactly where he had left it. Out of habit he gave it a quick look underneath before he slipped behind the wheel. He checked the wires under the dash and everything seemed just as he'd left it. He started the engine and waited for the Mercedes to appear from the gates of Grapponelli's house. He looked at the luminous dial of his watch. It was a few seconds short of nine thirty.

By one thirty in the morning Phillip had followed Monique and her Latin lothario from the house to the exclusive restaurant, *Rondi's*, and finally to a night club. Phillip was unable to get authorized access to it, it being a private 'members only' establishment, but Phillip knew well that kitchens, stockrooms and staff entrances were notoriously lax when it came to security. Often the rear doors are propped open either to allow fresh air in or to let the smokers on staff come and go for their quick cigarette breaks.

This club was no different and Phillip was able to simply walk in the back door. He followed the noise of the kitchens and then the applause for an Italian crooner who Phillip surmised was undoubtedly singing about a 'lost love.' It's all they ever seem to sing about, he thought.

He followed a labyrinth of passages past rooms full of cased wine and bottled tomatoes, past staff changing rooms and toilets, until he found himself behind the heavy curtain of a small stage. From the side of the stage and shrouded in darkness he was able to scan the tables in front of the small stage.

He saw no sign of Grapponelli or Monique there. He strained his eyes to see into the dimly lit booths at the back and eventually he was able to make out the two of them sitting with yet another bottle of champagne. Monique appeared to be just barely winning the fight with Grapponelli over possession of her breasts, and Phillip had to fight back the strong urge to teach Grapponelli some manners. Had the blood not been surging through Phillip's veins quite so hard he might have heard the man who crept up very quietly behind him. His first inkling that he was not alone was when he felt the muzzle of a pistol between his shoulder blades. It was a curious security guard who approached Phillip.

"Who are you? What are you doing?" the guard said in Italian.

Phillip of course had no idea what the man had just said but had a fairly good guess and got somewhere near the man's meaning. No-one was supposed to be back there, especially as they appeared to be spying on the club's clientele who expected and demanded complete anonymity. Prying eyes were not welcome or tolerated.

Phillip heard the faint static click as the guard depressed the speaker button on his two way radio,

271

presumably to summon assistance. It was the last conscious act he would perform for several minutes as Phillip spun on his heels like a tightly wound spring uncoiling. With his left arm he knocked the man's .40 caliber Beretta to one side and planted his fist squarely in the man's throat. As his knees buckled and his hands went instinctively to his crushed larynx, he dropped both his radio and his Beretta. Phillip, in one continuous motion, brought his knee up to meet the descending chin of the security guard and rendered him completely unconscious. As the man lay sprawled on his back Phillip picked up the Beretta pistol and the radio and placed them both in his jacket pockets.

He assumed that the man would shortly be found so Phillip decided to make a hasty exit. He retraced his steps to the back door, which was still open. He stepped outside into the dark and litter strewn alley. Two waitresses were having their cigarette break leaning against the wall but seemed so engrossed in their conversation that they paid not the slightest attention to Phillip as he strode past them. Passing a large waste container where several king sized rats were dining on restaurant leftovers he tossed in the radio and the pistol and kept on walking back to his parked car.

Sitting in his car some minutes later he waited once again for Monique to emerge and he fervently hoped she would be able to convince Grapponelli to take her back to the Hotel Clara. The night air was balmy and once his adrenalin rush had subsided Phillip began to stifle a yawn. His sitting position in the small car was cramping his long legs and he was becoming more and more concerned that letting Monique get so close to Grapponelli was a serious lapse in his normally sound judgment. With relief he saw Monique appear at the door with Grapponelli. It was now almost two o' clock in the morning and Monique was nervously playing with her left ear lobe. The gesture was prearranged and meant that she was loosing the battle with Grapponelli and needed rescuing in the near future.

Phillip was relieved and would be happy to oblige. Macarini was close behind his boss who had his arm around Monique's slender waist and appeared more than usually on edge. He surveyed the street several times before he opened the rear door of the Mercedes and solicitously ushered them both into the back seat with some haste. By now several patrons were emerging from the club, all with the same look of concern on their faces. Phillip started his car as the Mercedes peeled out of its parking spot in front of the club leaving a trail of rubber and smoke in its wake. Phillip joined the flow of traffic and followed at a discreet distance just as an ambulance, lights flashing, turned into the street.

Inside the Mercedes Monique suggested a drink at her hotel and Grapponelli readily agreed. He imagined himself putting the final moves on his latest conquest and savored the prospect of screwing this little redhead. The chase was a necessary part but it was the final capture and putting the victim totally under his control that was integral to Grapponelli's enjoyment of the seduction process. He differed from most men in this respect because his final conquest had to be one of complete dominance and subjugation.

His love making was not gentle. He enjoyed violence in all its many forms and rough sex was what he enjoyed most. Rarely, if ever, did the women concerned feel anything but revulsion at his depravities and rarely, if ever, did they voluntarily go back a second time.

Phillip followed Monique several car lengths back and soon he realized, with some relief that they were heading for the Hotel Clara. As Macarini swung the

Mercedes up to the front entrance, Phillip drove straight around to the rear parking lot, the lot reserved for employees and deliveries. He raced through the kitchen entrance and appeared in the dining room much to the surprise of the waiters and the *major domo*. Brushing past the startled head waiter Phillip gave him a brief nod of recognition. He continued out into the lobby area just as Grapponelli and Monique came through the front door.

The most important thing an English gentleman learns in life is when to stop being one. Now, Phillip thought, was one of those times. Phillip lurched towards Monique in his best imitation of a man with too much drink on board.

" Ah-ha. Mish Langer, how lovely to shee you!" He hoped he didn't sound too much like a third rate impersonation of Sean Connery.

"Dr. Fairfax," she replied sweetly, "please let me introduce my friend Signore Nini Grapponelli. Nini, this is my boss, Dr. Fairfax."

"Good to meet you old boy," responded Phillip slapping the diminutive Italian on the back and ignoring his proffered hand.

Phillip stumbled slightly and noticed Macarini taking a step towards him but Grapponelli gestured for him to stay back.

"Whoa, I say, must have had a bit too much of the local vino, eh? Fancy another one with me, Mish Langer?" and without waiting for a reply, he put his arm around her shoulder and propelled her towards the lounge bar.

She gave Grapponelli an apologetic look and went with her 'boss'.

"Good night old chap. Arrivederci and all that. Thanks for looking after my girl here," he said over his shoulder to Grapponelli, whose face was now scarlet with suppressed anger. Grapponelli stood angry and abandoned in the middle of the foyer.

Phillip made no attempt at being cordial nor did he invite Grapponelli to join them. Instead he continued to talk in a loud voice about his imaginary evening to Monique. He kept up the pretence as he called the waiter over and told him to bring a bottle of his best local wine, except he called it *red plonk.*

Grapponelli did walk into the lounge bar however whilst Macarini stood at the entrance and glowered at Phillip. Before Grapponelli could open his mouth to speak to Monique, Phillip jumped in.

"So you're the chap who took Mish Langer out to dinner tonight, eh? S'pposed to have dinner with me, y'know old chap. Bad form, Sir. Damned bad form. Still never mind, you brought her back safe." Phillip was warming to his role of an overbearing, bombastic and slightly inebriated boss. "We have a lot of business to discuss," he continued, so if you don't mind buzzing off we'd better get on with it." He drained the small amount of red wine the waiter had offered as a taste. It was a ritual the waiter thought Phillip incapable of appreciating.

Nini Grapponelli, however, took the opportunity, as Phillip loudly smacked his lips and belched, to tell Monique that he would call her in the morning. He gave Phillip another look of disgust. Phillip merely sat there staring back and grinning very widely.

"Best to run along, eh?" said Phillip, adding more fuel to an already blazing Grapponelli, whose plans for a night of seduction and sex now lay in tatters. Spoiled by an insufferable English idiot.

Ignoring Phillip entirely, Grapponelli said to Monique, "I have to go abroad tomorrow, on business, but I shall call you on my way to the airport. I hope when I

275

return we can pick up where we left off and enjoy another evening together." Glowering at Phillip, he added, "Perhaps we can enjoy our evening without interruptions next time. Good night, Monique. I wish you sweet dreams."

"Thank you, Nini. I had a wonderful evening. I'm sure we'll meet up again."

"*Ciao*, Monique. *A domani*", he said to Monique, and ignored Phillip totally. He turned and strode out of the lounge bar. As he reached the doorway and the waiting Macarini, he turned and looked at Monique. "*A più tardi!*" he said finally.

"Until later!" she replied as he walked out of sight.

"Phew! What a night!" Monique exclaimed as she visibly relaxed and threw herself back against the soft leather padding of the booth seat. Turning to a grinning Phillip she said, "You do a very good impersonation of a drunk, you know."

"Well, I've had quite a bit of practice," he laughed.

"I bet you have," and putting her hand gently on top of his, she added, "thanks for rescuing me. He'd reached the groping stage by the time we got into his car and I didn't know how much longer I could have stood it without slapping him. Trouble is, he'd probably have enjoyed that and thought it was a 'come-on'. God, the man really is a bore." Her green eyes sparkled as she bristled with indignation.

"I'm happy to have been of service," said Phillip with a look of mock chivalry on his face.

He kept it up for about ten seconds before they both burst out laughing. Their mirth was only partly humor; the rest was relief on both their parts that Monique was safe and no longer in danger from the lethal lothario, Nini Grapponelli.

After a short silence when Phillip poured them each a glass of red wine, he turned towards Monique and asked, "Were you able to find out anything from Grapponelli that might pertain to the Leonardo?"

"Nothing concrete, no," she replied, "but I did try to listen to a telephone conversation he had at the beginning of the evening. He went into the house to take it. All I could make out though was that he was talking to someone called Ikar, which is a Russian name. Also that he was bringing a 'surprise' to Pulkovo, which if memory serves me, is the name of the airport in St. Petersburg. But beyond that nothing. I was nearly caught listening at the door by that creep Macarini, but I said I was looking for the bathroom. I don't know if he believed me, but there wasn't much he could do except show me where it was."

"Yes, I did wonder where you'd gone," said Phillip.

"You mean you were watching me?" she sounded slightly incredulous but none the less rather pleased. "I didn't see you. Where were you?"

"You weren't supposed to see me," said Phillip. "That was the whole idea. In fact I was in the garden next door, which thankfully was very overgrown. Good cover, but I had a great view of you sipping your champagne."

"Jealous?"

"No, the company you were keeping wasn't to my liking and I don't like champagne enough to put up with the likes of Grapponelli."

"Come to think if it, neither do I."

They sat silent for a few minutes each thinking about the evening and trying to figure out what, if anything, they'd learned. Monique realized she still had her hand on top of Phillip's and withdrew it. He looked at her and whispered, "It wasn't bothering me, y'know...your hand, I mean." She gently put it back

FORTY

After a four hour flight, Grapponelli and Macarini stepped off Alitalia's Flight AZ540 at five o'clock in the evening local time in St. Petersburg, Russia. Ikar Volkhovsky was there not only to greet Grapponelli but to guide him through the customs hall. It seems his sphere of influence included the customs officers who merely waved the trio through without even a cursory glance at Grapponelli's bags.

Within twenty minutes they were seated in Ikar Volkhovsky's heavily armored Hummer and speeding to the center of St. Petersburg. Macarini sat in front with the driver whilst Grapponelli and Volkhovsky sat in the rear. Volkhovsky's huge body left little room for the slender Italian, so Grapponelli was somewhat relieved when they pulled up in front of the *Corinthia Nevskij Palace Hotel* on *Nevskij Prospekt*. It was an impressive hotel with an ornately carved 19th century classical stone façade. The front, however, was enclosed in glass with lush greenery dominating the lobby and atrium. Being only twenty minutes walk from the Hermitage it was a popular destination for tourists and businessmen alike.

St. Petersburg, formerly known as Leningrad during the Soviet era, was now a major financial center and at one time had been the capital city of Russia. It proudly bore the title of 'World Heritage Site'. The people were friendly and seemed a lot more cheerful than their fellow compatriots further south in Moscow.

This beautiful city on the far north west of Russia was known for its network of canals and the over one hundred bridges that crossed them. To some, it was known as 'the Venice of the North', but to everyone it was known for the famous Winter Palace of the Tsars, which is now the site of the famous Hermitage Museum.

Although Ikar Volkhovsky had his main residence in *Pushken*, a suburb of St. Petersburgh, and very close to the Grand Palace of Catherine the Great, he maintained a suite at the Cornithia Palace Hotel where he could negotiate his many and varied business deals. It was to this suite he now headed with Nini Grapponelli. Grapponelli's small valise, which contained the portrait of *"The Girls in the Red Dress"*, he kept firmly in his grip. Macarini and Volkhovsky's man followed and brought his suitcases which contained nothing more than his clothes and toiletries.

As they entered Volkhovsky's plush suite, the large Russian headed straight for his bar. Opening his refrigerator, he pulled out a bottle of vodka and taking two small glasses from under the counter he marched over to the large sofa. Sitting the glasses on the low table, he poured the thick clear liquid almost to the rim. He handed one to Grapponelli and with a quick toast of *"Na zdarOv'ye*, enjoy" he tossed it down his throat in one.

Grapponelli tried to follow suit but only managed half of his glass. Before speaking, Ikar refilled their glasses and then broached the subject that he'd been dying to bring up since Grapponelli's arrival in St. Petersburg.

"You have the painting, Nini?" he asked in his booming voice, pointing to the leather valise that Grapponelli had lain on the sofa next to him. Grapponelli sat with a firm grip on its handle.

"Of course, Ikar. I have it here and I shall be happy to show it to you, if you like."

Volkhovsky swallowed his second vodka in one gulp again and replied, "Damn right, Nini! I have been waiting all my life to get my hands on something like this.

A Leonardo da Vinci in my collection! Of course I want to see it." Volkhovsky stroked his big black beard and assumed a more serious tone. "However, you know I am a business man as well as an art lover, so I must first know what you are asking for it and secondly, I must have it authenticated."

"I have, of course Ikar, had it authenticated myself, in Rome, by a man who for many years was in charge of the paintings of the *Musei Vaticani*. I'm sure you know that it has one of the finest collections of 15th and 16th century work by the Italian masters. But if you feel happier having your own person inspect it, of course, I shall have no objections. Providing it does not leave my possession for this purpose," he added in order that the ground rules of the transaction were clear to Volkhovsky.

"I do not think that will be a problem, Nini. I have a well respected member from the conservation laboratories of the *State Russian Museum* here in St. Petersburg willing to look at our painting. He assures me it will take a short time only for him to verify its originality. I am aware of its provenance," he raised his bushy eyebrows and fixed Nini Grapponelli with his piercing blue eyes, "but that is of little concern to me. I do, however, expect that to have a bearing on the price you are asking, which is how much?" he added.

"I paid a great deal myself, Ikar," responded Grapponelli. "Perhaps too much considering its recent history. But for such a prize, such a 'once-in-a-lifetime' opportunity, I think the normal rules do not apply." Grapponelli pressed home a perceived advantage. "I have perhaps two or three other business associates who I am sure would agree with my sentiments, and who would love to own such a treasure themselves. But," he paused for effect, "my good friend Ikar was my first and foremost thought and I would let no one come before him."

Nini Grapponelli leaned back on the sofa and crossed his skinny legs, satisfied that he had Ikar well and truly hooked. Now all that remained was to reel him in.

"Very well, Nini, but you still haven't told me how much you are asking." He stopped and poured them each another vodka.

"I do not necessarily want even one *ruble* for the painting, Ikar, my friend. I would be just as pleased to accept merchandise. Perhaps cocaine and maybe a few cigarettes. I think you will find that quite a palatable price."

"It depends, how much cocaine you want, Nini. After all, I have to buy it myself and have all the costs involved in its transportation. So tell me what you are asking and I shall give you my answer."

Nini Grapponelli picked up his glass and took just a small sip this time of the neat vodka. He was not used to such raw drinks and it burned his throat as he swallowed.

He had grappled with the price during his four hour flight from Rome. Too much and Ikar might be put off making such an acquisition. Too low and he was doing himself out of profit. In the end he went with his gut instinct and said, "Ikar, my friend, for you I can accept twenty five million euros which I shall take solely in cocaine and another five million euros in American cigarettes."

Grapponelli scrutinized Ikar Volkhovsky's face. It was unlikely that the Russian would not haggle but he needed to know how much was his usual bluster and how much was genuine inability, or unwillingness, to pay the thirty million euros he'd asked.

The Russian's face was impassive as he stared back at the Italian. He picked up his glass of vodka and drained it in one, all the while fixing Grapponelli with his steady blue eyes. He put his glass back down on the table and refilled it. A small scowl spread across his face.

"Nini, I would not have believed that you could treat me this way. Are we not friends? Good friends! And yet you seek to rob me by asking so much for this painting which, as you well know, I can never allow anyone else to see."

"I honestly doubt, Ikar, that you can show anyone half the paintings in your collection. I'm not robbing you, I assure you. It is a lot of money, I agree, but it is not expensive."

Grapponelli knew by the look on Volkhovsky's face that it was a 'done deal'. He continued to press home his advantage. "It has been estimated that at auction it could fetch over one hundred million euros. Maybe even as much as two hundred million euros. Surely you must see that my price is very reasonable…even in light of its 'recent history'.

Grapponelli took another sip of his vodka. "But as you are my good friend, I will tell you what I shall do for you. I will accept twenty five million euros in cocaine and the cigarettes I shall purchase from you. I cannot possibly be any fairer with you than that."

Once again he sat back on the sofa and watched the big Russian. He would be very pleased with his days work if the Russian accepted his terms.

After a few seconds, the Russian engaged one of his bellowing laughs. The suddenness and severity of it made Grapponelli almost jump out of his seat. The Russian slapped his thigh and laughed again.

282

"Nini, you know my weakness for good paintings. If it is as you say, and my expert verifies this fact, you shall have your cocaine and I shall have my painting. Come, drink up, we must toast this deal and seal the bargain."

Once again Ikar Volkhovsky filled both glasses with vodka and the two men sank the contents in one gulp. The negotiations had been easier than Grapponelli had expected and, as he always did on such occasions, he wondered if he had started too low and dropped too quickly. Had he misjudged the Russian's enthusiasm for this painting and his ability to pay? He may never know, but he consoled himself with the knowledge that he had made a fairly swift profit, more than doubling his original outlay. And he'd make a big profit on the cocaine. He visibly brightened at this prospect and even found the vodka more palatable.

"For various reasons, Nini," the Russian interrupted Grapponelli's thoughts," we shall be taking the painting to my contact, Ivan, at the State Russian Museum laboratories. We will go after eight o'clock when only he will be in the building. Besides, the odd guard or two, who'll probably be drunk by then. It is easier for him to use his equipment there. For twenty five million euros I have to be very sure. The man we are seeing is an acknowledged expert but sadly he has developed a nasty cocaine habit. As I supply his needs, which are considerable, I can be assured of his discretion."

In fact, Ikar Volkhovsky had planned to cut Ivan's next purchase of cocaine with the toxic agent, *Potassium chloride*. This drug will disrupt the electrical impulses essential to heart function and once ingested, along with the cocaine, will kill within one or two minutes. If in the event an autopsy was performed on Ivan's body, it might show a heart attack, which after taking cocaine would not surprise any pathologist. Ikar will then have assured Ivan's silence was permanent and his death will be ruled a result of cocaine abuse. Very neat. Ikar lived in a violent world. He thrived and survived in it only because he was devoid of sentiment and never left loose ends hanging, unless it was by their necks.

By the time Volkhovsky had had two more shots of vodka and had discussed with Grapponelli a mutually agreed plan for delivering the cocaine to Rome, he announced it was time that they left for the laboratories of the State Russian Museum.

The two men rose with Grapponelli still firmly gripping the bag that contained the painting of "*The Girl in the Red Dress*." As they stepped out of the glass enclosed lobby of the Corinthia Hotel an icy blast hit Grapponelli in the face. It appeared winter came much earlier in this part of Russia and Grapponelli was wishing he'd worn warmer clothes. Luckily Volkhovsky's bullet proof Hummer and his driver, accompanied by Macarini, were waiting for them. Grapponelli was thankful that the driver had the heat turned up full blast.

They drove past the Winter Palace and the Summer Gardens, where the Tsars of all the Russias once strolled, and continued on to *Ligovsky Prospect*. Passing the metro station the car turned onto *Inzeneria Street* where the State Russian Museum laboratories were situated. They had only travelled about one and a half kilometers.

The driver pulled past the front of the building and then turned down a dark side street. He stopped by a large metal door that had no handle on the outside. He kept the engine running. A distant clock tower chimed eight o'clock and within seconds the metal door opened a few inches. A bald head with a shock of grey hair above the ears poked out of the gap and peered into the back seat of

284

Volkhovsky's Hummer. Recognizing Ikar Volkhovsky's large frame and face he beckoned him, with hurried gestures, to enter the building. Both men in the back seat quickly exited the car and shot through the now half opened door. It closed with a loud bang that seemed to echo throughout the maze of corridors that greeted them.

Ikar was the first to speak. "Ivan, this is my colleague, Nini from Italy. Nini may I present Dr. Ivan, an expert on medieval paintings."

The two men perfunctorily shook hands without saying a word. Ivan turned and in Russian said, "Please follow me," and Nini and Ikar followed.

After several turns, when Grapponelli was convinced they were back close to where they'd started, Ivan stopped in front of a solid looking wooden door and produced a large bunch of keys from his white lab coat. Opening the door, he silently gestured the two visitors into a largish room that seemed well equipped with tables, lamps and a variety of machines whose functions were not at all obvious to the two visitors.

Ivan flicked several switches on the wall and lights came on along with several of the machines. They hummed and displayed various blinking colored lights as they warmed up for whatever tasks they were to perform. Both Volkhovsky and Grapponelli were amazed by the sheer magnitude of technology that surrounded them, but Volkhovsky's impatience won out over his curiosity.

"Ivan, let's get going with this, shall we? Nini, May I now please see my painting?" His voice was not loud but he still managed to convey his growing annoyance at the lack of progress.

Ivan replied that the various machines would take up to ten minutes to warm up but that he saw no reason why the painting could not receive its first critical exam from the naked eye of the expert.

Nini Grapponelli placed his bag on the top of a clean stainless steel table and gently withdrew the painted panel. Carefully removing the protective covering, he laid it flat on the table. Ikar Volkhovsky pushed his large body forward and picked up the painting. He stood with it at arms length and held it beneath a strong overhead light. A large beam spread across his face as he set his eyes on a real Leonardo da Vinci portrait for the first time in his life. And, but for a minor consideration of twenty five million euros, it was his. His to share with no-one. Ikar Volkhovsky was a happy man.

After a few minutes spent by Volkhovsky in marveling at his new acquisition and Grapponelli wishing he'd had a pee before leaving the hotel, Dr. Ivan said that he was ready to start the examination of the painted panel. Volkhovsky reluctantly handed over the treasure to a seemingly nervous Dr. Ivan. Grapponelli wondered if his nerves were due to being in the presence of someone as menacing and powerful as Ikar Volkhovsky or whether he needed another hit of cocaine.

Ivan looked at the painting, also under a bright light suspended from the tall ceiling and gave Vokhovsky a quizzical look but said nothing. He examined it under a large desk mounted magnifying glass as Volkhovsky hovered over him. At one point, when the proximity of the large Russian began to hamper the efforts of the picture expert, Dr. Ivan spoke up. He suggested that Ikar might be more comfortable in his office where he had a full bottle of vodka. That tipped the scales and the two men were shown into a fairly sparsely furnished but moderately comfortable office with two leather armchairs.

Dr. Ivan placed a bottle of vodka and two glasses in front of them and left to resume his work.

Nini Grapponelli was not happy at being separated from his painting and immediately stood up and watched the nervous Russian through the clear glass window in the door.

Ivan put the panel through various tests, one of which included taking a swab from the very edges and from the center of the painting. The tightly curled cotton swabs were then immersed in a test tube half filled with a clear liquid. Grapponelli had no idea what was being done to his painting but he instinctively trusted that the little Russian knew what he was doing.

Ivan's movements were quick and precise and he seemed to accomplish his tasks with a practiced ease. Grapponelli continued to watch the panel as Ivan placed it into what looked like a photo copier, only three times the size. What came out looked like a long ticker tape only instead of being punched with holes; it had a series of printed numbers. Grapponelli thought how much more technical and sophisticated the Russian's equipment was compared to that of his expert in Rome. None the less he had every confidence that the outcome would be the same. A clean bill of health and Nini Grapponelli would be a great deal richer, or at least his Camarra bosses in Naples would be.

When the tape had finished ejecting itself from the machine, the little Russian spent several minutes looking over the numbers. Once or twice he glanced up and saw Grapponelli fixing him with his beady eyes but his face remained expressionless.

To Grapponelli's surprise, Dr. Ivan repeated the exercise once again, and again the machine spewed out its numbered tape. When it stopped Ivan compared the two tapes side by side. He appeared unsure of what to make of the result. He literally scratched his bald head and stood staring at the painting. After a few minutes he picked up the painting and walked into the office where Ikar sat working his way through the bottle of vodka. Grapponelli stepped aside to let the little man in.

"Ah, Ivan, you're finished at long last." Ikar spoke in Russian.

Replying in his native tongue, he said that he had, but was somewhat confused by the results. "I have dated the poplar panel and it is without question from the 15th century and quite in line with what Leonardo would have used. A minute fleck of paint from the outer edge also registered correctly for 15th century oil and paint pigments but the center of the painting, in effect, the entire portrait area, has given me a different result."

"What the hell do you mean, 'different result'?" boomed Ikar, as he breathed vodka fumes over the frightened Russian.

"I mean, it shows pigments that all show strontium 90. Now at first I thought that this might be evidence of major restoration but the black light showed no obvious retouching and the x-ray showed no other under painting. Sadly, I can only come to the conclusion that the painting has been skillfully faked. Painted no doubt by a superb artist but these machines do not lie. I regret to say that your painting is a complete fake and worth nothing. Except as a very good copy. Even, I might say, an exceptional copy, but a copy none the less."

Ivan took a half step backwards away from Volkhovsky. He was afraid that the news he bore might end in pain. His pain. Volkhovsky was not above killing the messenger of bad news.

Ikar's eyes bore into the little Russian like lasers. Ivan visibly wilted beneath this deadly gaze.

"A fake!" he boomed, "You're honestly telling me this Italian bastard tried to sell me a fucking fake?" His voice grew louder as the impact of this news gradually dawned on him.

Nini Grapponelli stood watching this confrontation not understanding a word of what was being said. But he fully understood that Ikar Volkhovsky was not a happy man. Wisely he chose to stay quiet and hoped that whatever had so upset the big Russian would soon blow over.

Ikar Vokhovsky recovered his composure somewhat after his outburst. He spoke more softly now to the little expert although there was still a menacing edge to his voice.

"You are quite sure, Ivan? No mistake, no doubts?" He even managed a smile.

"None. I even did the test twice to make sure. I can show you the numbers, if you want." He sounded somewhat relieved at Ikar's more composed demeanor.

"No, no, Ivan," he patted him on his shoulder with his huge hand. "I don't think they would mean much to me would they? No, I have complete confidence in you and your machines. If you say it's a fake, then a fake it is."

He took the painting from the little man and looked at it, this time with a different feeling in his heart. Ikar turned to Grapponelli, "Please, Nini, hold onto this magnificent painting so that I can admire it again."

The Italian took the proffered painting and held it in both hands against his chest. Ikar Volkhovsky tilted his head one way and then the other. He adjusted Grapponelli's hold slightly so that the painting was completely level. He stood with one hand cupping his elbow and with his other he stroked his heavy black beard as if in deep contemplation.

Both Dr. Ivan and Grapponelli looked at each other. Somehow Ikar's behavior seemed oddly out of place. Gone was his previous excitement at beholding one of the world's great masterpieces. Instead it had been replaced by a studious and quite frankly out of character appraisal as if he were a professor contemplating a great artistic conundrum.

At last Volkhovsky spoke. "It is, indeed, Nini, a fine painting"

With a speed that stupefied not only Dr. Ivan but also Nini Grapponelli, the big Russian's hand shot out from his chin and with a fist the size of a ham hock he smashed into the fragile antique panel. He added, "Such a shame it's a fucking fake!"

The force of the blow literally lifted the slightly built Italian off his feet. He shot backwards and being unable to get his feet under him in time, he ended up on his backside, clutching in each hand, a half of his painting. He stared slack jawed at Ikar Volkhovsky trying to catch his breath and make sense of what just happened.

Grapponelli's surprise and alarm was two fold. Firstly, at being so violently attacked and secondly to be told that his painting was a fake. All this sudden information flooding into Grapponelli's brain was too much for him to process. He sat on the floor wheezing and holding the two remnants of what he believed was a priceless Leonardo da Vinci painting. He was unable to assemble his thoughts or to make sense of this sudden turn of events.

FORTY-ONE

If the Marquis de Manville's plan had one flaw, it was this. The more expensive the painting, the more scrutiny it will be subjected to by prospective purchasers. Perhaps the Marquis and more specifically, Leila Diab, had not expected Grapponelli to sell on his newly acquired treasure quite so soon, but even if they suspected he might, there was only a slim chance that there would be any comeback on them. They mistakenly assumed no-one would admit to trying to purchase a stolen work of art. This would ultimately be a costly misjudgment on their part.

FORTY-TWO

Phillip and Monique had one last day in Rome where they enjoyed as much as they could of what that venerable city had to offer. Monique, who had spent several months in Rome during her university days, enjoyed being Phillip's tour guide. They not only visited some of the major attractions like the Coliseum but also some of the smaller and lesser known collections of art and antiques. Phillip especially enjoyed their visit to the small but unique *Museo del'Alto Medioevo* in the suburb of Eur.

It is a small archaeological museum specializing in the period from the end of the Roman Empire to the 14th century. It only had a few rooms and two were solely devoted to grave goods, a subject Phillip was surprised to find Monique knew quite a lot about. His special interest was in the large collection of elaborate weapons and armor. For once, Phillip was able to enlighten Monique on the history and development of some of the items on display.

That evening they enjoyed a superb dinner in a romantic setting. A few times the conversation became 'personal' in nature, which slightly unnerved Phillip. Not that he really minded Monique's enquiries into his non-business life, in fact he rather enjoyed her interest, but it was an unaccustomed experience for him and he was surprised at his own openness with her. His usual 'closed book' persona totally melted under the hot gaze of her sparkling green eyes. What made him slightly uncomfortable was his willingness to talk about subjects he'd hardly even thought about in the past few years. He often thought about Isabel and the void she'd left behind but he had never put voice to those feelings with another

woman. All in all he found the whole evening with
Monique totally enjoyable and cathartic. So much so that
when they were walking back to the car after dinner it
seemed quite natural for them to hold hands.

Arriving back at the hotel neither of them really
wanted to end the evening but they had an early departure
in the morning and an appointment with the Marquis de
Manville and with the chameleon, Miss Leila Diab. Phillip
had not yet announced his intentions to either of them. His
visit was going to be a surprise and he hoped that once and
for all he'd be able to end this saga of the 'stolen' Leonardo
da Vinci painting. He was eager to get back to Oxford and
the restoration of his beloved Riley.

FORTY-THREE

Nini Grapponelli had not slept and when he boarded his flight the next morning for Rome, he was totally exhausted. His head throbbed and his sternum still ached from the assault by Volkhovsky. He had spent the previous evening explaining the situation to Ikar Volkhovsky, assuring him consistently that he had no intentions of cheating him.

As Ikar's anger subsided, Grapponelli's rose. Not at Ikar but at the realization that he had been well and truly duped by the fat, bumbling Basson - although he knew him only by an alias - and by that cold bitch, Jasmine.

As soon as Ikar seemed to accept that Grapponelli was also a victim in this debacle, he resolved to forget the incident. He insisted Nini join him in several vodkas to help restore their tempers and their friendship. Reluctantly Grapponelli agreed to the drinking session which, in large part, contributed to his feeling ill that morning. During the flight Grapponelli said very little to Macarini although they were seated side by side.

It was two hours into the flight before Nini Grapponelli had formulated his plan for revenge. Only then did he outline his idea to Macarini who he knew would relish the idea of extracting information from that fat little French weasel.

First, of course, he would need to find out who he was and where he lived. For that he would need Macarini to revisit the hotel Condotti. Maybe, if Grapponelli's luck improved, the French bastard would have at least signed the register with his real name.

Thinking this was the best place to start; Grapponelli leaned over and told Macarini that he was to check out the hotel immediately upon landing in Rome. He told him who he was looking for and that he needed a name and address.

"No need, boss," said Macarini with a wide grin that showed off his array of gold teeth. "When I patted him down that time you met up with him, I lifted his business card."

He waited for a stream of praise from Grapponelli. It didn't come and Macarini's feeling of accomplishment, along with his grin, quickly dissipated.

"Good," was all Grapponelli could muster by way of a reply. "That'll save time."

"He lives, or at least works, in Nice. In France." he added as if Grapponelli had no idea where Nice was.

Macarini continued trying to elicit praise from Grapponelli. "I can't remember his exact address but I have the card at home. I thought it might come in handy one day." He was now going outright for words of flattery for his skill and foresight but as was so often the case with Macarini, he was disappointed.

"Do you remember his name...the one on the card?" asked a somewhat distracted Grapponelli.

"Er, no boss. Not off hand, but I think it started with a 'D' or was it a 'B'? Anyway he is an advocat; that I do remember."

"How do you know it's his card?" asked the small Italian of Macarini. "Maybe it was one someone gave him and it's not his name, address or occupation at all."

The thought had, surprisingly, occurred to Macarini and he was able to reply with some authority, "Because, boss, he had several of the same and all businessmen carry their business cards in the top pockets of their suits. Don't you?"

Grapponelli instinctively felt his top pocket and sure enough, he felt the small lump of five or six of his business cards. He nodded his agreement to Macarini and mumbled something about it having saved him some legwork. At that he closed his eyes and said no more to Macarini until they had landed at Rome.

It was now gone eight o'clock in the evening local time and Grapponelli wanted nothing more than to crawl into his bed.

FORTY-FOUR

The day had started off badly for the Marquis de Manville and had steadily got worse. He had tried in vain to convince Leila Diab to keep some of the money from the sale of the fake painting to Grapponelli. She steadfastly refused so that by the time they sat down to dinner they were openly quarreling.

"You have become seduced by all this easy living. Just look at you, surrounded by all this opulence...all these old paintings and antiques." She gestured vaguely to the walls around her. "Have you forgotten who put you here and why?"

By this time Leila was warming to her theme and her voice rose as she spat out her words of contempt. "It was my uncle and my father that installed you in this castle instead of the rightful son of the Marquis." The Marquis was well aware of this fact and never enjoyed being reminded that he was an utter fake.

She continued her onslaught. "They killed the real one, the real heir, so you could be here in his place. They didn't do it for you!" she screamed.

She fixed the Marquis with her cold dark eyes.

"They did it for the cause. The fight to free our people from those Zionist bastards that stole our lands, '*Insh Allah*', not so you could live in the lap of luxury!"

"I've done my bit!" The Marquis was not going to let her score all the points.

"Your bit! Your bit!" she openly scoffed at his feeble words. "What exactly have you done, this 'bit' you talk of? Have you ever got your hands dirty? Have you ever had to wash the blood off your hands? Have you?

No, you haven't. You've sat here in this old pile of stones
and *entertained!*"

By now Leila's fury had reached fever pitch. She
stood up from the table and leaned in to the Marquis. Her
face, red with fury, was only inches from his.

"If you hadn't looked so much like the Marquis'
son, the real Claude Chapon, you wouldn't have been
chosen for this mission." She allowed the uncomfortable
truth to fully register with the Marquis. "You'd still be
back in Lebanon living in the same squalid, rat infested
hovel like my Uncle Tariq does." Her stare was so
discomforting, so menacing that the Marquis looked away.

"If he'd looked like the son, he'd be here now." She
took his face in her hand and forced him to look at her.

"He'd have been the one to drive the Chapons
around and eventually take the place of the son and heir.
Or my father, if he'd looked more like Claude Chapon,
maybe he'd be alive now and living here. You've done
your 'bit!' I spit on your 'bit'."

Leila swept the glasses of wine, the half touched
plates of food and the solid silver cutlery onto the floor.
Her distain for the Marquis had reached new heights and
she couldn't let it go. She continued her venomous attack.

"You didn't even have the guts to do the killing
yourself. Even that you left to my father and uncle. They
were the ones that pushed the car off the road. They were
the ones that took all the risks and caused the bodies to
burn so that they were unrecognizable, unidentifiable."

For many years she had stored up her feelings and
now they came tumbling out, unchecked.

"Do you imagine they did this so that you could sit
in the lap of luxury? No, they didn't! And you have the
nerve, the unmitigated gall, to tell me, 'you've done your
bit'!" She slammed her fist on the table with such force

298

that the wine bottle fell over and spilled its ruby contents all over highly polished surface.

The Marquis looked at her and realized some of what she'd said was true. If he'd been honest with himself he'd have had to admit that *most* of what she'd said was probably true. But he still bristled at the verbal assault and sought to defend himself.

"You think it's been easy, holed up in this place with just Albert for company? Yes, I've entertained periodically but only so that our glorious cause could benefit, *Mash Allah.*"

He looked away from Leila. He could not bear to see the hatred in her eyes. But he gamely continued, "The people I mix with are not my people. They're not the people I understand or that understand me. I can never have a close friend, a friend I can confide in. A friend I can pour my heart out to. I'm just here to be used by the cause when they have need of me." He paused and using his linen serviette he attempted to mop up some of the red wine.

"I take people in for them. I don't know who or what these people are that I'm hiding. Or what they've done. Or who they've killed! I do it without question." He now looked around for something to put his sodden serviette on. Finding nothing close at hand he merely threw it back down on the table. He realized he didn't care anymore if it stained or not.

He still had Leila's attention so he continued. "I've hidden guns and bomb making equipment. Half the time I'm expecting the stuff to blow up and send me on my way to Allah with a big bang. This is what I do for the cause. It's not glorious and I don't kill people but it's my *bit.*"

Leila looked at him. She realized that he wasn't a warrior and never could be. If those who understood more

299

than she had decided he was useful, was contributing, then who was she to argue. Leila's fury slowly abated whilst the Marquis looked sullen and toyed with his wine soaked serviette. Eventually she spoke and broke the silence.

"Perhaps I was a little harsh. And we shouldn't quarrel." She attempted a smile but the Marquis was staring at his puddle of wine. He was sulking like a rebuked child.

"We have another painting to sell the day after tomorrow, *inch' Allah*, and I shall have to prepare myself for the banker in New York."

She thought that an injection of optimism might bring the Marquis out of his funk. She needed him to continue to play his part so she added, "I think this one will be easier to deal with, unlike that slimy little Italian. Basson said that he seemed very eager to buy and had funds for an immediate purchase."

The Marquis shrugged his shoulders. "I don't know how these bankers get so rich," he said rather petulantly. "They don't make anything, except paperwork. They just shuffle paper around on their desk and somehow it generates millions of dollars for them. It baffles me, it really does," added the Marquis.

"I know it does, but as you're most unlikely to ever become a merchant banker, I shouldn't worry about it. At least they know how to move money around the world so quickly it can't be traced and that's something that's definitely useful. To us, especially."

By now Leila's voice had a note of conciliation about it. She was quite fond of the old man, really, but the fire in her breast ignited by the wrongs she and her family had suffered at the hand of the Israeli state sometimes drove her to become overly passionate. By her own admission she was fanatical for the cause. She never understood why other people, including the Marquis, didn't feel the same way.

Tomorrow was another day and it was going to be a busy one. The captain of the fishing vessel that had so neatly dispatched the nosy Interpol agent, Daniel Masilionis, was due to arrive and collect cases of AK47 rifles with ammunition , several hundred kilos of Semtex explosives, some mining grade dynamite and some detonators. It had been stored in secret rooms in the castle. The Marquis had once again done his *bit*.

The captain was someone Leila could trust. She had used him numerous times over the years and he had never let her down. He had smuggled people in and out of Lebanon, Syria and Gaza. He had transported arms, ammunition and bomb making equipment and had even killed on her orders, and not once had there been a problem.

Tomorrow he would pick up the arms and ammunition and ship them to the operatives in the field so that they could more readily carry on the fight. Leila felt, as she headed upstairs to her room, that everything was falling into place very neatly. Her plans were coming together nicely and the fight against Israel and its' allies in the west was beginning to make headway.

Despite her disagreement with the Marquis earlier, she readied herself for bed with satisfaction bordering on contentment. She prayed to Allah for continued strength and guidance in the days to come, especially on her journey to New York. She also asked Allah to smite her enemies and soon fell into a sound sleep.

FORTY-FIVE

The following morning Phillip and Monique checked out of the Hotel Clara and ordered a taxi to the airport. In another part of Rome, and at the same hour, Nini Grapponelli, Macarini and two other henchmen in his employ, the Albi brothers, headed to Rome's Termini train station. They were to catch a train to San Remo on Italy's northwest coast, very close to the border with France.

At San Remo they planned to rent a car and drive the fifty kilometers to Nice, where they hoped to find Basson. A few discreet questions and they then hoped to locate the blond woman who had sold Grapponelli the fake painting.

The 'discreet questions,' however, were very likely to be accompanied by some violence from Macarini and friends. Grapponelli had found in the past this invariably speeded up the information gathering process.

As Phillip and Monique boarded their plane to Marseilles, Grapponelli and company were settling themselves down on the fast train to San Remo, changing in Genoa. By the time Grapponelli was signing the paperwork for the hiring of an E class Mercedes Benz saloon car at *Magesto Car Hire* just a few hundred yards from San Remo town center, Phillip and Monique were approaching the main gates of the Chateau de Manville in Baux de Provence.

Much against her impetuous will, Monique had agreed to wait in their hire car in the Marquis' driveway. Phillip had decided that the interview with the Marquis and Miss Leila Diab - her red VW was also parked in the drive - was better conducted by him alone.

Whilst he felt no physical threat from either the Marquis or Miss Diab, he doubted the interview would be pleasant or the outcome harmonious. It was seldom, if ever, that anyone accused of being a thief, a cheat and a liar, took the accusation philosophically. Phillip also expected some hostility from Leila Diab as he suspected she either knew about, or was complicit, in Daniel's sudden and mysterious disappearance.

Phillip rang the door bell beside the large oak doors of the Chateau. It took several minutes before he could hear the shuffling footsteps of Albert Guion and the bolts to the door being drawn back. As the door opened and Albert peered at the visitor, there seemed to be no sign of recognition from him.

"*Oui, Monsieur?*"

"*Bonjour,*" said Phillip, "It's Monsieur Guion, isn't it? We spoke a short while ago. How is your head wound?"

"How can I help you, Monsieur?" He ignored Phillip's enquiry regarding his health.

"I need to speak with Monsieur le Marquis and Miss Diab. I see her car is here."

Albert did not reply but opened the door a little wider and stepped aside allowing Phillip to enter the castle. Phillip continued into the great hall and waited while Albert re-bolted the front door. When he'd finished, he walked towards Phillip and without looking at him he said, "Wait here"

He loped along through the huge main hall and headed to what Phillip remembered as the doorway to the Marquis' study. Albert knocked and entered. It was a good four or five minutes before Albert re-emerged and ambled towards Phillip.

303

"He will be out soon."

And with that he turned away and headed towards his kitchen.

Phillip could faintly make out an aroma of cooking garlic and rosemary wafting from below stairs. It made him feel hungry and, he reasoned, that his arrival had probably interrupted his lunch preparations which might account, in part, for Albert's sour demeanor. Although, in reality, he suspected that Albert's attitude was always sullen.

After ten minutes of waiting, Phillip was finding himself bored with looking at the Marquis' long dead ancestral portraits that covered the walls, and wondered if the Marquis was indulging in some childish gamesmanship. It was probable that the Marquis had guessed at the reason for Phillip's sudden arrival. Had he thought Phillip was bringing good news about his 'lost treasure' he felt sure an innocent Marquis would have been much more eager to greet him. As it was, Phillip could only guess at what was keeping the Marquis' attention. Was Leila Diab with him? Were they working out a plausible story? But surely they would have had a story ready before this!

Phillip was still mulling over the various scenarios when the Marquis appeared from his study. In the dim light of the castle interior illuminated only by two large standing candelabra, the Marquis appeared even swarthier than Phillip had remembered him. He had a slight build but his movements somehow seemed awkward. Gone was the smooth and graceful dandy that he had previously encountered. He seemed ill at ease and not at all pleased to see Phillip standing in his great hall.

"You've found my painting I take it, otherwise why would be so rude as to appear in my home without notice and at the precise time I take my luncheon?"

Although the smoothness had gone from the Marquis' manner, his arrogance was still very much intact.

"In a manner of speaking, yes, I have found your painting," responded Phillip.

If the Marquis had no time for pleasantries and courteous behavior, Phillip was happy to dispense with them too.

"What do you mean, 'in a manner of speaking'? Have you found it or haven't you?"

"I seriously doubt it was ever lost in the first place."

Phillip stared at the Marquis as the later did a barely passable impersonation of outrage and indignation. It was not totally convincing.

"I'll even go further, Marquis, and suggest its 'loss' was part of an elaborate scheme to defraud;" continued Phillip, pressing home his initial advantage, "Quite how, I'm not totally sure, but I strongly suspect that you were hoping to sell faked copies. How close is that, Monsieur le Marquis?"

By now Phillip was standing within five feet of the Marquis and the difference in their height and build became more marked. Surprisingly, it didn't seem to intimidate the Marquis, whose face broke out in a thin smile. He clapped his hands together slowly as he looked at Phillip with the kind of expression that was normally reserved for a backward child who had eventually figured out a simple puzzle.

"Very good, Monsieur Fairfax," said the Marquis in mock appreciation. "It's true I still have the original and it is true that the quite brilliant copies that I plan to sell are the reason for my *'having the original stolen'*!"

Phillip was surprised at the Marquis' candor and self implication in a crime.

"I take it your first victim was Signore Grapponelli in Rome?"

"So, you have been busy, Monsieur Fairfax. Bravo! But I fear it will do you no good."

"Oh, I think the police and Interpol will be very interested in your little scheme. Not to mention Nini Grapponelli, a man, I suggest not best pleased at being played for a fool."

"Quite possibly, but they'll never hear about it."

Phillip was, quite frankly, a little baffled by the Marquis' *'laissez-faire'* attitude until he heard a familiar sound behind him. It was the sound of an AK47 semi-automatic assault rifle being cocked with the sliding bolt. Phillip new a bullet had been chambered and it was ready to fire. He had no doubt that it was aimed directly at his back.

The Marquis moved away smiling.

"You see Monsieur Fairfax, no-one will find out about our ingenious plan because you will not be able to tell them. My friends behind you will see to that. Now if you'll excuse me, I think my luncheon will soon be ready. *Au revoir* Monsieur Fairfax. Or more precisely, goodbye."

Phillip's first thought was for Monique who was sitting outside in the car. He hoped to God, they hadn't seen her. Maybe if she heard gunfire she'd have the sense to drive off and alert the police.

Phillip slowly turned around to see who and what he was dealing with. Two men, both Middle Eastern in appearance, stood with their rifles pointed at Phillip. The taller of the two men, who wore a blue peaked cap, was the captain of the boat that had killed Daniel Masilionis, although Phillip had no idea of this connection. The other man, shorter and missing most of his teeth looked equally as menacing, as he too, brandished an AK47. His evil grin

was a little lopsided and his left cheek seemed swollen.
This was courtesy of Daniel's parting blow but again, this
fact was unknown to Phillip. The captain was the first to
speak.

"On your knees, *zubb*."

Phillip thought he would test the man's resolve and
replied, "Go fuck yourself!"

It was a dangerous gambit but Phillip desperately
wanted to know the caliber of the man he was dealing with.
He also wanted the man to get closer. He might then have
an opportunity to strike out and dispossess him of his rifle.
But the captain was wiley and stood his ground. Phillip
tried again to make him loose his temper. He knew a man
in a temper was not as effective in a fight as one with a cool
head

"You want me on my knees? So come and make
me, you filthy piece of dog shit."

"Oh, I don't think that will be necessary, but you
will pay for your insolence."

At that precise moment Leila Diab appeared from
an alcove beneath the stairs, as if she had been hiding there
all the time. She hadn't because the alcove concealed yet
another entrance beneath the castle.

It seemed that the castle had been modeled on a
large rabbit warren. Phillip's face dropped when he saw
Leila Diab, for no other reason than she had a .45 caliber
pistol pointing at Monique's head.

Monique's mouth was covered with a wide piece of
tape and her hands were tightly tied in front of her with the
same white surgical tape. As she was unable to speak, her
eyes spoke for her. She seemed to be saying, "I'm sorry."
Phillip smiled reassuringly at her and spoke directly to
Leila Diab.

"She's got nothing to do with this. Why don't you let her go and I'll cooperate with you?"

Phillip knew even as he spoke that it was a futile attempt as well as grossly unoriginal.

"You'll cooperate anyway," said Leila, "of that I am quite certain. In fact, you have no choice. As for *your new woman* here, she will suffer the same fate as you."

Phillip was slightly taken aback by her use of the phrase 'your new woman', and could not immediately figure out what she meant by that. Maybe, he thought, it was because he had not brought her on his previous visit to the castle, but the reference seemed more personal than that.

"I think now you will kneel, *kufr* scum," interjected the captain.

Before complying, Phillip spoke to Monique.

"Don't worry. You'll be O.K. I promise. These characters know they can't get away with this. They're all mouth and no trousers." Again he smiled reassuringly and winked at her before he knelt on the floor.

"Put your hands behind your head."

Slowly Phillip complied as the captain nodded at the toothless one, who rested his rifle against the arm of an elaborately carved and gilded chair. He approached Phillip cautiously in a wide arc and came up behind him. Even standing, he wasn't much taller than the kneeling Phillip and it would have been easy for Phillip to have overpowered him but the thought of the .45 pointed at Monique's head was sufficient for him to practice some restraint.

There would, no doubt, be another opportunity when Monique wasn't in such immediate danger. And when that time came, Phillip was determined to make all of them pay dearly.

308

"Your pet monkey stinks," he said looking at the captain, as the toothless one approached Phillip's back. The captain merely smiled but the insult infuriated 'the monkey' who took a wild swing at Phillip's head. Phillip knew it was coming and he leaned back into his assailant's chest as the round house punch flew over the top of his head. Phillip's right arm shot upwards at the same time and his fist connected with 'the monkey's' swollen jaw. The man let out a scream of agony and began kicking Phillip's back.

Phillip knew a reprisal was inevitable but he enjoyed scoring the point. The resulting blows were worth the satisfaction he got from inflicting pain on the toothless tyrant. He also wanted to register with the captain and Leila that he was not going down without a fight.

"Enough, Ahmed," barked the captain as the toothless sailor pounded Phillip's back with his feet. "You'll have plenty of time to get your own back later. Maybe I'll even reward you by letting you have his woman for an hour or two." His face contorted in an evil smile. "But for now just tie up the *eben ahbe*."

Out of breath and now with a throbbing face, he cautiously snapped steel manacles on Phillip's wrists behind his back. As a parting gesture, and dangerously in defiance of his captain, he gave Phillip one last kick in his kidney before he went back to retrieve his rifle.

Phillip ached after this encounter but nothing on his face or in his demeanor suggested that he felt the slightest twinge of pain.

"When you have finished loading," said Leila towards the captain, "you can take these two with you. You know what you need to do. No trace, remember, and far away from here. Meanwhile, lock them securely in one of the old cells below until you've finished loading the truck."

Phillip realized that whatever the Marquis and Leila were up to, it went well beyond the sale of a couple of faked paintings. His mind shot back to what he'd seen on his first nocturnal visit to the castle. Another piece of the puzzle fell into place.

FORTY-SIX

Andre Basson was sitting behind his wooden desk surrounded by legal papers and folders. He was due in court the following day to defend the young son of a wealthy local banker who was accused of raping a neighbor's fourteen year old child. Since working as advocat for the Marquis de Manville his clientele had come from the higher echelons of society but their crimes were just as heinous and distasteful. In some cases they thought their wealth bought them rights over those less fortunate; rights to merely take what they wanted. Sometimes Basson hated his job.

It was lunch time and his secretary and receptionist, Cecile, had left for her customary rendezvous with her friends at a small restaurant close to the shore. Andre Basson sat alone in his office and occasionally took a large bite of baguette and cheese. As usual he wore the bread crumbs down his shirt front and tie. Occasionally he'd pop an olive into his mouth from the bowl that sat on his desk. His oily fingers he absentmindedly wiped on his trouser legs as he continued to prepare his notes for the hearing.

He hardly noticed when the outer office door opened. He assumed, in his subconscious that it was Cecile coming back from lunch. It wasn't. When the door to his office opened, Basson did not look up from his paperwork. Instead he asked Cecile for a large black coffee. Irritated when the door slammed loudly, he was about to scold Cecile when he noticed three men standing in the doorway.

"How may I help......." he started to say when realization suddenly dawned.

It was the man from Rome and two other men, big men, he did not know. He knew by the look on their faces

that this was not a social visit. But how did they find him?
He had checked into the hotel under a false name. He'd
paid with cash, and he had made no phone calls. The
question pre-occupied Basson when in truth he should have
been more concerned with his immediate predicament
rather than with the past.

"I am not a happy man, Monsieur Basson."
Grapponelli scowled at the little man behind the large desk.
"Yes, I know your real name. You and your partner in
crime have caused me much inconvenience and more than
a little embarrassment. So, now" and Nini Grapponelli
leaned on Basson's desk, looking him straight in his eyes,
"I want you to tell me who and where this so-called
Jasmine lives."

Basson's mouth gaped as his brain tried to come to
terms with what was going on.

"She has some of my money, Monsieur Basson, and
I am thinking that I would like it back."

"But *Signore*, I know nothing; nothing of the money
or about the painting. I was merely a 'courier,'…..a mere
messenger. Please, I implore you; I know nothing about
this Jasmine. Nothing, believe me."

"Really, Monsieur Basson? I am sorry to hear this
but my friend here,' he gestured towards Macarini, "is quite
pleased. You see he enjoys, how shall I put it? He enjoys
'jogging' people's memories and it's remarkable what
results he gets."

"But Signore Grapponelli, you must believe me, I
am just a small cog and I have been told nothing!"

Basson was playing for time. Slowly he began to
withdraw the center drawer of his desk. Inside he kept a
small .38 caliber revolver. He'd never actually fired it and
couldn't remember why or when he'd acquired it, but today
he was glad it was there. He just hoped he could put his

hands on it before Grapponelli started getting rough. With a swiftness that even surprised Basson himself, he pulled open the drawer, found the gun almost immediately, and stood up pointing it at Grapponelli.

"Oh, Monsieur Basson, what a stupid thing to do! Now I'm afraid I will not be able to control Mac here." He gestured with his thumb in the direction of Macarini. "He strongly resents having guns pointed at him."

"I don't care. I don't care," stammered a frightened Basson. "I don't know anything and I want you to leave - now - or I'll call the police."

The gun shook visibly as he pointed it, moving it in a small arc as the three men gradually moved further away from each other.

"But Monsieur Basson what have we done to warrant a call to the police? Surely we have only come to you to seek information?"

"Yes, well, I've told you, I don't know anything, so get out...all of you."

Not only was his gun shaking but now his voice shook, too. In a split second a four inch knife flashed through the air from the direction of Macarini. It embedded itself into Basson's right forearm and he lost all grip in his hand. The small revolver clattered onto the desk and bounced onto the floor.

Basson stood wide eyed staring at the inch of blade and black metal handle that protruded from his arm. Blood soaked into his jacket in an ever expanding circle. Basson watched mesmerized as the blood began to drip from his wrist onto his desk top. He also became aware of another warm, wet sensation as he realized he had lost control of his bladder. His pee ran freely down his leg and there was nothing he could do to stop it.

Macarini stepped over to Basson who was rooted to the spot still staring at his arm with the protruding knife. Macarini grabbed the handle and pulled out the knife. Grabbing hold of the damaged arm by the wrist, he forced Basson's hand flat onto the desk and with one swift movement he drove the blade through the back of Basson's hand, pinning it firmly to the desk.

Basson screamed with agony. His other hand that had been trying to staunch the bleeding from his right arm desperately fumbled with the knife handle. Macarini once again grabbed Basson, this time by the other wrist. Producing a second knife, he hammered that through the back of Basson's left hand. Now both hands were painfully and securely nailed to the desk.

The screams that emanated from Basson reverberated throughout the room. He pleaded between sobs and howls of pain to be let free. The pain he was experiencing was excruciating, unlike anything he'd ever felt before in his life. He tried to lift one hand off the desk, but the pain intensified a hundred fold and he gave up immediately.

Nini Grapponelli, being careful not to let his silk tie fall into the puddle of blood that pooled on the desk top, leaned a little closer to Basson. He asked once more who Jasmine was and where could she be found. Basson sobbed with pain as he looked into Grapponelli's emotionless eyes. He pleaded to be released from his agony but he received no quarter from Grapponelli who merely repeated the question. At the same time, Macarini placed the blade of a large hunting knife against Basson's right thumb. He bore down just enough to break the skin and when Basson did not immediately respond to the question, he exerted strong downward pressure. The sharp blade severed the entire thumb, right through the bone. Basson was very close to passing out and the smell of defecation filled the area around him. Grapponelli asked one more time for the information he needed.

Basson, who by now had become almost numb to the pain as his body fought the shock to its system, mumbled. Grapponelli leaned even closer to Basson to catch his breathless, whispered words.

"Leila. She's called Leila….Diab", his faint words were slurred slightly as white foam and saliva ran down his chin.

"And where can I find her?" Grapponelli snapped.

Slowly Basson formed the words Grapponelli needed to hear. "Château….at the Château…Manville….Leila."

Fredo, the third thug in Grapponelli's party had been waiting outside the office and had been sitting in the receptionist's chair. Cecile returned from an enjoyable lunch with her friends, and looked somewhat annoyed to see a stranger lounging in her seat with his feet on her desk. He was picking at his teeth with a straightened paper clip.

"Monsieur, that is my desk. Would you please get up? Are you waiting to see Monsieur Basson*?"* She naturally spoke in French and being someone who abhorred bad manners she pushed his feet off her desk.

Fredo did not understand the words but her incensed look and her petulant action conveyed her point quite clearly. He rose slowly from the swivel chair and held it out for her, as a '*maître-d'* might do at an exclusive restaurant. He smiled and bowed slightly as she placed her handbag under the desk and sat in her chair. She noticed it was still warm from Fredo's bum and found that singularly unappealing.

No sooner had she taken her seat than Fredo grabbed a full handful of her shoulder length hair and jerked her upright. She yelped in pain and surprise. Her head arched back as he pulled hard and propelled her towards Andre Basson's office. Opening the door with his free hand, he pushed the squealing girl into the room. Her head was still tilted towards the ceiling as she fought to minimize the pain in her scalp.

At first she didn't see Basson, as he lay crucified on his desktop. She was aware of other people in the office but it wasn't until she heard Basson's moans of pain did she realize the gravity of the situation she found herself in.

"Look what I got, Boss," beamed Fredo, "a little bird who doesn't like other people putting their feet on her desk!"

Grapponelli gave a nod to Fredo's brother, Bruno, who until now had been surplus to requirements. Bruno knew what was expected of him. He withdrew a Beretta pistol from beneath his brown leather jacket and screwed a long silencer onto the barrel. He stepped up to the girl who was now sobbing uncontrollably and placed the gun to her temple. He squeezed the trigger. It made a small *'phut'* sound. The exit wound on the opposite side of her head spurted a short jet of blood and she crumpled to the floor, dead.

"Time, I think, for us to leave," said Grapponelli. "Bruno…Fredo! Bring the car to the back door. Mac, do what you have to do. We've got what we came for and need to get moving."

Macarini nodded to Grapponelli and stepped behind Basson who was slumped, barely conscious, in his chair. His two hands still firmly nailed to the desk. Basson's head, two inches above the spreading pool of dark blood, tried to follow Macarini, but the effort was too great. He stared through closing eyes, straight ahead instead and looked at a grinning Grapponelli who came in and out of focus on a random cycle.

Basson offered little resistance as Macarini pulled his head back. With one quick slash of his razor sharp hunting knife he sliced Basson's throat almost to the bone. His severed carotid artery pumped an arc of blood into the air in a regular beat for several seconds until it slowed and stopped as Basson's heart shut down for good.

As a final barbarous act, Macarini used the blade on his knife and fished inside Basson's gaping throat wound. Finding the tongue, he pulled it from inside his mouth and flipped it out through the wound. It hung in a gory mess and laid over Basson's blood soaked shirt.

This method of leaving a victim has popularly been known as a 'Columbian necktie' but its origins were far from South America. It was a gruesome tradition embraced by the Napoli Camorra long before the Columbian drug cartels made it their calling card. It was a tradition Macarini liked.

Retrieving his two knives from Basson's limp hands, he wiped the blades on the dead man's jacket and put them into their leather sheaths. He would clean them thoroughly later.

FORTY-SEVEN

The Captain, Leila and the toothless sailor, Ahmed, were joined in the Great Hall by two other men, equally as unkempt but a great deal larger and stronger looking than 'the monkey' Ahmed. They, too, were armed with AK47 assault rifles which they had slung over their shoulders. The Captain addressed them in Arabic.

"Is the truck in position?"

"Yes, my captain," replied the tallest of the men. "We can start to load up whenever you and Allah command it."

"Good, but first I need you to go with Miss Diab and escort these two meddlesome *kufrs* to the cells beneath the castle. She will show you the way. Watch the tall one; he thinks he's a tough guy. He punched Ahmed in his broken jaw. If he tries anything like that with you, just shoot the bastard."

The two newer arrivals nodded and turning to Phillip, they grinned in anticipation of causing him a great deal of pain in the near future. Ahmed was told to follow, too, and sit outside the cell door until they were ready to leave.

Both Phillip and Monique were patted down by the taller man. He lingered as he allowed his hands to investigate Monique's blouse. Cupping her breasts in his rough hands, he looked again at Phillip grinning, his tongue all the while flicking like a snake's. The gesture was meant to incite Phillip's fury so that they had an excuse to beat him, but Phillip remained passive, his face a study of indifference.

Monique, however, did not react quite so nonchalantly to the liberties being taken. In a sudden burst of energy she brought her knee up into the man's groin producing a cry of agony as he cupped his testicles in both hands. Bending at the waist in a vain attempt to ease the sickening pain that coursed through his body, he staggered backwards trying to catch his breath.

Within a couple of minutes, he had recovered enough to step up to Monique and deliver a hard slap across her face. Leila Diab reinforced the rebuke by digging the barrel of her .45 caliber pistol hard into the base of Monique's skull; a warning 'do that again and your brains will cover the castle walls.' Like Phillip she felt satisfied that she had made her point and took the stinging slap to her face as the price she had to pay.

Phillip smiled at her, acknowledging her feisty attitude and said,

"Nice one, Monique but don't give them any more excuses. Next time it might be a bullet."

"Listen to lover-boy," said Leila between gritted teeth. "Next time, bitch, it *will* be a bullet and nothing would give me more pleasure than to bury *another one of his women.*"

The words, at first, did not fully register with Phillip. If she meant what she'd just said, was she the person who'd murdered Isabel? The idea just did not compute. Phillip stared at her looking for some explanation. Some reason that he could comprehend.

And why? What possible reason could she have to do such a thing? Even if Isabel's death was a mistake and it was meant to be him, it still made no sense. His head reeled with this new knowledge and he hardly even noticed as the tall sailor carefully patted all parts of his body checking for hidden weapons. Phillip's mouth was dry as he stared fixedly at Leila Diab. She looked back at him and eventually spoke.

"So, have you figured it out, eh Mr. Fairfax? Or as you English say, 'has the penny dropped yet?"

"But why? What do you mean by saying that?" Phillip's voice was hoarse and a little above a whisper. "What could you possibly know about Isabel? Why on earth would you do something like that to Isabel – or to me, for that mater?" Phillip was visibly shaken.

Seeking to make some sense of what had just been said Phillip continued to verbally bombard Leila Diab. "Our paths didn't even cross until recently. I'd never met you before. I've never even set eyes on you before I came to this place. Why in God's name are you saying this?"

"I'll tell you why, Mister Fairfax. I took from you something you'd taken from me. Quite simple really. You kill my lover. I kill yours."

"That's simply not possible! I have only killed soldiers, never civilians. Isabel was a civilian, dammit." Phillip struggled to understand what he was hearing. Struggled to make sense of Leila Diab's admission.

"I admit I was in the Falklands War, and I was in Northern Ireland, but even terrorists are soldiers - of a sort. The Irish Republican Army were terrorists but we treated them as if they were enemy *soldiers*, at least. But what the hell has this got to do with you? You're not IRA for God's sake, and you're not Argentinean. I don't exactly know what you are but you're sure as hell not IRA. So, what's the connection?"

It still made absolutely no sense to Phillip. She had to have made a mistake. Either then or now.

"It was in Gibraltar, Mr. Fairfax. Gibraltar 1988. March 6th, to be precise." said Leila, matter-of-factly.

"What about it? They were IRA…." Phillip stopped and after a few second's thought continued,

"….you mean Danny McCann or Sean Savage was your lover?"

"No, not them, nor the woman, Myraid, but the fourth one, Malcolm. The man they left guarding the car by the Spanish border. You were the one that found and killed him. You were the bastard that shot him through the face and I swore from that day, I'd make you pay, *inch Allah*."

As she spewed out her venom she dug the muzzle of her pistol hard into Monique's neck. "Yes, killing your wife was my revenge and killing that baby she was carrying was a bonus. And now I have you, too. Revenge, Mr. Fairfax, is very, very sweet. Very satisfying."

"What in God's name were you doing with Malcolm O'Brian? He was hard core IRA and whatever rag tag outfit you're with hasn't got anything in common with the Irish."

Phillip still struggled with this new information but any doubts that he had had she was telling the truth were evaporating.

"You're pure religious *jihadi*, maniac murderers in the name of Allah." Phillip was now enraged.

He shouted. "You're all afraid to think for yourselves. You're afraid of co-existence. You're blinded by your dogmatic faith. You are nothing but a bunch of murdering, xenophobic zealots."

"No. We're freedom fighters," she protested. "I don't owe you any explanations but as you are soon to die yourself, I will tell you. We met in a training camp in Syria. We had a lot of Irish come through there. And *Bader Meinhoff* and the *Red Brigade*. They all got trained by me and others like me. We understood their struggle against the corrupt governments of the West, the Jew lovers."

Leila Diab's belief in her cause was unshakable.

"But you could never have married him! He was staunch Catholic and I'm bloody sure your bunch wouldn't have allowed it either."

"What we had was good, and you took it away! You stole him from me." Leila Diab's dark eyes burned in hatred as she stared at Phillip. "The British killed my parents and you killed my one true love. And soon I will have you and your whore killed too to even the score."

Phillip had so many thoughts rushing through his head he could hardly think straight. He relived, again, the horror of that day when he saw Isabel's destroyed body. He thought back to the warm afternoon on 6th March 1988.

He and an active service squad of SAS took out three IRA suspects who were reported to have planted a 500 lb. car bomb near the British Governor's residence. It was on the small British Dependency of Gibraltar, an isthmus on the border with southern Spain. He even recalled the name, '*Operation Flavius*.'

Certainly he remembered shooting Malcolm O'Brien in the face. It wasn't something he'd ever forget. The SAS thought that they had only three suspects but something seemed out of place to Phillip who was leading the operation. Although everybody started running when the shooting started, one man could be seen walking away with a backpack over his shoulder. It seemed odd to Phillip at the time that the man was walking, unconcerned about what was going on around him.

When the man swung his backpack in front of him and thrust his hand inside, Phillip challenged him. The man spun around and simultaneously pulled his hand out of the bag. Phillip fired before it was halfway out and took the man's face off with two head shots.

Afterwards it was discovered that whilst the first three were unarmed, Malcolm O'Brien had not only two pistols in his bag but also a remote trigger for the bomb. It had been a *justified* shooting. A righteous killing, if such a thing ever existed.

He stared back at Leila Diab. He had dreamt of the day he would find the person who had murdered his wife and child, and now he had. But this was not how he had imagined it. In his dreams they had been at *his* mercy. Now that the day had come, he found himself at a distinct disadvantage. He was at the mercy of a fanatical killer and a rag-tag group of Arab terrorists. Added to that he had the burden of protecting Monique, a task he was failing at miserably.

"Take them downstairs and lock them up," ordered Leila. "We've more important things to attend to than argue with this piece of filth."

The sailors led Phillip and Monique away down a long flight of stone stairs and along several narrow passages. All Phillip could think about was how much he needed to escape.

He knew once Leila Diab had left the castle, the chances of finding her again was slim, and he desperately wanted...desperately needed...to bring closure to that gruesome chapter of his life. Besides, he also knew that whatever plans Leila had for him and Monique, the end goal was obviously their deaths.

His death he might be philosophical about but not Monique's. He had brought her into this situation and it was up to him to take her out of it.

After a few minutes they came to a series of three small cells. Each had a solid oak door with iron studs and huge black iron strap hinges. Inset was a small opening barely large enough to pass through a cup of water or a hunk of bread. It, too, was iron grilled. The 'monkey' produced a large key which he gripped with his whole fist. The two larger sailors kept their rifles trained on the captives.

Opening a door with some effort, Ahmed motioned Phillip and Monique inside, hitting Phillip on the side of his head with his fist as he passed.

The rusty hinges screamed as they grated on the large iron pivots that were hammered into the rock walls. It smelled musty inside and the walls and corners were festooned with spider webs. It was a room that had not been used for decades. It was lit by one very small window hole no more than six by twelve inches. In contrast to the darkness everywhere, one rectangular shaft of light from the sunny day outside sliced the room in two.

Vestiges of old straw lay strewn on the rough floor and mice could be heard scuttling into their little burrows in the rock walls. Like the first room Phillip had investigated on his clandestine nocturnal visit to the chateau, this cell, too, seemed to be hewn out of the solid limestone rock that the buildings above sat upon. It offered very little hope of an escape. As Phillip's eyes grew accustomed to the darkness, the door closed noisily behind them and they could hear the old key turning painfully in the lock.

As the sound of footsteps and Arabic chatter receded, Monique tore the tape off her mouth with her taped hands. However, getting the surgical tape off her wrists wasn't proving to be so easy.

Doing a passable imitation of Laurel and Hardy, she turned to Phillip and said, "Well, this is another fine mess you've gotten us into!"

"Yeah," said Phillip, "you're right, there." But he could not manage a smile.

"Any ideas?' she asked as she struggled to free her wrists from the tape that bound them.

"Try to find a bit of stone sticking out of the wall and rub the tape against that. It should fray pretty easily. If you carry on like that you'll just end up with sore wrists."

Without a word Monique set about running her hands over the walls to find some protruding rock.

"Christ, this place is covered in spider webs. Do you mind spiders?"

"No, not really," said Phillip and added, "I think they're the least of our worries at the moment."

Presently Phillip heard a scrapping sound as Monique worked on her ties, and soon she announced that she was free.

"Good! Now you can help me get out of these cuffs. Come around and undo my belt."

"Why, Mr. Fairfax, I do declare!" she mocked in Scarlet O'Hara fashion.

"Quite a one for the voices today, aren't we Miss Langer? You'll find when you've taken my belt off that it unfolds and inside a little pouch are some lock picks, but I'm going to need your help." They both kept their voices deliberately hushed.

She did as she was asked and had soon located the picks.

"What do I do with them?" she asked.

"I'll stand in the shaft of light so you can see." He moved out of the shadowed area of the cell, allowing the light to illuminate his back and his cuffed hands.

"OK. Find the pick with a forty five degree angle at the tip. It's about the thickness of a large paper clip."

"Found it," she said after a few seconds."

"Good. Now find a small round hole which should be on the top flat area of the cuff and insert the angled pick into the hole. Not all the way. Just about half way in."

"Now what do I do?" asked Monique with a furrowed look of concentration on her brow.

"I need you to turn the pick in a clockwise direction and feel for a lever."

Monique did this several times and although she felt the odd piece of resistance at the end of the pick, the cuffs remained firmly in place.

"Keep going," whispered Phillip in encouragement. "When you feel something, don't be afraid to apply a bit of pressure; the pick won't break."

As soon at Phillip had given this little tip to Monique she felt what she assumed was a lever. She applied pressure and within seconds the right hand cuff became loose.

"Great job," whispered Phillip slipping his hand out of the steel manacle. "If I can have the pick, I'll take the other one off."

This he accomplished in about four seconds. Looking at the cuffs he said quietly,

"They're Smith and Wesson M100's. I'll keep them. Never know if they might come in handy later." He tucked the open cuffs into the back of his trousers and then gently pulled Monique into the shaded area of the cell.

"I don't know if that little goon is outside or not. He was told to keep an eye on us I think, so I'm assuming he's out there somewhere. I'm going to look through that small window up there and see if I can figure out exactly where we are." His voice was barely audible.

Phillip reached up and grabbing the ledge, he pulled himself up to the window hole. The bright light of the sunny afternoon made him screw up his eyes but when he became accustomed to the light he saw a familiar site. They were approximately forty feet or so beneath the main castle on the side that dropped steeply down to the village of Baux de Provence about two hundred and fifty feet below them.

The rock face on that side was steep and only an experienced climber could make it up or down. Phillip remembered looking at it from the garden when he and Daniel Masilionis had first tried to find a probable entry point into the castle.

He dismissed it then and he dismissed it now as a viable way out of their predicament. Not that he, or even the slender Monique, could get through the small aperture that served as their window.

Lowering himself gently to the ground he told Monique in hushed tones that their only way out was through the door in front of them. Examining his lock picks, he chose the heaviest and strongest one he had. The lock was obviously old and probably had a simple locking mechanism but he knew it was pretty rusty and that would make it hard to move the levers.

"Monique, look around on the floor, on your hands and knees if you have to, and see if there's any piece of metal, an old nail or something, lying around. I think I'm going to need something stronger than my little picks."

As Monique started searching, Phillip refolded his belt and put it back on.

"What are we going to do if we can't get out of here?" she asked Phillip as if, for the first time, she realized they were in deep, deep trouble.

"Well, in the worst case scenario we'll just have to wait until they come to get us. We'll have to act quickly when an opportunity presents itself, but don't worry. I got you into this predicament and I'll get you out. Promise."

"Yes, Phillip, I believe you will, but don't worry about me. I'm tougher than I look."

"I do worry about you - and I believe you about being tough. I saw what you did to the guy upstairs." He smiled at the recollection of the man bent double in great pain but Monique was too intent on her search for metal that she didn't notice.

While Monique continued her search, Phillip examined the lock but could see virtually nothing in the dark. He did, however, hear the sounds of their jailer snoring a few feet away along the corridor. Far enough away, Phillip thought, that if they did get out of the door, he'd have time to react. Phillip realized that somehow they needed to get him to the door.

"There's nothing here, Phillip," whispered Monique, "I can't find anything except mouse turds and a couple of old bits of wood."

"Let's try the walls. There might be something hammered in to hang onions or whatever on. I'm pretty sure this used to be a storeroom."

Phillip joined in the search on the opposite side of the cell. They both searched thoroughly and in silence for a couple of minutes before Monique whispered.

"Hey, Phillip, I think I've got something. It's high up but you'll be able to reach it o.k."

Phillip stepped over to where Monique stood on tip-toe and followed her arm up to the metal peg that protruded from the wall. The contact with her bare arm brought an intimate feeling that was only heightened by their current predicament. When Phillip reached the peg he placed his hand over hers and for a brief second they stood like that.

"It'll be OK., Monique, I promise. We'll get out of here….somehow."

Phillip let go of Monique's hand and grabbing the protruding piece of metal he pulled down hard on it. It moved, but only infinitesimally.

"Can you get it out, do you think?" asked Monique nervously as she watched Phillip pulling down on the piece of metal with all his weight.

"Yes, maybe, but it's well and truly embedded in the rock. If I put too much pressure on it, it might snap off."

He continued to wiggle it upwards, downwards, and side to side, all the while trying to pull it out of the rock wall. It took fifteen minutes of this manipulation and the sweat began to bead on his forehead. His armpits and back became wet with the exertion but he kept going.

After another ten minutes he felt it give a little more and then suddenly the piece pulled straight out of the wall as if it had suddenly given up the struggle to stay implanted.

Phillip stared at the almost foot long piece of iron and realized that his hands were sore and bleeding, but it made an awesome looking weapon. It was square and had a lip at one end, presumably to stop a wooden shelf from sliding off. At about the six inch mark it began to taper and ended in a point so sharp he felt it would pop a balloon. The shank was rusty and not very smooth but Phillip was delighted that they had at least one solid weapon.

"I think this will come in very handy. Great job finding it. Any luck finding a nail or anything to try in the lock?"

"No, nothing at all. I've been looking and I think I've covered every square inch of this place and I haven't found one piece of metal. How in hell are we going to get out, Phillip?"

Phillip began to detect a note of desperation creeping into her voice. He couldn't blame her, he felt it too. Monique's voice betrayed her mounting fear, and Phillip attempted to reassure her by putting his arm around her shoulder.

"I have an idea but it involves a bit of acting on your part. It will be just as bad, if not worse, than with Grapponelli but you won't have to keep it up very long. We need to get that grubby little Arab to put his face to the window in the door, and the only thing that I think will bring him close is you. Can you cope with it?"

"Yes, but I don't know exactly what you want me to do."

"Entice him, but how you do it, I'll leave up to you. I wouldn't have the foggiest notion how to go about it. I need him to be pressing his face against the cutout in the door. Can you do it?"

"Well, I'll give it a bloody good try."

The fire was back in her voice as she prepared herself for 'center stage.' Phillip flattened himself against the wall by the door and extended his right arm to gauge the exact distance to the center of the door's cutout window. In his fist he held the metal spike which he now held resting against his breast bone. When the time came to strike it would be one fast arcing backhand that hopefully would find its target. He would only get this one chance.

"Ready when you are," whispered Phillip. Monique composed herself and cleared her throat.

"Ahmed! Oh, Ahmed!" she sang softly. "Please, I need to go to the bathroom. Can you let me out, Ahmed?"

"Piss in the corner," shouted Ahmed. "I'm not interested in your problems."

"I have got something that does interest you, though Ahmed! I'll take my blouse off if you'll just let me out for a minute or two…"

"I'm not opening the fucking door, so shut up."

"I thought you liked my breasts, Ahmed,"

"Sure, I like your tits. I like all tits, but I'm still not opening up the fucking door."

Phillip was pleased to notice that Ahmed's voice seemed to be getting closer as Monique kept up her unpleasant role of seductress. Suddenly Ahmed was outside the door but standing back from it by a good two feet as far as Monique could tell. She kept up her talk with renewed enthusiasm.

"See, Ahmed, I'm undoing my blouse. Can you see me? As I'm sure you noticed earlier, I'm not wearing anything underneath. Get closer Ahmed. Come and see my breasts. Maybe if you want, I'll let you touch them. You'd like to wouldn't you, Ahmed?"

"I'm not opening the door, but yes, I want to see you naked," and then almost as if he'd spotted a trap, he added, "Where's that ass that's with you?"

"Shhhh Ahmed, he's sleeping in the corner. Don't wake him up. This is just for you, Ahmed. You're such a strong man, the way you kicked him after he hit you, I knew then you were the stronger man."

Ahmed had never before been flattered by a pretty woman and his reaction to it would have been painful and pityingly embarrassing in anyone else. But to Ahmed it was a long overdue acknowledgement of his true worth. He beamed and showed an irregular set of diseased gums interspersed with the occasional tooth, as he pressed his face up to the window to better see the woman who was so attracted by his manliness.

330

Slowly Monique began to unbutton her blouse. She did it slowly and provocatively and swayed her hips to and fro as she did it. Ahmed took in the sight of her slow, revealing undress and licked his lips as she finally reached the last button. She slowly shrugged one shoulder and then the other out of her blouse and let it fall.

At that very moment, Phillip unleashed his backhand with astonishing swiftness and drove the long iron spike through the gap in the door and into Ahmed's forehead. The sound was like an egg being dropped onto a tiled floor magnified fifty times.

Phillip held onto the spike as Ahmed kicked a couple of times in involuntary spasm and then he felt Ahmed's dead weight hanging on the end of his iron dagger. He could hold him no longer. As the spike tilted downwards, Ahmed's head fell off it and made a sucking sound like Jell-O being emptied out of a mould.

"That little shit got exactly what he deserved, but I'm sorry you had to see it," said Phillip. He had complete empathy for someone who was witnessing their first killing.

Monique just stood there staring at the hole in the door where Ahmed had been standing only a second or two before.

She had no feelings other than ones of contempt for Ahmed and his murderous friends but his brutal killing in front of her very eyes made her feel sick to her stomach. She turned away and retched.

Phillip put his arm around her to comfort her but she shrugged it off. He left her to her own thoughts for a couple of minutes and then made her get back to the task in hand, namely getting out of the cell that imprisoned them.

Phillip began examining the door. He noticed that there was about a two inch gap at the top and it stood about an inch off the floor. It swung on two pivots like large iron 'L's hammered horizontally into the rock wall. He tried to lift the door by the central cross member that ran the whole width of the oak door. It was extremely heavy but it moved slightly. He tried again and lifted it a little higher this time, but there was no way he was going to be able to lift it off the iron pivots. They were just too high, and there wasn't enough clearance at the top.

By now Monique had recovered enough to see what Phillip was attempting.

"Can I help? What do you want me to do?" she asked, buttoning up her blouse.

"How big did you say those bits of wood were? The ones you said were on the floor," he replied somewhat breathlessly.

"They're only about a foot long and, oh, I don't know, about as thick as my arm. They looked like they were for a boiler or something. Not really big enough for use in a regular fireplace."

"See if you can find them. If I can lift this door up, maybe we can wedge them underneath," said Phillip as a plan began to formulate in his mind.

Monique began feeling around in the dark again for the small logs and soon found them. She brought the smaller of the two over to Phillip who examined it quickly.

"It seems to be solid enough. Now if I can lift this door up enough for you to slide it underneath we might be in business."

Phillip braced himself for the lift. He faced the door and took a firm grip on the wide cross brace, his legs placed about a foot apart.

"OK. Ready when you are," said Phillip.

"OK, too. The log's ready to slide underneath," replied Monique from her squatting position on the floor.

Phillip lifted with every ounce of strength he could muster. He grunted with the exertion as Monique tried to slide the log beneath the door.

"It's too bloody thick! Can you get it any higher?"

She shoved with all her might but couldn't get the piece of wood in the narrow space. Phillip heaved but couldn't get it even another millimeter higher. He let it drop and the metal hinges complained loudly.

"Shit!" He kicked the door in frustration.

"How about the other piece; is it any smaller?" he enquired.

"No. If anything, it's thicker," she replied the worry showing in her voice again.

"O.K. then, we'll just have to make this one a bit smaller." Phillip's practical side took over. He took the metal spike he'd used to dispatch Ahmed and drove it into the side of the log. It stuck in about a quarter of an inch.

"This wood is hard. Probably oak or ash but if I can get a slice off, we'll be able to jam it under the door," and with that Phillip picked up the log and pounded the spike onto the stone floor. After four or five hard hits the spike split a slender tapering slice off the log and clattered onto the floor. He retrieved his spike and tucked it into his belt.

"Handy little tool, this. Like a mediaeval Swiss Army knife," he joked trying to recapture a light mood

Feeling around for the log, he then handed it to Monique and said, "Once more into the breach, dear friend; once more!"

They each took up their positions again.

"Ready?" asked Phillip

"Ready!" said Monique, and once again Phillip heaved the heavy oak door upwards.

This time the log slid in easily and Monique rammed it in until it would go no further.

"I think that's as far as it's going to go," said Monique as she dusted her hands together and stood up. Phillip was relieved to let the door go and happy that it stayed in its lifted position.

"Now what?" she asked.

"Now," answered Phillip, "I'm going to see if I can get my arm under the door and find Ahmed. If I can pull him close enough I might be able to get his key, always providing he's got it on him. I'm hoping he didn't hang it on a nail or let one of the others take it with them."

Phillip lay down on his stomach on the stone floor which was cool and felt good after all his exertions. He pushed his arm under the door as far as it would go which was just below his elbow. With his finger tips extended, he could just feel Ahmed's clothing, but was unable to grab hold of anything.

"I can feel him. He's only about eighteen inches away from the door, but I can't grab hold of anything. My arm's too thick," he said with frustration.

"Let me have a go. My arm's a lot thinner," responded Monique as she lay down on her stomach next to Phillip.

She pushed her arm under the door almost up to her shoulder and felt Ahmed's leg. She recoiled at this first touch of a still warm dead body, but screwing up her courage, she tried again and was able to grab a fistful of trousers. She tugged hard and succeeded in pulling his leg closer to the door.

Phillip now was able to get a good hold on the limp body and he felt around for Ahmed's belt. When he found it, he felt for the key that might be tucked inside. Nothing! He started to roll the body over until it hit the door and running his finger tips down Ahmed's right leg, he felt the outline of a large key in his pocket.

"I think I've found it, Monique! It's in his pocket. See if you can hold him in this position while I fish it out."

Monique grabbed hold of Ahmed's clothing and pulled it towards her. The body's angle and dead weight wanted to roll it back, but with determination she held on. At last Phillip was able to get the key out of the dead man's pocket and dragged it beneath the door.

He held it up in triumph and turning to Monique as they both lay on the floor, he said,

"And that's how you get out of a locked prison cell!"

"Thank God! Let's get out of here before the others come back and find Ahmed's body."

"You'll get no argument from me, but we'll have to let the door down first. I'll lift again if you can pull out the log."

And with that he braced himself for another lift. The log slid out quickly and Phillip let the door down with another resounding crash as the iron hinges hit the pivots. He immediately put the key into the old lock and turned it. It was stiff but he heard the lock disengage. Phillip leaned against the heavy door and pushed it open, rolling Ahmed along with it. He cautiously peered around the door but saw no-one. Listening for a second or two, he was satisfied no-one was coming down the corridor.

"OK. Let's get out of here," he whispered to Monique, and taking hold of her hand, he led her out of the cell, stepping over the Arab's body and the pool of dark blood that was seeping onto the stone floor.

Once out in the dark corridor, Phillip examined Ahmed's body. He retrieved a knife with a sharp six inch blade and a spare magazine for an AK47 rifle. He tucked both items in his belt. They walked cautiously along the dark corridor and almost immediately tripped over

Ahmed's rifle which had been propped against the wall. It fell with a loud clatter but Phillip doubted anyone heard it. They were quite a way underground, but all the same he stopped and listened for the sound of approaching footsteps. Picking up the rifle, he checked the magazine. It was fully loaded. Now he felt happier that he could deal with the terrorists in terms they understood. It had been a long time since he'd held an assault rifle in his hands but it felt good to have one now. Feeling their way, Phillip and Monique continued along the dark corridor looking for a way to the outside.

FORTY-EIGHT

Nini Grapponelli, Macarini and the two other henchmen, the brothers Bruno and Fredo Albi, drove away from Nice and headed west towards the Chateau de Manville. They arrived in the small town at about four thirty in the afternoon. The sky was dark and heavy with rain. The clouds had gathered over the coast and had drifted inland making this part of France uncharacteristically somber.

Grapponelli instructed Macarini to drive up the winding road towards the castle perched on the summit. A little ways before they reached the entrance to the castle there was a cutout in the road and Grapponelli ordered Macarini to pull over and park the Mercedes.

The two men in the back seat exited quietly and opened the trunk of the car. Inside were two large canvas bags. They unzipped one and withdrew two Polish made PM98 submachine guns; a sort of cross between an Uzi and an AK-MP5., three Beretta M96 .40 caliber pistols and one M4 carbine. The second bag contained fully loaded magazines for each gun. Fredo and Bruno each put a Beretta pistol in their pocket and passed the third one to Nini Grapponelli. Macarini had his assortment of knives but also grabbed the M4 carbine and two spare magazines.

No-one had, at this point, spoken. It was a scenario they had gone through many times before, although Grapponelli had made his wishes known on the fast drive down from Nice. Everyone in the Chateau was to die and the painting – the real painting – was to be found. Nini Grapponelli thought of it as his property. He had paid handsomely for it. It would probably be necessary, however, for Macarini to use a few of his persuasion techniques to locate it. But after all, that was his specialty.

The four men hugged the rock face on the castle side of the road and slowly walked up towards the front gates. The larger of the two thugs, Bruno, took the 'point' position with Macarini close behind. Grapponelli was next in line, with Bruno's brother, Fredo, taking up the rear.

After a good five minutes uphill slog they came to a section of stone wall about forty feet from the main gates. The point man stopped and with an agility unusual in a large man, he climbed up the rock wall and slipped over the top into the Chateau gardens. The other three waited. Seven minutes later they spotted the 'point' man by the large pillars that anchored the huge iron front gates. Keeping in a low crouch, he ran back to where the other three Italians were waiting.

In hushed tones, Bruno explained to the others that they might encounter some opposition. There was a truck parked in the drive, supposedly from a Marseilles catering company with someone asleep in the cab. It was parked very close to the front door. Also three other vehicles, all empty. They decided that the safest route into the Chateau grounds was over the wall.

Bruno again lithely scaled the eight foot wall and laying flat on his stomach atop it, he held out his hand to help Macarini and Grapponelli. Fredo he left to his own devices and with an agility that seemed to run in the Albi family, he too was up and over on the other side in a matter of seconds. Grapponelli and Macarini stayed in the shadow of a large shrub whilst the brothers Albi were sent to find a suitable point of entry into the Chateau.

Ten minutes and they were back. Bruno explained that he had found a rear door which would be the best way in, so the four set off in single file, keeping low and close to the old stonework of the castle building. As they were nearing the door, Bruno held up his hand.

A man with a rifle, an AK47, slung over his shoulder sat on a low stone wall smoking a cheroot. Luckily for the Italians, his back was toward them. Silently, Macarini stepped forward and without making a sound, he approached the broad back of the man smoking. In one deft move he grabbed the man's hair with his left hand and with his right, he sliced the bared throat. A muted gurgle was the only sound as Macarini held the almost severed head and let the body slip to the ground. One down. It was a start, but no-one knew how many more were in the castle. Macarini wiped the blade of his knife on the dead man's shirt as Bruno and Fredo headed to the back door.

Turning the large iron handle, they opened the door and stepped inside the small hallway. On the left, steps led down to the kitchens. Cooking smells and the crashing of pots and pans announced that someone was down there engaged in their culinary labors.

The four Italians stood still and listened for sounds of approaching feet. There was none. Grapponelli decided their best hope for finding Leila Diab and the Marquis lay in the main rooms of the castle. It was a dangerous undertaking to go wandering around not knowing who or what lay behind each door but Grapponelli was in no mood to be put off. His quest of finding his painting and punishing Leila Diab was uppermost in his mind. The prospect of causing Leila great pain and suffering he found most appealing. He very much looked forward to their meeting.

In a well rehearsed routine the Albi brothers approached each door, stood and listened and then opened the door quickly. The entry, although quiet, was swift and anyone inside the room would have had little time to react. At the third door Bruno heard talking coming from within. They were outside the Marquis' study and Bruno whispered to Grapponelli that he heard a male and a female voice inside. Perhaps now Nini Grapponelli would get the answers he was looking for.

As they entered the study there were not as quiet as they had been before. The sudden intrusion made the Marquis spill his coffee whilst Leila Diab shot up from her seat and grabbed her black briefcase which she attempted to hide by the side of the desk. It was to no avail. Grapponelli had seen it. Her instincts were right but her reactions too slow. She backed away from the desk as Fredo leveled his Polish made sub machine gun at her. Bruno covered the Marquis with his. It was Nini Grapponelli that spoke first.

"I hardly recognized you, Miss Diab, or do you still prefer me to call you 'Jasmine'?"

The Marquis, who up until this point had no idea who the intruders were, shot a glance at Leila who kept her eyes focused on the sub machine gun and the man holding it.

Grapponelli continued, "Your disguise, as alluring as it was, was hardly going to stop me from finding you. Especially, when you employ someone as totally inept as the *late* Monsieur Basson. Oh! Did I forget to tell you? He went the same way you will both be going, just as soon as you've handed over my painting and…" Grapponelli paused for emphasis, "the return of my original investment, just as an acknowledgement that you underestimated me."

"Fuck you, grease ball!" spat Leila Diab but without taking her eyes off Fredo and his gun.

"I expected something along those lines from you, but I'm afraid your bravado will soon be broken and you *will* show me respect." Grapponelli's grin grew with his confidence. Finding Basson and Leila had not been as difficult a job as he had imagined it might be.

"I am happy to die if it is Allah's will. I do not fear you or your little faggot friends here. You will get nothing from me!" She literally spat in contempt although her phlegm fell well short of its intended target, Grapponelli's face.

"Ah! Somehow I am not surprised at your boldness, Miss Diab."

Grapponelli felt totally in charge and was now beginning to enjoy himself. He sat down in a large leather chair and nonchalantly withdrew a cigarette from his gold case and lit it.

He continued, ".....but I suspect our friend, the Marquis here, is less brave. Shall we test my theory?"

The Marquis who had said nothing until this point, mostly because his vocal chords were inoperable through fear, gained a little strength from seeing his god-daughter's defiance and added, "I, too, shall be happy to go to my grave knowing I do Allah's will."

His words were bold but they lacked any conviction. Grapponelli saw this and turned to Macarini.

"Shall we see, Mac, whose will is stronger? Mine or Allah's?" he said, and Macarini took up the challenge.

Pulling a knife from its sheath, he threw it with lightening speed and it embedded itself into the Marquis' chest. The Marquis gasped in horror as he looked at the handle sticking out of his sternum. Fear filled his whole being but it was his face that registered the pain first; his voice, second. He screamed. It was a high pitched scream and anyone outside the door hearing it might have mistaken it for Leila's voice.

"Still ready to die for Allah, Monsieur le Marquis?" There was derision in Grapponelli's voice.

"*Eben ahté*," screamed Leila as the Marquis tried to staunch the flow of blood from his wound. He felt faint and fell back into his well padded chair behind the desk.

Macarini stepped forward and took hold of the knife handle that protruded from the Marquis' chest. He twisted the blade in the wound and what was previously excruciating pain became unbearable. An electrifying scream from the Marquis ended in a whimper as the Marquis passed out.

"I suggest Miss Diab that you tell me where I can find my painting which I suspect may be in your black briefcase. For that, I believe, I shall need the combination."

Grapponelli nodded to Bruno to pass the case, which he did. It seemed no longer necessary to keep his gun trained on the Marquis so Bruno now stood facing the study door, his sub machine gun ready to shoot anyone who entered. Grapponelli placed the briefcase on the leather topped desk and turned to Leila.

"I'm waiting, Miss Diab! The number, if you please." Grapponelli's sarcasm was tinged with viciousness.

"*Kis Amuk!*" was the reply Grapponelli received, although he had no idea what it meant. Nor did he care much. But it was the vilest Arabic oath Leila could think of.

He sighed. It was going to be a long and tedious process after all but he knew before he'd finished with Miss Diab, she'd give him anything he asked for.

FORTY-NINE

Phillip and Monique retraced the steps they'd taken earlier when they'd been escorted down to the cell. The passage came out under the main staircase of the chateau, the place where Leila Diab had earlier emerged with a bound and gagged Monique.

Another shorter passage went off at a 90° angle and Monique whispered to Phillip that this was how she had been brought into the castle. This short passageway ended in a stout oak door that was no more than five feet tall that led out onto the gravel driveway.

However from the main driveway it was obscured by a low wall and several large shrubs. The problem, however, with using this to get away from the castle was that it emerged directly in front of the parked truck by the side of which three men, including the Captain, stood smoking cheroots. They had finished loading the 'catering van' with the rifles, explosives and boxes of detonators and hand grenades that had been stashed in the underground room Phillip had discovered on his first visit.

Phillip considered their options and decided that the most sensible route out was through the kitchen, into the pantry and then down the long steep flight of stairs. They would eventually emerge onto the footpath that would take Monique down to the village of Baux. His main problems, however, were twofold. First, they had to cross the Great Hall and secondly, they had to get into the pantry without being seen by Albert, or anyone else for that matter. Phillip decided it was worth the risk.

Holding Monique by the hand he led her quickly and quietly across the Persian carpeted floor of the Great Hall. The Great Hall was lit by two large floor standing candelabra in ornate black ironwork. On each were over a dozen fat candles that emanated a soft glow that threw long shadow up the stone walls. In more pleasant circumstances the subdued light would be calming but on this dark afternoon it just made the room eerie. A small flame flickered in the fireplace but did little to light up their surroundings.

Phillip and Monique kept to the shadows and close to the tall smooth stone walls. A light could be seen under the door of the Marquis' study. As they got a little closer, Phillip heard conversation from within followed by a loud shriek. They froze but no-one emerged from the room and no-one from outside came rushing in. The thick walls of the chateau had kept the noise contained.

Phillip held the AK47 in readiness as they made their way past the library and ever closer to the short flight of stone stairs that led down to the kitchen. They stopped outside and listened. There was no sound coming from the kitchen. Hopefully that meant Albert was occupied elsewhere in the castle.

Still holding his newly acquired rifle at the ready, Phillip slipped through the doorway and swept the kitchen with the barrel of his AK 47. Apart from a skillet on the stove top that was obviously full of shallots judging by the aroma, all was quiet.

Phillip beckoned to Monique and together they slipped into the pantry and gently closed the door. Within seconds Phillip had located the latch and he gently swung the whole door, complete with laden shelves, into the dark passage. Leaving it open for his return, the two of them went as quickly as they could down the steep stone stairs.

"How in God's name did you know about the door in the pantry and this passage?" questioned Monique, in a

345

coarse whisper, as the two continued to race quickly and quietly down the dark steps.

"Something I stumbled across last time I was here. I was doing a bit of poking around after Albert had mysteriously disappeared from the foot path only to re-appear inside the castle a few minutes later," said Phillip. "I think the place must be full of secret passages like this."

In just a few short minutes they'd passed the locked door that Phillip had once looked in. It now stood empty with the door wide open. Within a couple of minutes they arrived at the end of the stairway and into the small chamber that led to the outside and safety. Phillip opened the stone door as he had done once before and felt a strong breeze waft in the damp air and scents from the hillside.

"This is where we part company," said Phillip as he cupped Monique's chin in his hand.

"I want you to make your way down to the village. It's about two and a half miles and I want you to be very careful. Don't twist your ankle on the loose rocks. When you get there, call the police and explain what's going on up here. When you've done that, call Sir Robert at home and fill him in too."

"But Phillip, aren't you coming with me? Please come with me" she begged.

"I have some unfinished business in the castle. You'll be fine now and I need you to do this for me." He bent down and kissed her gently on the lips. "Now go on and be careful."

"You be careful, Phillip. I couldn't bear it if anything happened to you."

"This is something I have to do, Monique, but I promise I won't take any unnecessary risks."

"Promise?"

"Scout's honor! Now please go."

Immediately Phillip turned back into the dark passageway to climb back into the castle. Monique watched him go and wondered if she'd ever see him again. Tears welled in her eyes before she could stop them.

FIFTY

"Miss Diab, we can do this the easy way or the Macarini way, but do know this, you will, absolutely and without any doubt, give me what I ask for. Do I make myself clear?

"I understand what you're saying, you prick, but you won't get anything out of me. You can kill me, you can even kill the Marquis for I care, but I'll never give you the combination to my case. Oh, and if you don't put in the correct number first time you try to open it, the case will destroy anything inside." She was lying but it seemed plausible. She was desperately trying to buy some time.

"Same thing goes if you try to force it open. So you see, you little greasy 'meatball,' you don't hold all the cards."

Leila thrust her chin forward in defiance while Nini Grapponelli weighed his options. Coming to a conclusion, he withdrew his .40 caliber Beretta from his pocket and re-attached the silencer. Aiming it low, he fired once. The bullet missed its intended target and embedded itself into the lower book shelves that lined the walls. His second shot, that followed almost immediately, found the spot he'd been aiming at.

Leila Diab's kneecap shattered and sent her flying backwards. Unable to keep any balance, she fell hard on her back as she clutched at her disintegrated patella. Bone and flesh protruded through her fingers from the bloody mess that had once been an integral part of a flawless pair of legs. Leila Diab cried out as the pain shot through her whole body. It was so intense and all pervasive that it was difficult for her to tell if she had been shot elsewhere too.

"*Vaffanculo pote,*" yelled Grapponelli at the prone and crying Leila Diab. "Unless you want to be a total cripple, I suggest now is a good time to give me the fucking combination. I'm running out of patience, *puttana*"

Perhaps in his anger and impatience, Grapponelli had forgotten Bruno's earlier warning that there might be an unknown number of other people in and around the chateau. His use of the Beretta, whilst not nearly as loud as one without the attachment, could still be enough to alert the smoking sailors outside. Phillip, too, thought he heard the muffled shot as he appeared once again in the pantry.

The three sailors, led by the captain, walked back into the Great Hall. They had not heard the shot but it was time for them to get moving. They still had to unload the truck in Marseilles and stow it safely on the boat.

A stranger's voice could be heard screaming from the direction of the Marquis' study. The captain gestured to one of his sailors and in Arabic, told him to knock on the Marquis' door and tell them we are ready leave. The captain needed to know if he was expected to take the two prisoners below in the cell with him now.

From inside the study he heard Leila Diab swearing at someone but his knowledge of English was not sufficient for him to understand. Perhaps, he thought, she was chewing out the old Marquis again.

In an act of sheer nosiness he thought he would investigate. Holding his AK47 in one hand, he turned the knob of the study door and stepped inside. Bruno was waiting and a short burst from his sub-machine gun sent the inquisitive sailor flying backwards, his feet not touching the ground until he'd traveled almost three full yards. His hand automatically squeezed the trigger of his rifle as he flew through the air. He emptied half the magazine into the

349

ornate ceiling of the Marquis' study and the smooth domed ceiling of the Great Hall.

The Captain and the one remaining sailor dived behind the tall backed sofa and winged armchair but did not return fire. They knew that whoever else was in that room so was the Marquis and the revered Miss Diab. Bruno kicked the door shut again and stood in readiness for another attack.

Phillip heard the blast of gunfire too just as he was standing in the pantry. He gently pulled the door closed and stood silently in the semi darkness, listening. He heard nothing more for at least thirty seconds and decided to take a cautious look into the kitchen. As he peered around the door post, Albert stood there staring at him. Phillip swung his rifle around and leveled it at Albert's chest. The two men stood for a second or two and looked at each other.

Had he been one of the sailors, Phillip would not have hesitated in pulling the trigger, but Albert he felt, was probably an innocent victim caught up in something he didn't understand. Phillip lowered the muzzle of his rifle and spoke.

"Albert, I suggest you leave here now. This is not a good place to be. Take yourself down to the village. The police will be coming here soon and I expect there will be a lot of shooting. Go Albert, please."

"Monsieur, I thank you for not shooting me, but I cannot leave. There are bad people here and they have loaded the truck outside with many guns and explosives that the Marquis was hiding for them. We must stop them, Monsieur; they will do bad things with these guns." Albert's face had the look of a pleading child and he held his hands out in supplication. "Help me, Monsieur, to stop them!"

This was an unexpected turn of events. Phillip had expected to leave the police to deal with the Arabs and their arsenal of weapons. What he wanted was a little one-on-one chat with Leila Diab. In fact, he didn't really care if they chatted or not. He merely wanted to put a bullet between her dark soulless eyes. He could not afford the time to go chasing Arab terrorists when his wife's killer was liable to slip through his fingers.

"Albert, where is Miss Diab and the Marquis? Are they in the study?"
"Yes, I believe, but a little while ago when you and the other lady were running through the hall, I was listening from the cupboard in the next room. It's only a thin piece of wood that separates the two rooms there, and I heard another man talking. He was not French and I didn't recognize the voice, Monsieur, but I think bad things are happening there, too."

Phillip didn't know whether to be more surprised at discovering that Albert had seen him and Monique sneaking through the Great Hall or that Albert had appeared to take on another persona. Even his thick Provençal accent seemed less pronounced.

"Albert," said Phillip, "I heard gun fire just now. Where did it come from?"

"I think, Monsieur, the Marquis' study."

"OK Albert. I am going to go outside. If you're not going to go to the village then do something for me. Get me a bottle of brandy or something that will burn well and a rag. Soak the rag and stuff the neck of the bottle with the rag."

Albert said nothing but just nodded.

"If you want to help, somehow get to the front of the Chateau, light the rag and throw the flaming bottle into the back of the truck. But make sure the bottle breaks."

"I understand, Monsieur. A Molotov cocktail."

"*Precisament* ! A Molotov cocktail."

Phillip ran up the few stone kitchen steps but instead of turning left into the main hall, he turned right and headed for the back door. He cautiously stepped outside into the growing darkness and almost tripped over the body that Macarini had left lying by the low wall. The thick blood from his opened throat had pooled on the flag stone courtyard. Phillip avoided stepping in the sticky mess as he quickly and quietly slipped into the garden.

FIFTY-ONE

Macarini knelt beside the prostrated body of Leila Diab as Grapponelli stood over her. With his hunting knife Macarini slit her blouse open from the waist to her neck. He placed the razor sharp blade on her bare breast and with a slow movement of his wrist, he severed her left nipple. She cried out in pain. The blood flowed freely as Grapponelli asked her again for the combination to her brief case. Nothing but a stream of oaths in Arabic.

Macarini performed his trick again on her right breast. Grapponelli once more demanded the combination. Between coughs and winces of almost unbearable pain she managed to whisper her reply.

"Go fuck yourself, grease ball."

Macarini then began to work on cutting off her entire breast. He enjoyed this part of his work best of all. Leila Diab's scream only added to his enjoyment. But still she refused to give Grapponelli the combination to her briefcase.

Grapponelli placed his foot on her shattered knee and pressed down. She screamed again but the sound was almost lost as Phillip came crashing through the glass panes of the large French doors.

Bruno, who had been keeping an eye on the door to the Great Hall, expecting another Arab sailor to come charging in, was too slow to react. Phillip's first burst of gunfire as he jumped through the glass caught Bruno squarely in the back. Phillip rolled on his right shoulder and came up on one knee. From that low position he fired a quick burst that caught Fredo squarely in the chest.

Phillip would have taken out Grapponelli next, but his gun jammed at the crucial moment and in the split second it took him to react, Macarini was throwing himself full length at Phillip. His hunting knife firmly held in his right hand, he drove it into Phillip's thigh and rolled away just as Phillip caught him on the side of his head with the butt of his rifle. The blow was not enough to completely stun Macarini who got to his feet quickly.

Lunging with a second knife he had produced from a sheath strapped to his waist, he tried to stick Phillip in his gut. Phillip stepped into the attack instead of away from it and slightly to his right. He avoided the flashing blade and at the same time, he delivered a crushing blow with his fist and smashed into the bones on the back of Macarini's knife hand. His knife fell to the carpet. With his other hand he simultaneously delivered a palm-heel strike to Macarini's temple and this time he succeeded in dumping his attacker on his back. Macarini was dazed.

Phillip's movements were greatly hampered by the hunting knife that now protruded from his leg. He took a step towards the desk where the unconscious and dying Marquis still sat. Macarini had left his carbine propped against it and Phillip thought to grab it, dumping the badly maintained and jammed AK47. Too late. As Phillip had been dealing with Macarini, Grapponelli had to temporarily give up on Leila Diab and had stepped into the fray. As Phillip turned to retrieve the carbine, Grapponelli stuck the muzzle of his Beretta into Phillip's cheek.

"Well, if it isn't Dr. Fairfax! You are the last person I expected to see, but since you are here I can dispose of you all at once. You, I have no further use for, so I think you should be the first to go. Miss Diab and I still have to have a meeting of the minds. I fear she will need to suffer a little longer until she gives up her little secret."

Grapponelli had to reach up to press the gun into Phillip's face as he stood in front of him with the black briefcase in his left hand. Phillip could smell the cordite from the recently discharged gun. He contemplated an attack on Grapponelli, who under normal circumstances would have been easy prey, but the loss of blood flowing freely from his leg wound was causing Phillip to be a little light headed. He doubted he could move fast enough before the little Italian was able to pull the trigger and ventilate his head.

Somehow people always have an urge to speak before they dispatch someone in cold blood. Maybe they need to build up the courage or maybe they have some notion that they are doing God's work and the victim deserves an explanation. Either way, it generally proves to be an error. In this case, it was. Leila Diab, who had been lying in her own blood on the floor, had slowly dragged herself towards the fireplace. She picked up the iron poker that the Marquis used to constantly jab at the fire with. It was a habit that always annoyed Leila, but at this moment she was glad he had the useful piece of equipment around.

Taking it up in her left hand she swung it with all the energy she had left. It crashed into Grapponelli's left hand and broke every bone in his wrist. The black briefcase fell to the floor. The look of shocked horror on Grapponelli's face gave Phillip that split second advantage. With fading energy and strength, he grabbed Grapponelli's other wrist, the one holding the gun, and twisted it away from his own face. The gun fired but the bullet lodged harmlessly into the wood paneling that decorated the room.

Macarini had now recovered sufficiently to get to his feet drawing another knife from his belt as he did so. Phillip would have finished off Grapponelli then and there but at that very instant a noise so loud, so deafening shook the castle and everything in it.

In what seemed like slow motion to Phillip, every ounce of air was sucked out of the room and a split second later was returned as flying debris. Anything that wasn't nailed down seemed to be flying through the air. The solid mahogany door was splintered into a million pieces and flew into the study as small lethal darts. This was followed by a ball of flame that engulfed the room, singeing anything and anyone in its path.

Macarini, who had stood up and was about to exact full revenge on Phillip, received a large proportion of the darts in his back. A gilded leg that had once been an integral part of an 18th century armchair protruded from the back of his skull. His lifeless body fell on top of Phillip and far from finishing him off, actually served to protect him from most of the flying stone and mortar and the fireball that followed.

Grapponelli had been thrown by the blast and ended up underneath the upturned desk of the Marquis, out from under which, he crawled some moments later towards the shattered French doors that led to the garden.

When Phillip came round, the room was totally silent. Only when it dawned on him that he couldn't even hear his own voice did he realize he had been deafened by the explosion.

He pushed Macarini off him and felt around for a weapon. He was still unsure what had happened and knew that he was still in great danger. But nothing was where he thought it should be. The room was full of dust and smoke. Try as hard as he could, he could not fathom in which direction he should crawl. His leg still had the heavy knife embedded in it and his head felt like it had been used as a punching bag. Blood trickled down his face from a gaping wound in his forehead and the back of his right hand and arm was covered in sharp shards of wood that protruded like porcupine quills. Slowly, as his head cleared a little, his hearing began to return. A muffled sound like distant gunfire or fire crackers filled the air as the heat began to rise.

As Phillip lay on the floor of the Marquis' study he saw flames licking up the walls of the Great Hall and huge chunks of stone masonry falling from above. The ancient wool and silk tapestries that hung from floor to ceiling burned, giving off an acrid and choking black smoke.

It was obvious that the castle was truly alight and the only thought that Phillip had now was one of survival and escape. The prone body of Leila Diab lay only a few feet away but any thoughts of revenge were superseded by a need to get outside and away from the choking smoke. The blaze had now begun to engulf the study.

It looked as if the satisfaction of revenge would be impossible anyway. Leila Diab looked as lifeless as Isabel had as she lay in the pool of her own blood. Phillip crawled towards her and reaching out he felt on her neck for a pulse. There was a very slight one but it was obvious from the amount of blood on the floor that it was only a matter of a few short minutes before she would die.

"Burn in hell, Leila, burn in hell!" Phillip hoped it would be the last words she would ever hear.

Phillip crawled on his belly over the top of the dying Leila Diab and away from the flames. When he encountered large shards of glass on the floor he felt sure he was nearing the French doors and an exit to fresh air and safety. He kept going although unconsciousness was not far away. His survival instincts propelled him as he dragged his body inch by inch across the floor.

Besides the scorching flames, large pieces of stone masonry began to fall all around him. There was nothing he could do about that so he continued his torturously slow journey to the open air and safety.

After crawling and dragging his bleeding leg for what seemed like a lifetime, but was only a matter minutes, he felt the corner of a smallish object touch his fingertips. It moved as he tried to grasp it. His first thoughts were that it was the corner of one of the Marquis' collection of old leather bound books that had been blown off the shelves by the blast. But moving his fingers gently along the spine he encountered a handle. He grasped it firmly. It was Leila Diab's briefcase and something Grapponelli seemed prepared to kill for.

Feeling for the hand cuffs that he had earlier slipped into his belt he snapped one cuff on his wrist and the other on the handle of the case. If it was that important to Leila and Grapponelli it must be worth saving. He dragged it, along with his battered body, to the door sill where fatigue began to overcome him. His eyes slowly began to close.

The paneled walls either side of him were now a mass of orange and yellow flames and the air was thick with smoke. Masonry continued to bombard the lower floors as the chateau began to collapse. He knew if he succumbed to the desire for sleep he would never make it out alive. He willed himself over the threshold of the door and continued to crawl over the smooth, cool flagstones that were strewn with shards of glass and rock.

Eventually he felt soft, fresh grass beneath his fingers. It was the last conscious feeling he would have that day.

358

FIFTY-TWO
Two weeks later

Monique sat in a chair, her eyes closed but deep sleep eluded her. The slightest sound would wake her and she would sit bolt upright and stare at the body of the person lying just a few feet away. It was generally a nurse going about her duties or a cleaner mopping the floor but it was enough to snap her wide awake. The smell of disinfectant filled her nostrils and she felt nauseous.

She hadn't eaten much in the last two weeks but had lived almost entirely on coffee. She had rarely left Phillip's bedside as he lay quietly in a medically induced coma. A small screen on a chrome stand constantly blipped as it monitored his heartbeat. Digital numbers flashed in the corners that kept track of his blood oxygen and pulse rate. Phillip was in the Intensive Care Unit where an arterial line constantly measured his blood pressure. Monitors at the nurses' station out side his room kept a constant vigilance over all his vital signs. A nurse appeared every hour or so and adjusted his medications or his intravenous fluids.

Once one of the leads to his heart monitor had come off and the machine 'flat-lined'. Monique woke up with such a start when the rhythmic bleep stopped that she almost flat-lined herself. After a moment's panic, the offending lead was reattached and the reassuring rhythmic bleep continued.

Sir Robert appeared most days but mostly to check on Monique rather than Phillip. He called constantly, however, and spoke to the doctors who assured him that nature must take its' course and that when Phillip's body was capable of coping without help they would reintroduce

358

consciousness. Phillip had, they explained, taken a severe blow to the head and the swelling of his cerebral tissue needed time to heal and subside.

The wound to his leg was severe too and had caused much blood loss, but luckily the artery had not been severed. Had Phillip tried to remove the knife himself, however, the result could have been a great deal different, the doctor explained. Whether he would be able to run long distances in the future was, however, still in doubt.

The other injuries included several hundred splinters that had pierced his hands and arms. They took time to remove, but apart from some minor scarring, they would heal completely.

On day twelve of Phillip's barbiturate induced coma the doctor's had gradually started to reduce his dose of Pentobarbital. Phillip was slowly being brought to a state of full consciousness.

By day fifteen Monique hadn't even gone to the hospital cafeteria for coffee but had stayed constantly by his bedside. At two o'clock in the afternoon Sir Robert arrived with a hot thermos flask of coffee and a sandwich of brie, lettuce and tomato for Monique. She drank the black liquid thirstily but after only one bite of the sandwich, she put it down. She could not eat.

At two-thirty, Dr. Alice Favre arrived to look at Phillip's progress. His vital signs looked good and she told both his visitors that he could wake up at any minute. The doctor placed her finger in Phillip's hand and asked him to squeeze it. The response was slow at first but gradually it became stronger.

Phillip's first inkling that he was still alive was when he heard Sir Robert's voice. He was talking quietly to Monique but his words were meaningless and unintelligible. The sound, however, was comforting and Phillip drifted back to sleep without opening his eyes.

He had no idea how much later it was when he heard the voice again only this time it was mostly Monique's voice that he heard. He tried to move his lips but no sound came out. They felt dry and cracked. His eyes still remained shut but mostly because it hadn't occurred to Phillip to open them. When he tried, the bright light of the room made him close them almost immediately. In fact, the light in the room was fairly subdued and his blinds were closed but to Phillip it seemed like being in the headlights of a truck. He tried again.

Slowly he let the light filter through his dark eyelashes as he gingerly opened his eyes a little at a time. By the time they were fully opened Monique was out of her chair and was sitting on his bed. She took hold of his bandaged hand gently and kissed him on his dry lips.

"Welcome back to the land of the living," she said smiling.

Sir Robert stood next to her and laid a hand gently on Phillip's arm.

"You had us all worried there for a bit, you know, old boy. Ought to have a bit more consideration for your old uncle," but his beam spoke for the joy and relief that he felt inside.

Phillip tried a word or two in reply but only a croak came from his lips. Monique dipped her finger in a glass of water and gently laid it on his lips. Phillip savored the single drop of cold water that wet his lips. She had been instructed not to give him water by mouth until he was fully awake.

"Thanks," he said after a while, "that was the most welcome drink I've ever had."

Sir Robert had by now pressed the red rubber button that summoned the nurse on duty but it had been unnecessary. Phillip's vital signs on the monitors told them that he was now conscious and they wasted little time in paging his doctor. Dr. Favre appeared within a minute and examined Phillip. When she'd received several assurances from Phillip that he felt 'just fine' she left but not before telling Sir Robert and Monique not to tire the patient out. They both nodded and started speaking to Phillip at once.

"One at a time," croaked Phillip, and Sir Robert gallantly let Monique go first.

"I thought you promised not to take any risks," she remonstrated. Phillip just smiled with an impish grin.

"I said I wouldn't take any unnecessary risks. Everything else was just bad luck," he whispered huskily, his voice gradually getting a little stronger.

He reached for his water but Monique beat him to it and guided the straw into his mouth. He took a grateful sip, as they looked into each other's eyes. The look said everything that needed saying. Phillip was home and Monique was never going to let him go again.

Sir Robert took the opportunity to interject. "Now it's my turn." He looked at Phillip with his steely blue eyes. "There's quite a lot of catching up to do, so I'll keep it brief." He paused to marshal his facts into small easily digestible pieces of information and then continued.

"The Chateau de Manville is now, sadly, a pile of charred rubble. I doubt it will ever be rebuilt, even if it could be, and at first we all thought the *"Girl in the Red dress"* had gone up in smoke with it. But, and here's the really good news, the black briefcase that you had cuffed to your wrist contained a computer. Once the French authorities, the Surite it was, were able to open it and download the files, they were able to trace money transactions from Nini Grapponelli's bank account through several other banks to Beirut in the Lebanon. They were able to freeze those funds. Best news of all, they were able to nab Grapponelli. Colonel Bodoni will be investigating but there's every chance they can get Grapponelli on tax evasion, money laundering and no doubt several other things. They picked him up two days ago with his arm in plaster and they've got him banged up in Rome."

Sir Robert studied Phillip's face and saw a smile spread across his dry lips. Feeling Phillip needed to know everything he continued to feed him as much information as he could.

"The French found several bodies at the Chateau after the fire," said Sir Robert popping one of the patient's grapes in his mouth. "I don't think they've got round to positively identifying them all yet, but one looks almost positively to be the Marquis himself. He went down with the ship, so to speak. Another body they found was wearing more knives about him than a butcher's convention."

"That would be Macarini, one of Grapponelli's henchmen." Phillip's voice sounded weak but he brushed off any suggestion that perhaps they should wait until later to have the de-briefing. Phillip needed to know.

"Get to the good bit," urged Monique, "Tell Phillip the really good news."

Phillip raised an eyebrow and it hurt like hell.

Sir Robert continued, "Well, anyway, the really good news is that whilst the Surité was examining the brief case they found two secret compartments. One was empty but the other - I really should have a drum roll here – contained nothing less than the Leonardo da Vinci painting. It wasn't burnt after all!"

"That's great news," whispered Phillip but the smile on his face expressed what his voice could not. He asked, "So who does it officially belong to now?" He beckoned again for some water.

"This is where it gets interesting," answered Sir Robert. "The old Marquis, the one that died back in the 1950's had a sister. She joined a religious order in her late teens, just before the war. She's in her nineties now but they tracked her down to the Convent of the Benedictine nuns of the Blessed Sacrament, or some such name, near Craon in northwest France. Not far from Le Mans." Sir Robert stole another grape before continuing with his tale.

"Anyway she became the rightful owner of the Leonardo but, as she pointed out, she has no need of worldly possessions. The French government is hoping to have it donated to the nation. They'll probably get their wish."

"She'll be the richest nun in the world if they do," said Phillip as he tried to move himself a little further up the bed. The exertion exhausted him and he gave up.

"They did offer to buy it from her of course but do you know what she asked for in exchange?" It was a rhetorical question and Sir Robert kept going. "You'll absolutely love this Phillip. In exchange for the most valuable painting in the world, she would accept nothing less than a new minibus for the nuns at her convent!" At this Sir Robert roared with laughter and despite the fact that it hurt like hell, Phillip laughed too.

"I think she should have held out for a new roof for the convent too." Sir Robert was still amused at the thought.

"Blessed are the meek," whispered Monique.

"Just one more question, Robert," croaked Phillip. "The explosion and fire at the chateau; I know it was explosives that the Arabs were loading into the truck but how did it happen? What set it all off?"

"When you were sorting out the Italians and some of those Arab types, Albert Guion, the faithful old retainer, took it into his head to create a Molotov cocktail...." He paused.

"Might he have had the idea put in his head by someone...?" Sir Robert looked questioningly at the bandaged form that lay in the bed.

Phillip looked a little bashful as the memory of his instructions to Albert slowly returned to his consciousness.

"Oh, I see!" Sir Robert looked at his nephew and chuckled. He continued with his story. "Well, Albert apparently used a lighted bottle full of lamp oil and tossed it into the back of the truck." Sir Robert picked off another couple of grapes and popped them in his mouth before he returned to his story.

"It burned quite well for a few minutes, until some mining grade sticks of dynamite ignited and blew the truck up and the chateau down. The fire trucks and police couldn't, or wouldn't, go near the blaze for quite a while because ammunition was going off like a Chinese New Year celebration. So by the time they felt safe enough to get near the chateau, it was beyond saving."

"Yes, Albert was quite a surprise, I must say," said Phillip.

"Yes. By all accounts he's a bit of a dark horse. Albert had been around as a young lad just after the war when the old Marquis came back from his incarceration at the hands of the Nazis. Albert was fond of the old Marquis and decided to stay on at the chateau when he died. He looked after the latest Marquis, but in recent years he began to get suspicious about some of the odd goings-on at the chateau.

He eventually went to the police and after being questioned by their anti-terrorist lot, he agreed to continue as the Marquis' servant and to report any strange happenings to the authorities. Apparently, he turned out to be quite a useful informer."

Phillip was about to express his surprise again when a commotion in the hallway outside his room caught everyone's attention. A nurse was insisting that visitors were no longer allowed in after two o'clock and that he had to wait until six o'clock that night to see the patient. There seemed to be a lot of negotiating going on outside but Phillip was too tired to care. Until he realized who was making all the fuss.

I might have known, he thought, just as the large frame of Daniel Masilionis filled the doorway. He was on crutches and his face was peeling from excessive sun burn but still intact was his infectious grin.

"Where in God's name did you come from?" said Phillip, holding out his bandaged hand from which clear plastic intravenous tubes stretched into plastic bags of clear fluid.

"Ah, my friend," roared Daniel, "I went for a long swim courtesy of some Arabs and Miss Diab." He stepped forward to embrace Phillip but when he saw the state he was in he pulled back and patted the only bit of skin he could see that wasn't either bandaged or bruised. He gently laid his huge hand on top of Phillip's.

"But what my friend, have you been doing to end like this? I think you have been having too much fun without me. *N'est pas?*"

"It's a long story and I'll tell you all the gory details later. But I need to know about you."

Phillip was buoyed to see Daniel still alive and kicking and gratified to know that whatever he'd been up to hadn't been fatal.

"Ah! I was visiting with Mademoiselle Diab. She invite me and I was stupid, I go." Daniel gave one of his Gallic shrugs, as if to say it was *kismet*, fate. He had no choice. "She drug my drink and next I am in a boat in the middle of the big sea."

By now Monique, Sir Robert and Phillip were all listening intently to Daniel's adventure. He enjoyed an audience so Daniel started to lay it on a bit thick, as he continued with his saga.

"When I wake I see we are far from land but I have a strong need to escape!" He looked at each person in turn to gauge the impact his story was having. Satisfied they were all hanging on his every word he continued.

"There were plenty big bad people on the boat. Maybe twenty or even maybe thirty people"

By tomorrow, thought Phillip, the number would probably be fifty or sixty. But he allowed Daniel his moment in the spotlight.

"I demand to have speak with the captain! After some time, they take me. When I see my chances I attack the captain and his peoples. I fight maybe six or eight big men at once and then when they are all hiding from me, I jump out of the boat into the sea." He looked around to see the reaction. Monique was the only one who looked at Daniel wide eyed with admiration and awe. Phillip, smirking, looked at Sir Robert who winked.

Feeling at last he had a fully attentive audience in Monique, Daniel now spoke directly to her as he continued his tale of daring.

"I swim away fast but the bullets they get very close. Then the captain he decide to cut me up with the engine! As he come at me I hold onto the front of the boat and they think I am dead! But I cheat death. I am Daniel Masilionis, brave Interpol agent."

Phillip didn't have the heart to burst Daniel's bubble. He was obviously enjoying himself so Phillip decided to let him spin his fanciful tale to an enraptured Monique. He could wait 'til another day to get the real story.

"I was nearly food for the fishes. I swim in the sea for many days when a delightful young lady sail by in her boat and pull me out of the water. I was nearly dead but I am strong. Even I don't be so good for some days and she say, this angel lady who save me, I make no sense when I talk…."

"Nothing new there, Daniel," smiled Phillip.

Daniel ignored the comment.

"Ah, but I sleep for three, maybe four days and talk this nonsense. Eventually she take me to a island and there a doctor he help me. Now I am back and I bring my angel lady who rescue me. Come, come, my *babe*."

Gesturing wildly towards the doorway he waved his hand, furiously beckoning 'his angel lady'. In walked a lovely, tanned and sun bleached blonde that was Daniel's new love and savior.

After introductions all round Phillip smiled a contented smile and closed his eyes. He was relieved that Daniel was not dead. And apart from a few bumps and bruises, he was going to be fine too.

Monique bent over his bandaged head and kissed him full on the lips. Phillip was safe and soon they'd be home in England.

"Sorry to break up the party but my boy needs his rest and Monique you need to get some real food inside you and have a proper sleep yourself. Tell you what I'll take you back to your hotel. Give you time for a quick shower and I'll stand you some dinner.OK?"

" Yes" replied Monique, "Suddenly I'm starving." She bent over Phillip and kissed him lightly on the lips. "I'll see you in the morning. Sleep well."

369

FIFTY-THREE

"I'll pick you up in thirty minutes," said Sir Robert as Monique slipped out of Sir Robert's car in front of her hotel. Monique waved as she skipped up the steps. Monique felt elated. The worst was over and Phillip was going to make a full recovery. She'd see to that.

Five minutes later she felt the hot shower start to wash away not only her hospital grime but her tiredness too. She was now totally ravenous and the promise of a good dinner with Sir Robert was more than appealing.

Monique had only just finished showering when there was knock on her door. She was wearing a bathrobe and her wet hair was still wrapped in a towel.

"I thought you said you'd give me half an hour" she called through the door.

"Room service, Mademoiselle," came the reply.

So it wasn't an eager Robert after all. She looked through the spy hole and saw the uniformed waiter with a trolley bearing a big basket of flowers and an ice bucket with her favorite champagne. It must be from Phillip. He must have had Daniel arrange it. Smiling broadly she opened the door and the young man stepped inside.

"Bonjour Mademoiselle," he said politely, "would you wish for me to open the champagne?"

He wheeled the cart into the centre of the room.

"No. No thanks," she replied as she took the card from the large arrangement of flowers. She eagerly opened the envelope and extracted the small stiff card from inside just as the waiter's hand disappeared beneath the linen serviette that lay folded on the trolley.

He withdrew a silenced pistol and aimed it at a startled and confused Monique. Two muffled shots instantly found their mark.

Monique fell back against a blood splattered wall and slowly sank to the floor. A single shot exactly between her eyes and one through her heart killed her before she even hit the floor. She sat against the wall still with the startled expression on her lifeless face and still holding the card that came with the flowers. It read, *"With Compliments, Leila Diab."*

THE END